CONFUSION OF THE HEART

By: Douglas L. Maples

Only the ambitious arrogant mature and gifted lawyer can make a roster of a picture perfect firm. Shirley Thomas is a lawyer trying to define herself in a man's world looking and searching for the perfect man to be her companion and her only confusion is finding the right man who is suitable to meet her means.

Her friends Rachelle and Renee are looking for the same desires as their friend Shirley and even though they are gorgeous women they are still confused and searching for true love. Rachelle is a hair stylist and part owner of a popular salon Mother's Hair Salon and Renee is a manager at a grocery store chain.

Shirley is seeing a married man Thomas Patterson until she finds out that he is seeing another woman besides his wife. Shirley takes on another project by the name of Sam , but in the mean time she steps outside of her demeanor to sleep with a guy name Sharan who is not her type because of his complexion to get revenge on Thomas and she ends up getting pregnant.

Suddenly the stakes are much higher when Shirley realize that Sharan is actually her soul mate and he has been trying to get with the hottest African American lawyer who is very pretty, smart, witty and confused. Can Shirley's heart overcome her attraction to be with light complexion men?

Based upon evolution and other theories , persons physical attraction doesn't make the attraction compatible and those looking for physical attraction most likely end up unhappy in a relationship., that's my opinion.

Also coming soon by Douglas L. Maples
Delight
Entrance Part I II III
Bonita
Well-Bred
The Lies From The Inside
The Circle Par

This is the work of fiction. All characters , organizations, and events portrayed in this novel are either products of the author's imagination or are used fictitiously.

First Edition May 2012

Maples, L. Douglas
Confusion Of The Heart/ Douglas L. Maples- 1st ed.
1. Love story-Fiction 2. African American-Fiction. 3. Sexual orientation-Fiction. 4 Cincinnati 3(Ohio)-Fiction. IMANI BOOKS

Edited by: Billi Jo Louden

Cover and Graphic Design by: Tre Griffin (Black Star Graphics & Promotions/ griffintremayne@gmail.com)

CONFUSION OF THE HEART
ACKNOWLEDGEMENTS

To my family in Alabama, Memphis, Atlanta, Philly, Chicago, Mississippi, Detroit, Cali, anI would like to give praise to God Almighty for giving me the borrow times to display my talent and passion. This Book is for the Weave Master Sharon and Denise Moore, please keep inspiring others in the cosmetology world and in life.

I would like to thank Ebony and Twizzle, Regina Mason, Jamaya Murray, Nikki Calendar, Lutisha Jackson, Catrese Jordan, Kelly Wiggins, Dr. Carol Hubbard, Reco Walker, Creshonda Davenport, Teressa D. Heath, Chanda Walker, Lashonda Collier, Jimmy (Bo) Davis, James(Bo) Johnson, Quincy Singleton, Angela Travis, Tracey Booker, Leah D.Shippy, Marguerite King, Annie Mae Hutcherson, Denise Hodge, Ken Bailey, Shirley Thomas(Dayton Ohio), Cynthia Lee-Sanders(Dayton Ohio), Sarah Pope, Montoya Noel, B-Nati, Tyra Warner, Michelle Brookins, Helen (Tweetie) Nelson Charles Stargill, Reco Johnson, Andrea Dudley-Houston, Tamencia (Puff) McNair, Jamasha Hardy, Javana Jenkins, Shirley Harris, Tina Lynch, Mike Wilson, Torrice Rice, Keisha Washington, Tamu Johnson, Karen Allen Lightfoot, Kelly Brown, Lavina Coleman, Tanya Davis, Eric Brown, Connie and Kelly(Elkhart IN), Keva Kincaid, Silvia Trice, Kathy Forte, Shannon Glover (INDY), Jean Hall and Brooke Tonee McPherson, LaShauna Evans-Turnage, Latoya and Evon Hutcherson, Kyma Boyd, Marlo Smith, Veronica and Quida Staley, Baron(Sonny Red), Denita Harmon, Karla Miller, Karence Wheeler, Amy Hartly, Crystal McClelland-Manley, Nia, Adrian Marshall, Tameeka L. Hairston(Columbus, OH). Thanks to Trap Boy Entertainment (Ronald, Christopher and Saquan)

To my partners, Shannon Chambers, TaaShaun Smith, Lamont Green and my Web designer Tre Griffin.

To my daughters- Daysha L. Maples, Khalia I.R. Maples, LaShayna Murray, Montoya Noel and my step-daughter Janeay.

To my sons- Dwantai S. Maples, James A. Smith and DaShannon A.L. Hutcherson.

To my family, The Pitts, Maples, Lummus, Blackmons, Cobbs, Andersons, Marshalls, Gaithers, Normans, Jackson's, Drains and Lewis.

d D.C.

To my homies on serious lockdown Hosea Thomas, Andre Thomas, Jakuba Lewis, and O

Prologue

Shirley was attending a party at Rachelle's house in Amberly Village. The likes of Sharan Chambers were at the party with his friend Pedro. Shirley had been avoiding Sharan for several years now. Even though they would double date with Rachelle and Pedro or take trips together as a couple to accommodate their friends, Shirley wouldn't give him the satisfaction of any type of affection or intimacy, because of his complexion. She wasn't attracted to him physically at all being he was dark complexion like she were. Her attraction was to light skinned complexion men which was the complexion of the married man she was having a long term relationship with.

Sharan stepped towards Shirley and Rachelle even though he was kind of tipsy he managed to make a pass at Shirley. She ignored him refusing to respond.

"Okay Ms. Thomas, you don't have to answer, but if you get lonely Sharan will be sitting over there on the sofa." said Sharan.

She looked at him and rolled her eyes with an attitude she replied,

"Okay Sharan, now could you please leave me alone?"

Rachelle looked at Shirley hard and long, as Sharan made his exit. "Shirl that was cold hearted," as Rachelle turned up her nose at Shirley.

"Chelle, he's not my type I've told you, Pedro and him for years now. I'm not feeling him at all." Shirley told her.

"Shirl, you are stuck on stupid, because he's not light skin. He's very respectful, no kids, and no baby mama drama. No girlfriend or wife, he's not using or dealing drugs. He has his own business and if I wasn't fucking Pedro I would have him as my very own," said Rachelle.

"Well Chelle, he's not my type and I'm not going beneath my standards for anyone," said Shirley.

"Alright, you think Thomas is your answer to everything. Hell you'll always be number two to him, remember he's married with children Shirl," said Rachelle.

"He takes care of this," as she looked Rachelle up and down waving her hand across her body. "Plus he's light skin, those brothers are making a come back Chelle."

"I like dark complexion men myself, but I also like a man who values my opinion and respects my mind. Someone I can call my own and I don't have to share. Someone I can wake up to everyday and not just days when he's available." Rachelle looked at her convincingly.

Shirley turned her nose up at Rachelle once again. She knew her friend was right for the most part that she would be second to a married man. Shirley didn't look at the picture that way. She saw another vision a rainbow on the other side.

"Yeah, yeah Chelle I don't see you making a serious commitment with Pedro."

"One day I will Shirl, but I'm not confused either and he's not married, even though I'm probably not the only woman he's sleeping with, I'm not second to none neither," said Rachelle.

"I'm content with whom I'm dealing with in my life and I'm happy Chelle," said Shirley.

"Shirl quit fooling yourself, you're not happy when his wife thinks you are messing with Bob, Thomas white friend. The nights when Pedro is here you be wishing that Thomas is at your condo with you. So let's not fake it, just open your eyes and give someone else a chance at your heart who wont bring about confusion, that's all I'm saying Shirl."

Shirley nodded her head to her friend's advice. She then walked over by the sofa couch and sat in a near by chair. She was exhausted as she removed her shoes to relax. She was checking her nails when Sharan was hovering over saying something that she couldn't understand. When she looked up at him he had laugh lines in the corner of his eyes. She tilted her head in defense.

"What Sharan?" she was back being defiant with him. He pointed his finger at her, not knowing what to say, hell he couldn't say anything because he was nauseated. Then out of nowhere he vomited all over Shirley. It was in her lap and on her blouse. She was in disgust, as she sat there and screamed to the top of her lungs. Everyone in the party was at a standstill. Rachelle came to her friends rescue and laughed hard when she saw what had happened. Sharan had passed out on the floor in front of her. Pedro was next to Rachelle and asked her what happen.

"Chelle what happened to Shirl?" Pedro asked.

"Sharan threw up on her ass. That's what she gets from always acting mean towards him. Get your boy and I'll attend to my girl," said Rachelle.

That night would be a memorable one for Shirley Thomas and would band Sharan from ever getting close to her.

CHAPTER ONE

Confusion

Daylight soars over the beautiful condos in Symmes Township, a small suburb outside of Cincinnati, Ohio. In a queen size bed, lying spread eagle on satin sheets is a woman. She's beautiful, independent, spontaneous, and artistic. Wearing nothing but a silk maroon spaghetti strap nightgown. Next to her bed is her lazy boy chair which held her yellow sarong and a pair of matching yellow thong underwear.

The woman is a lawyer for a major law firm in Cincinnati. She is a single black woman with no children or a husband. In the court house she was often referred to as being a real

"Bitch". She was just good at her job and her male counter parts just couldn't handle it. A brisk of cold air shoots between her legs from the patio doors of her bedroom. The wisp of cold air awakes her. She was only wearing the silk gown and was moist between her thighs from last nights escapades. Looking over at her answering machine the red light was flashing, meaning she had messages.

She gently reached over to the answering machine and hit the play button.

Beep!

"Hello Shirl, it's me Thomas, I had a wonderful time last night. Sorry I had to make an early exit, but you know my situation. Call me when you get up."

Beep!

"Hey it's me again I just wanted to see if you were up yet, I guess not. Boy you were drinking like a fish last night and it showed at your place. Anyway I'll try later bye."

Beep!

It's now 12: 15 in the afternoon and I already left two messages. I hope you are alright. Please give me a call Shirl."

She hit the end button on her answering machine. "Shit I'll let his married ass beg some more before calling him back." She said out loud to herself.

She looked at the digital clock on her nightstand and it was 12:45 in the afternoon. She gathered herself and grabbed her small black book to record her rendezvous from last night. She tried to protect herself by keeping counts of her intimate encounters with the men she slept with, but at this time it was only Thomas Patterson.

She moved her hour glass figure across the white and gray wool carpet towards her bathroom in her room. She needed to take a shower and wash the sex from between her legs from last night. She would moisturize her skin and touch up her juice box with the feminine likes of Summer's Eve. Her body tickled under the softness of the warm water and the mixture of the gentle perfumed soap she used.

After her shower she wrapped herself in a huge cotton towel that swallowed her up. Placing a blue set of matching bra and thongs across the bed, she put on Laboratoire Remede's lotion on her face that helped her skin stay moisturized. She put on some cocoa butter lotion all over her body. She followed by putting on her bra and thong that she had laid out. She sprayed herself with the sweet smell of E. Marinella perfume which she got from Naples Italy. She had a hair appointment later so she put her hair in a bun.

She grabbed a pair of white Capri's, a white and blue Old Navy t-shirt and her navy blue crossing strap Chanel sandals.

Shirley put on her Pascal Locroix bracelet which was enhanced by the half karat diamond,

And she put on her two karat Crisscut ring with matching earrings. She placed her time keepers Chariot watch laced in diamonds on the opposite arm to complement her other jewelry.

At exactly 2 p.m. Shirley grabbed her car keys, Prada purse, cell phone and headed out the door. She walked down the stairs from her condo and she could see her dark blue 2002 four door Lexus LS 430 sitting in her private parking space under a large canopy. It was a nice breezy day outside in the beginning of April. She got in her car and immediately gave herself a massage in the pulsating seats that it offered. She placed her luxury Sedan in drive and roared over four speed bumps before entering into the oncoming traffic from Cole Dr. to the 275 west ramp. She picked up her cell phone to call the hair salon to inform Rachelle her stylist she was on her way. Her appointment was at 2:30. The phone rung several times before someone answered.

"Hello Mother's where we do hair like no other, may I help you?" The receptionist said.

"Is Rachelle in Anitra?" Shirley asked her.

"Who is this, Shirley?" Anitra asked her.

"Yes this is me girl." She responded.

"Okay, hold on girlfriend I'll get her," as the phone went blank briefly.

"Hello, dis is Rachelle, how may I help you?" The voice was loud and strong.

"Bitch it's me, what's up? I'm on my way and I hope you got a mild relaxer or do I have to stop at Sally's and pick up one?" Shirley said to her long time friend and hair stylist.

"Shirl, I'm surprised you are up after going home with that tired ass negro last night. Bring your ass on I already got the perm and Renee is over here crying and shit."

"Chelle, I'm not on her shit today. She needs to find her a man and get her some. And don't be talking about my boo either, Thomas got it going on and you know it," said Shirley with a fake laugh.

"All I know is the mother-fucker's married with children, but c'mon I'm waiting." Rachelle said with a low tone.

"Okay Chelle I'm about to turn onto the Norwood lateral now, bye."

She hung up her cell phone and was listening to Kelly Price *"Soul Of A Woman"*. The song "Friend of mines" was blasting through her speakers. She was singing out loud along with the music as she turned onto the lateral that would take her to the Reading Rd. exit by the Bondhill showcase cinema.

'She was a friend of mines, she left with my man. She lied, cheated, took all I had. She was a friend of mines, she used what she knew. She lied, cheated and left me confused.'

Shirley was singing to the melody enjoying herself and then she spotted a white Escalade EXT that pulled on the side of her from her peripheral vision. It was four guys in the vehicle bobbing their heads to whatever they were listening to. Shirley caught eye contact with the front passenger. He was light skinned complexion. He winked at her and threw up his hands to say, "what up" to Shirley. She pointed to the Reading Rd. exit sign and the truck slowed up to get behind her Lexus.

She merged onto to the exit ramp signaling to turn right going into Bondhill and the truck followed. She eased her car into the oncoming traffic driving about a mile up the road. She came to the light of Reading Rd. and California Ave. She turned left at the light, KFC sat on one side and the Quick Stop sat on the opposite side of California Ave. She drove

on down the street passing Bondhill Elementary school before she came to Mother's hair salon on her right. She turned into the small parking lot and the Escalade was right behind her. The truck pulled beside her and Shirley got out her car looking good as ever, even though she wasn't looking her best. The guys saw the beauty that stepped out the luxury Sedan.

All four of the guys mouths dropped instantly. The passenger stepped out and came around the truck to meet up with Shirley and she quickly sized him up. She broke him down to a science with one thought.

'Baggy jeans, Enyce shirt, Timberland boots, platinum jewelry and diamond studs in his ears. He's either a thug, drug dealer or an older guy trying to act young. Oh my God his nails are dirty'.

Shirley was in disgust even though the guy was of her likings, because he was light complexion. He wasn't going to make the cut with his nails being dirty. He smiled at Shirley and had a mouth full of diamond and white gold teeth. She really lost all control of trying not to be defiant, and more lady like when she denied him any possible conversation. He spoke to her. "Hello miss lady, my name is Mack," he said.

'Mack, what kind of name is that?' Shirley thought!

"I'm sorry Mack, I thought you were somebody I knew." Shirley quickly replied. She was quick on her toes when it came to someone she wasn't interested in.

"But'em can I get to know you?" He asked her smiling showing her his teeth again.

"Sorry I'm married and I don't cheat." Shirley pointed towards her ring which wasn't even on her ring finger. He wasn't giving up though.

"C'mon ma, holla at your boy. Everybody knows Ren Mack from College Hill. I'm an artist. I'm the next big rapper coming out the Nati." He told Shirley.

Shirley didn't care at all. She couldn't resist putting him in his place.

"Rapper, please I wouldn't be caught dead with you, your nails aren't even clean."

Ren Mack quickly looked at his fingernails. He laughed a little and replied.

"Oh I see you are funny, but you ain't no Janet either dig that."

"You sure isn't Tupac and this ain't no scene from Poetic Justice," as Shirley rolled her eyes turning her head and she walked off switching her hips leaving him standing there. Ren Mack turned around and headed back to the truck. Shirley headed for the salon where her friends Renee and Rachelle were looking out the huge store front type of glass at her talking to the guy. Shirley came in the door and her girls started drilling her.

"Girl who was that lil cutie out there?" Renee asked her first.

Rachelle had her hands on her hips. "Yeah Shirl, who might that be?"

Shirley looked at her friends and answered them. "Girl I don't know, some negro name Ren Mack who was sitting in the passenger seat of that Cadillac truck. We made eye contact when I was on the highway, he was probably a drug dealer or something and his nails were dirty. You know me hell to the na'll."

"Shirl that was Ren Mack? He's a rapper from College Hill." Rachelle let her friend know the truth behind the guy she just was conversating with.

"Shirl, you're always judging someone, at least he's probably not married." Renee told her and started walking back to where Rachelle's chair was at past the rest of the stylist.

"At least I don't have cob webs on my pussy Renee." Shirley yelled back at her glaring at

the back of Renee. She didn't respond and ignored Shirley and gave her the finger.

Rachelle slapped Shirley's arm. "Shirl, that wasn't nice at all, that's our girl."

"But damn Chelle, she's always in my business trying to check me about who I'm getting dick from and she's not getting any at all."

"Rachelle shook her head. "C'mon girl, back to the shampoo bowl. I gotta make you fly we are going out tonight." Rachelle told her.

"Is sista Theresa going with us?" Shirley asked her. She was referring to Renee.

"Yes girl, she needs to get out and flirt, get her feet wet." Rachelle said.

They started walking towards the back of the salon. Shirley spoke to Meco, Ms. Angie, Anitra, Ebony and the customers. Meco was part owner together with Rachelle. She was an older woman who was very cute, a red bone with nice size proportioned lips. Her nickname was Auntie.

Shirley, Renee and Rachelle had been friends since middle school. They all graduated from Western Hills High School at the top of their class. In the order of one, two and three. Shirley was valedictorian and had got accepted to Harvard Law School. Renee was salutatorian and attended the University of Cincinnati. Rachelle opted out of her scholarship to attend hair school, because that was her passion.

Renee was doing alright for herself now, she was a manager at Kroger's grocery store chain. She had a nice apartment not to far from the hair salon on Ryland Ave. She still had trouble trusting men after she was raped by ten guys from the U.C Football Team when she was in college. In order for her to cope with it she had to get psychological help and she resorted to smoking marijuana.

Rachelle had given birth to her son while they were in high school their senior year. Her child's father was a top basketball player in the State of Ohio his senior year and was going straight to the pro's, skipping college.

Tragically after the first two games of his pro career he was killed in a car accident. His

11

agent had provided Rachelle and her son with a nice lump sum that he was entitled to. Rachelle and Keith Caldwell Jr. were taken care of and Rachelle invested some of the money into Mother's hair salon which she is the co-owner. She used the rest to help purchase a home in Amberly Village and to buy some stock. She was a single parent just looking for someone to love her and her son.

Shirley was a powerful lawyer who had more then one attraction. She liked the arts, fashion and light complexion men.

Shirley was dark complexion, around 5'5", well shaped with the cutest face known to man. She stayed in designer clothes and jewelry. Her personality was good and she could get real nasty both ways if needed. She didn't have any low self-esteem like her friend Renee.

Rachelle was light complexion, around 5'6". She had an enormous butt, with a small waist line. She was pretty, real delicate with a sense of humor. She also was a heavy drinker and loved to fight. She was about her business and cared deeply for her friend-ship with her girls. She wanted more then what life had to offer and she wanted to settle down and be a family orientated woman.

Renee was around 5'6" regular built with no special features. She was plain Jane when it came to fashion and living a free-will life style.

In high school she was the most popular and wore all the latest fashions. But now the tables had turned and she was just old Renee. The rape had taken her whole demeanor down. She was still beautiful with a nice body and had a good attitude even though she and Shirley would quarrel, she loved her friend.

No matter the physical response she evoked, and perhaps especially because of the others, more complicated feelings she inspired, nothing couldn't come from it. The sooner they finished this wild goose chase about different opinions concerning attractions towards men, the sooner Shirley hair would get done. She ignored the thought to entertain her friend's curiosity about her love life even though they already knew. Hours passed and the three closed the hair salon that Saturday evening. All three women split up going their separate ways, but would meet up again shortly that night.

They were going to a popular nightclub called "Skipper's" located in Roselawn on Reading Rd.

At 10:30 p.m. Shirley and Renee went to Rachelle's house since it was closer to Roselawn. Shirley was dressed in an egg shell white two piece Cole Han outfit, with a pair of black toe out Cole Han sandals. She also had on a fine jewelry collection.

Shirley was now the one who was the most extravagant when it came to fashion. Renee had on a dark brown and tan Louis Button skirt with a blouse to match. Her suede Louis Button sandals where a perfect match to her skirt.

The two women sat in Rachelle's living room sipping on Bacardi Limon while she was getting dressed. Renee rolled her a marijuana stick, because she needed to feel relax since she was about to go into battle with the male specie that she feared now from her sexual

Assault back in her college day's. Lucky for her that Keith Jr. was at Rachelle's mom house, because she knew her friend would not let her smoke it from of him.

"Renee, let me hit your smoke I'm trying to get my buzz on before we even get to Skipper's."

"Girl you're a lawyer." Renee had a confused look on her face. Why should someone in Shirley position chance doing drugs?

"They don't piss me Renee. I'm not going to suck your shit up, I just want a few puffs to get the party started.," said Shirley.

"Alright," as Renee handed the joint to Shirley and then Rachelle walked into the living room. Rachelle was dressed in a gold sarong with gold Giorgio Armani mules, and a matching purse. She also had on her promise ring that Keith Sr. gave her that he was going to replace it with a wedding ring. Rachelle grabbed her a glass of Bacardi and downed it before they headed out the door for the night out at Skipper's nightclub. Rachelle decided to drive them in her brand new 4 door M-5 BMW. She was feeling good about her new purchase. She already had an Acura SUV. They pulled into Skipper's parking lot and it was packed. The line for the entrance was down by the Circle K convenient store. Skipper's was a popular nightclub in Cincinnati where Pro athletes, business CEO's, major corporation personnel and drug dealers came to play. They had to opt out and park across the street from the club in the plaza parking lot. The three women crossed Reading Rd. to get to the club. Several cars blew their horns admiring their appearance as they quickly walked to the other side of the street.

Shirley had V.I.P. at Skipper's, because she was one of the bouncers lawyer. Having V.I.P. meant they didn't have to wait in the long line to enter the club. It was a five dollar coverage charge, but they didn't have to pay. When they walked in the club Ja-Rule "Always on time" was playing. The dance floor was packed. Shirley spotted an empty table near the restroom and they headed towards it. Shirley knew by being close to the restroom they could see a lot of men going and coming. They sat down and a waitress came to take their order. "Excuse me, what can I get you ladies tonight?" She asked them.

Renee ordered first. "I'll have a Corona with a lemon and a flaming Dr. Pepper." Rachelle said, "And I'll have a strawberry daiquiri with Seagram's gin, a double please."

"Can I have a 190 Octane and make sure it's real slushy please," as Shirley was going through her Coach purse. The waitress left to place their orders at the bar.

"Damn Chelle, who are you trying to give your shit up to tonight?" Shirley asked her.

"Yeah Chelle, you know you get real freaky when you drink gin," said Renee smiling at her friend.

"Nobody, you two heifers are crazy, always thinking negative." Rachelle put a lot of emphasis in saying that comment. "I just feel good tonight, but if a nigga gets lucky then he'll be a happy camper." Rachelle told her friends.

"Please, both of ya'll will probably be some guy fiesta tonight." Renee was looking around when she made that comment under her breath, but Shirley caught it.

"Sista Theresa, you need to be someone's toy tonight, so you can get the webs off of your lonely ass pussy." Shirley gave a little laugh.

Shirley and Renee were always at each others throat even though they had love for each other.

"If I do heifer it won't be with a married man." Renee played her trump card knowing it would sting Shirley's nerves.

"I hope it's with a man period, instead of three speed vibrator man Mike." Shirley told her and Rachelle almost fell out of her seat laughing from Shirley's assault on Renee.

"Don't go there Shirl." Renee looked at her friend. Shirley had to keep going though. "I know you get tired of buying batteries for that damn thing."

"At least its mines, my property that I have papers for and I don't have to share and he can stay weeks even months. He doesn't have to hit it and get home to wifey, how about that smart ass." Renee said snapping her fingers.

Shirley was furious behind that statement. She didn't have any fire power left, her only defense was. "Yeah a receipt."

They all just giggled as the waitress came back with their drinks. The waitress made sure she gave all three women their proper drinks. Their total came up to twenty one dollars.

"I got it," as Rachelle went inside her purse and pulled out twenty-five dollars.
She handed the waitress the bills telling her. "You can keep the change."

"Thanks and you ladies have a nice evening. If you need anything else call for me, my
name is Ronnie." The waitress gave a huge smile.

"Okay Ms. Ronnie we will." Shirley answered for the three. The waitress made her exit
from the table. "Damn bitch you really do feel good tonight huh?" Shirley said to
Rachelle, as she sipped her 190 Octane.

"Girl who are them cuties sitting at the bar? They are looking this way." Rachelle
tapped Shirley to show her the three good looking fella's that were sitting at the bar.
One guy was dark skin, with a stud in one ear. He was dressed nicely in a brown funnel
stitch sweater, cotton corduroy pants and a pair of dark brown Gucci loafers. One of his
friend's was light complexion with curly black hair and a thin mustache. He was
dressed in a cactus suede shirt, scout sweater, scout viscose pants all by Bally and a pair
of Bally loafers. The last guy amongst the three had a caramel complexion. He was
dressed in a blue Marc Echo track suit and an all white pair of Nike Airmax 95's. He
was more flashy then his partners with his jewelry.

Rachelle caught eye contact with the dark complexion one and waved them over to
their table which had three empty seats. The trio made their way to the ladies table,
Rachelle pointed to the dark skin guy. She wanted to make sure that her girls knew
that's who she was interested in. It was always the same for the group of women when
they came across a trio together. Rachelle was light skin or a red bone as she was referred to. So she always chose the dark skin guys. Shirley was dark skin so she always
chose the light skin guy. Renee was caramel complexion, but she always got the left
over's.

She most likely didn't get involved with the person and just conversed with the guy
until her friend's mission was accomplished. The guys came over and sat down with
their new found companions. Rachelle started off the introduction.

"Hi my name is Rachelle, these are my girlfriend's Shirley and Renee." She pointed at
the other two women as she said their names.

The dark skin guy spoke for the trio first. "Nice to meet you miss Rachelle, my name is
Roy, that's my partner Casey and that's Lamar," as Roy eyes lingered on Rachelle, as
everyone else at the table said their hellos.

"So Rachelle, what are you ladies doing out alone?" Roy asked.

"We just are chilling having a little drink." She answered adding, "And ya'll?"

"Oh we just out trying to see what's going on in the Nati night life." He responded.

"That's what's up." Rachelle said.

"Rachelle would you like to dance, so I can talk with you privately?" Roy asked her.

"Sure Roy, why not?" Rachelle and Roy pulled back from the table. Casey looked at Renee. Renee looked away though. "Miss lady would you like to join them?" Renee eyes met with his. "No thanks, I'm cool I just want to sit here and enjoy the scene," she said.

Shirley knew her friend was being defiant and uneasy as she watched Renee sip on her Corona.

"Well Lamar would you like to dance?" Shirley invited him to the dance floor. Lamar smiled showing his pearly whites. "Sure Shirley, but I'm no pro when it comes to dancing," he said.

"Don't worry as long as you let me grind on you." Shirley was being naughty as they both shared a glare and a smile. They pulled away from the table leaving Casey and Renee by themselves. The club speakers were now bumping Jaheim, and the dance floor was packed. Rachelle and Roy were wrapped up in each other seductively. Roy had his hands all over Rachelle's very round bottom. Her sarong made it possible to see and feel every curve, plus she was wearing a thong and her trunk was cellulite and dimple free.

Shirley had her back pressed up against Lamar's front. They were grinding hard and having a good time. Renee and Casey were making small conversation with each other, but weren't really crossing any barriers. Renee refused to let her guard down. She was now feeling the alcohol she was consuming. When she did finally give him room to move, out of nowhere a woman approached the table where they were sitting.

Renee instantly notices that the woman was upset. She looked at Renee hard and long before saying anything. She snarled at Renee giving her much attitude. Renee became aware of the situation and was about to ask the woman what the problem was. Before she could the woman lungs opened up and she spoke. "Hey Casey where's ya boy at?" She asked. Casey's voice was raspy and nervous kind of. "Umm…Vikki, umm -umm."

"Quit stuttering negro, and don't lie Casey, because I'm already going to tell your wife Monica that I found you up in the club with some strange bitch." Vikki sucked her teeth and her words connected with Renee's womanly senses. It was like an alarm going off. Renee didn't waste anytime responding. "Bitch, who in the hell you calling a bitch? You horse mouth bitch." Renee looked the woman up and down.

"The bitch sitting with my husband's partner, that's who." Vikki looked around to see if she could locate her husband. Renee hand started shaking, because she wasn't the drama type like Shirley and Rachelle. She stood her ground though.

"Na'll I ain't no bitch. You don't know me like that and you better watch who the fuck you are talking to slut." Renee confidence shot to the roof.

Vikki pointed towards her crotch area. "I got your slut right between my legs BITCH!" Renee started to get up, but Casey grabbed her arm holding her back.

"Hey ya'll chill out with all that." Casey stated to the both of them.

As the commotion was taking place at the table Rachelle saw the strange woman pointing in Renee's face and she separated herself from Roy. She grabbed Shirley all in one motion and they headed to their table. Lamar and Roy followed not knowing what was going on. Roy didn't recognize his wife in the mix. When they reached the table Rachelle looked Vikki up and down. "What's up Nee, what's going on?" Rachelle asked her friend.

"This crazy ass lady right here is looking for her husband," as Renee was now standing up. She continued while pointing at Lamar and Roy. "He's probably one of them tired ass nigga's ya'll were dancing with."

Roy looked at his wife and knew it was her. Vikki focused in on him .

"Roy is that you? I thought ya'll were going to Bogart's to play pool, but I see ya'll are trying to shoot in a bitches hole instead." Vikki was now upset even more.

"Umm Vikki, we just stopped in here to have a few drinks." Roy said.

"I'm tired of your shit Roy. Do I look stupid? You stopped in a nightclub to have a drink Negro, and Bogart's sell drinks." She paused. "Na'll ya'll stopped in here trying to catch something from these home wrecking bitches." Vikki said folding her arms.

Rachelle kicked off her mules, because she wasn't taking the verbal abuse from this strange woman. "Hold up girlfriend, who you calling a bitch now?" Rachelle asked her.

"The bitch and slut who responded." Vikki said.

With no other words spoken Rachelle swung and hit Vikki in the mouth. Roy immediately jumped in between them before Rachelle could get another blow in.

He also did that so that he could protect Vikki from the outraged females. Lamar and Casey grabbed each other arms making a barrier in front of Shirley, Renee and Rachelle.

Vikki moved her hand from her mouth and looked at the blood in her hand and said. "I'm going to kill that bitch, she busted my lip."

"Let her go Roy," as Rachelle started removing her jewelry.

"Yeah Roy, let her ass loose, so we can stomp this bitch lights out." Shirley was removing her jewelry and sandals. Renee was just hugging herself, because she didn't want any parts of the drama for real. She was tipsy too.

"How we supposed to know they were married men? None of them are wearing rings." Renee let it be known as her words were slurry, but could be heard clearly.

"Roy you don't have your ring on? You must think I'm a damn fool. Save your breath trying to explain this shit to me." Vikki was still trying to attend to her wound.

Rachelle was trying to break loose. "What up bitch? That's what I do to hoes that run they mouth to a bitch like me." Rachelle told her.

"I'm going to get you yellow bitch, watch out Roy," as Vikki was trying to get loose also. Roy knew that his wife wasn't built for this type of battle so he didn't let her go. Security approached the scene by this time. Shirley explained the situation and by Vikki still carrying on like a mad woman they kicked her out and Roy and his partners left with her.

The three women sat back down at the table and Renee was crying a little.

"Seee…That's why I don't be bothered with no man now. They all are dogs girl." Renee's slurred speech was getting worse.

Rachelle looked at her nail and, "Damn I think I cracked a nail on that heifer's mouth, I Need a fill in."

"That bitch just don't know how close she was to a beat down." Shirley was putting her jewelry back on.

"If that was my husband I would have knocked his ass out and not trying to jump fly with the next bitch." Rachelle said.

"I know that's right Chelle." Shirley was checking her cell phone. Then she asked her friends. "So what's up, ya'll want to go to Perkins and get a bite to eat. I know you're famished after the knock out Chelle?"

"You got jokes Shirl, but yeah I'm down for some Perkins." Rachelle responded.

"Look Thomas ass is blowing my phone up girl. I bet he's on my voice mail too." Shirley was now shutting her cell phone. Renee was slumped over and they knew it was time to go. Rachelle was helping Renee get up. "C'mon Nee let's go."

Shirley helped Rachelle their friend. When the three women exit the club Rachelle and Shirley notice Roy and Vikki in the parking lot still arguing. They laughed at them. They dodged through traffic back across Reading Rd. to the Plaza where Rachelle's BMW was parked. Just as Renee was about was about to get in the car she vomited. Rachelle and Shirley took that as their cue to take their friend home for the night. When they reached the inside Renee's apartment they stripped her down to her naked-ness and placed her in the shower under cold water. After the cold shower they made her drink some 7-Up. They put her in the bed butt-naked with a sheet over her and placed a rotating fan directly on her. When Renee passed out they let themselves out of her less spacious apartment. It was about 2:30 a.m. when they pulled up in front of Per-kins in Correyville.

Shirley and Rachelle simultaneously checked their make-up in the vanity mirrors on the back of the sun visors. Their make-up and hair was still flawless. They stepped out the M-5 and shook their clinging clothes loose from their bodies. It was semi packed inside of Perkins, but that was the usual when the clubs let out in Cincinnati. You either went to Perkins, Chili Time, or White Castles for a bite to eat.

The hostess quickly sat the two at a booth by the window and from this view Rachelle could see her car. Shirley excused herself and went to use the restroom and make a call to Thomas. Shirley entered the restroom, and two women were having a discussion at the sink looking in the mirror. Shirley found a stall and entered. "Damn these toilets are nasty looking at least they have toilet paper." She mumbled to herself. She grabbed a hand full of toilet paper and then laced the toilet seat nicely. She undid her pants and pulled them down with her panties half way. She then positioned herself over the toilet not sitting down on the seat.. She started urinating and heard one of the females say,

"Girl ole boy was fine as hell in Brandy's, and did he give you his number?" Shirley was enjoying the pressure being relieved from her bladder and wasn't paying the women any attention. The other woman responded. **"Yeah girl, his office and cell number."**

"Where he said he worked at?" The woman asked her friend.

"He said he worked for Proctor & Gamble."

"And what kind of car was that he got in? His whip was nice as hell." The friend told her girl.

"Girl that was one of them foreign joints, an Aston Martin. The color was beauti-

ful a marble blue that looked black, can't you see me rolling that and us in it?" The female said.

Shirley woman senses picked up on that last response, because Thomas and some old white man were the only two who had Aston Martins in the city. Plus Thomas car was marble blue. Shirley was vexed and could feel her blood pressure rise a notch.

"Did you see that watch he was wearing girl? I mean damn the brother knows how to dress." The woman told her friend.

"All those crushed diamonds, girl I saw that watch, you caught a good catch tonight Alexis."

"I know Dominique."

Shirley was pissed. They had the nerve to be discussing the four thousand dollar watch she bought him for his birthday. She quickly wiped herself, pulled her clothes up and fixed herself. She then flushed the toilet and walked out the stall to see which one of these women was talking to her lover and boyfriend. Shirley reached a sink by them. The two women spoke to her. "Hi."

Shirley acknowledged them with a smile and a hand wave. She turned the water on in the sink and played like she was really washing her hands thoroughly. The women continued their conversation.

"So what was his name again Alexi?" Dominique asked her friend.

"Thomas, Thomas Patterson, that's my future husband girl." Alexis responded.

Shirley twitched at the female's last comment. Her mind was running wild a mile a minute. Upset wasn't the emotion she was feeling at this time. She couldn't describe how she was feeling. A thought came. "Bitch only if you knew he's already married and I'm his mistress. You're stupid and ugly as hell. Alexis you look more like a Volkswagen. Damn Thomas you could have tried to fuck something better then me, because this bitch is tired."

Shirley was extremely catty when it came to someone she was sleeping with. Her insides turned upside down in her stomach. She smiled at the two women and exit's the restroom. Her eyes were now kind of watery, but she didn't cry. Shirley sat back down at the booth across from her friend. Rachelle saw the glare in her eyes and knew something was wrong with her friend. She looked at Shirley long and direct before questioning her.

"Shirl, what's wrong? You look like you are about to cry." Rachelle said.

"Chelle, guess what, this lame ass Negro done gave his number to some dusty bitch, I

20

mean ugly as hell," said Shirley.

"Who Shirl?" as Rachelle had a look of concern on her face.

"Thomas bitch ass. I got him though. I think it's about time to go public on his ass."

A single lonely tear dropped from her eye. Then the waitress came to their booth.

"Hi, my name is Tasha I'll be serving you all tonight. What can I do for ya'll?"

"Nothing right now please," as Shirley eyes began to water even more.

"Hold up Tasha I would like the number two breakfast, my eggs scrambled hard with cheese," said Rachelle while looking over the menu. She made sure that she was giving her the exact order of what she desired.

Rachelle closed the menu and the waitress asked her. "What would you like to drink?"

"I would like two glasses of orange juice and some coffee please." Rachelle said.

"Would that coffee be decaf or caffeinated?" The waitress asked Rachelle.

"Decaf please." Rachelle answered.

"What can I get for you miss?" The waitress asked Shirley.

"Nothing for me, I'm not hungry." Shirley replied.

"Okay. I have a number two, eggs scrambled hard with cheese, two glasses of orange juice and coffee. I'll be right back with your order shortly."

The waitress grabbed the menus and left the booth. Shirley let the tears flow Rachelle retrieved a Kleenex from her purse and handed it to her friend.

"Girl I'm telling you, I'm going to let his wife know everything, how he's been fucking me, the trips, how her bedroom looks, and the whole nine yard." Shirley said as she wiped away the tears from her eyes.

"Shirl, it's not that serious to break up his home. I told you not to mess with him from the jump, but na'll you had too. I told you if he'd fuck around on his wife, he'd fuck around on you. I also told you not to fall in love with him, but you did. You confused lust with love and now look at you."

Rachelle was now upset at her friend that she would wait till Thomas did her wrong to tell his wife. She was acting like one of those Hollywood celebrity chicks.

"Chelle, I didn't fall in love though." Shirley confessed.

"Yes you did Shirl, yes you did. That's why you are hurting the way you are. Just exhale and move on. The shit get's old boo. You are successful without him in your life. What can he do that you can't do for yourself?" Rachelle said.

"But'em-," Rachelle cut her off before she could finish. "There is no but; you're always going to be number two to his wife Shirl. Nothing more, nothing less."

"I want my shit back!" Shirley said with the most devious voice.

"Girl that man done spent over a hundred grand on you easily over the years ya'll been fooling around. Trips to Italy, Hawaii, Japan, Egypt and France. He paid your condo up for two years when you first moved in. Bought you all types of jewelry and damn near paid for your Lexus. Let him have the shit you bought him, you got the better deal. He gave you enough hush-hush money to quiet a small village in the Congo's." Rachelle was caressing her friend's hand trying to calm her down.

"Yeah Chelle, but he played me like boo-boo the fool. You should see this bitch he gave his number to. I mean she ain't got shit on me." Shirley told her friend.

"That's just in a man's nature, they don't care who they fuck as long as it's some new pussy. Remember that shit down there between a woman's thighs don't have a face, only some lips to suck a brother in." Rachelle explained to her friend.

Shirley got quiet and then she spoke again, "Chelle, I guess I did fall in love with him. I accepted his marriage and still was in denial."

"it's going to be alright, we some bad diva's with that red snapper." Rachelle told her. Rachelle gave her friend a high five and they laughed. They sat in Perkins for another hour talking and discussing how they wanted their lives to be in the next five years. Shirley expressed to Rachelle how she wanted kids and to be married in the future. She also stated that she was trying to get pregnant by Thomas on purpose, but it seem like something was wrong with him, because she was fertile and could produce.

Under certain circumstances Shirley knew that Rachelle was right about her getting the better end of the deal during her and Thomas' relationship, and the fact she was living a lie as well as Thomas by living a double life herself. She could no longer argue that fact or make excuses for neither side. All she could do was move on and try to have a relationship of her very own dealing with less confusion. They say that daddy's raise their daughters, while mother's raise their son's. Shirley seen a splitting image of her dad in Thomas. His work ethics and his character. She couldn't figure out what his wife had that she didn't. Then it dawned on her, *"kids"*.

CHAPTER TWO

Revenge

That early Sunday morning the sun light came through the window's of Rachelle guest room. Shirley was sleeping until the sun hit her directly on her eyelids. The strong sun rays awoke her. She was sleeping in a long Nike t-shirt. Shirley squinted from the sun, wiped her eyes and grabbed her Geneva Cellin watch from the nightstand. It was 10:30 a.m. She stretched and yawned cracking her toes. She had stayed over from last night after they left Perkins. She got up and headed for the restroom so that she could release the waste from her bladder. After wiping herself she washed her hands and then turned on the shower. She went back to the guest room to grab her small bag that held her toiletries.

She then went to the hallway linen closet and grabbed a wash cloth and towel. Shirley walked back towards the bathroom and Rachelle passed her wearing a beach towel. They spoke and kept going. Shirley had obligations with her granny this Sunday morning. After her shower Shirley grabbed her pink duffel bag and got out her Baby Phat shorts which were khaki, a navy blue Baby Phat t-shirt and a pair of white on white Reebok classics with her little cute footy's.

'Her hair was still in the style that Rachelle fixed it the day before. She put her jewelry on and sprayed a little of her Apple perfume. She packed her bag with her dirty laundry and headed to the front door. She stopped briefly in the kitchen to see what Rachelle was doing. Rachelle had the stereo blasting Total "Kissing You" while she was cooking a good old fashion Sunday meal. Shirley continued on to her car. She put her overnight bag in the trunk and headed back in the house. She saw that Renee's dark green Nissan Maxima was gone, meaning she came and got her car sometime this morning. Shirley came back into the house, to help Rachelle briefly before leaving to go attend to her granny in Price Hill on the west side of town.

Rachelle was making fried chicken, broccoli with cheese, Mac & cheese, turnip greens, candy yams and cornbread. Rachelle was also making a pineapple upside down cake. She smiled at Shirley as she was mixing the sharp cheese in the macaroni.

"What's up girlfriend, where are you going today?" Rachelle asked her.

"I have to go run a few errands for my granny."

"Tell her I said hi and I love her too." Rachelle told her.

"I will, I let her know that her other granddaughter loves her too," as Shirley started to walk off. Rachelle stopped her.

"Shirl?" Rachelle called out. Shirley turned around.

"I love you and keep your head to the sky. Remember we some diva's out here, no man can dictate our happiness. Crying is a sign of weakness so stay strong and don't give him any of your precious tears. Call me later." Rachelle told her and Shirley nodded her head to what her friend was telling her. She got all emotional and had to embrace Rachelle for giving her that much advice. She knew she cared dearly. She went and gave Rachelle a hug. "Thank you Chelle, I needed to hear that."

She left from Rachelle's house and she immediately called her granny from her cell phone. Ever since her parents and sisters moved to New Jersey, the only family Shirley went around was her grandmother. Even though she had aunts, uncles and cousins that still lived in Cincinnati and the Dayton area.

She was only close to her grandmother. Her extended family always felt as though Shirley was stuck up, because of her education and career. Her grandmother wanted her to run a few errands. She wanted to get her grandmother's business out the way early so she could go home and relax. Shirley was heading up Glenway after turning off of Grand Ave. in Price Hill when her cell phone rang. Figuring it was probably her granny again she answered without looking at the caller I.D. "Hello," as Shirley answered sweetly.

"Damn girl I thought we were getting together today?" The voice said.

"Who is this?" Shirley knew the answer already, but she couldn't believe that Thomas would have the nerve to call her. But why wouldn't he? He wasn't aware of what Shirley now knew about him giving his number to a female while he was out last night. You could hear Thomas smile through the phone. "Don't play girl, you know it's big daddy." He said.

Shirley was already pissed at him, but that remark sent her over the edge.

"Steve Harvey not and my daddy is in New Jersey. Look Thomas I'm not feeling you today. I'll call you when I need some." She said with much attitude. He was confused behind that remark. "What's up with the attitude Shirley?" He asked her.

Shirley smirked. "Check your voice mail. I ran into that ugly bitch Alexis you gave your number to last night." She was really boiling now.

Thomas kept his voice even and cool. "Why are you tripping? I don't know any Alexis and don't have a clue what you are talking about."

Shirley was tapping her steering wheel. She was now furious because she knew he was lying. She said out loud indirectly to the side. "This Negro must think I'm stupid." She paused briefly. "Well Thomas since you don't have a clue, let me give you one." Shirley hung up the phone in his ear. She kept driving steady up Glenway Ave. Thomas called right back, upon Shirley pushing the talk button on her phone she could hear him say. "Shirley can we talk please, it must be a mix up or misunderstanding somewhere." She had to give him some more of her mind. "All this time Thomas I've been only fucking you knowing you have a wife, being faithful to your ass telling other men that I'm married living in fantasy world. Damn I was a naïve bitch. Not no more, I'm going out and find me some new dick."

Shirley almost began to tear up again.

"Come on Shirley baby let's talk this out, how about dinner tonight?" Thomas was begging.

"How about you have dinner with your wife or Alexis. I'm no longer involving myself with you, and please don't call my cell phone, office and house anymore. How about that." Shirley hung up her cell phone before he could respond. She was now pulling her car up to 1613 Iliff, her grandma's house. She got out of her car and her grandma was sitting on the porch. Shirley walked up the steps and was greeted by her elderly grandmother with a big hug and a kiss while she was still sitting down. Her granny had on her cotton housecoat and slipper's. Shirley sat next to her in a chair on the porch.

"Look at my grandbaby, just as beautiful as ever with yo black self. When you gone have me some great grand chittling girl?" Her grandmother had her eyes locked in on her. Every time Shirley would visit her grandma she would ask her the same question.

"Granny I'm focusing on my career right now, and you know this. I guess I'll have some whenever I get married, one day." Shirley knew she wanted a child more than anything, more than her granny wanted her to have one. "Pumpkin is you still meeting with that man with the fancy car?" She called her by her nickname she gave her when she was little. But she knew she was acquiring about Thomas. Shirley didn't want to answer her, but she did. "Yes ma'am Na-Na." Shirley answered her granny by calling her the name that all the grandkids called her.

"Pumpkin I don't like that man. Something is spooky about him. Ya'll don't live together and haven't had any kids in four years. I hate to say it, but the Holy Spirit tells me that he's not being honest with you baby. He's married or something child living one of those doubled lives. So watch yourself child." Shirley knew that her grandmother was right. She didn't tell any of her family members that Thomas was married, only her friends

Knew the truth behind her relationship with Thomas Patterson. "Na-Na we are just taking things slow."

"Well you be careful. I know this young handsome man at church who could give you a lot of chittling's, he single to Pumpkin. He sometimes runs errands for me when you are down at that Court House." She smiled at Shirley. Shirley laughed, because her granny was trying to hook her up again.

"Granny I'm okay, I don't need for you to find someone for me."

"You know granny got the hook up gal," she smiled at Shirley showing off her open face gold tooth that was apart of her dentures. Shirley changed the subject. "So what can I do for you today Na-Na?"

"Let's see, get my prescription from Walgreen, go by Pastor Cooper house in Hartwell, his wife made me a plate for Sunday dinner since I couldn't make it to church this morning. I need three money orders and here is a list of things I need from the grocery store." Her granny told her.

Shirley grabbed the list and scanned over it quickly. "Okay Na-Na I'll be back shortly." Shirley said as she put the list in her purse and headed back down the steps to her car. Shirley didn't mind doing things for her grandmother. She was grateful for her, because She had help pay a lot of Shirley's bills while she was in college. Nothing was greater then giving back to those who helped get her to where she was at in her life now. Shirley did everything her granny asked of her. She stood in the house drinking a glass of water. She was a little tired and she had a case to handle in the big court house tomorrow morning and she knew she needed a little rest.

"Oh Na-Na, Rachelle told me to tell you hi and she loves you."

Her grandmother looked over her glasses at Shirley. "Tell Rachelle she can visit me too and she needs to come and braid my hair for me. Shit I'm to old to be trying to get around like I use to."

"I'll tell her Na-Na. I'm about to go, I have to work in the morning. Do you need anything else?" Shirley was sitting the glass in the kitchen sink.

"No honey child, call me later and don't forget what I told you about that man, the spirit don't lie. Watch him now grandma done spoke child." She told Shirley.

"yes ma'am I will," as Shirley gave her a hug and a kiss. When Shirley pulled away from her granny house it was like 2:00 in the afternoon. She was having a hunger headache and was a little tired. She was driving down Glenway Ave. when her cell phone rang, this time she looked at her caller I.D. before answering it. It was Rachelle.

""I'll do her hair sometime this week, but every time I go see her she's always talking about you havingHello." Shirley was putting her Mary J. Blige CD in the changer.

"Shirl, what up? Are you coming back this way to eat dinner?" Rachelle asked her.

"I didn't plan on it. I'm tired from running around Cincinnati for Na-Na." Shirley told her.

"Girl she would do it for you." Rachelle replied.

"I know, and she told me to tell you that she needs for you to braid her hair and you could visit some times." Shirley told her.

 a baby girl." Rachelle put emphasis on her comment.

"I know she was just trying to hook me up with somebody from the church. She is too funny, but I do need to eat something I have a hunger headache. So I'll be over there in a few, I'm about to get on the E-way now." Shirley said.

"Okay good, can you please stop and get me a twelve pack of Michelob?" Rachelle asked her. Shirley smiled. "What for you don't drink beer?"

Rachelle sighed. "Shirl, just do it for me."

"You got that Negro over there don't you?" Shirley knew her friend to well, she knew without a doubt that Rachelle wanted the beer to entertain her male guest.

Rachelle chuckled and said, "Something like that and someone's here for you too."

"Where is Keith Jr.?" Shirley asked.

"My mom is going to keep him until Thursday."

"Alright heifer, but you think you are real slick Chelle."

"Bye I love you Shirl," as Rachelle made a whispering sound in her ear. She hung up her cell phone. Shirley knew that Pedro was probably over her house or some new guy she probably met and was trying to hook her up.

Shirley eased off the exit on Paddock Rd. She turned left at the light going to California Ave. She then turned right onto California Ave. going pass Sonny's bar and Mother's hair salon. When she got up towards Reading Rd. she turned into the parking lot of

Quick Stop convenient store. She saw a 4 door Honda Accord with a vinyl top that had a big dollar sign on the rear window and the third window on the sides. The car was dark blue and the top vinyl was white. She parked on the opposite side to where she had to go around the car to get into the store.

It was a guy sitting in the driver's seat. Shirley walked pass the car, the drive's window was down. The guy sitting in the driver's seat was resting his head against the white leather seat. He was on his cell phone, but he took out the time to notice Shirley and gave her a little smile. He was light skin and she gave a smile back. Shirley went on inside the store and made her purchase. When she exited the store another guy was standing outside handing out flyers. "Come see the hottest new local talent in the Nati at the Ritz nightclub this Saturday night. The Trap Boys featuring Ren Mack and Boobie. Show this flyer and get in half price." The guy shouted out. He saw Shirley and tried to give her one. "here you go miss lady the hottest rap group in the land." He tried to give her one, but she declined. "No thank you." Shirley kept moving towards her car. The owner of the Honda Accord was now standing outside the car leaning up against it. She quickly gave him the once over. He was light skin, well built and about 5'9" in height. He had his hair cut in a low fade and his goatee was well groomed. He was dressed in black and red in a Cincinnati Reds jersey, he also had a platinum David Yurman watch and a crushed diamond pinky ring.

She liked what she saw. He spoke to her giving her the opportunity to speak to him.

"Hello beautiful lady." He said admiring Shirley's face and figure.

"Hello, your car is cute. Oh I'm sorry you're a guy I need to say something more manly about your car. Your car is tight, I like the design, and it's original."

Shirley was using her flirtatious voice. He smiled at her. "Na'll miss lady you can say it's cute. Thank you, I put a lot of time into this car." He told Shirley.

"I bet it cost a pretty penny." Shirley said looking the Honda over once more.

"A small fortune, but nothing is too great for one that seeks his or her desires." He winked at her. She got in tune to his lingual.

Damn this Negro got a little mouth piece on him and his nails are clean, keep it together Shirl. Yeah keep it together girlfriend.

"So what's your name may I ask?" Shirley asked him.

"Sam, my name is Sam and yours?" He said.

"My name is Shirley, Shirley Thomas to be exact." Shirley smile was flirtatious.

"So what's your profile Miss Thomas?" Sam asked her and Shirley was confused by his question and she asked him. "What do you mean by that Sam?"

"Your status, your age, just stuff that makes you complete and me aware of, if I can get up close and personal with you." Sam looked Shirley over one more time licking his lips like L.L. Cool J. He continued on. "I can look at you and tell you are fine, but I want to know what comes with that beauty." Sam smiled to himself, because he knew he had intrigued her with that line.

"Well I'm twenty-nine, I'm single and I'm a lawyer." She smiled at him. Sam was shocked to find out she was a lawyer. "And you?" She asked him.

"I'm twenty-six, single, I own a Detail Shop to customize cars on Eighth and State. I'm also a promoter and the manager of the hottest rap group in the Nati. The Trap Boys, Ren Mack and Boobie."

She turned her nose up a little remembering meeting Ren Mack yesterday at the Hair Salon. "Oh for a minute I thought you were one of my potential clients. You know a statistic without a real job." She gave him a half smile.

"Na'll Shirley I'm legit with my gig. So you don't listen to rap music?" Sam asked her. She baffled the question at first and then answered it.

"I do, but I like good rap music not all that shoot'em up crap." She said to him.

"My group is about real life structure and not about gun play." He replied.

She changed subjects. "Umm so you don't have a female companion, a woman or something of that nature?" She asked him.

"I'm going to be real and straight to the point with you Shirley. I date from time to time, but I'm not in a relationship." She respected his answer because she knew that a guy with swag like his was getting some action somewhere.

Shirley asked him. "So where do you live?"

"I live in Evanston, down the street from Purcell Marian Catholic High School." He was looking dead in the pits of her eyes when he answered her. Shirley got straight to the point. "Do you have a number Sam?"

"Yeah Shirley, I have a number."

Shirley cocked her head to the side. "Well can I get it?"

"Before I give you my contacts, where about do you live?" He asked her.

"I'll tell you everything and anything you want to know when I call you. I'm kind of in a rush Sam." She told him.

"Alright." Sam opened his car door to retrieve a pen and paper out of his glove box. He wrote the information down on a piece of paper. "Here you go, here's my pager, cell phone and home number. I gave you a code for my pager so I'll know it's you when you page me."

"I hope you don't live with your parents or some chick." Shirley said.

"Na'll I got my own spot," as he was now walking her to her car. He opened the door for her. He watched her climb into her vehicle carefully admiring what he saw from that view. She got settled in putting her seat belt on. She rolled down the window and looked up at him. "I'll call you Sam."

"You do that Miss Shirley." He smiled at her and she started up her smooth engine, put the car in drive and was off heading towards Rachelle house.

Shirley turned into Rachelle's driveway, it was a turquoise Saturn SUV sitting behind her BMW M-5. Shirley got out and sat the bag of beer on the roof of her car, and then she went into the trunk and grabbed her small hygiene bag just in case she had to freshen up.

Shirley didn't use the doorbell or even knock she just walked into the house. You could hear the sweet sound of Sade coming from Rachelle's day room. Shirley headed for the kitchen to put the beer in the refrigerator. Shirley swore she smelled marijuana in the air as she headed to the day room. She stood in the entrance way of the day room she saw a guy sitting on the dark green sofa chair. He was dressed in the latest Roc-a-Wear fashion and had on a few pieces of jewelry. The guy who was hugged up with her girl Rachelle on the couch was in DKNY and sandals. Shirley recognized the two men. It was Sharan who she really didn't care for and his partner Pedro who was from Mt. Healthy and owned a few local drive-thru stores. Rachelle had been getting her feet wet from him for about four years now. They had an opened door relationship. Even though he was twenty-seven and established, he had told Rachelle he wasn't ready to be serious and get married. Since day one when they hooked up they were trying to hook Sharan up with her. Sharan notice

Shirley in the archway of the day room. "Rachelle your girl is here," as Sharan pointed to her. Rachelle looked up at her. "Hey Shirl, did you get the beer?" She asked her. "Yeah I got it. I put it in the fridge." Shirley was still standing in the archway of the entrance way.

"We already ate, the food is on the stove." Rachelle told her.

"I'm not hungry right now," as her eyes glanced over at Sharan briefly.

Shirley hadn't seen Sharan in like a year and a half since a party at Rachelle's house.

"Shirl, you remember Sharan don't you?" Rachelle said knowing she did.

"Shirley looked over at Sharan again. "Yeah I remember him, how could I forget?" Her eyes went back in her friend's direction. Sharan was brown skin complexion and Shirley didn't care for his complexion. He was good looking, well built and well-mannered. He had a good personality and good ambition. He use to sweat her and the fact he vomit in her lap at Rachelle's party and that was the last time she saw him. That day she would never forget. He was drunk that night and she was in disgust with him ever since.

"Well excuse me." Shirley said to the group. "I need to take care of something."

"Hold up Shirl, I need to get my man a beer, do you want one Sharan?" Rachelle asked Sharan as she got up from the couch. "Sure Rachelle." Sharan said.

Shirley was looking at her friend with crazy eyes, because she had on some tight coochie cutter boy shorts and a bra. Pedro patted Rachelle on her behind as she walked off with Shirley. The two walked into the kitchen together. Shirley whispered to Rachelle.

"Chelle, why ya'll keep trying to hook me up with him?"

Rachelle grabbed two beers out the fridge. She sat the two beers on the counter and looked Shirley in the eyes. "Shit that nigga likes you Shirl. Plus he's single with no kids and he has his own business." Rachelle hand was on her friends shoulder.

Shirley raised an eyebrow. "A kids clothing store Chelle."

"At least he has an honest job Shirl, he's not doing or selling drugs." Rachelle told her. Shirley insides were rubbing her the right way.

"Yeah-yeah." Shirley said knowing her girl was right.

"I'm not saying to just fuck him and marry him, but you could give him a chance. Shirl instead of being a brutal bitch." The look was long and pleasant that Rachelle gave her.

"You know what Chelle maybe you're right. I need to get Thomas off my mind. She let me freshen up and I'll take Sharan his beer." Shirley told her.

"Alright then." Rachelle winked at her friend.

"One more thing Chelle, bitch you bold as hell walking around in those boy shorts and bra." Shirley said.

"This is my shit Shirl, I can walk around this piece naked if I wanted to. My man and I about to go get our freak on, so be nice to Sharan." Rachelle grabbed the beer and left Shirley standing in the kitchen. Shirley gave her friend a snarl look as she walked off in her tight boy shorts and bra heading for the day room to get Pedro.

Rachelle got to the day room and stood in the archway and said, "Come on Pedro let's got to my room, and Sharan my girl is going to bring you your beer."

Pedro got up and brushed off his shorts and followed Rachelle to her room. Sharan sighed in the air before him………………………………………….....................................

Back in the kitchen Shirley womanly senses kicked in and revenge was on her mind. Even though Thomas probably hadn't gone through the actual process of cheating, but his intentions were to get him some new action.

Shirley was now going to do her. She was courageous and she was curious to how it would be to get down with a darker complexion brother on the down low not letting her girls know she went outside what she believed in. She knew Sharan was a good looking guy, but he wasn't light skin complexion. Her stomach did somersault's remembering when he threw up on her. But they did have some good times together double dating with theirs friends and never engaged in any type of intimacy. They would debate and argue all the time, and that was good to Shirley because she never let her guard down. Shirley sighed and exhaled. Taking her friend's advice and wanting to experience different, she was going to jump off the edge with Sharan. Right now she was vulnerable and emotionally out of sink. She has Thomas on her heart, Sam on her mind and Sharan on her conscious. Was she to be a total wreck? Or was she to be a strong individual and move on?

Shirley went to freshen up in the places she needed and sprayed herself with a 'Touch of Romance' by Ralph Lauren. She changed out of her clothes putting on the long Nike t-shirt she slept in last night. She left out the guest room and went back into the kitchen grabbing Sharan's beer and her a glass of water. She entered the archway and Sharan could smell the scent of the perfume she was wearing as it tickled his nose. It smell, real good to him. Shirley placed the water and beer on a coaster that sat on the small table in front of the couch. She then went and turned down Sade a notch.

She sat down on the couch and with her index finger she called Sharan over to her. He came to her and sat beside her. "So what's up with you Sharan and where's your girlfriend?" She asked him. He was caught off guard because she was never this nice to him. He looked at her and laughed a little.

"Are you serious Shirl?" He asked.

"Yeah I'm serious, so who is she and don't lie." She confessed wanting to know. He looked at her once more with puppy dog eyes, and then cleared his throat.

"I'm on E flat." Sharan laughed. "And I don't know about a girlfriend Shirl, but have you seen her?" He said that with sing song harmony.

"C'mon Sharan I'm serious." Shirley bit her bottom lip..

"Seriously Shirley, I don't have a real girlfriend in my life."

"So who are you sleeping with then?" She asked him.

Sharan glanced down at her. "Damn you are getting personal I'm not in your business like that."

"Oh so you can't answer my question?" Shirley was looking into his eyes.

"I can answer it, but why is that so important, and why all of a sudden you being nice to me?" He asked her.

"Can't a woman have a change of heart? Remember you are the one who vomited on me crazy," as she touched his hand. "Plus if you answer honestly, you might get to fuck me right now." Shirley couldn't believe the words that just left her mouth, but she didn't fret.

Sharan ears didn't believe what he just heard. "Excuse me." Sharan said. Shirley said it again.

"You heard me. I said if you answer honestly, you might get to fuck me tonight." She bit her bottom lip seductively. It encouraged him to answer her question.

"Oh yeah?" He said.

"Yeah," as she continued to search his soul looking in his eyes.

"Well Shirley to be perfectly honest. I was sleeping with this female name Gaye who worked for me." He stopped but Shirley wouldn't allow him to. "And what happened?" She asked him. He looked at her with a confused look and said, "Don't ever mix business with pleasure, that's all I'm going to say Shirley. It didn't last." Adding. "Damn Shirl, you smell good as hell, what are you wearing?" He asked her now holding her hand.

"A little something by Ralph Lauren called a Touch of Romance."

By this time Shirley was positioned all in Sharan's face. She was confused, so she took a chance to sip her water. She collected her thoughts and grabbed him by the head and kissed him soft and gently. He kissed her back longer than a few seconds. Shirley broke his kiss and took him by the hand to lead him to the guest room. He didn't believe what was going on. Dumb founded like a little goofy kid he felt on the inside. He didn't question her next move, he just went with the flow. He had laugh lines following her to the guest room, but never laughed. He grinned to himself though. Eagerly they stepped into the room and she closed the door behind them. Sharan stood there froze as Shirley went and positioned herself on the bed on her back sitting up a little. She urged him to her by pointing her index finger to him telling him to come and join her on the bed. Reality kicked in.

He came to her and laid between her legs as she spread them for him. They began to kiss

one another passionately, and then Sharan took one of his hands and went under her t-shirt to massage one of her breast still being held in her bra. Shirley moaned seductively from his touch, urging him to explore other places on her physical attire. He then took the same hand and investigated between her legs rubbing that area covered by the fabric of her nylon panties. Sharan then removed his clothing and jewelry except for his boxers.

They started kissing again, now they were chest to breast and boxers to her pussy. He then placed his fingers on her pussy to enter her passage which was met by warm wetness.

She moaned pulling Sharan closer to her. Sharan began to ease out of his boxers. Shirley stopped him. "Hold up Sharan, do you have a rubber?" She asked him.

"No not on me." He replied.

"You should have one on you at all time, you never know." She said.

"I don't be out there like that Shirl." That comment made Shirley insides tingle with excitement. She knew he wasn't out there promoting his sex like the average guy in his twenties. "Hold up , let me go see if Rachelle has one on hand. I like practicing safe sex until you know…," as she looked at him and got up off the bed. She grabbed her Nike t-shirt and put it back on. She left from the guest room and headed towards Rachelle's room. When she got to Rachelle's door she could hear her screaming out moans and grunts, meaning that Pedro was being intimate with her sexually. "Oh Pedro fuck this pussy baby. Oh shit black ass Negro I'm about to cum."

Shirley didn't care that her girl was in the heat of the moment. They use to have sex with guys in the same room when they were younger during their teenage years. So she knocked on the door anyway.

BOOM-BOOM-BOOM-BOOM! Shirley knocked aggressively.

"Who-who-who-is-is-it?" Rachelle's voice was skipping pace.

"It's me Chelle." Shirley yelled out.

"Oh shit Pedro, what Shirl? I'm trying to get my swerve on, come back later." Rachelle's breathing was uncontrollable.

"I'm trying to do what you're doing, but I need a condom." Shirley yelled from the other side of the door.

"Open-the ooh shit-doo-oor-and look-in-the-oh God dresser-and-get-one, damn Pedro take it out and let me suck it." Rachelle was loud with it as Pedro was digging deep inside her passage with his Tribal piece from behind.

When Shirley opened the door Rachelle was facing her in the doggy style position grabbing the sheets and Pedro was still grinding inside her passage. You could see the fuck faces Rachelle was making. They kept on going not paying Shirley any attention.

"Where at Chelle?" Shirley asked her.

"In the second drawer on the left side under my panties." Shirley followed her directions to stash of condoms. "Yes-yes-Pedro right there baby, harder, harder," as Rachelle was balling her fist with a hand full of the sheet she was grabbing. When Shirley was leaving out, Rachelle screamed real loud meaning she was having an orgasm. Shirley didn't waste anytime getting back to the guest room. She was now horny from witnessing her friend in that position. Her clitoris was throbbing. Sharan was lying naked when she returned to the room. Shirley notice he was large between his legs, way larger then Thomas. Her stomach twirled in panic, but she was going through with it.

She took her t-shirt off and laid beside him and handed him the condom. He opened the package and placed it on his Tribal piece which it went half way over the head and body. Sharan laid on top of Shirley and she grabbed his tribal piece and helped him guide it into her soaking wet passage.

"Umm-easy big boy." Shirley told him trying to take him inside her, he was half way in her, but it felt like he was already in her stomach. "Right there," said Shirley.

Sharan was moving gently and slow inside her. "Shirley is that good baby?" he asked. She tensed up and didn't answer him. Then he asked her again thrusting deeper inside her. "Shirley is that good baby?"

"Yeah," her voice was screechy and low. Her eyes went in the back of her head. Her eyes went in the back of her head. It felt good and it hurt at the same time as his tribal piece stretched her vagina walls completely. Sharan began to thrust inside her, she lifted her legs up further and Sharan was dripping wet. "Oh God-uh-God-on shit," as she uttered every gesture grabbing his arms tightly. She thought by telling him to sex her the pain would go away, but it didn't . "oh Sharan fuck me. Fuck me harder, right there, right there," as her eyes were rolling in the back of her head. Her vagina grew use to his large manhood and the pain started to feel more like sensation.

"Shirley you got some wet-wet," as his manhood slipped out. "No, put it back in, put it back in, I'm about to cum Sharan," her breathing was intensified. She grabbed it and put it back inside her.

He continued his massive drive pumping and pumping, harder and harder.

She was now grabbing the edges on the side of the bed, pinching her nipples, digging in his back as he gave her pleasure. "Yes Sharan, oh shit fuck me baby, right there, ooh-shit,ooooh, I'm Cumming, I'm Cumming, I'm Cumming Sharan," as she went soprano putting her nails in his back screaming to the top of her lungs. She never had an orgasm that powerful before, even when she masturbated. I guess her screaming triggered him, because he started his as well.

"Oh shit Shirl, I'm Cumming, I'm Cumming." He told her.

Shirley eyes got wide, because she could feel him shooting sperm inside her, meaning the condom broke. She immediately tapped him to get up off of her. She was shaking like crazy. Her body was incredibly drained. He looked down at himself and seen the condom had broke and saw all the sex fluids dripping from his tribal piece.

"Damn Shirley the rubber broke. I hope you're on some type of birth control." He told her.

"No I'm not, but I think it's hard for me to get pregnant. I hope you don't have anything I can catch Sharan." She said looking up at him.

"I'm not carrying anything you can catch and I hope you don't get pregnant, because I'm not ready to become a father, well I am, but the woman I want my kids by I would like for us to be married first." He said.

"Sharan I feel you on that," as she was still shaking below her stomach.

"So Shirl, where do we go from here?" he asked her.

"I guess to the shower and clean up, you handled your business. I'm good. If I would've known it was all like that I would have gave you some a long time ago." She smiled.

"Shirl, I was talking about between us, where do we go?"

"Sharan, I like you as a friend, but I'm not ready for a relationship right now. I'm just getting out of one, but thank you for making me feel good." She looked at him long and hard.

"Okay, but if you ever want for us to become a couple, I'll be available even if I'm in a relationship. I'll break it off just to be with you." He smiled back at her.

"What about if I just want some sex, can I call you Sharan?" She asked him.

"Yeah you can do that. So you and ole boy who drive the Aston Martin are through messing around?" he asked her, because he knew about Thomas. He got up and pulled her up with him. "Yeah it's over." She then started to remove the linen that had their sex fluids on it and they both went to the shower but naked together. Shirley placed the linen in the dirty clothes hamper in the hallway. They turned the water on in the shower. Sharan got in while Shirley went back down the hallway to grab them some towels and wash cloths. She returned to shower with him. They didn't mess around and just got clean and got out. After the shower they got dressed. Shirley made the bed up with fresh linen. Sharan went back into the day room feeling good about himself. Shirley went and fixed her a plate and wrapped it up with saran wrap to take home with her. She had to be at work in the morning and the orgasm she just had was making her sleepy. She grabbed her hygiene bag, plate and purse and went to Rachelle's room to let her know she was leaving.

BOOM-BOOM-BOOM! She knocked on her bedroom door.

"Come in." Rachelle yelled out. She eased the door open and stuck her head in the door.

"Girl I'm about to leave for home, it's almost 10:45 and I have to work tomorrow." Shirley told her.

Rachelle was lying across Pedro under the sheets watching T.V. with him.

"Alright Shirl, call me when you get home." She didn't even ask her did she sleep with Sharan.

"Oh Shirley, can you drop Sharan off for me? I'm spending the night over here." Pedro asked her lifting his head up off the pillow a little.

"Sure I can do that Pedro. Good night ya'll," as she shut the door behind her.

Shirley thought to herself, 'I sure can, especially the way he just put it on me.'

She went and got Sharan out of the day room and told him what Pedro asked of her. Then they walked to her car, she put the plate, her purse and hygiene bag in the back seat. She pulled away from Rachelle's drive-way she asked him, "Where do you live Sharan?"

"I live in Silverton on Plainfield Dr." He answered her.

"Good that's towards my way and I wont have to double back." Shirley said.

"Where do you live Shirley?" He asked her.

"I live pass Kings Island in Symmes Township," as she was now turning right onto Reading Rd. off of Section Rd. "Shirl, where are we going I live back that way?" He was pointing back towards the other way.

"I can go down Galbraith and get to Montgomery Rd. this way instead of going back down to Langdon Farm."

"I didn't know that." He said.

"Let me be the chauffer and you just give me the directions when I get to Silverton." She looked at him wide eyed.

"No problem," as he reclined his seat back.

She put Ashanti in the CD player and they both relaxed on the journey to his house. When she got to Silverton they passed the Silverton Plaza where Sharan's store was located. It was known as 'Kiddy Land'. He then told her to make a left on Plainfield Dr. She went a few houses down and then he told her to pull over by the light blue house with a fence around it. The house had two white and brown Akita's sitting in the yard. In the drive-way was a gray Yukon truck and behind it was a 2002 E class 320 Benz, it was all gray.

"Is this your house Sharan?" Shirley asked him.

"Yep, this is my little castle and when I find Ms. Right I will buy us a little mansion."

"Well you better be going it's getting rather late, by the way what's your number?" She asked him wanting to contact him for some more bomb sex if she needed it. He reached in his wallet and obtained a business card, and then told her to write his home phone number on the back which she did. HE kissed her on the cheek and told her goodnight. He got out the car and walked to the fence going in it. Shirley turned around and he was inside the fence and the dogs were jumping up on him happy to see their master. He waved bye to Shirley.

Shirley got home at around 11:40 and threw her keys and purse on the table in her living room. She put her plate in the microwave and went to use the bathroom. She washed her hands and took her clothes off, and then put her some comfortable sleeping gear on which was a pair of shorts and a tank top.

She went back to retrieve her plate and a glass of Sunny Delight orange drink.. Back to her bedroom she went cutting on her 57" flat screen to catch the end of Star Trek. She then called Rachelle to let her know she made it home.

"Hello Chelle," as Shirley heard someone pick up her line.

"Hello," as Rachelle answered.

"I'm home Chelle. Guess what I hit Pedro's boy." Shirley confessed to her friend.

"Why you little nasty bitch, Shirl you don't even know him like that girl," as they both laughed out loud.

"I know, but I'm glad I took your advice. That nigga is holding girl, he put it on me, had a bitch shaking and shit. Ten Thomas couldn't compare to Sharan. It's all good, I needed that." Shirley told her.

"So Shirl what's up with you and him?" Rachelle asked her.

"Girl you know he's not my type. I might just hit him a few more times though." Shirley told her friend.

"Alright Ms. To Nasty, I'll call you tomorrow. Pedro is trying to get me off the phone. I guess he's ready to serve mama again." Rachelle gave a fake laugh through the receiver.

"Bye Chelle," said Shirley.

"Bye Shirl," as they both hung-up the phone. Shirley ate her food and crashed to only be awakened by a blowing car horn in the morning.

CHAPTER THREE
Self-Esteem

Shirley went to her patio doors of her bedroom to see who was blowing making all that noise with their car horn this morning. It was Thomas. She had parked in the back to avoid him, but he found her car that was not parked in its usual spot. He had put some rose's on the windshield. She ignored him though and got in the shower. When she got out of the shower someone was knocking on her door, it was like 7:15. She had to meet with her client at 9 a.m. for a preliminary hearing. She continued on, because she knew it was Thomas from looking out of her patio doors again.

She put on her Victoria Secret cotton knit purple panties and bra set. Then she put on a purple sheet lace dress with a silk-chiffon purple slip by Diana Von Furstenberg. Some purple rayon and a purple ghost hat by Helen Kaminski. She put on her black leather sandals boots by Cesare Paciotti. She also put on some Mambo fragrance by Liz Claiborne. She placed her M+J Savitt and Rolex on. She added a little lip gloss on.

It was 8 a.m. when she left out the door of her condo with her Coach purse and brief-case. Thomas was sitting in his car parked by hers. He watched her unlock her doors to her car, and when she opened her door Thomas approached her. "Shirley can we talk?" "No Thomas, I have nothing to say to you," as she put her briefcase in the back seat of her car. "Please Shirl," as he begged her.

"I have to go to work, where you should be," as she was now grabbing the rose's off her windshield and put them in the back seat. Thomas was holding the driver door open. "Excuse me," as she walked around him climbing into her Lexus Sedan.

"C'mon Shirley," as she closed her door and started up her vehicle. Thomas knocked on the window, but she didn't let it down.

She put her car in driver and kept it moving leaving him standing there. She reached downtown Cincinnati at exactly ten minutes to nine. The traffic down I-71 was jammed packed at a slow pace. She parked her car in the garage on Main St. at about 8:55. Her office was down the street in the Nathaniel Ropes Building 917 Main St. suite 400. She was the only African-American in her firm and a woman. She grabbed her briefcase and purse then headed straight to the court house. When she walked in the courtroom it was 9:10 and her client was the first name on the docket. The bailiff called the case.

"The State of Ohio vs. Rodriguez Artiz." He said out loud.

Her client was looking around all paranoid until he saw the purple ghost hat that was very noticeable. Shirley put her briefcase and purse on one of the tables. She removed her hat and grabbed a folder out of her briefcase. She then waved Mr. Artiz over to where she was. Then prosecutor saw that Shirley was present and he then presented his case to the Judge. Shirley asked the Judge, "Your Honor can I approach the bench please?" Shirley asked him.

"Both of you may approach the bench. I don't have all day," as the Judge looked down at Shirley and the prosecutor. They both approached the bench to discuss the case privately with the judge.

"Excuse me your Honor, I have a search warrant by the Cincinnati Police Department which they confiscated 1,792 grams unit weight marijuana from my client. Now this is the lab report which my client's product was tested and weighed, but the lab only weighed in 26 grams of marijuana and not 1,792 grams which was supposed to have been confiscated from my client.

Now from me practicing law and knowing the law the police have not produced enough evidence to charge my client with drug trafficking. Now where is the alleged 1,792 grams? I don't know, but with these 26 grams my client can only receive a possession ticket. So let's not waste the tax payer's money or time with this case your Honor. I would like to move for an immediately dismissal." Shirley told the Judge.

The Judge looked at the Prosecutor and he nodded his head to agree with the dismissal. He then took his mallet and hit the gavel on the bench.

"The State vs. Rodriguez Artiz is dismissed of all charges pending, next ease please." The Judge said.

Shirley looked over at the prosecutor and winked at him. He looked back at her and moved his mouth to say, "I'll get you," but Shirley had to read his lips and she smiled at him. She leaned over to Rodriguez Artiz and said, "Don't be shy about dropping off the rest of my fee like today Mr. Artiz."

"No problem Ms. Thomas. I'm on my way to your office now," as he spoke with a Spanish accent. They both walked out the courtroom and she went to the records office to drop off some paper work and headed to her office. She walked in her suite and her secretary Pam gave her a memo with her messages. She had messages from a few new client's trying to retain her, Rachelle, her granny, Renee and Thomas. Thomas had called several times. She called her granny, Renee and the new client's first, and then she called Rachelle. Rachelle's home phone rung several times before she answered. The Hair Salon was closed on Sunday's and Monday's.

"Hello the Smith resident," Rachelle answered.

"Quit trying to be all proper, it's me heifer, what up?" Shirley voice was crisp and strong coming through the receiver.

"Nothing, how did court go this morning?" Rachelle asked her.

"You know I handled my business. I beat the case before it was even a case. I'm a bad black woman in the court of law," as Shirley laughed a little.

"You probably just let another criminal back on the streets." Rachelle sounded serious when she made that comment.

"Rachelle whether my client's are guilty or not, they pay me to do a job and that's to defend them in the court of law." She said.

"Yeah whatever Shirl, so are we going to lunch or what?"

"I'm going to pass today Chelle. I'm working a new project and I'm about to see if he would like to take me to lunch," said Shirley.

"Who Sharan? Ah bitch you probably done made up with Thomas punk ass." Rachelle was highly upset that her friend declined to have lunch with her. It was something they normally did on Monday's.

"Nope, wrong check yourself Chelle. It's neither one and I'll talk to you later, bye." Shirley said.

"Bye-," Chelle hung up in her friend's ear. Shirley smiled in the air. ***Sorry Chelle, but I have to see what's up with Sam I Am.*** Shirley said to herself out loud.

She knew her friend was upset with her, but she had to check out this new prospect. She begun to look in her purse for his number. She found it and paged him using her code to see if she would be that important this early in the game.

Things a woman do to test a man. About ten minutes went by after she paged him and her secretary buzzed in on the intercom. "Ms. Thomas, you have a call on line two."

"Okay Pam." Shirley picked up on the line hoping it was Sam.

"Hello Shirley Thomas, attorney at law, how can I help you?" she asked the person on the other end sounding professional.

"Shirl, can we talk now please?" It was Thomas pathetic ass calling.

"No Thomas, I'm in a meeting with a client, please quit bugging me, shit! You don't get it? It's over be a family with your wife," as she hung up in his ear. Pam buzzed in on the intercom again. "Ms. Thomas you have another call on line one and Mr. Artiz dropped off an envelope." Pam told her.

"See who it is on line one for me. If its Thomas Patterson tell him I'm not in my office. Open the envelope and to see how much money he left."

"Okay Ms. Thomas." Pam said. Shirley waited a few minutes and Pam clicked in.

"It's a man name Samuel Holston on line one and it's exactly thirty thirty-five hundred dollars in the envelope." Pam told her.

"Okay bring me the money and I'll take the call," as Shirley clicked over to line one to answer the call. "Hello, Shirley Thomas attorney at law, how can I assist you?' Shirley asked him.

"Hello Ms. Thomas, I see you decided to use my number. I didn't plan on hearing from you so soon." He said smiling from ear to ear.

"How can I not use your number and you gave it to me?" Shirley said.

Pam came into the office, Shirley waved her over to her desk and Pam handed her the envelope. Shirley reached in it and counted out five crisp hundred dollar bills and gave it to Pam. Then she whispered to Pam, "That's your bonus sweetie." She looked at Shirley and said, "Thank You."

Shirley waved her off telling her to leave her be. Pam left the office. "So Mr. Holston what's on your agenda for this afternoon?" She asked him.

"Nothing, what about you ?"

"I only had one case to handle for today and it's almost noon, meaning it's lunch time for me," she said to him hoping she could catch a line of potential male company.

"well I'm doing nothing sitting here in the shop about to detail a car around 2 or 3." he told her.

"So would you like to take me to lunch Sam?" Shirley asked him.

"Sure, I don't mind what time?" he asked her wanting to be sure.

"In about twenty minutes." She answered him.

"Are you going to meet me somewhere or do I have to pick you up?" he asked her. She sighed and then told him. "Yes silly I want you to pick me up." She replied.

"Where exactly do you work Shirley?" he asked her.

"I work on Main St. in the Nathaniel Ropes building. Do you know where that is?" She asked him. He stumbled at first then he answered her. "Yeah I know where that is."

"Well I'll be outside waiting on you. I shouldn't take you long coming from Eighth and

State. I'm dressed in purple with a purple ghost hat and don't have me waiting Sam," Shirley told him. "Okay Ms. Thomas I'm on my way, bye," as he hung up the phone. Shirley went to freshen up for her lunch date and she told Pam to take her messages and none from Thomas. She was standing outside the building when Sam pulled up in an all white 600 Benz with white leather bucket seats. It was dipped in gold from the grill to the emblem. He had 20" rims which were Lorenzo's dipped in gold. He saw her standing there in all purple with a purple hat. He blew the horn, but she ignored him, because she was looking for the Honda. Then he rolled down the passenger window to call her name.

"Hey Shirley, over here." he yelled out. He was playing Jay-Z the Blue Print, and you could here, "Girls, girls, girls," coming from inside the car. She didn't hear him so he called her name again. "Yo Shirley," as she turned her head, then looked from up under her hat to recognize Sam. She smiled and started walking towards the car. She got in and looked around the 600 Benz admiring the luxury car. "Hello Sam, I was looking for the cute little Honda, but this is real nice." She was still checking the inside out.

"The lil Honda is my toy and this is my business car. I only bring out the Honda on Sunday's or take it to car shows." He was looking at her.

"Oh I see, so how are you doing?" she asked him.

"I'm fine and yourself?" He replied.

"I'm okay, and I'll be even better when we get something to eat." She batted her eyes at him. He had turned the music down a little changing cd's, putting in Jagged edge. He could have sworn he heard her stomach growl.

"so where would you like to eat and how long is your lunch break?" Sam wanted to know how long he had to be in her company this afternoon.

"I have a taste for Chinese, and I'm my own boss." she smiled at him caressing his hand.

"Well that settles that. We could go to Blue Gibbon out on Tennessee Ave. for Chinese." he recommended.

"That's fine," as she leaned her seat back and started checking him out. His nails were still clean. He had on a Jim Brown throwback Cleveland Brown's jersey, which was brown and orange. Some orange and brown Bo Jackson cross trainers and some shorts. His hair was cut low with waves in it. He also had on a few accessories which were gold.

He rolled the passenger window back up. Even though it was the middle of April it was still a little breezy outside. It was a sunny forecast, with the temperature in the high 70's. He turned up the music a tab bit and then continued up Main St. to Liberty and turned right, and then turned left as the light going up Sycamore Hill cruising past Christ hospital in Mt. Auburn. He went thru Corryville to turn onto Martin Luther King Dr. and took it down to Reading Rd. turning left at the light of Reading Rd. and Martin Luther King Dr. He floated down Reading Rd. going thru Avondale and N. Avondale to merge onto Paddock Rd. where it made a "V" to either go down Reading Rd. pass the police station or Paddock Rd., because it was closer to get to the restaurant from Paddock Rd. then Reading Rd. They decided to order to go instead of dining in. Sam wanted to eat outside in a nice quiet spot keeping him close to his job. They ordered sweet & sour chicken, beef and shrimp fried rice with egg rolls. After getting their order he pulled out of the restaurant lot to turn right, and Sam went up Tennessee Ave. and stopped at the BP gas station that sat on the corner of Tennessee Ave. and Reading Rd. He bought them Kiwi fruit drinks and two bottles of Dansi water. They left the gas station going towards the Norwood lateral going eastbound.

He took the lateral eastbound to I-71 south taking that highway into downtown Cincinnati. Sam was now playing Musique Soul Child. Shirley had adjusted her seat even more to an incline position and placed her hand on his thigh singing along to the music and staring at him as he controlled the luxury car doing the speed limit. They got off on the Pete Rose exit and headed toward the Serpentine Wall.

When they reached the Serpentine Wall Sam popped the trunk to grab a small blanket. He carried the majority of the food and she helped. They found a nice quiet spot along the running water exhibit on a nice monument. He placed the blanket down and set the food down. She sat down holding her dress so it wouldn't rise. She didn't waste anymore time playing with the food as she fixed her a nice portion of food. Sam was more eager to play 21 questions. "So Shirley, where do you live?"

"I live in Symmes Township up by Indian Hills." She was still fixing her plate.

"So are you involved with anyone Shirley?" He asked her.

"No and what about you Sam?" She really wasn't looking at him at all asking him the question. He kind of knew too, because he already answered that question when they first met. "I told you when we first met, that I date from time to time, but there is no one special in my life." No eye contact at all.

"I forgot Sam, I'm sorry," as she put a spoon full of sweet & sour chicken in her mouth. "Mmm-Mmm, this is good try some," as she placed a spoon full towards Sam mouth to feed him. He took it. "That is good, almost good as mines."

She looked at him. "So you can cook Sam?" She asked. She couldn't believe it if he could.

"Yeah I'm pretty much skilled in the kitchen and one day I'll cook form you." He told her.

"We will have to see then, as she was still eating gracefully. Sam wasn't eating, he wasn't even thinking about eating.

"Shirley, I would like for you to come to the Ritz nightclub this Saturday night to see my group perform, plus Lil Jon and the Eastside Boyz are going to in town performing." Sam was still watching her eat. She opened her Kiwi drink and took a sip before answering him. She wiped her mouth and caught her breath.

"So you are asking me out on a date?" She asked him.

"I mean yeah, but you can meet me there. I just want you to see my guys perform. We might need to hire you some day as a legal advisor." He told her.

"Sam, I told you, I'm not a big fan of rap music." Her brown eyes were stuck on him.

"A free concert and it will give us a moment to chill." He told her not giving her a second to think.

"Why can't we have that moment alone?" She asked him.

"We can Shirley, but I really would like for you to see the Trap Boys perform, please." he begged her.

"Okay I'll come, but is it cool to bring my girlfriends?" She asked him, because she didn't feel comfortable going to this type of environment alone. She was still eating her food. "Sure that's cool, here's four V.I.P. tickets," as he reached in his pocket to give her the tickets.

"Thank you and I'll wear something sexy for you," as she smiled at him.

They finished eating their lunch and Sam folded the blanket and they went towards the drifting waterfall that ran down a concrete monument. They sat where you could wave your feet in the water. Sam removed her black sandal boots. He then massaged and washed her feet, so she could emerge them in the cool running water. She was like wow! But it wasn't anything new to her to have her feet massaged and washed. They laughed and talked for awhile. They even managed to share a small passionate kiss and after separating themselves Sam asked her, "Am I moving to fast Shirley?"

"No Sam, the timing is rather perfect. I just hope you don't have a hidden agenda."

"What do you mean by that Shirley?" He asked her being confused now.

"I hope you are since and not just trying to get in between my legs Sam." She said.

"Shirley, I am a gentleman and a scholar. So I'm looking for someone I can share and build with, not someone who can pleasure me for a brief moment, but someone I can please for a lifetime." His words were perfect to her ear, but she wasn't just a yo-yo on a string. "Okay we will see Sam."

"I'm serious Shirley." He was confident in his own words.

"Okay Sam, I hear you, but let's get ready to go, I need to get back to my office," as she was eyeing her Rolex.

Sam had dropped Shirley off in front of the Nathaniel Ropes building. They hugged and Shirley told him she would call him later. She still had thoughts of Thomas Patterson in the back of her mind and fresh thoughts of the sex her and Sharan shared yesterday. But her more profound thoughts were now reflecting Samuel Holston.

…………………………..
..

That Friday Shirley and Renee took off from their jobs early to go shopping in downtown Cincinnati at Saks Fifth Avenue. Shirley was buying her a new outfit for the concert Saturday at the Ritz. She bought her a $1,540 Paillete detailed Cardigan by Zac Posen which was black and white, a pair of $595 Vachetta leather sandals with the double strap collar all black. A matching bead embellished suede clutch purse by Giuseppe Zanotti which was $1,360. Shirley was feeling good about her purchase as she gave the cashier her platinum credit card. She just spent over 3 thousand dollars on an outfit, shoes and a purse. Renee thought her friend was crazy. Renee bought her a black silk & modal tank, a pair of classiques Entier Trellis sandals with a small heel and a large Shaw shopper purse. She spent a little over three hundred dollars after taxes. They left from downtown heading to Bond Hill to get new hair styles from their friend Rachelle and to show off their purchase they just bought.

…………………………...

That Saturday night Shirley, Rachelle, Renee and Meco were standing inside the Ritz nightclub in the V.I.P. section.

Meco was dropped dead gorgeous to be in her late thirties. She always hung out where the young crowd played exercising her right to be forever young.

The four ladies were astonishing , looking beyond spectacular. You would think they were attending an event on the Red Carpet and not just some rap concert. Sam saw Shirley and her group, and momentarily came to speak to Shirley briefly sending two bottles of Moet to their table. It was packed in the Ritz nightclub. The women were checking out the crowd feeling the vibe and the atmosphere.

Then Sam came on the stage to introduce the Trap boys. The women in the audience were going berserk for the rap group. Shirley saw the guy she rejected a week ago with his rap duo. Even her girl Rachelle and Meco were up on their feet. You could hear Meco say,

"That Ren Mack he sexy as fuck. I'm going to get his young ass," as an instrumental begun to play in the back ground. They were dancing on stage and jumping around to the music. They were throwing t-shirt out into the crowd.

"What up my people?" Ren Mack yelled into the mic. Female were yelling, falling faint and throwing their panties on stage. Security guards had to keep the female from getting up on stage.

"We are about to get the nasty Nati crunk, before my main man Lil Jon and the Eastside Boyz get on stage. Trap Boys are in the building." Ren Mack yelled out letting it be known.

"Yeah we in Da building. I be the Boobster," Boobie said.

"And I am the Mack, and we are the Trap Boys," as they both said the last part together. The music then died down and the light went off. They bowed their heads then a nice smooth instrumental came on thumping through the speakers and the light's came back on. Boobie started off rapping.

"I wanna go half on a baby, know that might sound crazy,

But I'm just used to getting what I've wanted since the eighties-

I might be the smoothest, haters copy each and every move,

Come on now can't lie, bout the fact yo boy cool-

I re-quire attention. I'm on my B.I.

Jail couldn't hold me back, fuck it I'll just learn to rap,

And make a profit off it, double every dollar I invest,

So me and you can have the time, to watch a couple sunsets."

Boobie let Ren Mack jump in. Ren Mack spotted Shirley in V.I.P. with her girls. He started rapping making his way to their table by skipping, because the V.I.P. section was right by the stage.

"Yes ma this is swag at its Pinnacle-

But the haters call it brag when I mention dough-

I am not here for the glitter-

I'm here to get it popping make it clear on ya twitter-

Yeah you tied to diss, but it's nothing I'm a class act-

E-class S-class can you pass that?" He was now in front of Shirley, Meco and Rachelle were trying to touch his arm going crazy to get a free feel. He was still giving Shirley his attention as he was rapping.

"I'm about to make it rain, did you bring your galoshes?

To my resort, to play tongue touching games as a sport-

It's yo fantasy, my show, so I'm ah fly into yo port.

Look my nails are clean, my Ice is shining, and I'm here-

Meet me back stage, so I can put a bug in yo ear.

Word to my mama, I need a woman in slow mo-

To share fuck faces with the Mack, at the end of the rainbows," as he walked off back to the stage leaving Shirley to wonder. She knew those lyrics were specifically for her she

just dropped her head. He was very popular, and Shirley felt foolish, because everyone else wanted him in the club and she turned him down. He amazed her with his talent. She immediately jumped on the bandwagon and gave him a smile. They watched Lil Jon and The Eastside Boyz perform. Now Ren Mack, Boobie and Sam were in V.I.P with Shirley and her girls. Shirley and Sam, Meco was under Ren Mack, Rachelle was talking to Boobie and Renee was all alone as usual.

The artist were properly introduced by Sam. Shirley and Ren would make eye contact then look in another direction. Ren gave Shirley an attitude, while Meco were steady putting intimate ideas in his ear. They chit-chatted over the loud music. Even though Shirley had somewhat met Ren Mack a week ago she felt a little sorry for not giving him a chance, but she didn't show any emotion as she stayed glued to Sam. So Ren figured he would give her friend the opportunity to close out the deal with him. When the club let out around 3:30 a.m. Sunday morning everyone went their separate ways accept Meco and Ren Mack. They headed for the Ramada Inn on reading rd.

………………………………..

.

Meanwhile at the Ramada Inn Ren Mack and Meco were isolated in a hotel room all alone. It was now like 4 a.m. and Meco had an itch that was growing increasingly and needed it to be scratched. She knew if only for one night, she could be a slut. The tension in the hotel room was almost unbearable to Ren Mack. "Go ahead Meco," he finally said.

"Take off your clothes." Ren eyes never left her, as she started to undress. Everything that was womanly shaped in her clothes stayed in place when she was completely naked. She was assured that her body was way more mature then those females he was use to being

with, more defying. She was already wet and ready.

"How do you want me?" She asked him.

"It's up to you," he said. "You're running the show." he added.

Meco then bent over on the bed showing her pussy from the back view.

"Here, come and hit it from the back baby," she said while licking her lips looking back at him.

Ren didn't even bother to undress. Brick heard in his jeans he unzipped his pants and pulled out his tribal piece. He didn't think about the condom he had in his pocket, as he lined his manhood up with her passage and entered her warm wet pussy.

He grabbed her by the hips and began to pump, pulling her backside onto him with every thrust. His hard young body and his enthusiasm made her even aware how good his sex was. She was thrusting back even harder against him as he tried to put it in her life. They both were yelling and moaning, making so much noise, that whoever was in the next room heard them. They didn't care, especially Meco. She wanted to tell that she did it with a rapper, even before he got famous, beyond fame. The episode of her having multiple orgasms, made him wonder how freaky this older chick really were. Then it dawned on him that he forgot to strap up. It was too late, and he kept going hoping she couldn't get pregnant, let alone had a disease. The smell from her vagina became faint all of a sudden. It got real fowl and unusual. Ren Mack notices the smell and pulled out from her passage. "What are you doing baby? I was about to cum again, put it back in," as her breathing was unsteady. She was looking back at him.

"Damn Meco, that's a fowl smell, yo shit is reeking with a bad fish smell. I hope you are

not carrying anything," as he was turning up his nose. She turned all the way around now standing erect in front of him.

"Excuse me, you got me fucked up boo. I'm not burning and I don't smell shit." She had an attitude.

"Stick your finger down there and smell yo shit. I'm just saying the last time I smelled a smell like that, I caught gonorrhea." He was looking her in the eyes. She eased a finger down inside her passage and pulled it out. Then she smelled it, and her nose turned up and she knew he was right.

"I told you, your shit had an odor." He was shaking his head when he told her.

"It must be coming from that new soap I just tried out. I must have gotten an allergic reaction. Something isn't right with my stuff. It has never smelled like this before I keep a fresh smelling pussy at all time. I'm sorry, but I don't know what it came from, but I can assure you that I'm not burning with a STD." She confessed.

"If my shit end up pussing, I'll be sure to let you know." He said.

"Please do, but I'm going to the clinic Monday morning and I'll call you to let you know how it went, and I'll make it up to you." She then reached for him to embrace him with a hug.

………………………………...
…

CHAPTER FOUR

Chaos

Even thought Shirley was dating Sam, she didn't participate in any sexual contact him and it was already the second week in May.

She was due to come on her period, but she was a week and half late. She thought it was stress at first, but she knew that she could possibly be pregnant. But who was the father if she were? Sharan or Thomas?

She knew in April around the 14th she slept with Sharan and the condom broke and she didn't use any with Thomas two night's before.

How careless she were she thought. Then she thought about all the times that Thomas never used any protection and she didn't get pregnant.

It was on a Friday night to days before Mother's Day and all three women were over to Renee's apartment hanging out watching "love Jones" and drinking Bombay Sapphire.

"Hey Rachelle slow down you know how you get when you drink light liquor." Shirley slapped her hand gently while Rachelle was pouring her drink..

"Go head on Shirl, if I get horny Pedro will come serve me up a batch of that good loving," as she gave a little laugh. Shirley looked at her tilting her head.

"Whatever bitch, don't forget you are driving and I need for you to help me with this pregnancy test."

Rachelle immediately put her glass down on the table. "Shirl are you serious? You done let that married faggot knock yo ass up?" Rachelle was pointing her finger in her face and she was loud.

"Shh-sh-sh, damn don't let Renee hear you." Shirley put her finger to her mouth.

"Girl she's in her bedroom with her toy probably smoking a joint," said Rachelle.

"Rachelle remember that Sunday night I gave Sharan some?" Shirley asked her.

"Yes I remember Shirl," as she was focused in on her.

"Well the condom broke and I don't know if I'm pregnant or not. I haven't came on my cycle yet and this is my time, but I'm late." Shirley was serious and her eyes didn't lie or hide the truth of the matter.

"How late Shirl?" Rachelle asked her.

"Like more than five days late, and I don't know if it's Thomas or Sharan's baby if I am pregnant. You're a pro so help me." Shirley smiled at her friend. She knew the ins and outs of this situation dealing with procreation, because after Keith Jr. was born she had other issues she had to resolve dealing with pregnancy. They disappeared to the bathroom. Shirley retrieved the pregnancy test from her Doone & Burke purse. She stood there for a brief moment holding it looking at Rachelle. "Well Chelle, what do I do?"

"Well you have to pee on the little strip and match the color of the strip when it turns colors to the color on the bottle where it tells you if it's positive or negative. If it shows blue then it's positive."

Shirley looked at her, and then looked at the bottle again. She carefully grabbed a strip out the bottle and carefully examined it. She then went and stood by the toilet and undid her pants, pulled her pants and panties down. She then started using the bathroom and at some point she managed to get a sample of her urine. She placed the strip on the sink nearby. She wiped herself after doing the business, flushed the toilet and washed her hands. After drying her hands she looked at the strip with Rachelle. It was already taking its color and how be damn the strip turned blue. Shirley heart dropped. She was nervous, but happy and sad at the same time.

Rachelle looked at her and said, "Girl I think you are about to become a mother." Shirley took the strip and threw it in the toilet and flushed it.

"Chelle I don't want this baby, knowing that there is a strong possibility that it might be Thomas' baby. I want my child to be around his/her father, not someone just dropping by every blue moon. But if it is Sharan's baby than that would be different."

"Shirl it might be his, you don't know." Rachelle was comforting her friend.

"And what if it's not Chelle I can't take that chance," as a tear began to form in the corner of her eye."

"So what are your going to do? Are you going to tell Thomas and Sharan?" Rachelle asked her. She was concern for her friend's well-being.

"I'm not telling Thomas shit fuck him he can kiss my natural black ass. I'm about to page Sharan and see if he would help me get an abortion and what he has to say, seeing what he would like for me to do."

"Shirl, what if he wants for to keep it if you are pregnant?" Rachelle asked.

The thought never occurred that he would from their conversation the night they both found out the condom broke. "Well we'll just have to see and I'll go from there." Shirley replied.

They went to Renee's living room and Shirley paged Sharan. She poured her another drink of the Bombay and it was a nice glass full. Rachelle looked at her and said, "Shirl, you can't be drinking like that if you are pregnant."

"I'm not keeping it if I am., so what do I care?" But deep down inside Shirley cared a great deal. She was juts confused and now disappointed that she had both encounters during the same time. Her mind raced as she waited for Sharan to return her call. She began to get impatient and she was about to call his cell phone and house phone. Then Renee's home phone rang.

Shirley screamed out to Renee. "I got it Nee." Not wanting her friend to answer her own phone to find out she was talking to Sharan. Shirley answered the phone with much excitement. "Hello," as she was hoping it was him and not one of Renee's strange friend's outside of their circle calling for her.

"Did someone page Sharan from this number?" He asked.

"Yes I did Sharan, this is Shirley."

"Oh, what's up Shirl? You sound like something is wrong." He asked her.

The phone went silent for a second. "Sharan I don't know how to tell you this, but I just took a pregnancy test and I think I'm pregnant by you."

The phone went completely silent and Shirley thought he hung up the phone.

"Hello Sharan are you still there?" She asked in panic.

"Yea-yea I'm here," as his pitch in his voice changed.

"Did you hear what I said? I think I'm pregnant by you." Shirley eyes looked up to the ceiling knowing a guys reaction when they hear news like this.

"Yeah I heard you, and are you sure it's mines?" He asked her.

Shirley began to let the tears flow and Rachelle knew something was wrong .

"Of course I'm sure. You are the only one I've slept with last month, you're the only one Sharan." She was crying from the hurt and her lying to this man who probably really cared about her. It was her desperation move.

She sucked her teeth and tried to control her emotions. "So what do you want to do Shirley?" He asked her.

"I'm not ready to be a mother or get married Sharan. I won't to have an abortion if I am pregnant. First I want to go see my gynecologist for a more precise result and I would like for you to go with me. If I am I would like for you to help me pay for the abortion." She sniffled and was wiping her tears away with the heel of her palm.

"Okay Shirley I will go with you and if you are I will pay for the abortion, it's my responsibility too." he told her.

"Well I'm going to make a doctor's appointment for the 22nd of this month. I think it's on a Tuesday if that's a good time for you?" She asked him.

"Anytime is a good time for me to handle my business. Now you quit crying everything is going to be alright." He told her.

"I will call you Monday after I make the appointment to tell you if I got in form that date." She told him.

"Alright Shirley, I'll talk to you later and take it easy." He said.

"Sharan, thank you. You're so remarkable, bye."

They hung up and she was devastated with herself. Rachelle looked at her friend long and hard wondering what had took place, but she knew it was good news for Shirley from the end of their conversation.

"So what's the deal Shirl?" Rachelle calmly asked her.

Shirley eyes were stained red. "He's going to the clinic with me. I can't believe I just lied to that man. Chelle I'm going to hell," said Shirley.

"No your not Shirl, so what did he say?" Rachelle asked her.

"Chelle he's a real man and I respected him dearly. He made me feel whole and complete, not alone and neglect," as she touched Rachelle's arm.

"Okay and Shirl?"

"He's going to pay for the abortion if I am pregnant." Shirley told her.

Shirley had puppy dog eyes. Rachelle smiled at her and said, "Girl I told you he's alright and just because he's not light skinned complexion you don't want to get with him on the relationship level. He even broke your ass off proper. Girl if you knew what I knew you would give him a chance," said Rachelle with a sassy look on her face.

"He did have some good wood girl, he put it down, but I don't know Chelle."

"We'll see how thongs add up when ya'll got to the doctor's office," said Rachelle.

"I will. I most definitely will and what the heck is Renee doing in that bedroom for this long?" Shirley changed the subject not wanting to feel any guiltier than she already were.

"Let's go and see Shirl," as they left the living room to go see what Renee was doing in her bedroom.

Boom-Boom! Rachelle knocked on the bedroom door. "Damn bitch what's up in there, did you sneak some nigga up in this piece?" Rachelle said standing back from the door now.

"Yeah Nee who un there with you, Shaba Ranks?" as Shirley laughed.

"Open up the door Nee so we can tell you the good news." Rachelle yelled and Shirley stared at her, like *what good news?* Shirley hands were on her hips. Rachelle just shrugged her shoulders.

"Hold up, here I come." Renee yelled back behind the door.

A few minutes went by and the Renee's bedroom door swung open. An unpleasant smell came from out of her room, plus it was smoky.

"Damn Nee what's that awful smell?" Shirley asked her.

The smell was like marijuana burning with some rubber. Shirley grabbed her mouth and nose, because she couldn't take the smell.

"Damn Renee why your eyes all wide and shit, and you're sweating like crazy?" Rachelle asked her grabbing her mouth and nose also.

"She was probably in there with her toy getting her some and done busted a nut," as Shirley laughed at her own comment.

"Shit whatever she was doing I hope her coochie doesn't smell like that." Rachelle was shaking her head when she made her comment.

Renee calmed down a little. "Na'll I was smoking some weed out of my weed wipe and accidentally burned the rubber piece on the side of it." Renee told them.

"Yeah whatever, you know Shirl is probably pregnant?" Rachelle told heinousness. Shirley was mean mugging Rachelle now. Renee eyes went straight to Shirley.

"Serious Shirl? What Thomas done finally knocked you up?" Renee asked her.

Shirley didn't bother to answer her, but Rachelle didn't have a problem as Shirley put her head down.

"She doesn't know if it's his or someone else's baby." Rachelle told the truth of the matter.

"You lying Chelle. What's up Shirl? Tell me what's going on." Renee looked her square in the eyes. Shirley brown eyes lit up with a desperation look.

"I just might be pregnant Nee. It might be Thomas or this other guys baby. I don't feel like arguing with you or hearing your smart remarks okay." Shirley turned her head.

"I'm not on that right now. I'm here for you Shirl," as Renee went to hug her friend. She let her go and Shirley told her the truth.

"Okay Nee, the other guy that the baby might be is Sharan." Shirley told her.

Renee couldn't believe her ears. "Sharan, Pedro friend?" Renee had her hands on her hips.

"Yes Nee." Shirley answer her.

"I thought you didn't mess with his kind?" Renee said.

"I don't. I found out that Thomas was trying to spread himself around, so I decided to give Sharan some on GP and the condom broke on me." Shirley explained to her.

"Why Shirl, you little nasty ass heifer you, so how was it?" Renee asked her.

"The shit was the bomb. He had a bitch shaking and shit." Shirley confessed.

"Why am I just now finding out?" Renee asked her.

Shirley and Rachelle responded at the same time. "Because you talk too much."

They looked at Renee and she gave a small grin.

"Shit I'm hungry now, let's go to Pizza Hut or Richie's," as Rachelle suggested pulling her panties out of her butt.

"Okay, but first you need to go wash your hands girlfriend." Shirley said.

"Whatever I'll rub it in your face." Rachelle reached out to her and Shirley took off running and screaming. "You nasty bitch." Shirley said.

The best of friends making good out of a situation that forfeited one of them stinging their life.

....

CHAPTER FIVE
Procreation

That Monday morning Shirley managed to make the Dr. appointment for Tuesday the 22nd. She called Sharan to let him know everything was set for the 22nd.

That Tuesday morning on May 22nd when Shirley pulled in the Madisonville clinic parking lot Sharan was already there. She parked beside his E-class 320 Benz. They went in as a couple. She was looking good and Sharan got all aroused from her personal appearance. He admired her even though she wasn't all that physically attracted to him. Shirley checked in with the receptionist and they waited for her to be called in the main lobby area of the clinic. It was packed in the waiting area with a lot of pregnant women and Shirley began to get emotional, because she really wanted the child if she were pregnant. Default by carelessness behavior and pressure of knowing it might be either Thomas or Sharan's child, she couldn't chance it.

The medical assistance called Shirley's name to place her in an examining room and Sharan followed her into the room. The medical assistance gave her a gown to change into.

"Hi my name is Mi-Mi and Ms. Thomas you'll need to get undress and put on the gown and hop on the examining table. I'll be right back to check your vitals." The medical assistance smiled at her and then left the room after Shirley replied, "Okay."

Shirley took the gown from her. She looked at Sharan and said, "Excuse me Sharan, can you turn around while I get undressed please?" She was handing him her Fendi purse.

"Yeah whatever Shirley, I've already seen your goods remember?" as Sharan turned around giving her the respect and space she asked for. She removed her Giorgio Armani heels and her blouse and pants all were turquoise.

She removed her white bra and panties and placed her panty liner in the trash can. While she was slipping on her gown, Sharan blurted out, "Damn Shirl, I didn't know your booty was that cute and round. I couldn't tell in the shower when the water was running down it."

"Sharan you suppose to be looking the other way, now come and help me on this damn table, you lil peep freak."

He smirked a smile and put her purse on her folded clothes then lifted her up on the examining table.

"Shirl you have some cute feet." Sharan commented.

"Oh yeah, are they cute enough to lick and suck Negro?" She asked him.

"You have jokes I see. I didn't drink your bath water or even eat off your fork, so what makes you think I'll suck your feet?" He looked at her.

"Negro, if I wanted you to lick my feet, my pussy or blow in my ass you would do it," as she looked at him with confident.

"Yeah you think so Shirl?"

"I know so," as she folded her arms. "Can you hand me that magazine off the table please?" She asked him. He gave her the magazine and she started fingering through it. She came across a small article in the Medical Reader's Digest, she was now viewing. It was an article on abortion. It had a little clipping that stated a message to mothers and expecting mothers.

'The precious gift to a child is a mother, the precious gift to a man, is the child's mother as a lover. Her uniqueness, style and grace, her strength, her smile and will to face the world. The way she motivates, collect and cares, her warmth and her ability to love & share.

The pain she adores when giving birth, she surrenders. To seek her love for her unborn child is like buried treasure. Men have scorned her, Mother Nature has warned her. The most skilled of mankind is born to her. Her will power and passion to succeed, amongst corruption, prostitution, liars, hustlers and thieves. Making her vulnerable and the love of living prey, that's why we set aside a Mother's Day.

Please stop abortion, because life is so precious. You were given a chance at life, so why should that little one growing inside you be murdered?'

Shirley eyes began to water and Sharan noticed her change of heart.

"Shirl what's wrong? You seem uncertain about something?" He asked her.

She wiped the single tear that escaped her eye. "Nothing Sharan, I just got caught up in something I was reading that's all," as she sniffled a little and smiled.

The medical assistance entered the room. She saw that it was something in the air.

"Excuse me, I can come back if I'm interrupting something." She said.

"It's okay I was just having a moment with my fiancé and got all emotional." Shirley responded.

"Okay I just need to check your pulse, blood pressure and take your temperature. Also I need for you to urinate in this cup for me." The medical assistance told Shirley.

The medical assistance did her small vitals check. Shirley gave her the urine sample she asked for and then she left the room. About twenty minutes later the doctor returned with a R.N. He had a chart in his hand. "Hello Mr. and Mrs. Thomas, I'm doctor Bosh, your regular doctor had an emergency," He said shaking Shirley and Sharan hand.

"Hi Doctor Bosh, we are here to find out if I conceived or not." Shirley explained to him.

"Well we'll find out. I need a small blood sample and I need to do a pelvic exam." He told her.

She thought about it and wasn't with this guy playing in her jewelry box. He didn't look right at all to her. She got furious. "A pelvic exam, I just had one two months ago." She rolled her eyes. Sharan knew she had an attitude.

"I normally do those when I'm checking to see if someone is pregnant Mrs. Thomas to make sure nothing else was contracted." Doctor Bosh told her.

"Well I don't need one Doc. I just want to know if I'm pregnant." Shirley crossed her legs and folded her arms sitting on the examining table.

"Okay, Tamu will draw your blood and I will bring you your results shortly," as he placed his large hand on one of her thighs. "See you in a little bit Mrs. Thomas," as he left the room.

The RN left the room behind the doctor and returned only in minutes with the things she needed to take Shirley's blood. Shirley wasn't feeling the thought to be stuck with a needle.

The nurse approached her. "Hold still Mrs. Thomas, let me see if I can find a vein," as the RN held her arm searching it for a possible. She took the rubber strap and tied it around Shirley's arm and then began to thump her arm searching for that special vein. Shirley saw the huge needle and began to panic.

"Oh-oh-no! I hate needles, please don't, please don't, stop," as Shirley became terrified. Sharan came to her aid. "Honey wait, calm down. Tamu is it? Let me talk to her," as Sharan grabbed her free hand and turned her head to look at him.

"Sharan don't let her hurt me." Shirley had fear in her eyes. Sharan wanted to laugh because all the times she played the tough girl with him and now she was face to face with her own fear.

"She's not going to hurt you baby. I'm here. Look squeeze my hand and think about the time when I threw up on you. Get mad." He told her.

"You're trying to trick me Sharan, it's going to hurt." Shirley said.

"Don't even think about it, the pain or the needle." Then he whispered to the RN Tamu. "Go ahead." Sharan told her.

Tamu eased the needle into Shirley's arm and she didn't even feel it. Shirley was pumping herself up to be stuck. She thought about Thomas reckless behavior instead.

"Come on nurse and do it I'm ready," as Shirley was trying to syke herself out by closing her eyes.

"Hold this cotton ball right there for me Mrs. Thomas and I'll be right back." The RN told her.

"Are you finished, or do you have to get another device?" Shirley asked her.

"I've been finished Mrs. Thomas," as she showed Shirley the tube of blood.

"You can get dressed Mrs. Thomas, because the doctor is not performing a pelvic exam." The RN left the examining room. Sharan smile was a mile long.

"You are a big baby Shirley." He told her.

"Forget you Sharan and hand me my damn clothes," as she had an attitude with him now. He grabbed her clothes and she snatched them from him. She was embarrassed that he saw that she wasn't a tough cookie after all. Shirley got dressed and fifteen minutes went by and the doctor came back into the examining room. He smiled at the two briefly.

"Well Mr. and Mrs. Thomas the test came back positive and you are pregnant, to be exact you are two and half weeks." He was looking at his chart.

Shirley folded her arms and then placed one of her hands on her forehead to hide her face.

"Congratulations to the both of you. What's wrong Mrs. Thomas you should be happy?" The doctor notice that she was hiding her face.

"nothing's wrong, I'm just surprised by the result." She lifted her hand away from her face. Looking at Sharan and then back at the doctor.

"So umm, are you going to sign up for our pre-natal clinic here? We have one of the best ones in Cincinnati." Doctor Bosh told her.

"No we were leaning more towards an abortion, do ya'll perform those here?" Shirley asked him.

"I'm sorry we don't, but I can assist ya'll to a specialist. His name is Doctor Heismann. He perform abortions on Auburn Ave." The doctor told her.

"Can you please give us the information to contact him please?" She asked him.

"Are you sure about this Mrs. Thomas?" The doctor asked her.

"Yes, my husband and I have already decided." She told him.

"Okay if you insist," as he began to write the information on a card. He looked at her and she smiled and then looked at Sharan and he smiled.

"here you go Mrs. Thomas, and what about some type of birth control?" He handed her the card.

"Sure whatever you recommend. I'll take it." She replied. Sharan just listen to the two going back and forth not adding a word.

"Well I would like to prescribe you Ortho-Tri-Cyclen birth control." The doctor said. She didn't waste anytime answering him. "Okay." Shirley responded.

"Well you have the number to contact doctor Heismann, and good luck to the both of you." He started for the door and Shirley stopped him with a question.

"What about the prescription Doctor Bosh?"

"Oh I'll make out an order and you can pick it up at your local pharmacy. It will be out at the front desk." He made his exit.

Sharan helped her off the table. She straightens out her pants. She put her Prada shades back on and they headed out the room. Sharan didn't question what just took place. For a few hours they were happily married and had decided to abort their child.

Shirley and Sharan left the clinic going their separate ways, but Shirley told him she would like the procedure to be done next week if she could get an appointment for the following week. She also wanted for him to go with her. She went home and called Rachelle to let her know she was pregnant. She cried herself to sleep.

Shirley was really upset with herself for the fact that she didn't know who the father of her unborn child that she conceived. Maury and Dana was definitely out the question. She felt so disconnected with herself for lying to Sharan knowing that he cared for her well-being. Her heart beat shamelessly uncontrollably out of control. She couldn't believe she let herself get in this type of situation taking responsibility, or did she?

The next morning at work Shirley called the abortion clinic to set up an appointment with doctor Heismann. She then contacted Sharan to let him know the time and day for her appointment. She able to schedule it for that following Wednesday on the 30th two Memorial Day.

That Monday they kicked it over to Rachelle's house for Memorial Day.

Shirley, Sharan, Renee, Pedro, Rachelle's mom Gloria and Shirley's granny was visiting.

Rachelle also got a chance to do Shirley's granny hair. It was a big secret about Shirley's pregnancy. Shirley and Sharan did manage to communicate better during this time and they enjoyed one another's company. Sam was in Arizona at a car show. Shirley didn't tell him about her situation. She figured after Wednesday that her life would be back to normal.

……………………………...
..

That Wednesday morning of May the 30th Sharan was blowing his horn in his E-320 Benz for Shirley. He was driving her to the abortion clinic. He had already been to her condo twice earlier in the week Monday and Tuesday.

It was 7:45 and Shirley's appointment was at 8:45 a.m. Shirley was already dressed waiting on his arrival. She came down from her condo to see Sharan handsome face sitting in his all gray 2001 E-320 Benz. She had on a black t-shirt, some black low Rida jeans and some all white Airmax. Her hair was pulled back in a ponytail, no jewelry just her black Coach purse, some shades and her Rolex.

Sharan got out the car to open the door for her. When he got back in the car he could sense something was wrong with her. He placed his hand on her thigh and said, "What's wrong Shirl?" She looked at him and said, "Nothing Sharan, I like this car its cute."

You could hear the crackling in her voice. He was determined that something was wrong and he knew that her eyes wouldn't lie. "Let me see your eyes Shirl." He asked.

"Why?" She responded.

"Because your eyes won't lie." He said.

"If you say so," as she removed her shades, her eyes were stained like an alley red brick.

"Shirl, you've been crying, look at your eyes." He told her with much concern.

"It's nothing Sharan," as he gently put the car in drive easing over the speed bumps to reach Cole Dr. When they got onto Cole Dr. he said, "Shirl, I'm worried about you."

"Sharan I just don't feel right killing our child. I've been up all night thinking about it, but I'm not ready to be a mother." She confessed to him.

"Don't think of it as procreation, think of it out of Wedlock." He told her.

"Are you sure Sharan? Are you really okay with?" She asked him. He was now merging onto the 1-71 ramp to go south heading into Cincinnati.

"Whatever makes you happy, like you said you're not ready to be a mother?" He was looking straight ahead.

"But'em-." She tried to respond but he cut her off. "Don't worry about it, I'm here for you and that's all that really matters right now," as he pulled her head to his chest and turned up his CD player which was playing TP-2 R. Kelly "I Wish" as he started down 1-71.

It was 8:00 clock when they passed the Red Bank exit, they continued down 1-71 passing Edwards & Smith exit, and then the Dana Ave exit. It was 8:20 when Sharan was getting off at the W.H Taft and Reading Rd. exit. He came to the light off the ramp he asked Shirley, "Are you hungry?"

She looked at him saying, "No."

It was a White Castle to his right which he turned into. He went through the drive-thru, because Auburn Ave. was off W.H Taft. He sat by the speaker with his window down waiting on someone to take his order. Then a female voice came across the speaker.

"Thank you for choosing White Castles, may I take your order please?"

"Yes I would like a large heavy-heavy and a sausage and egg breakfast sandwich.," as Sharan placed his order.

"Would you like anything else sir?" The female asked him.

"Hold on please, Shirl are you sure you don't want anything?' He asked Shirley and she shook her answering him saying "no" with her head motion.

"Umm-that's all." He said through the speaker.

"That will be $2.87 sir, please pull around to the first window." She directed him giving him his total for his purchase. Sharan whipped his Benz to the first window. He reached into to his back pocket and pulled out his wallet. He gave the cashier a five dollar bill.

"That was $2.87 out of $5, here's your change $2.13, please pull to the next window." The cashier told him. Sharan received his change and pulled up to the next window to receive his order. There were two other females that came to the window to see Sharan. He could hear one of the females say, "Kim that's the owner of that Kids store out in Silverton." They were eyeing him.

"Damn Alicia he's fine as hell, is anybody with him?" The other girl asked her. Shirley heard them and then eased forward a little so they could see her. She eased back into her seat and said, "I see you are a celebrity Sharan."

The females got quiet and then the one name Kim handed Sharan his order. "Thank you sir, please come again," as the girl kind of rubbed his hand handing him his food. Sharan looked at her and the female smiled at him. He shook his head saying, "Your welcome," as he tucked his order away and pulled off. The girls giggled out loud saying, "I hope that wasn't his girl in the car with him."

Shirley just looked over at him and then leaned back against the seat. She still had her shades on the whole time. He turned up the R. Kelly TP-2 once again to avoid the negative conversation that Shirley was trying to bring up. He turned onto reading Rd. going towards downtown getting all the way over in the right lane so he could turn right on W.H Taft. He road W.H. Taft all the way to the light of Euclid. He made a left onto Euclid that crossed McMillan and Euclid turned into Auburn Ave. He took Auburn Ave. up to McGregor and Glencoe Ave., and then he turned into the abortion clinic.

There were picketers outside the clinic as they sat in the car. Sharan finished his sandwich

and drank half his coffee. They got out the Benz and the picketers began to shout. "Don't kill one of God's creations." It came from the crowd.

Shirley was scared of the picketers.

"Procreation to build a nation, not abortion that's cruel torture and you'll be a murderer." The picketers yelled out.

Shirley got closer to Sharan fearing that they would get attacked by the picketers.

"Take it easy Shirl, I won't let anyone hurt you." He grabbed her in his arms and they continued inside the abortion clinic. They approached the receptionist desk and Sharan spoke for Shirley. "Excuse me Ms., we have an 8:45 appointment, the name is Shirley Thomas."

The older lady looked at the two and then down at a list. "Yes she's scheduled for 8:45, and you're right on time. So will it be cash or credit sir?" The lady asked him with a subtle expression. "Cash ma'am." Sharan reached in his left front pocket to pay the receptionist the money. She gave him a clip board with a form on it.

"Sir have your wife to fill out this form and return it to the desk and we will get her right in." The lady told Sharan also handing him a receipt.

"Okay miss thank you." Sharan grabbed the clip board and they went to sit down and Shirley filled out the form. Sharan was wondering how did the lady figure they were married. "Shirl, why did the lady think we are married?" He asked her.

Shirley looked at him with gloomy eyes and said,

"It was probably written down on the brief information I gave them when I made the appointment. They wanted to know will anyone be driving me home after the procedure and I said my husband."

Sharan just shrugged his shoulders not responding at all. Shirley completed the form and Sharan returned it to the desk. Moments later they called Shirley's name to be seen. Sharan waited in the waiting area for her return. Shirley returned at 10:20.

She walked out to Sharan in the waiting area. He immediately comforts her as they went towards the exit doors. She was crying as they stood at the doors and the picketers were still outside protesting.

God she didn't want to talk. She didn't want to think about it. She wanted him to wrap her in his arms, hold her close and hear him say that he cared with all his heart. Forgiving her for what she just did that could've bonded them together forever as well. Not that, that was the way their exchange was likely to be. The idea of having an audience watching her struggle to the car she kept her composure.

"Take me home please," she said quietly as they walked out pass the picketers and he was still holding her close. They reached the car avoiding the positive, but negative remarks from the picketers. He secured her snug and tight to the car and pulled away from the abortion clinic nice and slow. He was playing the jazz tunes of Kenny G, as he went back down Auburn Ave. and made a right onto McMillan and they rode McMillan down to where they could merge onto I-71 going north. Shirley put her head on his shoulder and went to sleep until they arrived at her condo.

Sharan took it upon himself to help her into her condo. She went and took a shower to relax and clean herself up. That's all she could hear ringing in her ear was the vacuum at the abortion clinic sucking in her insides. She was livid and couldn't understand why she was feeling so down.

Sharan invited himself to her kitchen and prepared her a grill cheese sandwich and tomato soup with a pickle on the side and a glass of sunny delight orange juice. Shirley was lying across her satin sheets on her bed when Sharan tapped on her door entering her bedroom.

"Here you go Shirl, you need to eat something." He came in and sat the food on her small table in the room. He looked over her lying still in her bed looking sexy as ever.

She had on a knee high silk blue nightgown.

"I'm not hungry Sharan," as more tears began to trickle down her dark face.

"Shirl quit crying everything is going to be alright." He told her.

"But Sharan, I just killed our unborn child and deep down inside I know it was wrong and it hurts." She explained with much emotions.

She knew her confining in the devil's work, not only was she a murderer, she wasn't telling him the truth behind why she did it. The pain was enormous and it stained her heart. If she was a movie star this would be her best role and would sure win an Oscar. More tears came about and Sharan grabbed her up to embrace her and gave her a few Kleenex to catch her tears.

"I'll stay here until you get to sleep and I'll let myself out." He told her. She nodded her head to approve of him doing so. Sharan tucked her under the sheets and he sat in the lazy boy recliner and ate the food he'd prepared for her watching the Maury Povich show.

"You are not the father," the T.V. was loud and Shirley heard the famous words that were so often announced from the DNA test they performed on the show. She cried more from hearing it as she suddenly fell asleep. Shirley didn't awake until the next morning, she checked her answering machine and it was full………………………………..........

CHAPTER SIX

Atlanta, GA. The Hair Show

She checked her answering machine and the calls that really matter was Sharan's.

Beep! "Shirl this Rachelle, how did it go? Give me a call."

Beep! "Girl this Nee give me a call."

Beep! "Shirl, hope you are feeling better. This is Sharan, call me."

Beep! "Pumpkin, this is your granny I had a dream about fish, so call me honey child."

Shirley tears resurfaced when her granny said that, because she knew when an older person dreamt about fish it meant someone close to them was pregna*nt.*

Beep! "Shirl, this is Sharan again and I realize that I really do care about you and we need to talk, so give me call."

Beep! "hey baby this is Sam, I've been trying to reach you since yesterday at work, at home, you cell and now this morning. I just wanted to know if you wanted to go to the Islands with me in about two weeks. Give me a call soon, because I have to book the flight."

"Beep-end of messages, please clear or save messages you would like, thank you beep."

Shirley picked her phone up to call Rachelle first. She called the hair salon.

The phone rang four times at the salon before someone picked up.

"Hello Mother's, where we do hair like no other, may I help you?" It was Rachelle answering the phone.

"Chelle, this is me Shirl, what's up girl?" Shirley asked her.

"Shit, I was worried about you. Sharan called me last night and told me to check on you." She responded.

"I'm okay Chelle, Sharan is so sweet, so perfect. Chelle I cried because I couldn't tell him the truth. I kept picturing him as my child father and he's the type of man a child needs in his/her life. The fact that , the vacuum was sucking all the living life out of me and the thought of it might being his was killing my soul, more than the pain from the procedure." Shirley sniffled.

"What's done is done and life must go on Shirl. I told you to pray and ask God for forgiveness and you'll prosper. But I received a call yesterday to be in the hair show that the Bronner Brothers are hosting this weekend in Atlanta. Are you up for going?"

Rachelle asked her.

"I'm suppose to be resting Chelle, but when are we leaving? I need to get away for a couple of days." Shirley told her.

"We are leaving out tomorrow morning, so we can kick it Friday night, because the hair show is Saturday. And yes before you ask, Renee is going." Rachelle shared that with her.

"I wasn't going to ask, but who car are we taking?" Shirley asked her.

"We are taking Renee's beat up Nissan Maxima," as Rachelle laughed.

"Yeah right," as Shirley sighed into the phone. "I'll ask Sam if we can take his 600 Benz

and leave him with my car." Shirley told her.

"That's cool, I did want to put the Beemer on the highway." Rachelle said.

"If Sam doesn't comply then we can take your Beemer." Shirley responded.

"Okay," said Rachelle.

It was a brief moment of silence. Rachelle thought about what had taken place in the salon a few minutes ago before Shirley called.

"Shirl, you just missed it. Ren Mack came in here going off on Meco. He was salty, because apparently she burned him, gave the Negro gonorrhea, it was funny as hell. She is over there with the I eat ass face now."

"For real Chelle?" Shirley asked her.

"Yeah girl. He dogged her out that one way. I know she feels real stupid, with her old tired ass, always trying to fuck some young guy. The bitch about to turn forty plus in July." Rachelle told her.

"So who are you using for models Chelle?" Shirley asked her.

"Probably Angie, Monica, Rita Summer, Auni and Janice. I got to beat the Weave Master Shanice. She's down at Transformations taking shit to another level. I ain't gonna hate, but the sister is a damn genius when it comes to styling hair. Then this little mother-fucker Eric J. in Atlanta has been winning the competition for the last two years. Those two are my only concerns, but I know I can beat them." Rachelle got hyper talking to her friend about the show and her competition.

"You can do it, I know you can beat them girl." Shirley gave her friend praises.

"That's what's up Shirl." Rachelle responded.

"Well I need to get up and take a shower, plus I have to go and buy me some more pads and call Pam at the job to tell her I won't be in until Monday." Shirley was explaining to her friend.

"Okay Shirl, bye."

"Bye Chelle."

They hung up from each other. Shirley called her job to tell her secretary she wouldn't be in the office until Monday morning. She called Sharan to let him know she was okay. Then she called her granny and Sam. Sam had agreed to let her use his car in exchange for her going on the trip with him to the Islands. After showering she got dress and went to Wal-Mart near her to buy her personal needs stuff.

She came back home and started to pack for her trip to Atlanta. She received a call from Renee while she was packing. Renee wanted to go shopping when she got off work at 2 O' clock that afternoon. Shirley decided to head down to Renee's job at Kroger's in the Hillcrest Plaza. Transformation hair salon was in the exact same plaza.

It was 2:10 when Renee walked out the grocery store. She followed Renee to her apartment so she could park her car and change out of her work uniform before they headed to the Mall. Shirley decided to get Sam's car from down at his job. They switched cars and Sam gave her five hundred dollars for her trip.

They went to Kenwood Mall to buy new outfits. Shirley called Rachelle at work to see if she needed a new outfit also. Shirley purchased her a tennis skirt and an halter top all white by French Connection. She brought some K-Swiss classics to compliment her outfit.

Renee picked out a pair of khakis shorts green, an all green Nike fleece shirt and a pair of black Nike slip-ons with the heel out. Shirley bought Rachelle a pair of tight Capri's the way her friend liked them. A nice pull up top that would show some of her stomach, all pink, some pink & white slide in three inch heels. They went back to Symmes Township after they left the Mall so Shirley could grab her bags she already packed . It was around 4:30 in the afternoon. They headed back down to Bondhill so Renee could pack her clothes. Renee was taking a shower when Shirley called Sharan again to thank him for there for her. When Shirley was on the phone she noticed a razor with a little chunk of white stuff on it lying on the end of the coffee table next to some marijuana Renee had exposed. She grabbed it to get a closer look and then Renee came out to the living room.

Shirley was holding the razor in her hand.

"Renee, what is this?" Shirley asked her.

"Shirl, give me that, it's nothing but some aspirin I use in my marijuana from time to time." She grabbed it from Shirley.

"If you need to resort to that, you need to stop smoking that shit." Shirley said to her. Renee disappeared again and Shirley yelled out. "Damn if a bitch needs to smoke aspirin, then she might as well graduate to some crack." She held the phone back up to her ear.

"I'm sorry Sharan, now what were you saying?" as she continued her conversation with him.

After Renee got situated and packed they put her things in the trunk of the Benz and headed around to Mother's Hair Salon.

It was now 5:30 when they walked in the salon and Rachelle was on her last head. Shirley walked down to her booth and Renee went into the restroom. All the other stylist were now gone.

"Hey Chelle, is she your last client?" Shirley asked her.

"Yes Shirl." Rachelle answered her. Shirley sat in a waiting chair by Rachelle's booth, and grabbed a magazine to read.

"Shirl, do you remember Puff who work for Anthem Insurance?" Rachelle asked her.

"Yeah I think so, how are you doing girlfriend?" Shirley spoke to Rachelle's client. The female turned her head to speak to Shirley. "I'm fine and you? Where is ya'll one friend at?" Puff asked them.

"Oh she's in the restroom." Shirley answered her.

"I thought I saw her one night up by KFC on California and Reading Rd. It was late out like 2 in the morning." Puff stated.

"Shit ain't no telling with her weird ass, you probably did," said Shirley.

"Puff do you won't for me to do anything else to your head?" Rachelle asked her client, turning her to face the mirror.

"No Rachelle it looks good. Thank you, how much do I owe you?" Puff asked her.

"Just give me sixty dollars." Rachelle told her taking ten dollars off her fee.

Rachelle spun her back around and took the smock from around her client. Renee came out the restroom and Puff spoke to her while she was paying Rachelle her money. Shirley was still fingering through the magazine.

"What up Nee?" Rachelle asked her as they watched Puff walk out the door of the salon.

"Nothing girl, something is not agreeing with my stomach." Renee told her.

"Why are you sweating like that Nee?" Rachelle asked her.

Renee wiped her forehead. "I don't know, but I'll be fine." She told Rachelle.

Shirley jumped in. "The bitch is just weird as hell Chelle."

Renee got an attitude with Shirley for that comment. "Fuck you trick." Renee told her rolling her eyes at Shirley.

"Yeah whatever weird ass bitch." Shirley had to get the last word.

"Ya'll chill out and help me close up," as Rachelle walked passed Shirley hitting her on the arm. Shirley looked at her crazy.

"Are ya'll bags already packed?" Rachelle asked them.

"Yeah we are packed and ready to go. Your outfit is in the car. I got the Capri one size smaller, because I know you like your shit tight. All pink with a pink pull up shirt and some pink and white slide in heels." Shirley told her.

They helped Rachelle clean up and close the shop. It was exactly six 6p.m. when they were walking out the hair salon. Rachelle was in shock to see Shirley going to the all white Benz trimmed in gold.

"Damn Shirl, I know this isn't that nigga Sam's car? So who are you fucking now?" Rachelle asked her still checking out the Benz.

"It's Sam's car," as Renee announced it from her folding her arms as if she was jealous of her friend.

"Damn bitch I can answer for myself, I don't need a ventriloquist." Shirley rolled her eyes at Renee. "Chelle I haven't slept with him, but this is what we are traveling in."

"I hope he's not a drug dealer Shirl," said Rachelle.

"I hope not either." Renee added.

"No he's not, he has his own detail shop and promotes concerts and manage that group the Trap Boys. He's legit." Shirley answered her friend's speculations of Sam's line of work.

"Okay Shirl." Rachelle nodded. Renee just rolled her eyes, as she went and got in Rachelle's Acura truck. Shirley was cramping a little, but she felt good about the situation.

Shirley followed them down to Renee's job so they could grab a few groceries for their trip. They purchased chips, bottled water, soda's, cold-cuts and pasta salad. Shirley had to buy some more pads, because she forgot the ones she bought earlier at her home.

Renee snuck off and bought her a Monistat kit, because she had a yeast infection from her dildo and drinking too much beer. They got to Rachelle's house and made sandwiches. Rachelle also fried some chicken for their trip and to accommodate her company before leaving. Pedro showed up that night. Rachelle also had to call her models to let them know what time the show started Saturday in Atlanta. They were coming down Friday instead of Thursday. Shirley had went to gas up the Benz and take care of a few more things she needed to handle. She met Sam for a brief moment to give him the key to her condo. She didn't ask him why he wanted the key she just gave it to him. When she returned at around 9:30 that evening things had calmed down in Rachelle's house. Renee was watching T.V. in the dayroom. Rachelle and Pedro were getting their freak on in her bedroom. Shirley went and took a shower.

When she got settled in her sleeping gear she entered the dayroom to do her nails and toes. Renee was sitting on the floor Indian style drinking Crown Royal and Ginger ale. When Shirley went to go use the restroom she heard Pedro giving it to her friend, because Rachelle was screaming in ecstasy telling him to give it to her.

Shirley just smiled and shook her head. When she returned to the dayroom she crashed on the couch. Renee was now out on the deck smoking her marijuana. She was hiding the truth from her friends.

Rachelle had set her alarm clock for 4:15 a.m. because she wanted for them to be on the highway before the early morning rush hour traffic.

They woke up and Renee was already dressed in a pair of jeans and a Polo shirt with her sandals. Rachelle and Shirley showered one after the other and got dressed.

Rachelle wore a Baby Phat pair of jeans, a Baby Phat t-shirt and some Mules. Shirley had on some Denim Apple bottom jeans and an Apple Bottom t-shirt with her leather Cole Haan sandals. It was like 5:20 when Rachelle was looking for the cooler to put the beverages in. Renee was watching the two run around grabbing item.

"I already put them in the cooler and the cooler is in the car all we need is ice." Renee told Rachelle.

"Let's start loading our luggage in the car." Shirley said walking pass them with hers. They followed with their stuff. Everything was set all they needed now was a bag of ice. They grabbed it at the Marathon gas station by Rachelle's house. They took I-75 south off of Summit Rd. leaving the gas station. Shirley drove first. They were listening to Jaheim as they crossed the bridge into Kentucky leaving Cincinnati.

They reached outside of Lexington city limits at about 8:05. They were making good time and stopped right inside of the Tennessee state line so Rachelle and Renee could use the restroom. Shirley and Rachelle switched seats, putting Shirley in the front passenger seat and Rachelle in the drivers seat. Rachelle immediately put in Mary J. Blige. "Take me to the ATL Mary," as she pulled out of the rest stop. Renee fell asleep when they were coming out of Nashville.

When Renee woke up she saw the sign that read 'Welcome to Atlanta, Fulton county'. Rachelle merged in the lane going towards downtown Atlanta. They were on I-85 and Rachelle was looking for the Martin Luther King Jr. exit. She saw it and merged off the highway to get directions to the Comfort Inn Downtown by the Greyhound Bus Station. They had reservations for a Presidential suite. It was 2:00 in the afternoon when they pulled up in the Comfort Inn. They got checked in and muscled everything to their shelter for the next four nights and three days. Shirley called for the shower first.

She took her shower and put on a cotton ruffle dress all white no bra and black panties. She was bleeding, but not to heavy. She still wanted to be careful and wear the black panties. She added a fringe scarf and her jewelry.

Rachelle went in after her and came out in her thong putting on her some daisy duke shorts all white, a pull up top with ruffles that were yellow, no bra, footy's and some K-Swiss classics.

Renee came out last and put on some khakis blue shorts, a Polo stripe shirt and some blue flats with the heel out to match her outfit.

It was 3:30 that afternoon when they left for the Underground Mall.

They went shopping, but didn't really purchase anything at the Underground Mall. Then they went to the Lenox Mall to shop, because they had a better selection. When they left the Mall after shopping for the latest designs they went to grab a bite to eat from Krystals.

The restaurant reminded them of White Castles. Renee got her something, but Shirley and Rachelle went to Burger King on Peach Tree. They met some guys and told them they were looking for a spot to party in Atlanta. The guys invited them to the Hot Spot. They didn't join the guys instead they drove around Atlanta for a little while. At 10:15 that night they started looking for a club to parlay in. They ended up at club 112. There they ran into Ren Mack and Boobie.

Rachelle was flirting with Boobie and Shirley just made conversation with Ren Mack. Renee was in her own little world. Ren order drinks for everyone and paying for it.

"What's up Boobie, what are ya'll doing in ATL?" Rachelle asked him, looking at him seductively.

"We down here on some business, about to get on one of Lil Jon mix CDs." He answered her.

"I thought this was a jumping club down here?" Rachelle asked him while she was bobbing her head to E-40.

"Rachelle, it is but they're clubs down here don't start jumping until after twelve." Boobie knew the facts about the clubs in Atlanta.

"Damn our clubs in the Nati be packed at this time," said Rachelle.

She sipped her drink and Shirley and Ren started talking.

"So Shirley you are messing with my dude Sam?" Ren asked her.

"Something like that Ren." She said.

"But ole Ren Mack wasn't good enough for you?" He asked her with a fake laugh.

"I mean you are cool, but what's up with you and Meco? I heard she's hot," as Shirley put her finger in her mouth and made a sizzling sound and then touched Ren Mack's hand and smiled at him.

He put his head down and then lift it up with a small smirk. "So you heard huh?" He paused and said, "Yeah she burnt me. I should have known with her old ass. She's always in the Ritz trying to get at a young player." Ren told her.

"Well Sam and I are dating, but I do dig your music and I hope ya'll do well in the future." Shirley told him.

"Thanks and I heard you are a lawyer. You don't look like you practice law," said Ren.

"How does a lawyer suppose to look? If you keep it up I'll sue you for slander the next time you direct your rap towards me." She smiled at him.

He laughed a little showing off his diamond and platinum teeth. Rachelle was rubbing Boobie's thigh trying to feel him up. She was drinking gin and she didn't won't to waste anymore time discussing premature issues. Rachelle had a slight itch in her panties and she was gaming to get it scratched.

"Damn Boobie, do ya'll want to get some drinks and go back to our hotel suite?" Rachelle asked him.

Boobie was ready and more certainly eager to go. "Sure, we don't mind and there's a liquor store down the street."

She looked at him and they decided to leave.

Boobie and Ren Mack followed them in Ren's F-150 truck sitting on 26" chrome rims. They stopped at the liquor store and bought four bottles of liquor. Then they stopped at a convenient store for ice, juice and soda's to mix with their liquor. When they reached the hotel suite Renee went up to her and Shirley room with the twin beds and rolled her up one of those marijuana sticks.

Rachelle kicked off her K-Swiss, grabbed some cups and started mixing drinks. She mixed Tequila with Bombay with a little orange juice. Shirley looked at her crazy knowing she gets buck wild when she drinks any type of light liquor and especially like this. Shirley and Ren Mack were on the couch in the living area of the suite drinking Martel and Coke. Rachelle and Boobie were on the Love sofa up under each other. There was a movie on the HBO channel, but no one was watching it.

Shirley was feeling a little light headed and needed some fresh air. She leaned over and asked Ren did he want to take a walk out by the pool area and he agreed to.

"Rachelle, Ren and I will be back in a few." Shirley told her.

Rachelle looked up at her and replied, "Where are ya'll going?"

"For a walk." Shirley answered.

"Okay, me and Boobie will be here chilling," as Rachelle looked at Boobie real cunning like. Rachelle and Boobie watched their friends leave out the door. Two downed two more drinks and Rachelle was now extremely horny. She grabbed Boobie by his man-hood in his pants and whispered in his ear. "Do you want to go upstairs?"

He swallowed deep in his throat. "I don't care." He told her.

She grabbed him by the hand and led him upstairs, but Boobie had to help her.

When they reached the bedroom Rachelle immediately stripped out of her shirt and her reddish nipples were rock hard. She pulled down her daisy duke shorts and thong to her ankles and came out of them one leg at a time. She threw herself onto the bed, while Boobie stood there looking at her thick body.

IIc thought about this chick name Aunika from Dayton he was digging. Rachelle moved with sinewy cat like grace as she sprawled on the bed, beckoning Boobie.

His thoughts came. ***"Damn I just want to spread her thighs and fuck the shit out of her."***

Even though her waist line was tiny, her ass and breast were enormous, the size of cantaloupes. "Come here Boobie baby," as Rachelle whispered to him. He jumped onto the mattress and started groping her. She giggled. Their hands were everywhere at once.

Her breast, his back, her hips, his strong arms, her long hair, and his engorged tribal piece in his shorts. They slowed down getting pass the initial giddiness. Boobie quickly undressed. Rachelle held his arms over his head gently pinned him and extended her tongue. She licked an agonizing slow path from his forehead, down the bridge of his nose, across his lips, chin and throat, to his chest and stomach. Finally she ended up at the tip of his manhood.

By this point his manhood was hard enough to cut glass. It gave a few bobs before the light complexion diva engulfed it with her mouth.

Boobie told her. "If you keep that up you'll get a surprise. Now I've warned you," as he smiled down at her. She released his tribal piece long enough to say, "Right!"

Then she immediately drew concentric circle with her tongue from the tip of his tribal piece, down the shaft to his testicles. She flatted her tongue, as she gave a long lick from the base to his piss hole, and then opened her mouth wide lowering it into his joint. Rachelle made several swallowing motions while easing his 10" tribal piece into her mouth one inch at a time. By this time her face was almost smashed into his pubic hair, he thought he'd gone to heaven and back. He was loving this diva. He tighten up his toes and said, "No one has never put all of me inside their mouth before," as he lay back enjoying the moment. His tribal piece must have been half way down her throat. She had dick crammed into her face, as she continued massaging his manhood with her tonsils.

It was too much, he held onto her head for support, and then pumped his hips erratically, and shot scalding wads of semen straight in her mouth as she swallowed. Rachelle held his tribal piece firmly in her mouth until it softens.

"Thanks," he said adding, "But I wanted to fuck you Rachelle."

She raised an eyebrow. "We still can Boobie, because I want to cum too."

"I want to eat your pussy first." He said.

She looked at him and said, "So what's stopping you?"

He then positioned her over his mouth, facing away. He took a moment to gaze at her tender rouge lips and the pink inside as she lowered her pussy to his awaiting tongue and mouth. The mere sight of her hot slit had him stirring a hard again. Rachelle's nookie was like the insides of some sweet fruit, ripen by the sun. It was warm and delicious, and produced a steady trickle of juices as he lapped steadily. She began to whimper and he pushed his tongue in as deep as he could while pressing her clit with his thumb.

She rocked back as he gripped her hips, rubbing her clit with his thumb and she rocked back again with his entire face in her pussy. When his nose tickled her puckered asshole she howled. "That's-it that's it right there Boobie," as he pressed harder on her clit and devoured her leaking wet pussy. She leaned forward and began jacking him off as her hips gyrated wildly.

Then she shouted in a shrill quivering voice. "I'm cumming, I'm cumming, I'm cumming!" as she fell forward to his thighs. She collapsed and he released her ass cheeks from his grip. Her body was motionless exact for the steady rhythm of her hand tugging his tribal piece. He was stiff again. He looked down to admire Rachelle's luscious body. She lay on her belly, her backside had perfect curves. Her massive boobs were spread out on both sides. "Mmmmmm-hmmm." She said turned around and sat up giving him a dreamy look. "That was a good nut I busted, I needed that," she whispered.

"Are you ready for round two?" Boobie asked her, because he was more than ready and the alcohol had him energized. She started at Boobie's hard thickness. She was ready, freaky as ever wanting him to fill her hole up with his love making device. He propped his head with a pillow and laid back. Rachelle hovered over him and impaled herself on his tribal piece in quick sinking motion. No condom of any kind, just bare skin. Flesh to flesh as she leaned forward with her delicious breast brushing his face. He grasped one and began teasing her nipple. "Ooh," she purred. "That feels good Boobie."

He held her hips and pumped upward, jamming his tribal piece into her passage as hard and fast as he could, still sucking her nipples the whole time. Rachelle screamed and squealed as he tongued her breast and pumped inside her vagina walls.

He was about to cum and Rachelle slowed her gyrations just enough to prevent him from cumming and then she sped up again. They continued to hump ravenously. Rachelle was a sexual acrobat and it was clear she knew all the tricks of the trade. He knew she was a pro, because of her experience. After switching positions several times, they went into the traditional missionary position with her legs hooked over his shoulders. He was able to grind into her pussy, while still plumbing her depths like an oil drill. He was able to find her G-spot, as they fucked in tandem for a long time. Finally Rachelle face twisted into a mask of ecstasy and she rubbed her long fingernail lightly over his back.

"Harder, harder Boobie," as she cried out and put her nails deeper into his back. "I'm cumming Boobie, I'm cumming. Oh shit I'm cumming and it won't stop," as she screamed to the top of her lungs and Renee heard her in the other room.

He rammed Rachelle until he couldn't hold back anymore and launched a solid blast of semen deep inside her pussy. Rachelle tensed up and released up and released a shuddering orgasm against of her own. Boobie indeed hit her G-spot. They ended up with a ton of kisses and declarations of passion. She was satisfied as they lay there butt-na-

ked...

....

..

Meanwhile Shirley and Ren Mack were out by the pool having a pleasant conversation under a jade moonlight. They were outside and weather was formerly being it was the 1st of June. The sky was clam under the veil of the moonlight. A romantic touch of an essence, if two lovers were storming up passionate emotional interest before committing the final score of being intimate.

Ren Mack had that glare in his eyes. Shirley was feeling the vibe, even though she was now interested in the likes of Sam Holston, but has an emotional connection for Sharan. She was now vulnerable and had confusion in her heart.

If she wasn't on her period, she would have probably let Ren Mack explore the uniqueness of her womanly possessions. Her stomach swam with butterflies and her mind fluttered in waves trying to control her vulnerability and stay within her means. Living past subtitles she remained unworthy of her heart. She held his hand to describe the way she was feeling towards anyone in front of her. Ren didn't understand the picture, but knew being in the presence was remarkable. He didn't rely on his go-getter skills and tried to understand her floetry and the style she possessed. He didn't care if she was involved with his manager/friend Sam, he desired her. She was a challenge indeed, because she had denied him in the beginning. Without a conscious thought, her hand raised a finger over his ear along the outline of his powerful cheek bone. And even more she wished she could touch his soul, soothe his ego, ease away all of fates tangles that lay between them. Unbidden her mother's voice echoed in her head.

'**Stay free, if you can, of passion that exists without a deeper foundation Shirley. Women tend to struggle not knowing the influences of what the man has on his**

agenda and being weaker vessel women tend to fall victim to the nonsense.'
Her eyes drifted in the back of her head. She snapped out of her trance. When words
needed to be spoken, they weren't. When desire needed to be handled, it fled. Her emotions ran wild unknowingly as she separated herself from him saying, "Let's just be
good friends Ren, because anything else would be complicated. He didn't referee her
call

Trying to argue the fact that he knew where she was going with this moment. Something was troubling her and he saw it on her face, Ren didn't question it and replied.
"No problem Shirley, I'm with that, and maybe who know, maybe some day we could
make some music together behind this moment we just shared," as he smiled at her and
she gave a half smile in return. "Let's go back inside to see what the others are doing,"
Shirley suggested. Ren waved his hand in front of them for her to lead the way. Renee
was in the other bedroom that she and Shirley were sharing playing with her magic
card. She was in her panties and bra sitting on one of the twin beds matching cards together. Her voice was low as she made pairings. " **Howls of the Night Pack, Sorcery
2/2, so the Giant Growth is +3/+3 can take out the Prize Unicorn which is 2/2. Na'll
the Deadly spider ½ and the Juvenile gloom Window 1/3-1/3 can protect the forest
of Basic Land. Fuck, Damn it this shit is complicated," as she threw the cards
down.** Her hormones were raving after hearing Rachelle and Boobie having sex in
the other room. She heard her friend screaming out in pleasure through the walls. She
decided to get her toy out and play with herself. She cleaned the bed off pulling the
comforter back. Then she went and got her toy from her bag. Checking the batteries to
see if each speed was on point, she then eased out of her panties grabbing a rag to remove the cream from inside her that was helping cure her yeast infection. She grabbed
her Penthouse Heat Wave lubrication out of her bag. She then lay back down and out
some if the lubrication on her juice box and lubed up her toy. "I hope I can get off, because I need to bust a nut bad." She said to herself letting out a sigh. "Do your thing
Mike," as she eased the dildo inside her passage giving her the sensation and satisfaction she was needing. After grinding it
Into her passage several times trying to heat her own passion. Renee got frustrated, because she couldn't find her clitoris to bust the but she desired. She pulled the dildo out
throwing it to the side. "This is some bullshit, a bitch need some real veins and a real
dick inside her. This shit is getting old," as she looked up at the ceiling in disgust.
Shirley and Ren Mack entered the suite room and didn't see Boobie and Rachelle and

Shirley knew where to find her friend. She told Ren he could have a seat so she could go get his friend. Shirley knew her friend to well and the gin did it all the time. She knew Rachelle would blame it on the alcohol. Shirley got upstairs and come to the door of the bedroom that Rachelle was occupying. She knocked lightly on the door. Tap-Tap= Tap! Rachelle heard the light tapping at the door. "Who is it?" Rachelle yelled out. "Hey Chelle are you busy, because Ren is ready to go?" Shirley asked her. "Not any more, hold up here we come, we'll be down in a minute" Rachelle told her friend. "Okay Chelle," as Shirley went back down the steps to attend to Ren Mack. Rachelle got up to go use the bathroom what was in her room. Boobie was already taking a quick shower at the tine. She wiped herself and flushed the toilet and then joined him in the shower. They got out the shower and dried off. Boobie got dressed and she put on her night gown and they headed back down stairs. Shirley and Ren Mack were watching videos. "Hey ya'll" as Rachelle got their attention. "What ya'll doing?" Rachelle asked. Shirley looked at her friend and knew exactly what she'd been doing. "Nothing, just watching videos waiting on Boobie." Shirley replied. '**Yeah heifer you been up there fucking up a storm I see"** Shirley smiled at Rachelle. Then she stood up and so did Ren Mack giving each other platonic hugs. Shirley and Ren walked towards the door Rachelle and Boobie followed. Shirley opened the door and Ren

Exited first waving and smiling at Shirley and she returned the same gesture. Boobie followed, but before his exit he kissed Rachelle in the mouth giving her much tongue action. Shirley eyes were now wide open. He waved at Shirley and left out the door. Shirley closed the door and asked her friend. "Chelle I know you didn't fuck him?" Her hands were now on her hips. "Yes I did, I had to get some of that dick. I have waited to fuck him since that night at the Ritz. Girl I had to get some from away from home." Rachelle cut her off. "Until that Negro put a ring on this finger, I'll fuck who I want too, and when I want too." Rachelle put emphasis on her statement. "Excuse me sorry for being in your business." Shirley looked at her. Rachelle walked off and went back upstairs to her room. She was feeling real jazzy. Out of all the trouble they went through Shirley didn't want to argue with her friend and let it go. What foolish behavior she displayed on their trip. The next day they went to Lenox Mall to meet with Angie, Monica, Rita, Janice, summer, Kissy and Aunie who were Rachelle's models in the hair show. The Bronner Bros. Hair Show was in Saturday at the Convention Center. They bought lingerie and outfits for the shoe. They drove to College Park and Decatur to chill. After eating at Dominquez later on that night Rachelle, Shirley, Angie, Monica,

Janice, Rita, Summer, Auni and Kissy got directions to club 112 on the Westside of Atlanta. Renee didn't go out with them as they as they all went partying on the streets of Atlanta.

Renee sat in the living area of the hotel suite and was reading a magazine sipping on some Tequila Patron while her friends were out trying to party in the clubs in Hot Atlanta. She came across an article talking about, 'How The Females Body work'. **Renee found out that her pubic hair, which she had a lot in that area, it had helped keep dirt and**

Germs away from a woman's genitals back in prehistoric days. She kept on reading. **'to find out that the most supersensitive organ of a woman's body is her clitoris, located right below her pubic bone. On the outer genital's it's tucked inside the top portion of the inner lips of her vulva. The clitoris continues on for about three to four inches inside women when is it fully developed. The part you see is the tip of the pink gland and is covered with a hood of skin. The clitoris contains about 8,000 nerve endings. It's sole purpose is for sexual pleasure'.** Renee found out some interesting things about herself and she kept on reading the article. "Now this sounds interesting, **'A Woman's G-Spot'.**" as she glanced at the page. It read, **'The G-Spot is the size of a quarter between her pubic bone and her cervix. It's approximately on the outer end of the woman's uterus. The G-spot is a spongy tissue loaded with blood vessels. According to specialist with PhD's. in Sex Education who conducted research they said, "when you stimulate the G-spot it produces brain chemicals that block out pain and induce pleasure". Stimulating the G-Spot will produce intense orgasms in females. The biggest problem is finding the exact spot.** Renee was puzzled, because she now knew that this was the problem she was having trying to locate this spot with her dildo repeatedly so she could bust. She'd done it before not knowing the facts. She kept on reading to get a better insight. **"If you insert your finger into the vagina and make that " Come here" motion you should feel it around in that location. If you do it too intensely it will make a female feel like she has to urinate. So Stroke it very gently at first. Even wait for about ten seconds before you stroke it again if you do it right she will feel the pleasure and get stimulated and have Multiple orgasms'.** Renee was impressed and started to get aroused from just reading. Her vagina was now throbbing from this information and she even began to get moist. "I need me some real dick in my life to hit this G-Spot. Or I'll try again with my finger and my toy. And what's this," as she looked on the opposite page of the magazine. I read,

'**The Length Of A Woman**'. She started to read the other page. '**A woman's vagina is approximately four inches long. The muscles of the vagina are very close together when she is relaxed. When she get's excited the walls widen and the vagina actually lengthens a few more inches to allow for penetration. Now that you know about G-Spot and where it's located try to hit it when having sex. One of the best ways to hit the G-Spot directly is in the doggy style position. Remember for the best results let him hit it from the back ladies'.** Renee closed the magazine and was ready taking deep breath. She got her purse, down the rest of her Tequila. She stepped to the door of their hotel room and closed her eyes. Please Lord, let me find someone outside these doors who can help me fulfill my needs." as she opened her eyes and let out a sigh, and then she opened the door heading out to the streets of Atlanta. She took a walk up Peach Tree where she came in contact with a guy standing on the corner at a little booth selling oils, incense and CD's. "Excuse me sir do you have any Frankincense? Renee asked the guy. "Yes I do baby girl," as he showed her a smile letting his two lateral bottom teeth expose his gold's. Can I please buy three?" She asked him. "Yes you may and what a beautiful lady like you doing out here all alone?" The guy asked her. Renee looked at him with her beautiful brown eyes and said, "I'm from out of town, trying to get into something. I like to smoke weed and just chill." She smiled at him. He glared at her. That question shot

Straight to her pubic bone. "That would be nice, but you are at work." She said. "I'm my own boss, I make my own hours," as he gave her a soft smile. "Okay I'm staying down at the comfort Inn about four blocks down the street with my girlfriends. They are out partying at one of these clubs down here." She had her head down like a shy school girl, but was ready to be a naughty girl with nothing but sex on her mind. "Well I'll shut down my booth and I can give you a ride back to your room. My truck is parked over there," as he pointed to an all black Range Rover sitting on 24"s chrome rims. The guy closed down and hauled his things to the truck. They both crossed the street and climbed in the truck. Renee didn't even notice he had Ohio plates. He turned up the music which was Janet Jackson and pulled off slow heading back down Peach Tree towards the Comfort Inn. They got to the room and Renee invited him in. He was around 5'7" medium built with short hair light waves in his cut, brown eyes and he had two small gold's on his bottom laterals. He was brown complexion with a goatee. Renee went to put on some shorts and a t-shirt. She returned to the living area and fixed them a drink of liquor that they already had in their suite. She made him a Martel on the rocks and she had another shot of Tequila. The guy pulled out a bag of marijuana in the Fonto Leaf. "So miss lady what is your name?" he asked her, because they never properly introduced themselves to one another. " Oh my God, I'm sorry my name is Renee, my friends call me Nee for short, and yours?" She moved a little trying to gaze in his eyes. "My name is Chucky Stargate and my folks call me Chuck." He was now licking the perfectly rolled Fonto leaf he just filled with the marijuana. "So where do you live Chucky?" Renee asked him. "I'm from Dayton Ohio the Gem city and where do you live?" He answered her after answering her .

Renee thought he was from Atlanta, but it didn't even matter he was man she could get some wood from. "I'm from Cincinnati about thirty minutes from you." She said. A sinful stare. "Oh the Nasty Nati huh. I use to be down there with one of my dudes who went to U.C." He lit the marijuana and puffed it slow.

"I graduated from U.C. about eight years ago." She told him. Chucky passed the Fonto to Renee nodding his head. She puffed the joint and started choking. "Girl don't kill yourself have you ever smoked Purple Haze?" He asked her. She shook her head "no" still trying to catch her breath. "No I haven't," as she gave him the Fonto back. "Well take your time miss lady" He said.

Renee got an instant head rush from the marijuana. She was felling herself and got bold with it. The alcohol and the marijuana started mixing and brought a chemical reaction to make her actions be known. She started stripping out of her t shirt and shorts. She wasn't wearing any panties or a bra now. Her bushy pubic hair was now inches away from Chuckey's face, being she was now standing and he was sitting. "C'mon let's go upstairs to my room," as she took his hand to lead him grabbing her clothes she just stripped out of. When they entered the room Renee was pulling Chuck's shirt off. "I hope I'm not being to forward Chuck?" she said to him while looking at his chest and stomach. He had tattoos of money dope and dope packages " Oh na'll Renee, do you." She examined him turning him around, looking at his butt and broad shoulders the she saw the massive tattoo across his back. It read! **'STAREGATE'** in big bold letter across the top. She turned him back around to face her. She took in a deep breath and said, "Whatever the reason I've waited to long, to make the first move." She lost Chuck with that comment.

She stood there breathing heavily, both of them were quite anticipating. He moved his hand around her back onto her bare bottom Renee gasped as he pulled her close to him, as he stroked gentle circles across her ass. Touches that advanced onto her hips as his fingers inched closer to her vagina. Renee caressed the side of his face.

"You turn me on like crazy Chuck," she said with a dirty smile. His fingers crossed her pubic hairs and went onto her pussy lips separating them. She bent her knees and began to move her body up and down. His tribal piece throbbed as he felt the honey from her sex begin to cover his finger. "Take me to the bed Chuck," she requested. He picked he up, kissed her on the lips and eased her on to the bed . He began to take off his Red Monkey jeans. "Can I do that," she asked him. She then stroked his hard on through the fabric of his jeans, her fingers glided softly up and down where his private part was positioned in the jeans. She unzipped his pants and began to pull his pants down. Chuck couldn't wait he helped her do so. Once he got out of them he was now in his boxers. She eased down his boxers, then puckered her lips and firmly pressed them against his hot flesh. She kisses his dick head several times, and then stuck her tongue out to taste the drop of pre-cum that has eased up through the slit. Renee smiled, then looked at him and moved his tribal piece across her lips with quiet moan. She lipped her mouth farther along his tribal piece across her lips from an "O" as she sucked his throbbing. Still looking up at him, she took his entire tribal piece in her mouth, He gasped. "Yeah, that's it, that feels good as hell." He said. She took long hard sucks after another. Repeating the technique over and over Chucky found himself about to cum. "I'm cumming now Renee," as a blast of hot semen squirted out of his tribal piece. His toes began to curl as he stood there at the edge of the bed looking down at her. She smiled at him, and then moved back up on the bed and opened her legs. She wasn't she about what she wanted. "You know what I'd like for you to do to me?" she asked him. "I'd like for you to put your face in my pussy and lick me with your tongue until I cum." He caught his breath from still cumming and moved

towards her sex. He spread her with his fingers and licked all over her vulva, smearing her wetness with his mouth, doing her slit at first using side motions, then changing to tight circles. After a few minutes, Renee moaned. "I'm going to cum Chucky baby" as she felt his fingers pressing that spot she read about earlier. She squeezed his head with her thighs, really putting her body into her orgasm. Then she climaxed covering his lips and tongue with her juice. She was shaking like crazy trying to catch her breath. "How was that Renee?" he asked her. She was still trying to catch her breath not believing she just had an orgasm. 'I loved it," as she laughed a little smiling looking up at the ceiling. He eased next to her and she smiled, then she reached over and started stoking his manhood until it started to get hard again. She moved on top of him and guided his tribal piece into her canal of love. "This feels amazing, oh my god. I almost for got how the real thing felt." Renee said. As she pumped her body up and down on his tribal piece pushing him deep inside her vaginal walls. Her heart was beating fast, as her blood was racing through her veins and her orgasm was building up again. He knew she was going to cum again from her motions. Her butt lifted in the air as he thrust upward putting all of him inside her. She gripped his chest with her fingernails holding on as she road him steadily. She began to sweat and it dripped down on his face and chest. Her grimace was unpleasant as she continued to ride him furiously. Her movement was wild and out of control grinding

hard on his tribal piece. Her moans were loud and utters were continuance, as she gave it all she had to cum one more time. His tribal piece had reached her G-Spot and the strokes were on time as her vagina and that spot was stimulated. "Oh god, I'm cumming, I'm cumming, I'm cumming," as she screamed to the top of her lungs. She squeezed his chest

Leaving her nail print in it. She triggered him and he was cumming inside her walls with no protection at all. She collapsed on Chuck's body shaking from spasms. Renee had over come her fear of sleeping with men again. She rolled over to go to the restroom. She stood in the mirror of the restroom down the hall smiling at herself. "You did it girl," as she looked down at her pussy. Then she realized that something was running down her leg.

She touched it with her finger. It was nut from chucky. "Damn Nee, you done did some bullshit. I hope this Negro ain't got no diseases. And I hope I don't get pregnant from this one night stand. I'll get his number and shit just in case." she wiped herself again, and then jumped in the shower. She wrapped herself with a towel and went down stairs to get two bottles of water and the remainder of the Fonto they were smoking and her Frankincense she bought from him. Chuck had put it in Renee's life again and she was feeling great about herself. They talked and then went to take a shower together getting freaky in the shower once more. This time he hit it from the back and he reached her G-Spot was this time and she let it be known the way she screamed in ecstasy. After they showered and had sex for the last time they got dresses. Renee put on a Loonies tune t-shirt and they regrouped in the living area watching T.V. He gave her his personal information to contact him when she got back to Ohio.

He was down in Atlanta attending the hair how also. They made a date to meet each other at the hair show tomorrow. Chucky had to make an early exit. It was like three in the morning. When she opened the door for him, Rachelle and Shirley were coming in and were startled. "Oh God you scared us Nee," Shirley said. Rachelle and Shirley gathered themselves. "I'm sorry ya'll, Chucky these are my best friends Rachelle and Shirley," as she pointed to each of them. "Hello,"

He said admiring both of her friends. "He's down here for the hair show also. Rachelle is one of the stylist competing in the show Chucky baby." Renee told him. But Shirley and Rachelle were confused, because Renee called him Chucky baby. They looked at her wide eyed. "Oh yeah, well good luck tomorrow perhaps," as he smiled at them and kept it moving, before doing so he reached over and kissed Renee. "Bye Nee." He said in a low tone. "Bye Chucky, I'll call you." She closed the door letting her friends in. Shirley looked her up and down, and then sniffed Renee up and down.

"Damn trick you been doing it? Good God Almighty, the bitch done got her some dick." Shirley said. Renee got an attitude. "Fuck you Shirl!" Renee responded. Then Rachelle asked her, "Nee did you get some girlfriend?"

"Chelle I don't kiss and tell, but he sucked the shit out of this pussy and fucked me real good" Renee smiled at her.

"Don't you still have the itch Nee?" Rachelle asked her

"If I do, he took it away," as she smiled even harder at her friends walking off going back up stairs. Shirley just eye balled her, and Rachelle looked at Shirley and smiled.

Renee went and lit her Frankincense letting the aroma spread throughout the room her and Shirley were sleeping in. Shirley and Rachelle took showers getting in their night gowns meeting back up in the living area suite. They were snacking on chips and drinking soda. They were having some good girly conversation. "Rachelle did you see Eric Sermon?" Shirley asked her batting her eyes.

"Yes girl, I saw Andre Rison., Michael Vick, Ludacris and Too Short. I sure would like to fuck him Shirl, without all that nasty rap he be talking about. I wonder if Too Short can really handle business in the bedroom." Rachelle said.

"I didn't know 112 is where all the celebrities go party at." Shirley said.

"Shirl we might have to come back down here real soon for about a week and just do us." "I know Chelle, this is the spot." Shirley was amp.

"Shirl it's getting late and I'm tired," as Rachelle yawned when she made that statement.

"What time is the hair show Chelle?" Shirley asked her.

"It starts at 1:00 p.m. but we don't go on stage until around like 3:00 p.m." said Rachelle.

"Oh, you better be trying to get some sleep then." as Shirley stood up and turned the T.V. off. They headed for upstairs. When they reached upstairs Rachelle told Shirley, "good night Shirl."

She looked at her friend and replied, "Good night Chelle." They both went into the doors of the rooms they were sleeping in. Shirley was sharing rooms with Renee. Shirley grabbed a few things she needed and didn't really stay in the room that long when she and Rachelle returned from the clubs. She took a shower in Rachelle's room. When Shirley entered the room this time she smelled an awful odor. She grabbed her mouth and left out the room in disgust. The Frankincense had made the room smell distasteful. She knocked on Rachelle's door. "Come in," as the door slowly opened. "Shirl what's wrong" Rachelle asked her.

"This bitch got the room smelling like ass, pussy and the Wilderness." Shirley was looking very confused.

"Well you can sleep in here if you lie or there's always the couch downstairs." She told Shirley

"What side of the bed do you like Chelle?"

"I'm on the right side, and here's a pillow," as she threw a pillow on the left side of the bed for Shirley. Shirley crawled in the bed with Shirley.

Shirley was looking up at the ceiling when she asked Rachelle, "Chelle how was it when you had Keith Jr.?"

"What do you mean Shirl?"

"I mean how did you feel? Having a child didn't make you fell different in any type of way?" Shirley asked her.

"It made me feel special bringing a life into the world. I guess it made me feel different. Why?" Rachelle asked her.

"Nothing I was just wondering, that's all. Well good night."

Shirley was emotionally distraught about not having her baby. Shirley closed her eyes. Rachelle knew that her friend was still troubled by the fact she had an abortion. Rachelle finally passed out her-

self...

....

The next day they went to the hair show where Rachelle was going to show off her new creations. The hair show was packed at the Convention Center in Atlanta Georgia. It was many booths set up selling all types of products from hair supplies, fancy bags, oils & perfumes, jewelry, cosmetics, t-shirts, magazines, books and other items.

Shirley, Renee and Rachelle walked in to see a lot of different events going on around them. Rachelle models for the hair show were already there.

There were a few celebrities in the crowd like, Too Short, Eight Ball & MJG, Andre 3000, Big Boi, Tyrone Hill, Dave Justice, Ike Reese, Trick Daddy and Trina.

Pastor Troy was performing when they entered the main section where the actual hair show was taking place. Rachelle left Shirley and Renee sitting out in the audience while she went to the back to set up. Monica, Summer, Rita Auni, Angie, Janice and Kissy followed her with their outfits and make-up kits. When they reached back stage getting checked in they walked passed Eric J party to see a marching band, half naked women and other props he was using for his show. Eric J was a male stylist, dark complexion, wearing a funny looking Mo-hawk hair cut with dye in it. He had on some high heel boots and some expensive eye wear. He was also real feminine. He nodded to Rachelle and her models, but Rachelle ignored him. They kept walking to see the Weave Master Shanice setting up. She had on a flashy short dress with the back out showing her flesh, and her curves were very presentable in place in the white dress. She had glitter on her face and portions of her body that showed her butter scotch complexion smooth skin tone. Her stiletto boots with a small heel trimmed in metallic gold off set everything on her body.

Rachelle and Shanice made eye contact and like females competing they rolled their eyes at each other showing no love at all. Rachelle kept it moving to her booth. She was nervous being this was her first major competition. She got it together as everyone changed into their perfect fitting outfits showing off their curves and a little flesh. Their make up was flawless and Rachelle was ready to show off her skills.

Rachelle put on a fitting skin tight all pink body suit, with some pink and white Stiletto heels. She didn't have any props like all the other stylist. Bronner Bros. was giving out $20,000 dollars to the winner. But Rachelle wasn't. even thinking about the money, she wanted the trophy and to beat Shanice out. She was still jealous of Shanice for a creation she did with a weave job that landed her on the Rikki Lake Show some years back.

She was known as the Weave Master throughout the Tri-State and the Mid West. Plus Shanice use to mess with Pedro. Rachelle shook the butterflies from her stomach and was ready to do her thang. Even though Rachelle knew that Shanice had something good up her sleeve for the show, she had some new creations of her own she was going to do out on stage. Shanice wasn't just some ugly duckling either, she was gorgeous and well put together. After Lil Jon and the Eastside Boyz performed the Hair Show started. Chucky and his friend Ken left their booth to attend the show and they joined Renee and Shirley in the crowd. It was three females in their view eyeing Chucky and Renee. They were giving hard stares and mean mugs. Chucky knew who they were. It was Aunika, Milan and Deona from Dayton, Ohio. His home girls who stripped at Majestic's Night-club in Dayton. Aunika was like 6'1, brown skin with brown eyes and a fat bottom with a slim waist line. Milan was around 5'7 with dimples when she smiled, long hair and kind of

chubby, but thick with it in all the right places. She sucked her thumb a lot. Deona was dark skin and thick with it standing at around 5'6. She had a cute smile also. Chucky was in disgust, because she was telling everyone in the Gem City that he had gotten her pregnant. Deona Everson was eye balling him thoroughly. She smiled at Chucky, but he ignored her. Solid was the gratitude and no formal introduction was needed. She rolled her eyes at him and "Fiesta" by R Kelly featuring Jay-Z came on as the first stylist came on stage from Dallas Texas. It was an older female who brought flavor in the beginning with a group of beautiful thick country girls modeling for her. Then she had a prop do-ing a hair style under water with one of her models. They finished up and then the Weave Master Shanice came out on stage parading to Nelly's "Country Grammar." She showed off a numerous of weave hair styles. She even showed off her new creation with a bouquet of arrangements that let real live Doves fly from it. She was hot and was gaining the crowd and the judges. When Shanice made her exit Jay-Z featuring UGK was playing "Big Pimpin," as she received a standing ovation from the crowd and the judges. She stared at Rachelle back stage and then rolled her eyes at her as to say top that. She was next. They came out to the tunes of E-40 "Captain Save Ah." Rachelle had her own mix CD that a local DJ in Cincinnati made for her. All her models stepped out stylish and beautiful getting the crowds attention. After a walk and strut through, they all sat in different chairs and Rachelle went to work on stage giving each model a different dazzling hair style. She was actually doing hair and not using any props like the first two styles before her. When she finished the last model Toni Braxton's "Breathe Again " was playing. Rachelle blew a nice kiss over her styling scissors and put them in her holster

belt letting the crowd know she was hot with it. She place her hands on her hips and then showed the crowd all her designs by walking down the line of models. The models stood up and then strutted around the stage showing off their new styles and cut that their stylist performed. Rachelle got a well deserved applause. Even Shanice was clapping for her when she exit's the stage coming to the back where the other stylist and models were waiting on the results of the competition. Rachelle gave her a wink and said "**Thank you.**" To where Shanice had to read her lips.

Eric J. was next and he had a live Marching Band from one of the local Black Colleges in the area. They were playing Petey Pablo's song and then started to do his models hair. He was the crowd's favorite being he was in his home town. Then some of his models exposed their breast giving the audience a strip show. Eric J. finished and got a standing ovation and the crowd was going crazy. But he soon found out that he would be disqualified for letting his team of women expose themselves showing their breast and vagina's on stage.

Even though Rachelle was the only stylist who actually showed her work on stage without any props, they gave a trophy to The Weave Master Shanice. Rachelle didn't hate and gave her praises. Shanice told Rachelle next year to get her some props to entertain the crowd and she would definitely take home the trophy with no problem. They all had a good time at the Hair Show.

It was 7:00 p.m. when Shirley, Renee, Chucky and Ken were waiting on Rachelle and the models to come form the back. Aunika, Milan and Deona walked pass them. Deona stopped and said to Chucky, "I see you got your cape out of the cleaner's. Remember you

have a baby in the oven nigga," as she pointed to her belly. "I'll see you back in the city, don't get caught up into that," as she then pointed to Renee and rolled her eyes. She then walked off with her girls and they were all laughing. "What's that all about Chucky?" Renee asked him. He looked at her with curious eyes. Then responded. "I don't know, but I will get to the bottom of it when I get back home. I mean ole girl has been trying to get with me for the longest and I haven't stepped over those boundaries yet. The other two Aunika and Milan are my home girls. So I guess she trying to be funny, because I'm with you." Renee didn't even questions the situation anymore, because she knew he was probably lying and sleeping with the female. She was just satisfied that she got a piece of action from him. Rachelle, Auni, Kissy, Monica , Angie, Rita, Janice and Summer came form the back to meet Shirley and Renee. They hugged their girl and the other females who participated in the competition giving them their praise and gratitude for a job well done even though they lost.

Later on that night they hit all the clubs they could in the night's grace of time. They went to Nikki's strip club on Beytal Ave. The Atrium nightclub on Memorial Dr., Gental strip on Metropolitan Ave., The Bounce on Bank Head, they even went back on the Westside of town to Club 112, Club 559 and the Foxy Lady strip club. Rachelle ran back into Boobie and got her an early morning session with him. Renee ended up sleeping with Chucky again and Shirley was just enjoying her early Sunday morning sleep in the living area all alone.

When the guest Renee and Rachelle departed the three got dressed and attended a church service on Old Norcross Rd. After the church service they went and checked out their

suite and then went to a restaurant nearby to eat a country style mean before hitting the highway going back to Cincinnati. While they were eating in restaurant Shirley received a call from Sam and he told her they were going to the Virgin Islands instead of the Bahamas. She didn't care where they were going, she just wanted to spend some time with him alone. They managed to gas up the vehicle successfully and merge onto the I-85 highway heading north out of Atlanta. It was around three that afternoon when they got on the highway going home. When they reached Nashville to get gas and use the restroom Renee did away with her toy, batteries and all. She even got rid of her lubrication cream. She has over come her fear and was destine to compete and mate again when given the opportunity. They reached the Cincinnati city limits at around 11:30 that night. They dropped Renee off first and they went to Rachelle's house. Shirley sat and talked to Rachelle for an hour or two before going home.

CHAPETER SEVEN
Bad Habits

That Monday morning things were back to normal. Shirley went to work and during her lunch break she took Sam in his car. When an employee of Sam's drove her car out of the shop, she was in disbelief . Her car had a make over. Sam added twenty inch chrome rims on her Lexus, a light tint on the windows and put a small kit on it. Her eyes lit up and she was stuck. Sam walked up behind her to greet her. " Hey baby, you don't like your car?" He asked her. She turned around and out of nowhere she kissed him passionately. When she released from his lips she caught her breath and said, "Sam I love it, but I can't afford

this," as she pointed to her car. "Don't worry baby, its on me, anything for the future Mrs. Holston." Then her inner thoughts took control of her and she thought to herself. *"I haven't even given him any sex, and he's doing this for me. Either I'm dreaming , or he's a natural sucker, or he's just a good ass Negro. He's already talking about me being his wife in the future. Whatever the case may be I'm all for it. Damn Shirl kiss the man, do something don't just stand there goofy."*
She gathered herself quickly and gave Sam another passionate kiss and told him, "Thank you Sam you are wonderful."
"Anything for you baby, and how was your trip?' he asked her.
"It was okay, but I was thinking about you the whole time I was there." She said letting her head down. He lifted her head back up by her chin.
"Did you meet any celebrities while you were down there?" Sam asked her. She looked him the eyes and said, "I didn't meet anyone, but I did see a few." He hugged her and said, "That's alright, are you still going to the Virgin Island with me?"
"Why of course baby, I'll go anywhere with you." She replied.
"Well it's the weekend of June the 23rd and we will be back that Monday on the 1st of July." Sam told her.
"Okay." She smiled at him.
"So what are you doing tonight Shirl?" he asked her
"Nothing, why?" she answered with a question.
"I want to spend the evening with you, take you out to dinner" He gave her a look.

"We can do that Sam, what time?"

"At around 8:00 this evening." He looked down at her.

"Okay, I'll be waiting and don't stand me up," as she smiled at him again adding a kiss. They separated and Sam helped her in the car. He shut the door and watched her pull off out of the shop. She was feeling good about herself. Thomas had been trying to get her to return his calls, but she didn't. She kicked back at her office for the remainder of the day.

…………………………………...

During her time in Atlanta Thomas had got in trouble at his home from messing with Alexis. His wife found out and kicked him out of the house. He had resorted to sleeping in his and car. He even started getting high, because Alexis was an undercover addict and she turned Thomas out.

Later on that night Shirley and Sam ate dinner at Dock Side 7 in Norwood. It was a restaurant in a predominately all white neighborhood that sat in the middle of Cincinnati with three or more neighborhoods surrounding it.

The restaurant was very elegant and nice. You could get anywhere from Seafood to a nice steak dinner. They were sitting at the table getting ready to order and Sam told her with a serious face while she was looking over the menu.

"Shirley, you have your friendship side of the menu and you have your fuck side of the menu." Shirley moved the menu from in front of her face and said, "Excuse me Sam." She had an attitude and was confused like her ears were deceiving her.

"I said, you have a friendship side and a fuck side of the menu, so be careful when you place your order." He smiled at her.

"And what the heck does that mean Sam?" She asked him putting the menu down.

"It means if you order from the friendship side it's platonic, meaning things on that side come up to fifteen dollars or less a plate. Then you have the other side which is the fuck side of the menu meaning if you order from this side which the plates cost twenty dollars or better you plan on giving up a little booty later on tonight," as he was showing her the menu.

She folded her arms and sat back. "Sam you must have me confused with one of those little hussies you are use to dealing with , because I can pay for my own meal." She made a noise with her lips.

"Shirley, I was just playing baby, calm down it was a joke. I will pay for your meal no matter what, I asked you out," as he reached over and grabbed her hand. She lost the attitude and they got back to enjoying their evening together. After dinner Sam stayed at her place that night. She wanted to give him some sex, but she was still bleeding a little. They just cuddled.

……………………………...

ON THE OTHER SIDE OF TOWN THAT NIGHT, Thomas had dropped by Renee's apartment on Ryland Ave. He was cooler with Renee then he were with Rachelle. He knew that Rachelle didn't like him to much. He poured out his feelings to Renee concerning Shirley and him getting kicked out of his house by his wife. Renee comfort him and ended up sleeping with Thomas crossing that fatal boundary of messing with a guy that her friend had been involved with. She didn't care it was an opportunity for her to get her some more action from a man. Plus she figured Shirley wasn't messing with him anymore, being she was involved with Sam now.

The next night Thomas found himself back over Renee's apartment. This time he came with his new habit. Thomas was now smoking crack trying to rid his problems. He had started to rent out his car to some drug dealers in Walnut Hills.

What Thomas didn't know that Renee had a habit also. Renee was sitting in her living room on the couch and Thomas was on the sofa chair. He placed a hundred dollar piece of crack on her coffee table. Renee looked at the funny looking object and then at Thomas.

"Renee, you don't mind if I get high, my nerves are bad?" He asked her.

"No I don't mind, as long as you are sharing," she said as her own palms began to sweat.

Her eyes lit up and the urge hit her. The funny smell that Rachelle and Shirley witness that night at her apartment when Shirley did her pregnancy test was the smell of crack cocaine being smoked in her marijuana. The razor Shirley found on Renee's coffee table didn't have chunks of aspirin on it, it was crack cocaine. Renee started using a harder drug, dealing with some females outside of her girls relationship.

"You smoke this shit Renee?" Thomas asked her.

"I put a little in my weed from time to time, smoking me a lace joint." She told him still eyeballing the piece of crack he laid out.

"Oh." he said adding, "Well do you have a razor so I can cut it up?"

She glance away from the crack momentarily and replied. "Yes right up under that ashtray in front of you."

Thomas reached up under the ashtray and grabbed the razor. He started cutting up the drug into pieces.

After he cut it up he pulled out a glass pipe and lighter. He played with the glass object for a second and then placed a piece of the substance on top of one end of the pipe.

He put his mouth on the other end and lit the end which contained the substance on it.

It sizzled and dissolved making the glass pipe foggy. Thomas inhaled the smoke and he held it in for a few seconds before exhaling it.

He coughed a few times and said, "Renee do you want to try this?"

She looked at him and was confused to see him actually doing drugs.

"No thanks Thomas I'm straight, you can just give me a little to lace my joint." She told him, but he still tried to convince her the way that Alexis did him.

"C'mon babe, just try it you'll like it." He was extending the pipe in her direction.

She folded her arms and took in a deep breath. Then she let out a sigh. "I guess it won't hurt to try huh," as she grabbed the object from him. Thomas went over to her to assist her.

He placed a piece of crack on the end he would light and he lit it. She inhaled it and then exhaled the smoke with a constant cough. She was hitting her chest trying to catch her breath. She was hooked just like that. She began to sweat from her forehead and got instant diarrhea.

She had to go shower after using it on herself and they ended up in her bedroom smoking the rest of the drugs and freaking at the same time. After they finished smoking the crack up, they were now sitting around with no money geeking like true dope fiends.

Renee looked at Thomas with a strange and deranged look of confusion. Her thirst for the drug was becoming enormous running through her system.

She didn't know why her system, now craved for the drug, but she had to have it.

She asked Thomas, "You can't buy anymore?" He looked up at her still trying to light the pipe that had no more crack on it. "Not until the morning when the banks open up." He was still trying to flick the lighter.

"You think I could sell a piece of my jewelry, like a ring or something for some more?" She asked him. His eyes lit up. "Hell yeah! I know a spot in Walnut Hills where some young guys will trade you some drugs for jewelry."

Renee didn't hesitate. "Okay let's go!" She grabbed a diamond and gold ring out of her jewelry box and they hopped in Renee's Maxima and headed down Paddock Rd. to merge onto Reading Rd. They took Reading Road. through Avondale all the way to Blair St. and went across the Blair St. bridge making a right onto Mather St. in the Setty Kuhn Projects. It was a housing complex that took up two streets that were very small. They were like town houses connected together with some four unit apartments.

Thomas got out the car when he saw a group of guys standing in an entrance way. He walked up to the group and asked them. "Excuse me, have ya'll seen Dante or Vino?" One of the guys stepped up and said, "They just left, why, are you looking for something?" The little short guy asked Thomas.

"Yeah a nice fifty piece." Thomas said.

The little stocky guy spit out pieces of crack into the palm of his hand from his mouth. "Pick any two for fifty." He told Thomas.

Thomas saw how big the pieces were and got excited. "Umm-umm I don't really have fifty cash, but my girl has a nice diamond ring she's willing to exchange for that." Thomas was still eyeballing the crack in the guys hand. The guy closed his hand and looked around. "Oh yeah, were she at?" The guy asked Thomas.

Thomas replied. "Hold up, let me go and get her."

Thomas left the entrance way to the curve and waved Renee to get out the car and to come where he was at. Renee got out and Thomas walked her back through the entrance way.

"Hey lil man, here she go." Thomas and Renee stood there.

The guy couldn't believe his eyes when he saw Renee. He couldn't believe this female was using drugs. Her t-shirt draped over her braless bosoms and her daisy dukes were screaming for attention. Renee looked damn good, well built with firm breast and long dark hair. Thomas told her to show the guy the ring. She showed him the ½ karat ring, but he was eyeing her instead of the ring the whole time. He was shopping for something else and that was, Renee. He pulled Thomas to the side and whispered in Thomas ear.

"Yo man fuck that ring, what's up with her is she willing to do a little something else for all this in my hand?" The guy flashed all the crack to Thomas again and Thomas got more excited. He put his finger up to the guy and said, "Hold up."

Thomas walked back over to Renee and grabbed her to talk to her. He looked at her square in the eyes. "Look Renee, he doesn't want the ring, he wants you. He want to have sex with you for the dope."

Renee put her hands on her hips with an attitude. She didn't like this idea at all.

"Excuse me, hell no. I'm not that gone off that shit Thomas you got me fucked up." She drifted to the side.

"C'mon Renee he's a young guy, he will cum quick and we out." Thomas told her.

"No Thomas, and if you cared about me you wouldn't be trying to convince me to do it." Renee put her hands back on her hips after waving her hand telling him how she felt.

He dropped his head momentarily and said, "Renee I'm trying to get high and I know you want to smoke some more. So c'mon we have five hours before I can withdraw money out of my account."

She grabbed herself together and thought about it for a long moment.

"Okay Thomas, I'll do it just this once, no more. Go ask him do he want an oral job or regular sex?" She asked him.

Thomas stepped away from her to find out what exact he wanted. He wanted both and she agreed. They went behind one of the complex behind a big bush to hide them.

Thomas was the look out for them. Renee was standing there with the guy and the both of them were nervous. "I hope you have a condom." She told him..

"Yeah, I got one." he told her.

Renee rubbed her sweaty palms on her blue jean shorts. "Well unzip your pants, and give me the dope," as she had her hand out to receive the drugs.

Thomas had told her to get her pay first. The guy dropped two pieces in her hand. Renee knew it was suppose to be four pieces of crack. "Hold up, where are the other two pieces at?" She questioned him.

"I'll give them to you when we are finished."

She then let him pull his private part out through the slit of his boxers.

She bent over to reach it. She took in a deep breath and let out a huge sigh. She placed it in her mouth going up and down a few times until he got rock hard which was in not time. She pulled it from out of her mouth backing up a little.

"Where is the condom at?" She asked him.

He gave her the condom he had already in his hand. She grabbed the Life Style condom and placed it on the guy's private part. She then pulled her shorts and panties down on him. She turned around and bent over so he could enter her from the rear. She helped guide him inside her passage making sure the condom was still on him. She was wet when he entered her and he grabbed her by her love handles, as he pumped himself inside her. Renee didn't moan or let him know she was enjoying herself.

"C'mon man, I know you've cum by now."

Renee commented while she was jerkin her body from his movement.

"No'op not yet, but I'm about to cum, Oh- oh there it is I'm cumming," as he shoved himself further inside her making grunts. She pulled away from him. She turned around to see if the condom had broken and it didn't. She quickly pulled up her panties and shorts. He was still standing there with his pants down when Renee opened her hand to receive the rest of the crack. He was sweating and breathing hard.

"Miss lady you are too beautiful to be smoking shit" As h gave her the other two pieces.

"Thank you" Renee was very polite. She actually enjoyed turning her first trick for the drug.

He replied. You deserved it. And if you need a connect for some more here's my cell number. "He reached in his pants pocket to give her a bootleg business card. "So your name is Yikes?" She looked at him.

"Yeah that's me Setty Kuhn's finest" He smiled at her showing off one of his gold's.

"Well if I need anymore, I'll call you" Renee gave him a smile filled with confidence. Thomas and Renee left from Walnut hills back out to Bond hill to Renee's apartment to get high.

……………………………………...

…

That Wednesday after Shirley got off work she found herself in Evanston at Sam's house. She had just stopped bleeding the day before. She knew she was going to spend the night with him, so she brought her feminine hygiene with her along with her over night bag and work clothes for the next day. She took a shower and gave herself a douche before lying down with Sam. She also started her birth control. The muscles in her stomach and hips ached as she pressed her knuckles into them while walking to-wards the king size bed in Sam's bedroom that he was already lying on. Her pretty feet entangled in the wool carpet, as she gained momentum towards him in her silk maroon night gown. She didn't have on any panties. She wanted his touch, but she wanted to protect her feelings also. She wanted to wait another month or two before giving her body, and then all of a sudden she got cold, then hot and even hotter. For an uncomfort-able moment they studied each other. This felt new and awkward, but it felt good. Sam offered his own smile and Shirley gave hers, as she eased onto the bed. Her heart pounding in her eardrum, she went on ahead so boldly with no second thought and re-moved her night gown letting him see her nakedness. He knew what she wanted and that their maturity was a given. Moments later Sam was putting on a condom after all the initial foreplay that just occurred between them. She gasped for air as he did also after they slammed over a period of time. It wasn't

Like the fireworks and Sharan had gave her in the bed, but it did release a little frustration and tension she was having. Shirley had given Sam some sex this night. She was having mixed emotions after sleeping with him. She faked one of her orgasms and he thought he had put her to sleep and he left out for a little while. He did this three nights in a row now. Shirley played sleep. When he returned and went to sleep, she still cared for Thomas and she had feelings circling for Sharan, even though she was now laying up and being involved with Sam. Her emotional wave was ramming through her body and it echoed making her insides hollow. She was indeed an emotional wreck.

CHAPTER EIGHT
Feelings

The phone rang several times before Rachelle picked up. "Hello", as Rachelle was woke up out of her sleep. "Hello Chelle it's me Shirl." The phone was quiet. "Shirl do you know what time it is?" She asked her.

"Yeah it's almost 4:30." Shirley sucked her teeth. She was still kind of snuffling. "Yeah exactly 4:30 in the morning" Rachelle replied.

"Chelle I need to talk to you," as she could now hear her friend crying.

"About what Shirl, and are you crying?" Shirley started crying again even more.

"Chelle, I'm confused. I don't know what to do. I still have feelings for Thomas, but I have an emotional side for Sharan and I'm building a side for Sam and I'm sleeping with him. How can I give Sam my all when I have feelings for others?" She was trying to calm down.

"Honestly Shirl, I don't know, but you need to figure it out and stop crying, it's going to be alright."

"Me and Sam are going to the virgin Islands next week, but I think he's seeing someone else Chelle"

"Why do you think that Shirl?"

"Because he left out in the middle of the night three nights in a row. We done spent the night together Monday, Tuesday and Wednesday and all three nights he's left making runs at all hours of the night thinking I'm sleep."

"Shirl does he come back?"

"Yeah he comes back "Shirley answered her.

"No, he doesn't. When I do drift off and wake up he be right by my side. I gave him some tonight for the first time. He left out and came back, and now he's in there snoring. He can't really do it either Chelle. He's not like Thomas and surely isn't like Sharan. The Negro used a Magnum like he could fit it. Please he knew he needed a damn Life Style. But I do like him Chelle." Rachelle laughed and it made Shirley laugh a little. "Shirl you are crazy, talking about the like that. The biggest thing is for you to be happy with less confusion in your heart."

"Hopefully I'll have it together when I get back from the Virgin Islands and this Negro ain't got a hidden agenda." Shirley confessed to her friend.

"Well you think about who will make you happy and complete Shirl. That's all that matters. Think about it while you are down there relaxing on one of those beaches girl-friend."

"I will Chelle, hey Chelle, I love you and thanks for being my best friend"

"Bye Shirl you old sentimental bitch you, I love you too."

They hung up and Shirley cried herself to sleep on Sam's couch.

....
...

The Virgin Islands was of Puerto Rico located in the Caribbean Sea. Saint Thomas, Saint Croix, Saint John and about 50 Inlets belong to the United States. The annual rainfall average is 1,016 and the average annual temperature is 78 degrees, because of the scarce of freshwater. St. Thomas is commercial center of everything that goes on in the Virgin Islands. St. Thomas has beautiful resorts along the Islands with several of beaches.

It is the perfect vacation resort for lovers.

That following week Sam and Shirley were in a yellow cab going to the Greater Cincin-nati airport. Renee had been missing in action since their trip to Atlanta. Sam and Shirley boarded a Southwest Plane heading for Miami. When they arrived in the Virgin Islands it was beautiful and the people there greeted them with a cow-tow showing an obsequious deference. The people were very respectful and gracious. They made their way to the Hotel they were staying in on the beach of St. Thomas. The resort was beau-tiful and ran down the beach for miles. That night they ate at the resorts restaurants and walked along the beach managing to make love on the beach under the moonlight. It was very romantic. The made in the back to their room and past out in each others arms. The next morning when Shirley awoke she was alone in their hotel bed. There was a note on the stand by the bed next to the phone. It read: '**Shirl I have a little business to Attend to in St. John, I'll be back in a couple of hours. I ordered you breakfast in bed, it should arrive at 9. Love you and I'll see you in a little while."**

She balled the note up in her hand and was wondering what h had to do in St. John where she couldn't go. She started to get upset and then there was a knock on the door. She looked over at the clock and it was exactly 9. She gathered herself and slipped on a t-shirt to cover her breast and her panties. When she answered the door she was greeted by a foreigner speaking a little Spanish.

"Good-Morning Senorita, your Pappi sent you breakfast Senor Sam." The guy looked over Shirley and she looked back at him.

"Where would you like this Miss Thomas?" as his accent took over Shirley's attention hearing her name roll from his tongue turned her on. She was in a daze for along moment. "Senorita" as he called out. "Where do you want your food?"

Shirley snapped out of her daydream. "Oh I'm sorry, over there please," as she pointed to the table by the sofa in the living area. The guy pushes the cart into the room and places the tray on the table. It was under a silver cloche and it was accompanied by an arrangement of flowers. He turned around to exit out the room and caught a portion of Shirley's figure and her panties hugging her cheeks a little, because her t-shirt had risen a little. He smiled at her after looking at her and she caught his eyes roaming and pulled her t-shirt down. "Thank you Senor" Shirley told him. The guy nodded his head leaving the room. She knew he saw her booty and she felt a little mannish. She closed the door and went to see her breakfast. She lifted the lid off the food and it was delightful sight. It was a continental breakfast. She covered it back up and went to brush her teeth and washed

her face. She came back into the living room and ate her food reading a pamphlet that was in Spanish. Shirley could speak Spanish and German. '**Como vivir con La Hepatitis C Cronica.**' That's what the front read of the pamphlet. She kept reading it. **"Casi 4 millones De Estadounidenses Estan Infectados Con el Virus de la Hepatitis C.'** She took a bite of her waffle and said, "Damn Hepatitis C is going on crazy down here too." She kept reading the pamphlet until her breakfast was completely gone. She then went and laid down for a little while giving her food time to digest. Afterwards she got up and took a long private bowl movement to release the waste from her insides. Then she took a long hot shower. She moisturized her skin and put on her thong underwear and bra set. She then put on a dark colored purple sun dress and her Gucci sandals. She placed her Rolex on and other little jewelry. She placed her Gucci shades above her head and was back in the living area fingering though another magazine. Hours had now gone by and Sam didn't show. She was getting impatient and bored so she finally decided to leave the room. She went window shopping for souvenirs and other small vacation items she could bring back with her. She found herself gazing up and down the streets of St. Thomas until night has snuck up on her. Shirley was walking along the beach outside the hotel thinking where could he be? She finally pulled up by the bar that sat outside by the pool and nearby Sauna that was outdoors. It was like yards away from the bar. She glanced over the Sauna because there was a group of people in it having fun. They were laughing and drinking. The women were half naked showing their breast. There were four women and three guys. She so happened to take a double look and she spotted Sam amongst the party. There was a female in Sam's lap with a cigar in In her mouth and holding a drink. She was very dark in complexion with a nice figure and her hair was done up nicely. Shirley thought to herself, **"Who do this Negro think he is Tony Montana or somebody, and that bitch he's with look like Chiquita the bitch from the movie 'Belly'. I don't have to take this shit. He got me messed up he's been gone all fucking day and now he's all up under some bitch."** She stood up and started pacing back and forth at the bar debating if she should confront him now or back at the room. She counted to ten to calm down. She decided to do it in their room leaving him with no lead way to get out of what she just witnessed. She didn't want to go there with the females knowing her girl wasn't there to have her back. She was smart playing her cards. She sat back at the bar and ordered her a few drinks. She had two Sex On the Beach with Martel and two 190 Octane her favorite drink. She was feeling good as the hour went by. Then some guy pulled up with an accent. She didn't pay him no mind until he spoke to her. She was still eyeing Sam and the others in the sauna. "Hello, a beautiful lady, why such a long face?" He asked her. She looked around asked him pointing at herself. "Yes you, there is no other beauty staring me in the face, but you" "Nothing's wrong with me, I'm just enjoying the night air." She had a buzz and now all of a sudden had revenge on hr mind. "Well do you want any company Miss lady?" He asked her. Shirley couldn't get the anger from her mind. "Hell I don't care, it's a big bar, room for everybody" He sat closer to her admiring her drunken beauty. "So what's on your mind and what's troubling you?" He was now in her face. She grabbed his hand and asked him, "Do you think I'm a beautiful woman to have a real man in my life, Mr. I don't know your name?" He gave her a slight squeeze at her own hand and replied, "Let me give it to You like this Miss lady, as long as you feel beautiful within yourself and have self- confidence you will be fine no matter what." He nodded his head. "By the way my name is Tajih," as he extended his hand to Shirley. She shook his hand introducing herself.

"May name is Shirley and I'm from Cincinnati, Ohio in the States." He released her soft hand and smiled. They sat their and ordered another round and chatted for an hour. She saw Sam leave with the company who was with him and the female who looked like Chiquita was on his arm. Shirley knew he was probably going somewhere to have sex with her. She was in position to be naughty herself with this Islander guy. All her morals went out of control. "So where do you live Tajih, around here?" Shirley asked him.

"I live in Florida, I'm just visiting. I have a room in this hotel."

"Are you serious, because I have a room with my male friend in this hotel also? We are on the third floor in room 322." She told him.

"My room is two doors down from yours, I'm in room 326, Shirley girl." He told her and she rubbed her thighs together getting the urge to go to his room. She was feeling herself. Angry and distraught was Shirley after seeing Sam leave with the party going towards a hotel on the other side of the sauna.

Shirley made her move. Her heart pounded in her chest as she pulled Tajih into her arms.

He was already hand with needs of his own. She did that to him, and she didn't even realizing it. The way she angled her chin, her laugh when she bit her lip touching his strong arms during their conversation. He was now just in much of a crazy lust as she was making sure if Sam was getting him some on the Island from a stranger she would do the same.

Eager to kiss her Tajih eased up her chin. Her sober expression stopped him, because he knew she was tipsy. She caught his stare in mid-air and knew what he really wanted to do. "Having seconds thoughts Tajih?" She asked him. "No." he said to her relief.

"It's just I don't want to take advantage of you Shirley." He added. She looked at him with her beautiful brown eyes.

"You're not, I want you too." She kissed him instead initiating the contact.

He smelled clean and fresh as her lips were pressed against his and it was a mint taste. She wasn't shy with her kiss giving him her tongue that had alcohol on it. A tremor shook through her body. She wanted him. Her eyes were closed and her lips were soft and full. An odd tender feeling filled her chest surprising given the force of her desire. Awed at the depth of emotion churning within, he cupped her turned face and reverent-ly kisses each eyes lid. Her eyes opened part way. They were lustful with hot desire.

"I want you to Tajih," she murmured in a throaty seductive voice. "We should go up-stairs to your hotel room Tajih." She explained to him.

……………………………………...

Next thing Shirley knew she was in Tajih's bed in his hotel. Shirley took off her jewelry and shades. She then removed her sandals and sun dress. Her thong and bra where still on as Tajih looked at her. Then she removed her bra exposing her incredible mounds of love. She put Tajih hand down in her thong. She was wet and, warm, and she started kissing him on the mouth. Then she tells him some off the wall stuff she would care for in a million years. It must have been the alcohol talking in her place. Her mind was in a daze, a constellation of thoughts that she wanted to express.

"I've never been fucked in my ass before and I want for you to be the first. Then I want you to put it in my pussy after that. That's my fantasy Tajih and I want to fulfill it with you tonight a total stranger." She glared at him long and hard while she eased out of her thong underwear. Tajih agreed to her wishes as he also got undress and took her to the bed. He had a form of lubrication at hand being some petroleum jelly Vaseline. He bent her over on the bed and greased up her anal area. Then he grabbed him a condom and placed it on his hard tribal piece. He had got rock hard from looking at her and touching her body. He then dug a finger inside her butt hole trying to widen it out a little know-ing that his manhood wouldn't fit off the rip. She felt very uncomfortable and uneasy.

"Hold up Tajih, I don't think I'm ready for this." She begged, but he kept playing around in that area now fitting two fingers inside her butt hole. It was painful as she bit down on her lip trying to block out the pain. He then eased the head of his tribal piece inside her.

"Oh my God Tajih, slow, go slow that hurts like hell, take it out please, please take it out." She begged him and once again he ignored her wishes. She was screaming to the top of her lungs as he pushed the majority of his tribal piece inside her anal.

It burned with pleasure giving her a sensitive sensation.

She grabbed the sheets and put a mouth full of covers in her mouth. He was ramming her hard at a steady pace and then he pulled out. She smiled loving this feeling now. He then placed his hard on inside her wet passage. She had, had an orgasm from him being inside her anal. They wiggled, whammed and grinded into each other for about an hour before she had a powerful orgasm, because Tajih had hit her spot from the doggy style position. Tajih had cum also and the condom caught all of his love babies.

After her breathing had calmed down she hurried up and got dress exiting Tajih's room unnoticed.

She entered their hotel room throwing her bag on the sofa and placing her shades on the table. Sam was sleep when she came into the bedroom.

She stripped down to her bare skin and jumped in the shower. She washed her pussy anal area repeatedly and was crying in the shower. She stared talking to herself.

'Damn Shirl what is wrong with you? Quit feeling sorry for yourself. You're miles away from home with a pretender or am I jumping the gun, because I just fucked a total stranger? Fuck how in the hell that Negro gone leave you unattended for hours and didn't bother to check on you. Fuck him you did what was somewhat right. So woman up and live with your decisions in life Shirl. Damn my asshole is hurting like hell," as she sniffled and laughed a little with her tears realizing she just done some courageous shit back in room 326 with Tajih Mohardy.

More tears raced down her dark complexion face. She put on a spaghetti strap night-gown and her comfortable panties. She then went and stood out on the balcony of the hotel room and stared out into the night air. The sea was calm and the air was nice and breezy. Her eyes lifted and she realized that her life was in a shambles. She wanted more and the fact she thought that Sam was now cheating on her and they just begun to have something special, she was in a world of confusion. She just wanted to get back home and figure out her next move leaving lust alone and seeking out her own happiness. She was a career woman with no kids and was ready to settle down to have a life of her own.

She let out a sigh and headed into the bedroom where Sam was asleep. She eased in the bed still sniffling, she was looking at the back of his head and then turned around and when she did Sam awoke. He turned to face her.

"Hey babe, I was wondering where you were. I'm sorry about today I got caught in a whirlwind of business with my main man Ox." Sam was touching her shoulder, as she turned around to face him. Her face was filled with hurt.

"Oh I was on the beach having a drink at the outside bar catching the Ocean breeze." Her eyes were glossy and stained with red. "Shirl, have you been crying, what's wrong?"

He asked her and her conscious was talking to her.

"Ask him Shirley. Ask him who were those people he was in the sauna with."

She didn't have the heart to ask just yet not wanting to confused anything , because she did just do an act out of revenge.

"I was worried about you Sam. You've been gone for more then two hours and I spent the whole day by myself. We suppose to be spending time together and not apart. So yes I'm a little upset and yes I've been crying worrying about you," as a single tear dropped from her eye.

He wiped her tear away with the heel of his palm. He kissed her and said, "I'm sorry I didn't mean to have you worrying about me and I got caught up. But tomorrow I'll make it up to you. We are going Kingston Jamaica. I want you to meet some people I know who had me isolated all day. Okay?"

She nodded her head and Sam held her letting her head rest on his chest.

She went to sleep not saying another word.
…………………………………..

The next morning they took a shower together and got dressed. Shirley had on a see-thru

Sarong light blue and had on some white thong underwear.

Sam was dressed in some Roc-A-Wear black shorts and a matching shirt. She had on some Chanel sandals and he had on some Kenneth Cole sandals.

They went to breakfast down in the hotel restaurant. After breakfast they took a cab to St. Thomas. Sam escorted Shirley on a huge Super Yacht a Sun Seeker. There were three females on board with bikini's and heels. They all looked beautiful with no make-up. The sun was bright and it made the ladies skin tone look marvelous. Shirley notices that one of the females was the one that was all on Sam last night in the sauna. The one who looked like Chiquita from 'Belly'.

Shirley was observing them to a science as she got the Yacht. They got closer to the women an older looking man surfaced from the lower level of the Yacht. He was tall and slim. He looked like Shabba Ranks with long dreads. He had on a lot of jewelry, some tight khaki shorts, and no shirt and leather sandals. Sam reached the three women first and introduced Shirley to them. "Good morning ladies, I would like for you to meet my girl. Tiysha, Compass and Quida this is Shirley." Sam pointed to each woman call-ing their names. Compass was the one who looked like Chiquita.

"Hello," as Shirley frowned with a smirk. She wanted some static, but knew she was on enemy grounds. She gave Compass a hard stare.

"Hello madam," as Tiysha extended her hand to Shirley and spoke with an Island accent.

She greeted her. "Hello," as Quida greeted her giving her an eyebrow.

"Hi there Shirley girl, Samuel has told us all about you yesterday, so you're the love of his life?" Compass asked her. Shirley looked at her like, **"Bitch please you was just all over my man with your jugs in his face last night."**

Shirley responded. "Yes I am her. So Sam has been talking very highly of me?" Shirley asked Compass.

"Yes last night we had a blast in the sauna by the hotel with my husband." Compass told her.

Shirley eyes got wide and with no control she blurted out. "Your husband?"

Shirley was in shock, because she now knew what she'd done last night with Tajih Mo-Hardy was out of order and out content.

"Yes my husband Ox standing over there with the chauffer of the Yacht." Compass explain.

Shirley eyes looked over at the older slim man knowing that he was at least in his forties.

Now she was puzzled, because Compass looked like she wasn't even twenty-one years old. "So who are the other two women your relatives or his daughters?" Shirley asked her.

Sam, Tiysha and Quida were now having a conversation of their own.

"They are his wives also, but I'm the head." Compass gave her a smile.

"Oh I see," as Shirley tried to sum it up in her head.

Ox was making his way over to the small crowd to greet Shirley.

"Hello, and Samuel this must be your diamond in the rough you've spoken so highly of?"

as he smiled at Shirley.

"Yes Ox, this is my girl Shirley from the States." Sam told him and Ox turned to Shirley and grabbed her by the hand.

"How do you do Miss Lady and welcome to the Caribbean," as he kissed the back of her hand. He continued. "So my lady, I hear you are a lawyer?" His question rolled off of his tongue with much accent.

"Yes I am." Shirley replied while feeling guilty about last night.

"So are you mainly a criminal or civil case lawyer?" Ox asked her.

"I can be both, whatever someone hires me for, I can handle the job. I'm allowed to practice all over the United States." She told him.

"Good, because I might need to hire you the way Samuel is ripping me off with the cars he detail for me." Ox gave her a smile.

Shirley smiled back at him and Sam was now on her side with his arm around her waist. "C'mon Ox my work is qualified and I'm certified." Sam told him.

"Well Ms. Shirley you are food Sam knows where ya'll sleeping quarters are and Compass will show you around. I need to borrow Sammy boy for a moment, and I promise I want keep him away from you like I did yesterday," as Ox and Sam went around to the other side of the Yacht.

"C'mon Ms. Shirley let me show you the rest of the Yacht," as Compass took her below the Yacht. There was some dance hall music playing. There were sofa couches position in a pit shape, a bar, a pool table and screen T.V. The interior wash brass and gold trimmed. Compass poured Shirley a drink of Bacardi 8 bottle, it was dated 1898. Shirley sipped the rich liquor and got a burn in her throat, but it tasted good. She caught her breath and asked Compass, "So Compass what do you do?"

Compass looked her in the eyes and said, "Miss Shirley I don't mean to be rude, but I fuck Ox and he likes to watch, Tiysha, Quida and I have sex. My life is some what made in the shade. We live together in a mansion in Kingston."

"That's very interesting Compass. Life with no worries and no career." Shirley commented the last part under her breath.

"Let me share with yah Shirley girl. See Ox saved me from my abusive step-dad when I was fourteen. He killed him and moved me in-." Shirley cut in. "What about your mom and other relatives Compass?" Shirley asked her.

"My mom had a massive heart-attack after my step-dad was killed. My dad fled from Jamaica when I was an infant. Plus my step-dad was molesting me as well as my uncles being I had blossom at a very young age looking way older then I was." Compass explained to Shirley.

Shirley saw the hurt on her face. "Compass you had a rough journey and I feel your pain."

Shirley tried to console her.

"It made me a stronger person Ms. Shirley. Ox took me in and made me finish school. He never touched me in a sexual way until I was eighteen and I urged that on trying to give him something in return. I'm only twenty years old and I've seen more than the average eyes have seen in a lifetime. I've been around the world dealing with this man."

"Compass, what about you having your own family with kids?" Shirley asked her.

"Shirley girl this is my family. Ox, Tiysha and Quida. I can't have any children , because my uterus was damaged badly from the STD's and not knowing I had them from being molested. That's why they are in the picture. Both of them are pregnant now carrying our children. They are young also, Tiysha is twenty and Quida is eighteen. Ox saved them also. So this is my family and if I wish to attend college I can. I did dream of a Doctor."

Shirley looked at her and said, "Compass you are a strong individual I must say and I'm glad that I met you."

"I'm glad I met a woman of your stature too Shirley. C'mon I'll walk you back to Samuel , because I have to get my husband for his noon massage ." Compass told her and Shirley nodded her head to say okay. "Compass, before we go back up on the deck, how far is Kingston from here?" Shirley asked her.

"We will be there by the morning time," Compass told her and they both ventured back ob the deck. They saw Ox and Sam standing looking over the side of the Yacht into the blue water.

"Hey Compass baby is it time for my massage?" Ox glanced over his shoulder to see them when he asked her.

"Yes it is time." Compass answered him. He shook Sam's hand and said, well Sam I'll leave you two love birds to be alone and explore. Oh Sam you know where everything is and the room if you need any privacy." Ox told him.

"okay Ox," said Sam, as Ox walked over to Compass and Shirley passed him to reach Sam. Ox and Compass disappeared. Shirley still had her drink in her hand. Sam greeted her with a kiss. "Hey baby what are you drinking?" He asked her.

"It's Bacardi 8 and the year on the bottle was 1898." Shirley looked at her glass telling him.

"Let me taste it." He asked her and she gave him the glass. He tasted the liquor and she hugged him and asked him, "Sam do you care for me and be honest?"

He looked her directly in the eyes and said, "Yes Shirl, I care for you, I love you."

It sounded authentic to her ears, but she wasn't going out like that. "Sam you don't love me." She replied adding. "You might like me a lot, but love me na'll it's to soon boo." She told him.

"Shirley my feelings run deep for you." He told her and she had this confused look on her face. It puzzled her for a brief second. "Sam, how deep?" She had to ask him not taking her eyes off of him wanting to hear his response.

"Deeper than your womb and deeper than the depths of the ocean." He didn't blink and his expression was serious. She couldn't detect false or lies at this point when he answered her. He was serious.

'Sam, would you kill for me?" She asked him and maybe the Bacardi 8 was talking for her.

"Yeah if my life was endanger too." he told her.

"Would you ever steal for me Sam?" Shirley was testing him with the questions.

"Yeah if the shit doesn't belong to you." He was sharp with his answers.

He answered her not knowing where she was going with the questions.

"Sam would you ever cheat on me?" She was now holding both his hands staring up at him, because he put the drink down.

"For what Shirley? You are all the woman one man needs in his life nothing more, nothing less." Sam was still serious.

"What if I ever cheated on you Sam, would you leave me?" She asked him.

"That depends on whether your cheating were deliberate or incidental." He said.

"Deliberately!" She quickly answered him.

"No because, your brain is a shut off mechanism and sometimes your hormones think for you, but your feelings remain innocent." Sam explained to her.

"What about Incidental?" She asked him.

"Love is pain and a suffering heart is worse than a broken leg. If I'm not doing my job physically, mentally or emotionally, then my love for you will turn into pain, because you will find what you need elsewhere. So I guess I would never leave you if you cheated. I would rather work on the flaws in our relationship first before resorting to breaking up." Sam told her with a straight face. Shirley eyes began to water.

"Hold me Sam," she asked, as they embraced one another and that tear escaped from the corner of her eye. They stood there looking over the edge of Yacht into the blue water. Then Compass came to the surface completely nude and asked them.

"Excuse me you two, Ox wanted to know if ya'll want to joint us in the bed for this orgy?"

Shirley eyes slowly looked at Sam like she couldn't believe what she just heard.

"No thanks Compass," as Sam spoke for the both of them. Compass disappeared.

"Damn Sam they are bold and outgoing huh." Shirley said to him.

"You're telling me. They are always friendly and touchy with me when I come down here. Real hospitality," said Sam.

"Have you ever slept with either of them Sam and don't lie?" Shirley just knew he did and that would put her at ease if he did from her little nonsense she did last night.

"To be honest, Ox want me too a couple of times, but I was down here strictly on business, but if I wasn't I probably would've. And like last night if you and I wasn't in a relationship I would have and that's the truth." He looked at her.

"At least you are honest Sam." She told him.

"Shirl, Compass probably wants to lick your nookie," as Sam laughed.

"I'm not going to even comment on that Sam," as she looked at him long.

"We will probably leave Monday for home if that's okay with you?" Sam told her.

"That's fine Sam, whatever you want to do baby." She kissed him.

They stood there on the Yacht looking over the edge out into the salt water.

…………………………………..

Later on that night they occupied a room on the Yacht together gaining intimacy while on the water. Shirley now knew what it was like to have a water bed. She ever got a little sea sick.

That morning they awoke and headed up to the desk. The Yacht was anchoring inside the harbor of Kingston. Jamaica was beautiful and Shirley knew she was in a tropical climate. Kingston was the capital and had a rich natural plant life. A string of resorts extended along the southeast coast in the natural harbor narrow peninsula where they docked at.

Montego Bay and Ochoa Rios was close by and Jamaica had resorts along the north coast too.

Ox Sun Seeker rested in the harbor, while they went and got in an awaiting gray 600 Benzes he had. His well trained body guards escorted them in the two Benzes.

They stopped in the inner city so Shirley and Sam could purchase clothing and other personal hygiene to freshen up for the day, because they didn't bring a change of clothes.

After shopping briefly they headed up in the mountains where Ox mansion was located. It was much cooler in the mountains and Shirley was loving the moment she was spending in this tropical region, thinking she was made for this type of adventure. It was more than pleasure principal, her idea of romance was beyond anything she'd ever dream of, being with Sam who wasn't or involved with anyone, made the romance appearance more realistic then the mirror image of anything fabricated.

After the morning hospitality with Ox and his companion, Sam and Shirley ventured into the natural plant life that surrounded Ox's mansion.

It was very interesting that Shirley saw that God created their bodies to demand a variety.

She knew if "He" didn't give them the variety they needed and crave, then their bodies would rebel. In essence to say, **"I can't handle this. You're giving me too much of this thing therefore, I'm going to get sick or have some kind of negative reaction every time you feed it to me."**

That wasn't the case at this point in her life at this very moment and she was craving more standing in this foreign land that wasn't foreign to her heart and the way she was feeling.

Sam hugged her from behind enjoying the natural plant life himself. His confidence was building being in her presence.

He knew she was the type of woman who could be easily associated with a Doctor, Dentist, a business man or anyone with a six figure career job. Instead she was in his presence and it was a tremendous feeling for him as that sudden rush raced through his body and he gave himself a smile.

He squeezed her in his arms tightly kissing her on the forehead. He knew he was being influenced by others and Ox was his teacher. They casually caressed each other gently trying to figure out each others passions.

That night after dinner Ox and his three wives took them to Kingston to a reggae splash that had a variety of artist performing. The crowd at the concert was polite and still energetic controlling the atmosphere.

Compass showed Shirley how to skank dance like the Jamaicans. Ox and some other guys were smoking big Fonto leaf joints like Cuban cigars. Shirley just took in the culture that surrounded her. This was different from the Wilderness or the Imperial Reggae spots back home in Cincinnati. It was very different from being secluded with Thomas while on a trip. She never got a chance to enjoy his company when they escaped to a secluded place alone in a different city or country, because normally he was there on business related terms and not for pleasure.

That night or early morning Shirley made passionate love to Sam. When she climaxed she shed a tear for her own happiness. It was complex, but her complexity of venue made her terms to negotiate this new found contract for a long term contract.

That morning after eating breakfast and showering they headed back to the Virgin Island on Ox's Sun Seeker with just the Captain and the navigation crew.

Ox and his three lovely young wives stayed behind.

That Saturday and Sunday, Sam and Shirley enjoyed each others company like true romancers seeking long term goals.

Even though Shirley was feeling Sam, she still protected herself during their intimacy using protection whenever they participated in sex. Her conscious sometimes wonder off to Sharan and her trip to the abortion clinic. It was still haunting her.

That Monday morning they were back on a flight to Miami and then to the Greater Cincinnati Airport. Shirley thought she had her life under control with less confusion in her heart making it clear that she was going to be serious with Sam. He was light skin, well-mannered and he had his own money. She didn't care that he didn't like the arts nor did he have anything really in common with her.

It did kind of puzzled her that Thomas and Sharan liked the arts and just about everything she did. Sharan and her use to enjoy the company they had when they went on little outings with Rachelle and Pedro in the past. Even though they never hooked up on a serious level involving each other intimately, he was very much compatible with her. He even managed to sex her real good two months ago when she got her revenge on Thomas for giving the strange female his number. But Sharan had the ultimate strike against him. He was a brown skin complexion brother.

That night when Sam and Shirley got back to their separate homes, Shirley called Rachelle to let her know she was back a week early.

CHAPTER NINE

The Truth

The phone rang several times at Rachelle's house before she picked up breathing heavy through the receiver. "Hello, hello," as she answered the phone aggressively.

"Hello Chelle, are you busy?" Shirley asked her.

"I was, but what's up Shirl? And why are you back so early?" Rachelle asked her.

Shirley could hear another person in the background trying to get Rachelle of the phone.

"Stop boy, can't you see I'm on the phone." Rachelle told the person who was bothering her.

"We decided to come back early." Shirley told her. It got quiet and then Rachelle said,

"Guess what Shirl, Pedro proposed to me Saturday night."

"You lying girl, how did that finally happen?" Shirley asked her.

"Friday night Boobie called the house and Pedro answered the phone. We got into a big argument and I let him know until he put a ring on this finger, I'm going to do what the fuck I want to." Rachelle was smacking her lips.

"Well congratulations Chelle." Shirley was happy for her.

"Will you be my Maid of Honor Shirl?" Rachelle asked her.

"You know I will. Where's Nee at? She didn't answer her phone before I called you." Shirley asked her.

"I haven't heard from her ass since you left for your trip and she hasn't been to work either. Also your boy Sharan is downtown being held by the Feds." Rachelle told her.

"Are you serious Chelle, for what?" She asked with much concern in her voice.

Shirley heart sped up a little. She was now feeling butterfly's in her stomach wondering what he was downtown for, especially being held by the Feds.

"Hold on Shirl," as Rachelle told her to hold on, but Shirley could still hear her voice.

"Pedro, what is Sharan being held for again, Shirley wants to know?" Rachelle asked Pedro, but she still had the phone to her mouth. It was quiet while she received the information from Pedro. "Oh he's being held for unpaid taxes and tax invasion. Also under investigation for allegedly selling stolen clothes. It's real messed up." Rachelle tried to explain to her.

"Damn that's messed up," Shirley replied and got quiet thinking about him.

"So how was your trip with Sam I Am?" Rachelle laughed.

"It was wonderful Chelle and Jamaica was beautiful girl." Shirley told her friend.

"I thought ya'll went to the Virgin Island Shirl?"

"We did, but Sam's friend Ox who's from Jamaica took us to his mansion in Kingston and it was pretty. I think I'm in love Chelle." Shirley confessed to her friend.

"Bitch please, there you go tripping again. This Negro done gave you some head on the beach and shit, and now all of a sudden you are in love, yeah right." Rachelle wasn't buying what Shirley was selling her.

"Seriously Chelle, our time together was priceless and I see potential in him." Shirley said.

"Yeah, yeah, we'll see, but it's late heifer and my man doesn't appreciate me being on our phone this late." Rachelle told her.

"What you mean our phone Chelle?" Shirley asked her.

"Like I said, our phone. Pedro moved in Saturday night too, so it's our phone." Rachelle said it with emphasis sucking her teeth.

"Well excuse me, Ms. Our phone. But we need to see what's up with Renee tired ass tomorrow and I'm going downtown to see about Sharan too," said Shirley.

"Right." Rachelle answered her.

"Well I'm not going in tomorrow, so I'll be at your job in the morning Chelle."

"Okay, I'm so in love now calm down." Rachelle told her.

"Bye yellow heifer," said Shirley.

"Bye to you too winch," said Rachelle and they hung up from each other.

Shirley's affection and guilt for Sharan started to race through her body and mind. She wouldn't feel right not going to his rescue to see if she could help him out. After all he was there when she needed him the most.

…………………………………..

That morning at around 10:30 Shirley entered Mother's hair salon with a Mood Indigo denim wrap dress made by Fubu ladies, a pair of Enzo Agiolini cork bottom wedge dark brown shoes showing her toes. Rachelle saw that her friend was glowing. Rachelle had on a Tommy tank top dress all white and a pair of Mystique thong sandals.

With no hesitation Rachelle grabbed her purse and told her co-workers she would be back in a few for her 11:00 clock appointment. They took Rachelle's Beemer to Renee's apartment.

When they arrived at Renee's apartment her car was there, so they went upstairs to her door and began to knock. Rachelle balled her fist and hit the door.

Boom! Boom! Boom! Rachelle put her ear up to the door to see if she could hear any movement going on. She heard the T.V. and some female voice she thought.

"What do you hear Chelle?" Shirley asked her.

"The T.V. and it sounds like some females are talking." Rachelle told her.

"Open up this damn door Nee, it's us," as Shirley confessed on the other side of the door.

But no one answered, so Rachelle just so happen to twist the door knob and it was unlocked. They slowly entered and there was two half naked women sitting in Renee's living room trying to light a glass instrument. Their hair were nappy looking, their lips were purple and dry. Renee's apartment smelled like sour garbage.

Rachelle and Shirley grabbed their mouths and noses trying not to absorb the smell through their senses. The two women didn't bother to attend to them or question them as the females still continued to light the glass instrument.

There were pizza boxes, dirty dishes and empty beer cans and 40 oz. bottles everywhere.

Renee's apartment never looked like this before, she was a neat a freak. This picture wasn't right at all.

"Excuse me, where's Renee?" Shirley asked the two women.

"She's in her bedroom," as one of the females took time out to answer her.

They looked like they been up all night and needed baths. Shirley and Rachelle went to her bedroom and opened the door and couldn't believe their eyes.

Renee was getting rammed by one guy and two other guys were standing on each side of her while she had their tribal pieces in her hand giving them oral pleasure.

Then it was a guy butt naked in the corner video taping the scene.

"Hell to the na'll, break this shit up. Ya'll got to go," as Shirley had her cell phone in her hand up to her ear.

"You got us fucked up slim, she owes us for our dope and she's paying us this way." The guy in the corner responded.

"Dope? She's not on any fucking dope." Rachelle responded with an attitude.

"Yeah the show is over, she's not being Cassidy Clay any longer, look the police are on their way," as Shirley was bluffing with the remark. The guy dropped the video camera.

"Five O, c'mon ya'll this bitch done called the law. We out of here," as he grabbed his clothes running pass Shirley and Rachelle. The other guys followed him. Renee sat up and was confused and high. Her room smelled awful, like ass, funky sex and sweat. "What ya'll do that for? Ya'll be getting dick, so why can't Nee get some dick?" Renee said. She was looking like the two women in the living room. Her eyes were big and wide, her hair was not done and the bottom of her feet were dirty. Shirley walked over to her and said, "Damn Nee, what on God's green earth were you thinking?" She hugged her.

"So all along you've been smoking this shit," as Rachelle picked up a bag of crack lying on her dresser. "That's why your eyes were big like that, sweating and acting all strange when you come out of your room." Rachelle added.

Shirley was still hugging Renee. "Yeah Chelle and we didn't even pick up on it, ignoring her cry for help, damn." Shirley was disgusted with Renee, but also concern for her. This was the bottom of the barrel.

"So you lied to me when you told me you were putting aspirin in your weed and all along it was crack. You played me for a fool Nee," as Shirley shook her head shedding a tear and then she came out of it aggressively.

"Get your ass up and go get in the shower you are going on Burnet Ave. I'm about to pack you some clean clothes, Rachelle go kick those dope fiend bitches out. We are checking her ass into the Detoxify Center at University Hospital." Shirley told her.

"What are ya'll doing? Those are my real friends." Renee questioned Shirley.

"Shut the fuck up Nee, we are your real friends. Girl before I, Uhh," as Shirley lifted her hand and stopped herself from hitting Renee out of anger and love.

"Nee go get in the fucking shower, go get in the shower now." as Shirley raised her voice and kind of gave Renee a push out of the bedroom. Renee walked out the bedroom holding her head down. Rachelle looked at Shirley and Shirley tilted her head to the side to say, "What." to Rachelle. She rolled her eyes at Shirley and went to the living room to handle her business. She grabbed a butchers knife out of the kitchen drawer and came into the living room waving the knife.

"You hoe's got to go." Rachelle told them.

"But Renee said we could stay here." One of the females said looking disfigured.

"Sorry, but you bitches room and board has been revoked, get the fuck out now before I get to using this." Rachelle was now pointing the butcher knife at them. They grabbed their clothing and instruments quickly. "This bitch is crazy Queen B," as the female told the other one as they left out the apartment.

Rachelle secured the door quickly by locking it. She then went to aid Shirley in the bedroom, but she wasn't there. She then looked down the hall to see the bathroom door open. She went to the bathroom to see Shirley sitting on the toilet with the seat down talking to Renee. Rachelle walked in and Shirley was crying. She rubbed Shirley's shoulder. Shirley was holding a towel for Renee. When the water stopped Shirley pulled the shower curtain back and Renee was standing there shaking in fear. Shirley handed her the towel and Renee began to dry off. After getting the majority of wetness from her body she wrapped herself with the towel and stepped out the shower. She looked at them and said, Ya'll mad at me? I'm sorry, I need help and sometimes I feel like I don't won't to live anymore,"

Rachelle and Shirley embraced their friend. "It's going to be alright Renee, we will get you some help and get you through this," said Rachelle. They all were crying.

Shirley separated herself from the two and said, "Go get dress Renee."

Renee gave her the puppy eyes, but she left with her head down. Rachelle turned to Shirley and said, "What about her apartment?"

"We will put it back together when you get off work today. I'm not going in." Shirley told her and Rachelle grabbed her by the shoulder and they walked out the bathroom.

'Plead my cause, O Lord, with those who strive with me, fight against those who fight against me. Take hold of the shield and buckler, and stand up for my help. Also draw out the spear, and stop those who pursue me. Say to my soul. "I am your salvation". Let those be put to shame and brought to dishonor that seeks after my life, let those be turned back and brought to confusion that plots my hurt.'

Shirley knew her friend needed her and she had to be there for her. Her prayers were silent remembering what her granny taught her growing up. They made Renee clean herself thoroughly by putting on clean panties and bra which she didn't have many that were clean. They did manage to find her a set. After Renee was dressed they grabbed her keys locking up her apartment as they left for the Detoxify Center.

Shirley decided right then that she would pay more attention to those who were close by her and she cared deeply for.

They stopped in the Avondale town center to buy Renee some new underwear, bra's and socks. Also some outfits and hygiene products for her stay at the Detoxify Center. Having to wash her clothes later and pack her a bag. Shirley also called Renee job to explain the situation to her Union to try to save her place of employment.

Imbalance and Boredom causes problems being unable to rest enough or laugh enough or maybe just working too hard. Too much stress frequent emotion upsets and a lack of variety in life can all have adverse effects on your behavior. This gives you the imbalance and boredom causing you to have problems. Renee was a person who was experiencing this imbalance boredom.

CHAPTER TEN

The Showdown

They successfully dropped Renee off at the University Hospital. Shirley put her bill on her credit card. They also gave the receptionist and drug counselors their numbers to contact them. After leaving Avondale and the University Hospital they went back to Mother's hair salon. Shirley didn't waste anytime hugging Rachelle and getting in her car heading downtown to the Federal Building to see Sharan.

She got downtown in no time finding a parking space near the building. She checked her face in the vanity mirrors on her visors. She got out of her car brushing her clothes off shaking the fabric from her dampen skin. She had perspired a little from all the activity from earlier. She grabbed her briefcase out of her trunk. She went in her purse and retrieves some change for the parking meter. When she entered the building she asked the receptionist what floor did they hold their prisoners under investigation.

She received the instructions and went up to the fifth floor and had to check in with another receptionist. There she was briefly held up and then two women came from behind some double doors. It was a dark complexion woman around 5'5" black hair and well-built. She had on an orange long sleeve blouse and flat front pants, with some orange heels by Nine West. The other woman was light skinned complexion around 5'6" with dookie braids that were black and maroon coming down her back.

She had on a crème color ruffle halter top with leather straps a long ruffle skin with side leather tie which matched the halter top and a pair of open toe crème colored quarter inch heels with leather straps. The dark complexion woman spoke first.

"Hello Ms. Thomas. My name is Renee Price, I'm with the Federal Bureau of Investigation," as she extended her hand to Shirley.

"Hi, I'm Eva Hawkins, I'm from the Internal Revenue Service," as she also extended her hand to Shirley.

"Hello, ladies, I'm Sharan Chambers attorney and I would like to speak to my client please." Shirley gave them a smile.

"But Ms. Thomas, his lawyer Harold Perkins has already talked to him, and we didn't know he had two lawyers." Renee Price told her.

"Well now you know, so may I please speak with my client?" said Shirley.

"We are getting him now Ms. Thomas." Eva Hawkins told her.

"Okay." Shirley replied as the three women stood there. Then a man in a security suit stuck his head out from the double doors. "Ms. Hawkins and Ms. Price we are ready for you." he told them and they nodded their heads to the man and led the way.

"Ms. Thomas follow us please," as Eva Hawkins led the way. They went through the double doors. Shirley was shook down thoroughly by Renee Price before she entered the room where Sharan was sitting at shackled in a chair.

He smiled at her as she entered the room. "You have an half hour Ms. Thomas," as Renee Price left the room. Shirley nodded to her.

Shirley sat down across from Sharan giving him a friendly smile of her own. It was a long stare before either one of them spoke. Then Shirley spoke first. "Hello Sharan." He just looked at her and then he repositioned himself in his chair a little.

"What brings you down here?" he asked her in a husky voice.

"You silly, Sharan what do you mean? When I heard you were down here in trouble I knew I had to be here for you." She replied.

"It's nice to know that you care Shirl, but what about your dude you escaped to the Islands with? Plus I already have a lawyer and I don't need any extra help, from you." Shirley's heart dropped, because Sharan knew her business and he neglected her help.

"Sharan, Rachelle told you my business?" She asked him.

"Na'll a little bird on the wire informed me. It's funny though we murder our child one week and then weeks later you are off in the Islands with a new Joe. All I know is it could've been his baby and not mines." Sharan told her and she could tell he was angry.

"Sharan that's not fair, why would you throw that up in my face?" She cried out.

"Shirley what the fuck you know about being fair? Huh tell me. What, tricking a nigga out of his morals and shit or letting someone pour out their feelings and then executing a fatal blow. What about loyalty and respect huh? Boy I should have never f*…" as he didn't want to say the rest, but she knew what he wanted to say. Shirley didn't understand his aggression, as her tears began to form.

"Sharan, I never told you we were together, so how can I display the act of not being loyal?" She asked him.

"Fuck loyalty, I speaking on respect Shirley. Respecting yourself as a woman, loving yourself first and for most. You just broke it off with a married man and then you fuck me out the blue. Then you take off to the Islands with some Joe, c'mon if that's not being real friendly with your shit, then what is?" Sharan told her.

Shirley eyes lit up in fury. She started shaking because he hit a nerve.

"Sharan, I'm not trying to go there with you, but I'm here for you no matter how you may feel about me or how upset you may be," as she sniffled telling him.

"Shirley you just don't get it." He paused a moment. "I love you and I care about you, but you've never stopped once and realized it."

She started crying even more not knowing how she really acted towards this man who really cared about her, not what she had , but about her. Sharan didn't stop he continued on getting a little sentimental.

"You know Shirl, sometimes I would sit and wonder are the decisions I make in life worth the results they bring and are the results ever really forgiven for a bad decision," as he paused putting his head down. "God knows I've made my fair share of mistakes and I wonder how the forgive part goes. I put myself on the other side of the fence and I wonder what kind of decisions are unforgivable, if any? Maybe the one we made to kill our child not giving it a chance. I'm not just blaming you it was a fifty-fifty decision." He rested a minute and continued on. "The lack of loyalty is probably not forgiven. Every beautiful thing in the world revolves around that word and that word only. Loyalty is picking one up, when metaphorically the other is too injured to move or carry on. Keeping one strong in a moment of weakness, or even better than that, never letting the other one hit rock bottom, because your there to catch them before they get that far," as he balled his fist tightly on the table making his jaw tight. He still continued.

"I can't deny that I have feelings for you and yes, that seven letter word is a difference between forgiven and unforgiving and even loyalty." He told Shirley .

"The reason I love you most is because no matter what the situation appears to be, I will never completely lose my loyalty for you, as you continue to do foolish things ignoring who really loves you Shirley. But it's cool and I don't need your help I'm good. Yo guards get me out of here." Sharan yelled out. He just dropped a bomb in Shirley's face. She didn't know how to respond. She was stuck and now even more confused.

Shirley tried to touch him, but he yanked away from her. "Sharan, please don't do this, please call me I'm sorry." She stood there in tears, as the guards took Sharan back behind the doors. Her heart was more troubling and torn apart. She didn't even bother to fix her face, as she left from the fifth floor of the Federal Building. She went to Mt.

Adams to get a piece of mind and to be at peace with herself trying to figure out her next move. She sat in Play House in the park listening to her mind and heart speak to her. She began talking to herself.

"Maybe Sharan is right, maybe I don't respect and don't display and loyalty to anyone who care's about me. Am I forgetting my morals? I'm independent or am I? Do I find myself depending on a man to make me happy.?

Because the only thing Thomas had done for me was pay my bills, shower me with gifts while he got his thrills off and went back home to his wife. He practically used me. Am I chasing a ghost, when my real soul-mate was just before my eyes?"

She thought to herself long and hard sitting there crying and wondering.

She recollected her thoughts and left Mt. Adams going down Victory Parkway and when she went around the bend by the United Dairy Farmers, she got pulled over by the Cincinnati Police. Shirley pulled her Lexus Sedan over and placed it in park. She waited for the officer to approach her vehicle and already had her license, insurance and registration out. He came to her window and she let her window down slowly.

Shirley took it upon herself to ask him the question.

"Excuse me officer what seems to be the problem?"

"I'm just doing a routine check to see if it's you in this car Ms. Thomas." He stated. He was looking down on Shirley making sure it was her.

"Why wouldn't it be? But yes it's me, did I do something wrong officer?" Shirley was now getting irritated.

"This is my area to patrol and I was wondering what a woman like you were doing in a couple of drug area in Walnut Hills late last month around this time." He told her.

Shirley knew that Sam had her car around that time last month.

"I was out of town late last month." She told the officer.

"Did you leave your vehicle with someone?" He asked her.

\She knew she didn't have to answer the question but she did anyway. "Yes I did." She told him in a sarcastic way.

"Well you need to watch the company you keep. Your car was spotted on Sesame St. and in the Setty Kunh Terrace two known drug areas. I thought it was a couple of drug dealers I knew with the flashy rims and tint, until I ran your plates in." He was still looking down on her. She looked up at him and replied. "I'll check it out officer and thanks for making me aware and being concerned officer." Shirley told him.

"No problem Ms. Thomas, you have a nice day and be careful." The officer told her.

"Okay," said Shirley.

The officer walked off and she rolled her window up.

"That damn Sam, I wonder what the hell he was into? I know he was doing something he had no business doing in my car." She said to herself pulling off.

……………………………………...

She went back up to the hair salon after she grabbed her something to eat from Richie's. Rachelle left the shop an hour early so they could go put Renee's apartment back in order. They clean her place to sparkle. Everything was back to normal at 5600 Ryland Ave. apartment #4. While they were cleaning up Shirley found Thomas watch she bought him. She knew it was his from the engraving. She cuffed it and didn't tell Rachelle she found it. She was now wondering what the hell Thomas was doing over to Renee's and Renee didn't tell her. There was some fishy stuff going on, and she would question it at a later date.

They were sitting on Renee's couch reminiscing about old times looking at pictures. Then Shirley got all mushy on the inside wanting to know why Rachelle told Sharan that she was out of town with Sam.

"Chelle, Sharan didn't want to see me, let alone want my help, after you told him I was in the Virgin Islands with Sam."

Rachelle saw the concern on her friends face. "I didn't tell him shit, maybe Pedro told him, but I didn't. Only thing I told Pedro that you were in the Virgin Islands and not with Thomas." Rachelle looked at her.

"Chelle, I told you to quit pillow talking about our business with Pedro. This Negro went off on me Chelle and I couldn't understand why." Shirley vented to her.

"Shirl, he has feelings for you and then you slept with him not having any emotions towards him," as Rachelle looked in her eyes.

"But Chelle I explained how I felt about what we did that night. We had sex and I had no other type of feelings towards him. The Negro gave me a hell of a speech on loyalty that made me cry with his punk ass. It hit home though and had me thinking ever since I left f

from seeing him." Shirley told her friend and was about to tear up again just thinking about her visit with Sharan.

"Shirl, you can't forget he has his own feelings and you can't determine his feelings or actions. Then he experienced you getting the abortion killing ya'll suppose to be child together. That shit can do damage to a guy, especially when they have feelings for the woman and he has mad feelings for you. He's just being stubborn right now." Rachelle explained to her.

"Chelle, he was very clear and cold hearted with his words. I cried in Mt. Adams not understanding why he hated me and was so distance towards me. I just want to return the favor of him being there for me Chelle." Shirley was emotionally.

"Shirl, things don't always work that way. The scars will heal in his heart. He just feels betrayed right now. Don't sweat it, I'll talk to him okay," as Rachelle rubbed Shirley's arm. She had started crying and just nodded her head to respond to Rachelle.

The loneliness was there in Shirley's heart. They sat around Renee's for another hour or so. Rachelle decided to take Renee's dirty laundry to her house and washed her clothes. They left Renee's at around 8 that night. Rachelle went home and Shirley decided to go over Sam's instead of driving home. She had a few clothes already over his house. She was spending the night with him and plus she wanted to question him about her car. When she parked her car in the drive-way behind his 600 Benz it was 8:35. Sam. Was home, but he had company. Shirley let herself in with they key he had give her. Shirley entered the living room they were in to see four guys smoking cigars, drinking and discussing business she suppose. She stood there for a brief moment before one of the guys notice her and nodded to Sam. He turned to see his girlfriend standing there.

"Hey babe, why didn't you call first?" Sam asked her.

"I was just in the neighborhood and didn't feel like driving all the way home." She answered him. She was exhausted and he saw it on face.

"Okay, give me about fifteen minutes and I'll be finished. There's some Ike's barbecue in the kitchen if you're hungry." He told her.

"Okay," as she left and went to his room. She kicked off her shoes and lay across his king size bed watching a re-run of "Martin" on TNT.

Sam came into the bedroom after "Martin" went off. He gently laid next to her and said, "So what's up Boo?"

She turned around to face him. "Nothing much, just a little depressed, tired and down."

"Why is that Shirl?" He asked her now rubbing her side gently with the most cunning stroke.

"I just found out my girl is on drugs." Shirley told him.

"Who Renee or Rachelle?" Sam asked her. She closed her eyes and said, "Renee." Trying not to bare the hurt by saying her name.

"So what are you going to do Shirl?" He asked her.

"We already and getting her some professional help over at University Hospital." She was now holding her head.

"That's cool and if there is anything you need for me to do, don't hesitate to ask me. Are you spending the night over here?" He asked her.

"Yep, unless you are going out, then I can go home. I need to be held Sam," said Shirley.

"Na'll I'm in for the night. Plus I'm still kind of tired from our trip," he said.

Shirley took this time to ask him why did he have her vehicle in those known drug areas when she left him her car. "Sam can I ask you something and will you be honest with your answer?" Shirley was rubbing his hand.

"Sure, go right ahead." He told her.

"What were you doing in Walnut Hills when I was in Atlanta and you my car?" She was looking him square in the face.

Sam thought someone was being nosey trying to discuss his other business to her that she wasn't aware of. But he answered her the best way he knew how.

"Well if you insist Shirl, my granny lives on Sesame St and I was dropping off a clients car in the Setty Kuhn Terrace, and why did you ask me that?" Sam hurried up and switched the game up.

"I was pulled over by the police earlier today on Victory Parkway and the police who pulled me over must have seen my car in those areas when you had it. He told me that they were known drug areas that's all." Shirley told him.

Sam was in relief hearing what he heard. "Shirl, damn near everywhere in this conservative ass city is a drug zone. He was probably just judging you car, because they think everyone riding rims is doing something illegal." Sam was defensive with statement.

"It's okay baby, calm down. Can you warm me up some food please? And where is my nightgown, the green one?" She asked him.

"It's in the top drawer along with your panties and bra. Your two outfits are in the closet,

I had them dry-cleaned." Sam told her.

"Okay I'm about to take a shower," as she stood up and started to undress. Sam left the room to warm her food up.

After her shower and eating, she made love to Sam trying to forget about her day that was so depressing. When she had her orgasm she collapsed on him falling asleep, because she was so exhausted.

……………………………………...
....
……

She went to work from Sam house the next day. Shirley was at work thinking about what went on yesterday with Sharan and Renee. She was in a bubble and her heart was in the mist of confusion dealing with the fluff she was surrounded by. **"I have a destiny."**

She thought to herself. She sat at her desk thinking and reminding herself she wasn't perfect.

'In other words we know that God love us because the Holy Spirit teaches us so. We put our hope in God because we are sure that He loves us and has a great future planned for us.'

Her morning hue of deliverance came from a scripture in the Bible as she sat in her office reading her Bible. In Psalm 84:11 she read.

"For the Lord God is a sun and shield; the Lord will give grace and glory: No good thing will He withhold from them that walk uprightly."

Shirley was confident that everything would pass and her life would prosper.

Then and there she took in a deep breath and vowed to move in a direction of Understanding making her life with Sam and her girlfriends mush easier and pleasant.

……………………………………...
....
……

The month of July was spent piecing out the recovery of Renee for Rachelle and Shirley.

Renee was coming around doing her programs and getting back on track. Shirley and Rachelle kept her apartment up while she stayed in a halfway house getting her drug treatment. Renee also found out that she was with child and was now a month and a half pregnant.

Renee was in a raw dilemma like Shirley was when she found out she conceived. She didn't know if her baby was Thomas or Chucky's from Dayton who she slept with in Atlanta during the hair show. She was looking good though. Her figure was back, she was drug free and her glow was back. She was the old Renee from high school and college before she was raped.

Even Chucky was coming to visit her in Cincinnati. She told him everything when she contacted him. She told him about her past of being raped and why she even started smoking marijuana up to her experimenting with crack cocaine.

He didn't judge her and especially that he was under the impression she was carrying his child. Renee didn't really know that he wasn't just dealing oils, incense and CD's, he was a very well known drug dealer in Dayton Ohio.

The stage was set and Renee was scheduled to get out of treatment and the halfway house in the beginning of August. She was happy and ready to get on with her life putting the past behind her. She thanked her girls for their support.

Even though her family was there for her, her friends were there the most.

…………………………………………..

August came and the summer of 2001 was a scorcher. Renee was released from the treatment center and her girls were right there to greet her. They took her out to eat and shopping. Renee's belly was beginning to show a little. When they took Renee to her apartment Chucky was waiting on her with balloons and gifts. He was digging Renee and her girls were happy for her.

Shirley and Rachelle relationship were in its best stages. The harmony was fascinating. Times were beginning to be like old times when everyone was doing good jamming to the beat. Renee had Chucky in her life, Shirley had Sam and Rachelle had Pedro. Rachelle and Pedro's wedding was scheduled for the spring of 2002 in April.

…………………………………………..

In the middle of August Sam and Shirley was having dinner at the Montgomery Inn down on the river by Sawyer Point with Boobie and Ren Mack and two female companions they knew.

Sam pulled up in the parking lot of the Montgomery Inn and Boobie followed him in his white Cadillac Escalade truck. They were in valet parking. Sam and Shirley got out the Benz. Sam had on Polo jeans, a short sleeve multi-colored soccer style Polo shirt with a collar and some leather sandals. Shirley had on a white silk mini-dress showing her cleavage and some black tie up stiletto heels. Her hair was cute in a cute style now. She had on her glitter lotion that was blending in with her jewelry.

Boobie got out and was fly as usual with Phat farm from head to toe.

His date Aunika from Dayton out by Northland was dressed in a tight green mini-dress with the back out, with some gold knock off Chanel pumps with the toe out. Her toe nail polish was chipped and she had corns. Her hair was done with glue traps and pro style gel. She stood at 6'1" and was light complexion. She had a nice round bottom. She was indeed ghetto fabulous.

His rap duo Ren Mack got out the back of the truck with his date, Aunika's best friend Deona. She was from the Desota Bass in Dayton. She was dressed in some women dress slacks all gray that were super tight making her booty look wide and flat. A blouse that looks like it came from Dots with fake ruby's down the sides and some two inch heels. She had on wig store accessories. Her hair was done nicely though.

She was dark skinned complexion with dimples.

Ren Mack had on Roc-A-wear jean and shirt outfit. He had on a pair of all white Air Force 1's. He was rocking his platinum jewelry.

They all entered the restaurant together and Shirley was cracking up on the inside at Ren Mack. He kept making faces at her making it seem like he didn't want to be with his date.

Aunika and Deona snarled at Shirley and she didn't even give them the satisfaction ignoring them and their childish games. They were seated and had a nice view of the restaurant. Sam recognized a few pro athletes who played ball for the Cincinnati Reds and the Bengal's.

Sam ordered champagne for the whole table. Aunika and Deona weren't familiar with the taste of Moet, so they ordered daiquiris.

The waitress came to their table and placed the menus in front of them.

Aunika was curious, hungry at the same time hearing her stomach growl. She was smacking on her chewing gum rambling through the menu. Boobie didn't wait to tell Aunika the deal on the expensive menu she was now fingering through.

"Aunika hold up," he said and she looked around her menu at him. "What?" She responded with an attitude getting everyone's attention at the table.

Sam and Ren Mack knew it was coming. Boobie looked at her long and hard, and then said, "You know you have your friendship side of the menu and you have your fuck side of the menu? So choose your meal carefully." He told her. She batted her eyes at him and said, "Boy-bye, I'm hungry as hell. I want this whole Rib dinner and their special sauce, so I guess I'll be a fucking and sucking bitch tonight."

Ren Mack cracked up and Deona said, "I'm not that hungry, so I hope the same rules don't apply with you Ren?"

Ren didn't say anything. Shirley looked at Sam and he shrugged his shoulders smiling at her. "Sam I wonder where Boobie got that from?" she whispered in his ear.

It was undesirable futuristic motivation from the energy that flowed amongst them in the Montgomery Inn that night. Shirley and Sam were flattered and entertained by their company. Shirley got to know Aunika and Deona a little better. They were younger than her, needing a womanly role model. Shirley had found out that from Deona that Chucky was a known drug dealer in Dayton, but she also found out that Deona was obsessed with him. She was stalking him, because she knew exactly where Renee stayed at.

It was funny to Shirley seeing how this young girl was acting having a crush on a guy like she once did when she was younger.

She just took everything in and let out a sigh in the air from being overwhelmed by her company. She was loving it. Shirley let her guard down to Sam and she was falling in love with him and so was he.

....

In September on Labor day Rachelle had everyone over to her house to eat and hang out.

Meco, Ren Mack, Renee, Shirley, Sam, Pedro, Boobie, Chucky, Ebony, Rachelle's mom and a few other people. They had a blast and Pedro didn't even know that Boobie was the one who called the house.

CHAPTER ELEVEN
Engagement

In late September Shirley was at work and she called Sam to ask him if he wanted to do dinner that night, her treat. He agreed and she made reservations at Christine Lenhardt's on W. Mc Millian in Clifton. It sat across the street from the Taco Bell.

It was a European cuisine restaurant, a German culture. They had reservations for 8:45 that night. They drove Shirley's Lexus Sedan to the event.

Shirley was dressed in a maroon strapless silk-lace dress with a maroon crotched cotton knit sweater coat all by Sully Bonnelly, and she had on a pair of suede cut out Stiletto heels by Christine Louboutin.

Sam had on a black viscose silk crepe suit with a short sleeve silk jersey crewneck, some wire frame Cartier eye wear and a pair of Allen Edmond loafers. They parked in the small lot of the restaurant and entered being greeted by the hostess.

"Hello, how are you all doing this evening?" The hostess asked them.

"Guten Tag." Shirley spoke in her foreign tongue telling the hostess good-evening in German.

"Guten Tag Fraulien, ich sehen Sie sprechen Deutsch." The hostess responded telling Shirley good-evening and that she speaks German.

"Jah Ich sprechen Deutsch und mochte ein platze vor zwei , meine name sind Thomas," as Shirley told the hostess she spoke German and she had reservations for two under the name Thomas.

"Jah, sie platze sind da, kommen sie bitte," as the hostess told Shirley their seats were over by the window and to please follow her.

"Danke schon." Shirley replied to the hostess telling her thank you.

Sam and her took their seats at a cozy table by the window that had candles burning on the table.

"Bitte, I will bring you two menus, but first what type of beverage would you like?" The hostess asked them.

She was a thin red hair woman about in her late thirties with freckles.

"I would like a glass of Cordon Blue please." Sam told the hostess.

"And I would like a glass of Red Zinfandel please." Shirley ordered her drink.

"Okay, I'll be right back with your drinks and our menu." The hostess walked away from their table to retrieve their drinks and the menu.

Sam looked at Shirley with confident eyes and was amaze that she spoke another language. "Shirl, I didn't know you German."

"Yes Sam I speak German fluently, I also speak French and a little Spanish." She was admiring him as well sitting across from her. He was handsome as ever and she continued to stare into his eyes.

He cleared his throat and gently touched her hand that a French manicure.

"Shirley, I would like to ask you something." Then he grabbed her hand.

"Sure Sam go ahead, what is it?" She told him. He relaxed a soft moment and then started to speak.

"You know that I love you and I know I can love you forever," as then started to massage her hand and with his free hand he went into his suit jacket pocket and retrieved a ring box. Shirley began to shake and tear up when she witnessed the ring box. She was now off balance not knowing where he was going with this conversation and the ring box.

She was thinking to herself, **I know he's not about to ask me to marry him, he couldn't.** She tried to calm down, but she couldn't as Sam continued to speak.

"Shirley, out of all the possible companions a man can have, I never had a woman of your stature before and my mother always told me when I come across the right woman make sure I try to keep her. So with all do respect Shirley Thomas, will you marry me?" He let her hand go to show her the ring. It was platinum one karat diamond ring. Shirley responded after starring at the ring for a long moment. "Are you serious Sam ? Oh my God. Sam are you serious? Don't be playing with my heart." She was looking at him. "Yes I'm serious Shirl," said Sam. She took a few more glances at the ring and said, "Yes, I'll marry you." She was in total shock, because no one ever proposed to her. Sam reached across the table and kissed her. "I love you Shirley." He told her after the kiss. Shirley responded. "I love you too Sam."

A waitress came back with their drink and the menus. "Hello, I'm Katie and I'll be your server for the evening. Who get's the Cordon Blue?" Sam lifted his hand. She placed the drink on a paper coaster in front of him.

"Then you must get the Red Zinfandel miss," as she placed Shirley's drink in front of her.

The waitress notice that Shirley was sniffling with a tear. "Excuse me Miss would you like a Kleenex?" The waitress asked her.

"Yes please," as Shirley continued to sniffle.

The waitress went to a nearby stand and retrieved a box of Kleenex . She came back and let Shirley get her a few out the box to wipe her tears .

"Thank You Katie," as Shirley was trying to clear her face.

"I will have to see some I.D for the drinks please its restaurant policy." The waitress told them. They showed their I.D. 's and Katie asked Shirley. "Miss is everything alright?"

Shirley looked up at her and said, "Yes everything is okay, my boyfriend just proposed to me." Shirley showed off her new engagement ring to the waitress.

"Congratulations!" The waitress told her.

"Well thank you Katie." Shirley was happy with her response feeling real good.

"Well do ya'll need a minute before placing your order?" Katie asked them.

"No, hold on please," as the both of them picked up their menus.

"We would like the fried veal dinner please" Shirley decided to order for the both of them. Sam didn't question her, because he never been in the restaurant, but he did eat veal. "Can I offer you any dessert tonight? The lady of the restaurant has made her special German double fudge cake." Katie told them.

"Umm, we would like the special German double fudge cake with a side of Vanilla ice cream. And can we have a re-fill on our drinks when our food comes out and two glasses of ice water with lemon please?" Shirley was in full control. It was fearless expedition to shoe her now she wasn't going to back up from the situation.

Shirley and Sam tackled their dinner and dessert offering each other portions feeding one another off their forks romancing each other. It was perfect, so perfect they went downtown after dinner by the Fountain Square to ride in a Chariot through downtown Cincinnati. The ended up back over Sam's house in Evanston being his house was closer to Downtown. Shirley thought in her mind to give him a sexual pleasure ha hasn't received from her engagement ring. She wanted to thank him properly. Shirley slid out of her Stilettos and silk lace dress. She was in her black thing when she eased in the bed with Sam who was flipping through channels with the remote in his boxers. She straddled him where he couldn't see the T.V. only Shirley's hard nipples and her womanly features was in his face that was soft and smooth. Her dark melon breast was upright staring at him. She worked her hand into the slit if his boxers ns squeezed her tribal piece. She eased down still holding his manhood in her hand, and the she pulled his tribal piece out and starting licking him. He grunted with pleasure, as she took him in her mouth until his head was wedged in her throat. Her tongue lashed at the underside of his tribal piece as she sucked it. "Mmm," she hummed making his body tighten. "I wanna be inside you Shirley," he gasped with a hard on. His testicles were reaching the boiling point of orgasm. She released him and he was erect, and the she rolled over to skim out of her

thongs and spread her pretty dark thighs for him. He got in position above her. She gripped his tribal piece while rubbing the head up and down over her slick vagina lips. "Fuck!" He blurted out feeling wildly transformed by her handy aroma and her teasing. Her legs snaked around his back, as he began to position himself into her. She molded around him like a second skin. He couldn't believe how tight her twat had gotten. She was wet and he started to increase his pace, pulling back until only the head was inside her, and then quickly slamming forward making her cream out with ecstasy. Maybe she was faking to stroke his ego. But Sam couldn't tell if she was. "Harder!: She begged him. He started to increase his pace even more, feeling her attempt to suck him deeper inside her wetness. Suddenly she tensed up, convulsing uncontrollably as she came. "Uhhggghh, oh my God, I'm cumming Sam," she groaned pressing against him. He continued to plunge his manhood as far as he could go inside. Hw was paralyzed with cum bliss, as he had on orgasm also. He gave a few more final thrust before pulling out. His breathing was heavy as he told her, "I love you Shirley," as he rolled over. "I love you too Sam." She got up and went and took a hot shower knowing she took an offer from someone who wasn't compatible with her, but was of her attraction. This was confusion as it's best. Shirley and Sam had planned their marriage ceremony for May of 2002. Sharan had received three years from the Feds and was placed in a Federal facility in Ashland Kentucky.

The next month they were over at the Newport on the Levy at the Funny Bone. Shirley, Sam Pedro, Rachelle, Chucky, Renee and Chucky's best friend Ronnie Roche girl Tayama. Ronnie Roche was a comedian out of Dayton Ohio. Tayama was a plus sized girl who was very beautiful. She was dark in complexion like Shirley with much style. Her hair was done nicely, her nails were perfectly manicured and she had on designer clothes. She was an Editor for a Publishing company out of Columbus Ohio. Renee was now four months pregnant and she was definitely showing. Bernie Mac and Delray were opening up for Ronnie Roche, because it was his tour.

They had a ball at the Funny Bone that night and went to Perkins afterwards to eat. Chucky introduced everyone to Ronnie Roche and they got autographs and pictures with the famous comedian.

The trend of commercial business and inspirational partnership was connecting the pieces to their life puzzle. Every turn made heads turn with whispering tongues of compassion not understanding the effects of the outgoing love that was building between couples searching for a way out. Like the royal Crown cola everybody wanted a sip of the good life. No one wanted confusion at this point, especially Shirley Thomas. All the ingredients Carbonated Water, High friction, Corn Syrup, Caramel color, Phosphoric Acid, Caffeine, Natural flavors, Acacia gum and Citric Acid made up the taste that would quench anyone's thirst in life and this dark bottle of Shirley Thomas was quenching Sam's thirst for her love and companionship. It was official; they were engaged only being involved for three and a half months. Shirley realized that you only live once and she wanted to show Thomas Patterson she was over him. Shirley and Sam were intimate over the next few months before going to New Jersey to meet Shirley's parents.

CHAPER TWELEVE
Meet the Parent's

It was a week before Christmas when Shirley and Sam got I-71 Northbound heading for Camden, New Jersey. It was good weather to travel in during this time of year when it was suppose to look like winter. They took Sam's 600 Benz. When they entered West Virginia they took pictures in the mountains all the way outside the Pennsylvania Turn-Pike. When they reached Shirley's parents house in New Jersey it was 8pm. It took them exactly fourteen hours to get there. When they pulled in the drive-way of her parent's house, Shirley's dog Lucky ran to the car barking and wagging his tail. "I hope he doesn't bite Shirl." Sam made the comment putting the car in park killing the engine. "Who Lucky? He's just hyper Sam." She got out the car and Lucky jumped on her. There wasn't any snow on the ground, but it was fairly cold out.

"Hey Boy, hey Lucky you miss me boy?" as Shirley was petting him and you could see her breath fog the air. Then her two sisters came to the door and opened it to see their big sister. "Mama, Daddy Shirley's here." Her youngest sister Trina yelled through the house. Shirley's other sister handed her sister her coat and they both came out the door together to go greet their sister. Sam was now standing outside the car petting Lucky. Shirley sisters walked up. She smiled at her sister. "Hey Shirl," that was Sherrie the middle sister who looked like Shirley. Shirley waved her hand and said, "Trina and Sherrie this is my fiancé Sam." They looked over Sam and he looked back at them. "Hi," as Sam put his hands in his pocket. "Hi, so you are my future brother-in-law?" Trina asked Sam. "Yeah that's me." He answered.

"Whose car is this? It's tight." Trina asked her sister.

"It's Sam's car Trina." Shirley told her, but Sam corrected her. "Trina this is our car," as Shirley looked at him crazy in complete chock. "Well let's go in it's freezing out here." Shirley suggested. When they got up on the porch her mom and dad were in the door-way. "Hey baby," as her mother greeted her with a hug and a kiss. "Come here Pumpkin and give your daddy a hug and a kiss." The man was husky standing at 6'5" around three hundred pounds. He grabbed his daughter in his arms swallowing her up. Sam was behind Trina and Sherrie coming in the house. He released her and said. "Now where this guy trying to marry my baby?" Her dad asked. "Yeah Shirley where is my future son-in-law?" Her mom asked. Trina and Sherrie stepped to the side and Sam stood there with Lucky. "Sam come and meet my parent's." Shirley waved him over to where they were standing in the front hallway. Sam walked over to where her parent's were standing. "Sam come give me a hug," as Shirley mom hugged him. "I've heard so much about you Samuel, glad to meet you." She released her hold from Sam. "It's a pleasure to meet you too Mrs. Thomas." Sam told her. "How are you doing son?" as Shirley dad extended his hand to Sam, and then he pulled him close to him giving him a big hug. "I'm fine sir and yourself?" as Sam was trying to catch his breath. "I'm good, real good. My name is Melvin. I don't go by that Mr. Thomas bull crap, just call me Mel. As soon as ya'll get washed up we can eat dinner." Her dad walked off adding, "Boy I'm hungry." He was holding his stomach. Everyone made their exit and Sam went out to the car to get their small hygiene bag and Lucky followed him. Lucky was a brownish red boxer mixed with a Rottweiler and his tail was clipped. They freshen up and sat at the dinner table in the

Huge dinning room. It had a small chandelier hanging from the ceiling. Sam pulled out Shirley's chair for her showing her parents he had skills of a gentleman. Positioned at the head of the table was Big Mel, Shirley's Dad, and to his right were Sherrie and Trina. To his left were Shirley and Sam. At the other end was Shirley's mom. There was six dishes on the table which consisted of Mac & Cheese, Spinach, corn on the cob, tossed salad, homemade biscuits and fried chicken. There was two pitchers on the table, one filled with water and the other one filled with Ice Tea and Lemons.

"Sam can you say the grace please?" Shirley's mom asked him.

"I will this is my house." Big Mel told his wife. "It's okay Big Mel, I can bless the food." Sam replied. Everyone reached around the table making an inclination by holding hands. Sam bowed their head and everyone else did the same in silence. **" Lord give us this Daily Bread to strengthen out bodies with nourishment. Let us take in this meal Mr. and Mrs. Thomas has prepared for us into our temple you created. And please Lord help those in need who still suffer from 911. With your everlasting love heavenly Father, Amen."** Everyone else at the table said, "Amen," as they lifted their heads. Shirley didn't know, and she didn't question his Faith.

"Annie Mae pass me the chicken, I'm starving," as Shirley's mom passed the chicken to Sam and he could shuffle it off to Shirley to reach her husband.

"Pass your glass around if you would like some Ice Tea." Trina told everyone, because it was in front of her.

"So Samuel, what do you do for a living again?" Big Mel asked him not taking his eyes of the food.

"I have my own business, a detail shop." Sam told him.

"So you maintenance cars. How much money you make a year?' Big Mel asked him.

"Well Mel, that depends on the season, but in a year of real good business I subject to make between sixty and seven thousand." Sam told him.

"Are you serious? That's a lot of money just washing cars." Mel said.

"Yes sir. I receive business from Louisville, Chicago, Cleveland, Dayton and Toledo. Parts of Indiana, sometimes St. Louis and West Virginia. I've had customers come from Detroit, L.A. and Texas to get their cars detailed. We just don't wash cars, we customize them also." Sam was proud of his business.

"What school did you go to?" Mel asked him.

"I went to Western Hills and then to Xavier University and received a B.A. in Business Communications." Sam answered him and Shirley eyes lit up.

He never told her his education back ground. She never asked.

"I went to West High myself. Shirley also graduated from there." Her dad told it all.

Sam looked at Shirley, because he didn't know that either. Did they really know one another to take it to that next step?

"So when is the big day Sam?" Shirley mother cut in.

"We are looking at May the 7th, right before Mother's day." Sam answered her.

"So how much will I have to spend on this wedding?" Her dad asked Sam.

"Not a dime sir, I'm going to pay for it." Sam announced to her family.

"No way Sam we would like to help out.' Shirley mom told him.

"Shut up Annie Mae, the boy wants to pay for his own wedding, so let him. Sorry about my wife I apologize for her rudeness." Big Mel told him.

"It's okay Mel, Mrs. Thomas I'll take care of everything." Sam assured her.

They continued to eat dinner talking and everyone had questions for Sam.

After dinner Mel and Sam went into the Den to have a drink. Then Mel invited him to go to Atlantic City for a little gambling. It was around 10:00 pm. The women cleaned the table and were washing dishes. Sam told Shirley he was going to Atlantic City with her dad. Shirley's dad had a gambling habit and that was his way to get out of the house.

They drove Mrs. Thomas 2002 XKR convertible Jaguar that Mr. Thomas bought her for her birthday. It was cherry red with low profile tires. The interior was white with white leather bucket seats. It was a two door Coupe.

Sam had on his leather and brocade jacket by Versace and he put on his suede Wallabee boots. While they were on their way to Atlantic City the women were finishing up in the kitchen.

………………………………...

"Mama what do you think about Sam?" Shirley asked her mom.

"Well, he's a gentleman from what I see, but he's probably to good to be true. Shirley I don't have to wake to him, you will." She told her oldest daughter.

I know mom, but I just wanted you and dad's blessings."

"Shirley you have our blessings, as long as you are happy." Trina cut in.

"Shirl hurry up so we can go upstairs to talk." Trina had her hands on her hips.

"Girl your sister will be here for two weeks. With your hot ass." Her mom told her.

"Here I come Trine." Shirley hugged her moms and said,

"Thanks mom."

---By this time Sam and Mr. Thomas was entering the Casino. "I'm going to the Black Jack table Sam, are you joining me?"

"Yeah Mel I'll try my luck." Sam followed him to the Black Jack table.

They circled around a few crap tables and passed a poker table before grabbing two seats at the Black table. "Can I have three hundred dollars worth of chips please?" Mel asked the dealer. "Do you want me to deal you in sir?" The dealer asked Mel. "Sure!" Sam just watched , as Mr. Thomas lost three straight hands. Sam saw another attraction going on in the Casino. It was a contest involving females. He left the table unnoticed circling back around the tables to the other side of the Casino. Females were every-where dressed in the skimpiest of clothes. All types of women.

It was the Urban Models contest presented by Kay Slay who was entertaining the crowd in fashionable bikinis. From Fendi Gucci, Vera Wang, Louis Vutton, Ralph Lauren, Baby Phat, Prada and more. The music was playing as the MC was announcing the models participating in the contest.

A model entered the small runway and the MC announced her.

"We have Ms. Avalon "Da-A-Game from Miami fl. By ways of Newark, New Jer-

sey. She's wearing a G-string one unit all white swimsuit. She's 5'7" with measurements of 34D-26-42." She strolled down the runway and back. "Next we have Ms. Ali Milan from Los Angeles California. She's in an all black G-string bikini by Baby
Phat. She stands at a towering 5'9" and her measurements are 36 DD-26-42," as the tall thick white girl strutted down the runway. "Next we have from the Bronx New York. She's rocking a blue short shirt and some white boy shorts. Her figure is 34-27-42." She looked like she was Latino. Sam was taking all this in getting aroused looking at these females.

"Coming to the stage we have beautiful and talented Ms. Montana Rite from Brooklyn New York. She has everything fella's, from a 34 c bust, 26" waist and succulent 43" ass-oops I mean around the hips. She stands 5'8" and has legs for days. She is wearing a Gucci bikini designed by Jua. Get a good look, because they don't make them like this any more." She was getting whistles and everything from the crowd, and more from the women who were watching.

"Last but not lest we have L.A. from V.A. wearing a white t-shirt half cut, some tight pin striped Boy shorts and heels. She stands at 5'2" with the figure of 34-28-46. She can definitely shake what her mama gave her." as she walked down the runway getting jiggy with it. She really made her booty clap. The Mc was fanning himself. "Boy on boy, I don't know about ya'll, but a player like me need a drink. Please give all the contestants a hand." Everyone was clapping and whistling.

"Please give a round of applause for our judges, The Elliot sisters Theresa and Daneen out of Detroit. The beautiful Jazz from Boston, Ms. Solea and Kyra Chaos from Hampton VA." He waited for the crowd to settle down. "Now let's bring out last years winner Ms Bianca Simms from London England." She came out in Baby Phat see-thru night gown all white. You could see that she had on a two piece underneath the gown which was all white. "Just for those who don't know, but Bianca won last year from the measurements of 34-25-40 standing at 5'5" when she reached the MC she hugged him. "Ms. Bianca would you like to say something to the ladies who are competing?"

She grabbed the Mic. and said. "Good luck ladies," as she smiled and waved her hand to the audience walking off the stage.

"There you have it people last years winner. Now who is going to be crowned 2001 Urban Model of the year? DJ let me get some Jay-Z before we crown the winner."

The DJ was playing "Girls" by Jay-Z.

"Can all the contestants please return to the stage." as all the beautiful ladies came back stage. "Cut the music DJ. Judges do we have a winner?" The judges nodded to the MC. Solea handed him a piece of paper. "Drum roll please. Na'll I'm kidding. The 2001 Urban Model of the year goes to Montana rite out of Brooklyn, New York." She was in shock covering her mouth in surprise. She walked towards the MC and Bianca to receive her crown after hugging a few other models she competed against.

Then Mary Jane a.k.a. the Cocaine cowgirl from Atlanta was performing in the Casino for this event. She had on a pair of Low Rida jeans, a loose fitting blouse some black Stiletto boots and a string of pearls.

Sam just looked and then walked away towards the bar. He was brick in his pants from watching all the contestants model. He saw an attractive blonde who was in a rouge bikini and matching heels sitting at the bar having a drink.

Sam eased up to the bar and ordered him a drink. This was the finest Casino bunny he'd ever seen. She looked familiar and he had to know if this blonde was who he thought she was. He tapped her on the shoulder. "Excuse me Maria, is that you?" She turned around half way looking Sam directly in the eyes. "Yeah it's me, and who the hell are you?" She asked him.

"I'm Sam, E's friend from Cincinnati, remember me?" Sam smiled at her.

"The Sam who was at the car show in Phoenix, with the lil cute Honda?" She asked.

"Yeah that's me, and what are you doing in New Jersey, especially Atlantic City?" She took another sip of her drink and said, "Shit I'm working, turning tricks trying to live." She took another sip of her drink throwing her head back.

"What's up with E?" Sam asked about her boyfriend.

"Shit I don't know. I got tired of fucking him and his home boys fro free, so I left Arizona." Sam had to shoot his shot. He been had the hot's for her.

"So are you busy right now Maria?" Sam asked her.

"Why Sam?" as she turned completely around opening her legs putting her hands on her thighs. Sam could see her print at this angle.

"Because I would love to see you naked." He smiled at her.

"Is that so?" Maria asked him.

"Yeah, I've wanted you every since I seen you over E's when I first started coming to Arizona in 1998." Sam took a sip of his drink.

"Well I just started my break. I have an hour, so do you have a room in the Casino?" She relaxed her hands on her thighs. " No, I'm here with a friend who lives in Camden." She eased off the bar stool. "Well I have a room upstairs, let's go and it's going to cost you." She walked in front of him showing her 38" hips. She was a 36DD-23-38 and her heels made her look taller than she were. Sam lust was building as they got on the elevator to reach the fifth floor. As soon as they reached the inside of the hotel room Maria took it upon herself to unbuckle Sam's belt and pull his pants and boxers down to his ankles. Sam was stiff as a dead man's body. "Ooh it's true. I expected your cock to be this fat gorgeous," as she squealed. He gasped out as she bent down, and then breathed heavily on his swollen head.

"Oh damn." He moaned. "You like that huh?" She asked him. "Oh hell yeah Maria." He stood there tensing up. "Well you'll really love this."

She started flicking her tongue over his tribal ridge, and then she took him in her mouth inch by inch. She began to fondle his balls, as she stroked him with her mouth.

She repeated this motion several times and then said, "Now I need you in me Sam." as she sighed. "Fill me up, fill my wet pussy up with your hot steamy cum. You hot faceable Stud you." she stood up and walked over to the bed.

She laid down pulling off her sting bikini. Seeing her huge hard pink nipples and cute cut little bush was more than he could stand. Out of no respect for his future bride, Sam didn't use any protection coming out of one leg walking over towards her falling down on top of her. He steadied himself to enter her cave of pleasure. He slid himself in, and felt her lips swell and moisten. He knew this blonde was ready for him. They moaned simultaneously as he pushed inside her. She grabbed him tight around his back and squeezed her thighs around his body. "That's it Sam fuck me!" she cried out.

"Keep fucking me like nothing else on the planet matters." She uttered every word with his pumps. "Oh Sam I love your thick fat cock." She gasped. Sam was pushing and pumping furiously inside her wet hot pussy. "Harder, harder," as she demanded him digging her nails into his ass and pumping upward to meet his thrust. She gave a final thrust against him. Gripping him tightly as she cried out contorting her flushed face, as she climaxed. They moaned so loud, because Sam was cumming inside of her, they thought the neighbors would hear them.

Meanwhile back at Shirley's parents house she was in a conference with her two teen-age sisters. Trina was sixteen and Sherrie was seventeen. Trina was courageous and very out spoken. "So Shirl, how old were you when you first had sex?" Trina asked her big sister. Shirley looked at her and said, "Girl I was fourteen, why you ask?" Trina put her down rubbing her thigh and replied, "Because I have a boyfriend and he wants to do it, but I'm scared it's going to hurt, and I told him I would just give him a blow job." Shirley rubbed her little sister's hand. "It's going to hurt breaking your hymen, you might even start bleeding. I know I did," As Shirley eased her own hand in her crotch area remembering how it felt. Her mind state was concern her little sister, but she knew eventually her little sister would experiment with sex. "Oh that sounds painful Shirley. So what about a blow job, can you teach me?" Shirley was in shock to hear her mention that. Her little sister was serious, because her eyes never left Shirley's face. "Girl a blow job? Trina you don't just go putting your mouth on any ole dick."

Even her older sister Sherrie had to comment on that. "Yeah Trina she's right."

Trina eyes removed from Shirley momentarily to respond to Sherrie. She snapped her head back and smacked her lips together. "shut up Sherrie you don't know anything, you're still a virgin too." She then turned back to Shirley saying, "Plus I love him Shirl." Trina gave her the puppy dog eyes and the saddest face. She was her baby sister and no matter how many times she would tell her no, she knew Trina would continue to ask or just go all out and try it on her own. "Alright Trina if you insist. Go get me a ba-nana or a carrot" Trina hopped up immediately and went to get what her sister asked for. She brought her back both running to the room they were in, which was Shirley's old room. Shirley couldn't quite remember how she mastered the art of giving a man oral sex, but she did. Shirley took the banana first and held it firmly in her hand. "Trina first you grip his thing like this after it's hard, and then you lick the top of the head gen-tly like this," as Shirley was demonstrating with the banana. . "Then you go to the sides like it's an ice cream cone going up and down. After that you ease off of it then make an "O" shape with your mouth gong down the top of it." She showed her the proper way to do it. "Don't try to take it all in at once or you'll gag. Make sure your teeth don't get in the way. Repeat this motion over and over, even go down and suck his testicles a few times, he'll let you know if your doing a good job with his moans and grunts. Now you try it with the carrot."

Shirley handed her the carrot. Trina was having second thoughts, but she went ahead and tried it. "Like this Shirl?" as Trina was performing the action.

"Yeah Trina, but it a little more definition." Shirley knew she was teaching her little sister right, but wrong and her parents would be disappointed at her for teaching her little sisters a sex act.

She thought if her siblings needed her, then she had to be there for them whether right or wrong. Sherrie was taking all this in for herself also. Trina all of sudden came up with another idea. She stops practicing and said, "Shirl, what if I watch you do it to Sam."

Shirley looked at her long and hard. "You'll love that. Na'll you can't watch me do my man girl. Shit you might as well watch an adult movie." Shirley told her.

Trina put her hand over her head and then said, "What's that Shirl?" She asked her.

Shirley was amazed, because Trina was already experimenting with marijuana, but was dumb founded to a lot of other things.

"It's a porno goofy." Shirley said.

Trina had a dumb look on her face. "Oh, will you get me one?"

Shirley didn't want to be a party spoiler, but she had to tell her no. "quit tripping Trina, you don't need to be doing it anyway. You need to be worrying about graduating and going to college and not sex. You need to see if that lil boy really likes you and not what's between your legs." Shirley told her little sister.

Shirley started kicking knowledge to her little sisters about the hearts of men and the evil they do to women. She dropped a ball on them making Trina have second thoughts about having any sexual contact with a boy until she was ready and the time was right. Shirley taught then sex acts, but flipped the game on them telling them about unwanted pregnancy and STD's they could contract from unprotected sex. It made Sherrie and Trina stomach's turn upside down. They laughed when needed and they got serious when it called for it.

. . . .

...

Back at the Casino Sam had separated from Maria and ran back into Mr. Thomas at the bar. The husky giant of a man was having a drink when Sam pulled up. He circled around him from the opposite side letting Mr. Thomas think he was coming from the slot machines and not from upstairs in one of the casino hotel rooms.

"Hey Mel, are you finished?" Sam took a seat right beside him.

"Yeah Sam I've been looking for you. I hit big at the black jack table. I won thirty-five hundred not counting the three hundred I lost. So where did you go?" He asked Sam. Sam wasn't really paying Mr. Thomas too much attention still not believing what he just did with Maria in New Jersey while he was with his fiancée dad. His head was down.

"Sam did you hear me?" Mr. Thomas asked him again.

He snapped out of his train of thought. "Yeah I heard you Mel. I was over at the slot machines and I lost like four hundred dollars." He knew this day would probably come back to haunt him someway, somehow. He always wanted to sleep with her, and so be it, it had to happen. A cheap thrill for nothing, because Maria didn't even charge him.

"Here," as Mr. Thomas gave him four hundred dollars.

"No thanks Mel, I can't take that." Sam told him.

"Go ahead, it's free money, it will replace what you lost." Mr. Thomas told him.

"If you insist Mel," as Sam took the money.

"Do you want a drink Sam?" Mr. Thomas asked him. Sam thought about it and declined.

"No thanks Mel, are you ready to go?" Sam asked him.

Mr. Thomas rubbed the rim of his glass firmly and then said, "Yeah let me finish my drink first." He turned the glass up to his lips and then guzzled the rest.

They left the casino heading back to Camden. They got in at around 3am and Shirley was in the den waiting on him. They walked pass the den and Shirley was up.

"Hey daddy I see ya'll made it back." Shirley said to them and her daddy didn't even look to acknowledge his daughter. He kept it moving up the stairs saying, "Good-night pumpkin."

Sam came in the den with a tired look. "Hey baby, I'm about to go get our bags from the car." He was trying to figure out how he would get in the shower to wash Maria's scent before Shirley would detect it. He knew he was playing with fire.

"Sam, I already got our bags while you were at the casino."

He was surprised. "Oh."

She was now getting up off the leather sofa chair. She grabbed him around his neck holding him. "So did you have a good time?" Shirley asked him.

Not wanting her this close to him before he cleaned up, he hurried up and answered.

"Yeah I enjoyed myself. Let me go take a shower I have casino smoke on all over me."

He was feeling guilty about his actions hours ago.

"Okay baby." She kissed him on the lips.

"Where are we sleeping Shirl?" He wanted to get undress and take a nice hot shower. "In my old room. It's upstairs all the way down the hall, the last door on the right. The bathroom is two doors up on the right from my room." She told him and he separated himself from her going upstairs to take a shower. Shirley went and got her a glass of water. She then went upstairs to check on him in the shower. She decided to get in with him. She started washing his back for him and then noticed a strand of blonde hair in his hair. "Baby, who you been kissing on, a white girl?" Shirley asked him. He turned around quickly, because he was caught off guard. "What are you talking about Shirl?" He asked.

She turned him back around to remove the hair. "Come here you have other people hair in yours," as she removed the strand of hair. He turned back around to see the strand of hair she was holding in her fingertips.

"That was probably one those females standing over me and your dad at the card table, because he was winning like crazy" He told her.

"For a minute there I thought you was cheating on me with a snow bunny," as she smiled at him. They got back to Shirley's room and she wanted to have sex, but Sam claimed he was beat, after all he drove all those hours to Camden from Ohio. She respected his wishes and they went to sleep in each others arms.

………………………………...

...The days grew vivid and long leading up to Christmas. It snowed two days before Christmas and Shirley decided to play with Sam in the snow. The Doppler Weather station predicted up to eight inches of snow. But it only snowed two to four inches. They took Lucky outside to build a snowman with them. Lucky was amazed from the snow like always eating the snow gracefully playing in it.

Enjoying each other they played in the snow like two teenagers dealing with puppy love. They almost caught frost bite before going back inside to warm up and get cozy by the fire place her parents had in the living room. They cuddled on the couch drinking co -co with marshmallows snuggled in a blanket. They were intimate during the week leading up to Christmas having several pleasurable moments of unprotected sex. Shirley started

taking her birth control, because she was sure to get pregnant from all the times Sam released inside her vagina walls.

It was Christmas Eve and Shirley was giving her mom and dad their gifts. She bought her mom a diamond Swiss Corum and her dad a David Yurman Watch with a black lizard leather band. She brought both of her sisters designer Tennis bracelets with their initials engraved in them. She also managed to buy Trina a Porn D.V.D. She got Lucky a solid three inch thick bone with marrow. Shirley made sure that the gifts were from her and Sam. She didn't give Trina the Porno in front of her parents. Her mom and dad brought Sam a leather Eel skin wallet by Perry Ellis and got Shirley gift certificated for fifteen hundred dollars.

Later on that night early morning around 2:00 a.m. Shirley and Sam were having sex. Sam was engulfed between Shirley's legs where she was grabbing the bed post enjoying Sam's tongue inside her. The door was now ajar and she seen a pair of mysterious eyes looking at them even thought it was pitch black in her room. Shirley wasn't startled because she knew who was watching them. She didn't give Sam a blow job, but she did perform for the watching eyes. The next day was Christmas and the Thomas family along with Sam had a wonderful Christmas. They ate gracefully and after dinner they played cards, sang Christmas carols and drunk eggnog. Shirley was happy feeling loved and making a sense of why she was now happy.

Two days after Christmas Sam and Shirley was packing the Benz with their luggage. When Sam was going back in the house Trina came out to the car with Shirley while she was positioning a few bags in the car. Trina stood there for a moment unnoticed and then

Shirley saw her sister. "Hey lil sis, what's up?" Trina batted her eyes and said ,

"Nothing, I'm going to miss you." Shirley hugged her sister and said,

"I'm going to miss you too Trina."

Trina felt the tight embrace. "Thanks for the D.V.D. Shirl. I think sex is over rated and those females in the move are too nasty. They take it in every hole with ease like it doesn't hurt. I know some of those guys things got to hurt. I think I'll wait until I'm grown before I experiment with sex." Shirley hugged her again. She wanted to hear that instead of a few months down the road that she contracted a disease or was pregnant. Shirley smiled and said,

"Trina you have a lot of living to do and you are not missing out on anything. You're right sex is over rated."

Trina smiled at her big sister. " I'm coming to Cincinnati this summer with you for my summer vacation." Shirley couldn't deny her that opportunity, but she was to let it be known to her that she knew she was the one watching her and Sam having sex.

"Okay, but I won't allow for you to be peeping in my room while I'm having sex with my man." Shirley said to her little sister and Trina looked at her crazy like she was busted.

"Shirl you saw me?" Shirley tilted her head and said,

"Yeah I saw your nasty butt, that's why I gave you a show, because I usually don't do him like that." Shirley told her and Trina blushed a little.

" Shirl do that feel good when a man eats you out?" Trina asked her. Shirley went back to square one dealing with her sister's curiosity. She didn't lie to her though. "Hell yeah girl, as a matter of fact don't ever do a man unless he does you." Trina took that part in.

"Well ya'll have a safe trip home Shirl and I'll call you, but I am coming down there this summer." Trina said and she hugged her sister again.

"Okay we'll be waiting on you." Shirley said.

Then Lucky, Sherrie, Mr. and Mrs. Thomas came out the house with Samto see them off.

CHAPTER THIRTEEN
An Unfamiliar Visit

Sam and Shirley left Camden, New Jersey heading back to Cincinnati. When they reached the outskirts of Cincinnati Sam dropped Shirley off at home in Symmes Township. She was more intuit about her new found engagement especially after him meeting her parent's. She was now relaxed in her own setting and it showed in her face, mind, body and soul. She thought out of the three, being Rachelle, Renee, and herself that she was happier and in control of her own destiny. Renee was now seven months pregnant and her stomach was way out there.

That following week on New Years Eve Shirley found herself with Sam in Brandy's nightclub. They were surrounded by the Trap Boys and their female companions. Boobie was with this chick name Star and Ren Mack was with his new girlfriend K.K. Pedro and Rachelle even showed up to bring in the New Year with Shirley. The nightclub was packed as everyone partied bringing in the New Year of 2002.

What New Year resolution was brilliant and going to get put into play? Who knew what the New Year had to offer better then those ready to fulfill their own destiny. Shirley had excused herself to use the restroom. While she was in the ladies room using it, she noticed an unfamiliar discharge in her panties on her panty liner. She was in disgust, as she removed her panty liner from her panties. She examined it closely and smells the discharge. It was awful.

"That's not right Shirl. Something is wrong with your coochie girl," as she disposed the panty liner. She wiped herself and it seemed like the smell more agitated after she did that. It was a bad odor. "Damn I hope I don't have a urinary infection or that Calgon done messed my stuff up," She fixed her clothes and washed her hands. She never gave the thought of her having a STD. She was too naïve.

When she came out of the restroom she saw Ren Mack standing alone. His girlfriend was on the dance floor along with Boobie and Star. Pedro and Rachelle were sitting at a table. Sam was discussing some sort of business at the Bar with a heavy set man. It gave Shirley time to talk with Ren. She liked his swag, because he spoke with much knowledge and respect. He always left her with a subliminal message. She stood next to him. Ren was focused on his girlfriend. K.K. was a redbone female standing at 6'1 with the possible measurements of 36D-26-42. She was stacked and her stomach was flat. Her white pants showcased every curve she possessed. She had on sleeveless blouse that tied around the neck and opened at her cleavage. Then her three inch heels made her even taller, but sexy. Her hair was done nice and he nails were carefully manicured. She was pretty. Ren was sure he had a Stallion, a super model, a sure winner in K.K. She resembled the Urban Model Cubana Lust from Miami, but she was much taller. Ren then so happens to take his eyes off his girlfriend to notice Shirley next to him. She smiled at him and he smiled back taking a sip of his drink. Shirley told him over the loud

music. "She's a handful huh Ren?" Because she saw that Ren had his eye on her. He didn't hear her clearly.

"What did you say Shirley?" he asked her,.

"I said she must be a handful."

He knew she was absolutely that and some. "She's more then enough for one man to handle, but I love her." he confessed to Shirley taking another sip of his drink.

"She's beautiful Ren, and I hope you treat her right. You know after every concert you do some female will want to give Ren Mack her body." Shirley smiled at him showing him her pearly whites.

"Shirl I'm through with that lifestyle. I'm on some grown man right now. And she's the reason to be. We've been dating for three months now and tonight I'm going to ask her to marry me." Ren said.

Shirley slapped him on the shoulder. "Are you serious Ren?"

"Yeah, I'm serious," as he retrieved a ring box from his pants pocket showing Shirley the ring.

"Ren that's beautiful. She's a good catch. I'm jealous." Shirley smiled at him.

"Well you only live once. You and Sam inspired me to have a serious relationship. Plus I want to sct an example to my son Lil Ren." He said and Shirley lifted her eyebrow a little and titled her head.

"Ren Jr.! There are two of you Ren" Shirley stepped back a little.

"Yep Lil Ren Mackie Jr. He's six." He told her.

"So you go by Ren Mack, that's short for Ren Mackie?" She looked at him with a stare.

"Yeah that's my government, Ren Mackie?' Shirley now wanted to know what his small conversation was about form earlier he was having with Sam.

"Ren what's a glass house? I heard you mentioning it to Sam earlier." Shirley was curious about him and Sam's conversation, because it sounded rather interesting to her ears. Brother J. and DJ Rob G. were the DJ's making the tunes come out of the speakers in Brandy's nightclub this New Years Eve.

They were mixing "Time for some Action" by Redman with L.L. Cool J.

"Mama Said Knock You Out" and then N.W.A's "Straight Outta Compton" and Eric B. and Rakim "I Ain't No Joke."

Ren looked at Shirley seriously and began to beak it down for her after taking another sip of his drink.

*"Shirley living in a glass house leaves you ignorant and numb to what's around you. With all the glass around you its easy to see objects outside the house, but you can't feel and know what the objects are about until you open a window and get smacked in the face by the win*d.*"* He paused a moment and the DJ was mixing a series of EPMD songs together.

"The wind brings the vibe of everything that exits outside your world. In this case every action has a reaction and with that reaction comes a vibe. The window that was open is really your eyes. The eyes don't always see what they think they do, in fact the glass house, most people choose to live in, could be considered to be a magician's magic box," as he sipped his drink once more. *"The box contains an illusion and perception which pollute the mind. If TV's need a converter box to better the reception, what's the*

answer for denial? If everybody is real, who is fake? If everybody sells drugs, who the users? It can't be stealing if there's no thief. The world is how we see it. It doesn't take 20/20 vision to see it clear. I know fire burns and I don't have to stick my hand in it to know it. So why deal with people who are capable of burning you." He was now pointing in Shirley's face making sure he had her attention.

"Shirley you are smart, but you are in the glass house, so be careful, because everyone is not who they claim to be. The fake person is willing to bet their real and solid, but only the real can admit their flaws. It's like smelling the rain before it comes. You're a lawyer and you can pretty much determine when a person is guilty or not from their reactions. So use your everyday life experience now in your life and you'll see through the glass house. Everything comes to the light." Ren downed the rest of his drink and K.K. was approaching them. Shirley was stuck, because she didn't catch the message he was telling her. She wanted to ask him more and to get what he was trying to tell her. He dropped her some jewels, but where was he going with it?

"Oh Shirl, that came from this guy name Chris White. I'm about to get another drink, do you want one?" He asked her.

She shook her head "no". K.K. arrived by them and smiled at Shirley and then kissed Ren. He formally introduced them and the two walked off leaving Shirley standing there.

What was he getting at? Shirley wondered. She was now curious, but her biggest problem for her now was this uncertain discharge she was having. She stood there with a blank expression on her face.

Sam came over to where she was standing to get cozy with her before the count down. He introduced her to his big cousin Sunny Red from Walnut Hills. Sunny Red wanted to retain her for future encounters he might have with the law, being he was the man, a major distributor of cocaine in that area including Avondale, Evanston and Mt. Auburn. They closed a deal and Sunny Red even gave her a retainer fee right there on the spot. 20 thousand in big bills, which Shirley secured it in her Gucci purse that matched her Gucci heels.

When the count down began Ren Mack was on his knee proposing to K.K. letting her know he wanted to take their relationship to the next level.

The night was fabulous regardless that she had a discharge and a bad odor coming from her vagina. She reframed from giving Sam any sex that early morning when they returned to his house. She told him she think she had a bacterial infection from the Kalgan she used the other day. They spent New Years day together.

....

The next day which was January the 2nd, Shirley went to work from Sam's house. After handling a few pro-bono cases as the firm, she called the clinic to make an appointment. She needed a pelvic exam and to renew her birth control. It was around 10 a.m. when she called and someone had canceled their appointment for 1p.m. that afternoon. So Shirley decided to leave work early and make that appointment. She wanted to know why her pussy was in this condition. She left her office heading to Madisonville. Her regular doctor was in this time. She checked in with the receptionist and minutes later she ran into Dr. Bosh.

"Hello Ms. Thomas, how are you doing today?" He asked her. Shirley looked up at him.
"Hello Dr. Bosh, I'm fine and yourself?" She said.
"I'm okay. So what brings you to the clinic in this weather?" He stood over her, because

she was sitting down.

"I'm getting a refill on the birth control you recommended and a pelvic exam, it's that time again. The birth control is working well too." She gave him a big beautiful smile. He placed his big hands on her shoulders. "I'm glad to hear that. I think your doctor is here today, is it doctor Michelle McDonald?" He asked her. Shirley wanted to remove his hands badly from her shoulders, but she stayed professional.

"Yes that's my doctor. Well Dr. Bosh it was nice seeing you, I think they are calling my name." She looked at him. He removed his hands.

"Okay, bye Mrs. Thomas and you take care." He replied. "I will." She said and watched him walk off. She gave a fake little frown and said, "Yuk! His hands are gross looking. And he thought I was going to let him play in my pussy with those huge wrinkle ugly hands of his, hell to the na'll." She said herself.

Then out of nowhere the same medical assistant from last year when her and Sharan were at the clinic came and got her from the waiting area. She placed Shirley in the same exact examining room. Mi-Mi introduced herself not remembering Shirley from her new hair due. She took the initial vitals that were needed. Then the same RN Lutisha came in the room to check other things from Shirley, getting a urine sample and blood. Then she took a sample from her discharge after Shirley told her about the smell and everything. She witnesses it for herself and the RN almost choked.

About twenty minutes later Dr. McDonald came into the examining room. Shirley was in a gown naked underneath lying on the examining table. Dr. McDonald made her spread her legs and started poking her fingers inside of Shirley with her surgical gloves and instruments.

"Ms. Thomas have you notice any difference in your urine or discharge lately?" She asked Shirley.

Shirley closed her eyes and said, "Yes, I just noticed it New years Eve." She kept feeling the doctor dig inside her vagina.

"It looks like you have some bacteria along your vagina walls," as she still had her fingers inside Shirley with the instrument and a mirror on the end of it.

"Is it bad Dr. McDonald?" She asked her.

"I don't know what it is until, the test comes back from our lab. I can treat it, but hopefully it's nothing to serious." The doctor came from inside her removing her gloves.

"We'll see what type of bacteria you have in a minute. Lutisha should be getting the results from our lab in a few. I'll be back." The doctor told her and left the room. Shirley sat up and was nervously waiting for the results.

Minutes later the Dr. and RN had returned with the results. The Dr. had a chart and the RN had a huge needle and a small bottle of vaccine.

"Ms. Thomas, we have a slight problem, you've contracted Chlamydia, but it's in its earliest stage and that's good." The doctor told her.

Shirley couldn't believe what she just heard. "What?" She said loudly. "Chlamydia?"

"Yes Ms. Thomas, Chlamydia. How many sex partners have you come in contact with over the last month and a half?" The doctor asked her.

"Only one," as a tear ran down her dark cheek bone. She was embarrassed and now angry.

"How many partners has that one had?" The doctor asked her.

Shirley couldn't focus at this point and the doctor was asking her a question that only Sam could answer. "I don't know, but I'm going to kill that son of a bitch." Shirley was mad. Her arms were now folded as more tears ran down her face.

"Well you need to contact him so he can be treated also." The doctor told her.

Shirley wanted to scream to the top of her lungs. "His name is Samuel Holston, he lives at 3061 Hackberry Ave. His number is 221-6-," as the doctor cut her off. "Ms. Thomas that's for you to do, to contact him and tell him he has contracted a STD that he has passed on to you and needs to be treated."

Shirley just nodded her head. She couldn't believe that he gave her a disease.

"It's The doctor told her. Shirley looked at her wide eyed and realized it was better to be safe than sorry. "Yes, that will be fine Dr. McDonald," said Shirley as she continued to sniffle.

"Well I need to give you this vaccine shot and I'll prescribe you an antibiotic along with your new birth control order. Lutisha will need to get more blood from you so we can run the HIV test." The doctor stood there with a concern look on her face for Shirley. Shirley just nodded her head and wasn't even concerned about the needles at this point, all she could do was think about letting Sam have it. The engagement was definitely off.

"Oh Ms. Thomas make sure you don't start the birth control until you finish the antibiotic first. And please start using protection." The doctor told her and she looked at Shirley hard and long, and then she gave her a soft smile.

"Okay." Shirley answered her.

"Now I need for you to turn on your stomach for me. Don't worry you want feel a thing." The doctor told her and Shirley turned on her stomach. The doctor flipped up her gown and squeezed a portion of her butt cheek and stuck the needle into the fatty tissue..

"Ouch!" Shirley blurted out. It did sting a little, but it didn't hurt.

"See Ms. Thomas, a little sting. I'm all done. Lutisha she's all yours honey." The doctor told Shirley she would call her to let her know how the HIV test went . Lutisha took her blood and Shirley got dressed. She received the antibiotic from the clinic pharmacy and left in a rage of hell. She called her job to let Pam know she wasn't returning to work. It was now 2:45 in the afternoon. She tried to call Sam, but she got no answer. The detail shop was closed after New Years, so he was running around town. They had plans that evening which was now officially canceled. She drove her Lexus down Madison Rd. heading in the direction of Sam's house. She had to vent to someone, so she called Rachelle at the hair salon. The phone rang several times before Anitra answered the phone. "Hello Mother's where we do hair like no mother, may I help you?"

Shirley was still crying. "Anitra, can I speak to Rachelle please?" Shirley asked her. Anitra sense that something was wrong with the person asking to speak with Rachelle. She didn't recognize it was Shirley. "Hold on please." The phone went blank.

"Hello dis is Rachelle." Her voice echoed through the receiver.

Shirley started crying even more through the receiver when Rachelle spoke through the receiver. "Hello, Shirl, Nee, who is this?" Rachelle knew it was one of her girlfriend's on the other end. But who? Rachelle had told Shirley about Sam before hand and that something wasn't right about him. She didn't get all the information from Boobie, but she got enough to know that Sam wasn't who he claimed to be.

"It's me Chelle, Shirl. You were right about Sam girl." Shirley sniffled.

"What's wrong girl?" Rachelle asked her.

Shirley collected herself and said, "This Negro done gave me fucking Chlamydia."

The receiver fumbled from Rachelle. "What?" Rachelle asked out loud.

"This Negro done zapped me girl, he burnt me, gave me Chlamydia. I just came from the clinic getting a pelvic exam, because I noticed a funny discharge in my panties and my stuff didn't smell right. I thought it from the Kalgan I used." Shirley explained.

Rachelle knew it, she knew he was a snake. It finally came to the light the real about this brother and Shirley saw outside the glass house and Rachelle was happy.

"So are you going to call off the engagement Shirl?' Rachelle asked her.

"Hell yeah it's over, fuck that Chelle. I'm no fool, I'm not fucking with his trifling ass. I was so embarrassed at the clinic. I'm on my way over his house now," as she continued to cry.

"Calm down Shirl and be careful. You can wait until I get off and we can beat the nigga down together." Rachelle told her and was serious.

Shirley laughed a little still crying. "Na'll Chelle, you crazy girl, but I got this." Shirley tried to clear her sniffles up.

158"Well stop over my house later I think Pedro said something about Sharan wanted for you to do his appeal for him." Rachelle told her.

Shirley was now sucking her teeth. "Okay, I'll be over later," as Shirley was driving down Madison Rd. pass Withrow High school. "Bye Shirl." Rachelle told her and they hung up.

She remembered the first time when she got burnt when they were in high school attending the Jazz Festival with Shirley's older cousin Bonita.

Bonita male friend invited them up to him and his partner suite they had in the Western Hotel downtown Cincinnati. Bonita's male friend partner Snake had slept with her and Shirley and Rachelle ended up contracting gonorrhea. She remembered the painful shot she received as she felt Shirley's pain.

....

...

'When a woman's fed up' was playing in Shirley's car as she drove pass the bank and Al's Nest park going through O'Bryanville , a wealthy community on the other side of Evanston. She came to the light of Hackberry and Madison Rd. and she turned right onto Hackberry. When she got down in front of Sam's house she saw a female sitting on the porch in the cold with her arms folded. When she parked her car she looked up to see the female smiling at her. R. Kelly had sunk in her head, because she was fed up. "What the fuck she smiling for? I'm about to tear this mother-fucka up," as Shirley put her keys and mace in her coat pocket. She took off her jewelry and put it in her purse. It was cold out, the snow had been pushed to the curves making the streets and sidewalk clear. She had on a pair of high heels all black stepping out the Lexus pulling her clinging clothes from her thighs. Her eyes were still stained with red from crying.

The wind hit her face, but she didn't stop. She headed for the porch hoping and praying that Sam was home. His car was in the drive-way. When she stepped up on the porch the female was sitting in a chair wearing a bubble coat, some jeans and some High Tech boots. She had a lot of earrings in her ears and a lot of rings on her fingers and thumb. She was real ghetto Shirley thought. She was a light complexion female.

Shirley was about to speak and ask for Sam, but the female was quicker to the draw.

"Your cousin isn't here right now he should be on his way in a few." The female said and smiled at Shirley.

"My cousin?" Shirley thought she said it to herself, but the female heard her.

"Isn't Sam your cousin? Aren't you a lawyer or something?" The female asked her and Shirley was really confused now. His cousin? What type of game was he on?

"Yes I'm a lawyer." Shirley answered.

"I remembered your Lexus when me and Sam went out to dinner and then out to your house when you were handling a case in Atlanta or Alabama, I can't quite remember." The female explained and Shirley wanted to hear more.

"Oh ya'll did?" She was being sarcastic. Shirley now had her hands on her hips after taking her hand off her mace.

"Yes girl, your cousin is my boo. I'm five months pregnant by Sam and we are engaged to be married," as she stood up to show off her belly by undoing her coat and then her ring which was the exact ring he gave her. Shirley was now vexed on boiling point status, but she kept her cool. "Excuse me, I didn't catch your name." Shirley told her. She wanted to make sure she knew her name when she confronted Sam.

"Oh my name is Chloe and what's your name again? He told me, but I think I forgot, isn't it Carol?" Chloe was now sitting back down in the chair she was sitting in.

"No it's Shirley, but they call me Shirl." Shirley told her.

The female looked up in the sky for a brief moment and then said, "Yeah that's it."

Shirley didn't let up trying to get the facts. "Chloe can I ask you a question, are you sure he took you out to my house?" She asked Chloe.

Chloe blinked her eyes and folded her arms on top of her belly. "If you live out past Kings Island in those fancy condo's, yep he did. Why, did we make a mess in your bed? He was supposed to have washed your satin sheets," said Chloe.

Shirley reached her hand in her pocket to make a fist she was so mad. She didn't let her true emotions show in front of Chloe. "Na'll Chloe, ya'll didn't mess my sheets up. It was nice meeting you. Tell my cousin I'll be to see him later." Shirley was now beginning to understand what Ren Mack was speaking on about the glass house the other night.

"Okay Shirl, I'll tell him, bye." Chloe smiled at Shirley

"Bye," as Shirley turned around and went back to her car. She knew she couldn't be mad at the female, because Sam was playing them both.

All alone he had a hidden agenda. She sat in her car for a moment and then started up her engine going down the street to the corner of Hackberry and Fairfax. At the light she started crying hitting her steering wheel.

"Why that bastard. He actually fucked some female in my bed at my house. That was some fowl shit. Who does he take me for? He has to pay, I'm fucking him up." She said and loud while sitting at the light.

She had to clean her thoughts. She drove downtown to Fountain Square to get a piece of mind. She sat down there feeding the pigeons in the cold weather. It was around 3:30 when she got back in her Lexus Sedan. She was numb and didn't even notice that she had a ticket on her windshield from the parking meter expiring. She tore it up she was so mad. She was so much in the mist of confusion she almost had a wreck driving out to Rachelle's house on Reading Rd. and Seymour Ave. by Hillcrest Plaza. She was turning into Popeye's between Walgreen's and Firestone tire.

Rachelle had left work early, because she only had two clients. When Shirley got to Rachelle's house they were all in the dayroom, Pedro, Keith Jr. and Rachelle. They were watching Harry Potter and it was a little after four and it would be getting dark soon. Shirley looked at Rachelle and started crying. Rachelle went to comfort her immediately.

When Shirley calmed down Rachelle asked her. "Shirl, do you want a drink?" Her sniffles cleared up a little. "Yeah a double shot of cognac would be nice." Shirley said. Rachelle let her go and headed out the dayroom, but before leaving out she turned around and said, "Remy or Martel?"

"Remy." Shirley replied.

Rachelle got her a drink and returned back to the dayroom. When she handed Shirley the drink she started crying again. "Chelle why me? I'm trying to be the best woman I can be." You could see the hurt on her face.

"Shirl it's not your fault, that nigga just fowl and lost out on something good." Rachelle knew it was probably the karma coming back on her friend from messing with a married man.

"Chelle the shit he gave me was bad, but to top it off I just found out he has another bitch five months pregnant who he also suppose to be engaged to also." Shirley paused. "He had the bitch out to my condo in my bed while we were in Atlanta."

Rachelle's mouth dropped. "You lying girl."

Shirley was wiping away a few tears. "I just ran into her when I went by his house earlier and he wasn't there. Her name is Chloe and he told that we were cousins." Shirley facial expression gave a series of twist and confusion.

"Girl fuck his trifling ass , I'm glad you found out now, before you took that step and then finding out later down the line that he was living a double life. People are sick in the head now a days Shirl." Rachelle hugged her.

"Chelle, how can I tell my parent's about this? I regret even letting him meet them," said Shirley. Rachelle brushed her shoulders off.

"Just do it Shirl and gone brush your shoulders off like Hova." Rachelle smiled at her and Shirley gave her a smile back kind of cheering her up.

"I'll call my mom tomorrow," as Pedro came into the entrance way of the dayroom, because him and Keith Jr. had made an exit when Shirley came in.

"Shirley, Sharan is on the phone for you." He said.

They both looked at him and Shirley said, "Okay."

Rachelle got up and retrieved the phone from Pedro. She handed it to Shirley .

"Shirl, I'll leave you to talk to him and are you staying the night?" She asked her. Shirley nodded her head up and down telling her friend yes.

She eased the phone up to her ear. "Hello," as her voice was low and dry.

She curled up under herself on the couch. "Hello Shirl. What's up? I heard you were getting married," said Sharan and the pain hit her again and she started crying.

"Shirl what's wrong, what happen?" He asked her and you could hear the sincerity in his voice. She calmed down a little to answer him. "I was, it was too much for me to handle, but I'm through messing with him." She told Sharan.

Sharan was concern. "Is there anything I can do?" The words sounded like relief and she needed to hear something positive.

"Sharan you are locked up, but I wish you were here to hold me." Her voice cracked a little.

"I wish I was there too." he replied. She was now confused , blinded by the fact that she played him and he was still willing to be in her corner.

"You're not mad at me Sharan?" She asked him

He let out a sigh and said, "Shirl I only was upset with you, because I care about you and my heart skips beats for you."

She realized right then he really cared for her. He wasn't the complexion she desired, but he was qualified to be a real man with ambition.

Camouflage in the rough main of society dealing with attraction, Shirley knew now that her soul-mate was a man that was a darker complexion not several shades lighter.

"I sorry I acted like a bitch over the years ignoring you Sharan." It was some certainty behind her statement.

"You don't have to apologize Shirl, remember I wasn't your type." He was being a little sarcastic.

"But Sharan, you are my type on the inside. You're everything a woman wishes for in a man." She told him and he was happy to hear those words coming from her. But he had other plans and business to discuss. "Well I fired my lawyer and I would like for you to appeal my case for me." He told her and her heart started to beat to a new rhythm of relief, because she already knew he wanted for her to appeal his case. She took it upon herself to initiate the call.

"I'll do it for you, free of charge Sharan."

He was caught off guard. "Why?" He questioned her.

"Because I like you and you are worthy of me doing so." She said.

He was really caught off guard with that statement. ***She likes me?***

"Oh so you like some Sharan now?" He asked her.

"I would like too, or even love some Sharan eventually," said Shirley.

The phone got quiet. "That might be possible." He was thinking about playing hard ball like she did for years, but why when he tried so long to be in this position to love her and be with her. Was she using him for a rebound, or was she really going to give him a shot?

"So are you going to send me a visiting form so I can come and see you Sharan?"

"You're already on my visiting list as my fiancée." he told her and she smiled through the phone. "What made you do that?" She asked him, but was happy he did it.

"I'm always thinking ahead, so when are you coming down?" He asked her.

"Well today is the 2nd , you write me and give me the address and directions and I'll be down there after I receive the letter." She said and it sounded official.

"Okay." he answered.

She took in a deep breath and said, "Well my homie lover friend I'll be waiting on my letter. Oh do you have my address Sharan?" She asked him.

"I remember the address, but what's the zip code?" he asked her.

"It's 45244." She smiled telling him her zip code.

"I got it, let me speak back to Pedro and you should be getting that letter shortly." Sharan told her and was confident .

"Okay Sharan, I miss you and can't wait to see you," as she was getting up to take Pedro the phone.

"Shirl I miss you too," as his words melted her.

Shirley reached Rachelle's bedroom and the door was open. Rachelle, Pedro and Keith Jr. was like one big happy family watching T.V.

"Pedro, Sharan wants to speak with you," as Shirley threw him the phone. Rachelle looked up at her, and Shirley smiled at her.

"How did it go?" Rachelle asked her by whispering. Shirley didn't answer her with words, but a wink and a smile let her know it went good.

"Auntie Shirl, can you take me to McDonalds please?" Keith Jr. asked her.

Rachelle answered for her. "No, boy you better go in there and eat what I cooked," said Rachelle.

"But mom, I don't won't any pork chops," as Keith Jr. stuck his lip out beginning to pout.

"Yeah I guess I can do that. Have you been good in school?" Shirley asked him.

"Yes ma'am." His eyes lit up.

"Well c'mon so we can go." Shirley told him.

He jumped off the bed to leave out with Shirley. She took him to McDonalds and when they returned Shirley decided to go home instead of staying overnight. She reached her condo at around 8p.m. that evening. She didn't answer her cell none when Sam was trying to call her after she left his house running into Chloe. She knew he was on her voice mail and he would probably be on her answering machine at home also. When she got in the house she took a nice hot bath and took two more pills of her antibiotic. After her bath she relaxed in her sweat pants and t-shirt tank. She checked her messages and Sam was on the machine several times. Beep!

"Shirl, I know you're upset, but I can explain Chloe, please give me a call."

Shirley didn't want to hear it. Busted and plus you gave me Chlamydia. Beep!

"Shirl it's me again and it's not as bad as it may seem, please call me."

After her last message she decided to call her parents and let them know the bad news. It was a nightmare for her, but she had to let them know.

The phone rang several times in Camden before someone picked up.

"Hello Thomas residence." Her moms picked. "Hello mom," as Shirley started crying.

"Pumpkin what's the matter?" Her mother asked her.

She was too fragile, but she went on ahead and tried to tell her.

"Mama, it's Sam," as more tears began to flow.

"What did he do baby?" Her mom asked and Shirley could her dad in the background.

"What did that you punk do to my baby?" He said.

Her mom told him, "Shh-Melvin, I'm trying to find out now. Go ahead Shirley and tell mama what happen." Her mom was all ears.

"Mama he gave me Chlamydia, he's engaged to another woman who's five months pregnant." She was calming down as she explain it to her moms.

"I knew it, I knew that Negro was too good to be true." Her mother said.

"Why me mama?" Shirley continued to sniffle.

"Girl quit crying and how bad is it?" Her mom asked her.

"They caught it in its early stage." She told her even though she was embarrassed.

"That's good don't be depressed over that man, there are better men out there baby. I'm glad you're not seeing that married man anymore either." her mother told her.

Shirley was surprised that her moms knew about Thomas Patterson. She didn't even question how she knew.

"Mama there's this guy who cares about me, but I've been ignoring him for years, because of his complexion. Other than that he has a wonderful personality and we are very compatible." Shirley felt good expressing the facts about Sharan to her mother. She felt like she was sixteen again instead of twenty-nine.

"So what's stopping you Pumpkin, his complexion or his personality?" her mom asked her.

"Right now he's in a Federal facility." Shirley told her mom and she snapped.

"Shirley Ann Thomas we didn't raise you to deal with career criminals and you know how your dad feels about drug dealers and things of that nature, that might be a bad idea." Her mother expressed to her with concern.

"No mama, he's not involved in that mess. He has his own business and his accountant for his store didn't report some of his transactions and they caught up with him." Shirley

tried to explain, as she caught her breath and continued on. "I'm going to appeal his case for him. You met him back in 2000 when Rachelle, her boyfriend Pedro, his friend Sharan and I stopped by the house on our way to D.C." Shirley told her.

Her mother thought about it for a moment. "Okay, I remember. So Sharan is the fella? He was well-mannered and he was kind of cute to Pumpkin." Her mother told her and her dad was in the background again. ***"Who was cute Annie Mae?" He asked her.*** Her mother ignored him though.

"So what you think mom?" Shirley just didn't want to hear some encouraging words, she wanted to feel them.

"All I can say is to be careful and follow your heart, but make sure you're in control having less confusion in your heart Shirley." Her mother told her.

Shirley heart was at ease hearing her mother give her the advice she gave her.

"Thank you mom!" as you could hear the lift in Shirley's voice.

"Your damn daddy is bugging me to talk to you girl, here Melvin," as her mother her dad the phone. His husky voice spoke into the receiver.

"Pumpkin do you want me to send my hit squad down there to take care of him?" Her dad asked her. Shirley smiled from her father's question. "No dad let me deal with it."

"Are you sure? Because you know I'll do it." He told her and she just hurried him off the phone. "Bye daddy, I love you and tell mom I love her too." Shirley hung up the phone with her parents and then she decided to call Sam and give him a piece of her mind. She had a quantity of explosive dialogue going through her head as the phone to Sam's house was ringing. Hello," as a female's voice echoed. "I got it, hang up." It was Sam's voice.

Shirley didn't waste another second. "You know Sam, you ain't shit, you are fowl as fuck," as he tried to cut her off. "Please Shirl, let me explain," as she cut him off.

"Fuck that Negro, explain what? The baby Chloe is carrying, or the part about me being you fucking cousin? Or the fact she's wearing the exact same ring you proposed to me with? C'mon Sam cut the games." Shirley was heated with emotions.

"I was going to tell you about the baby and I had proposed to her a year ago, which I broke it off after I met you. I didn't think you would mess with me knowing I had someone carrying my child Shirley." He confessed.

"You damn right, but it's funny, because she looked every bit of five months pregnant or more. So you had to still be fucking her Sam, while we were together. The bitch even told me you took out to my condo and fucked her in my bed on my satin sheets." So you are busted playboy." Shirley told him. Sam was now angry and you could hear it in his voice.

"She told you that? That heifer lying," said Sam.

Shirley wasn't buying it. "Not only that, now I got to take antibiotics, because your nasty ass done gave me Chlamydia that I found out about today. I gave the Health Department your information you nasty ass punk mother-uhh-I hate you," as Shirley screamed through the receiver. "Ooh , I hate you Sam, I can smell your nasty ass all the way out here." She was mad and then Chloe cut in. "This nigga gave you what?" Chloe said and no one knew she was even on the phone listening to their conversation.

"Chloe, he gave me Chlamydia and that's why I stopped by there today. So you better go and get yourself checked out if you're still fucking the Negro." Shirley told her.

"I kind knew you weren't his cousin and thanks Shirley. I'm going to the clinic tomorrow." Chloe told Shirley. Sam was now furious as he yelled again at Chloe.

"Get off the phone now Chloe." He told her, but she didn't.

"Well Sam, it's over thanks for the rims and everything else. The ring and rims will help pay for my doctor bill. You have a nice life, you Chloe and the baby. My things I have over there you can keep them, because you bought them. And please don't have me go and get a TPO for you, because I hate stalkers." She hung up on him.

....

She was now making the move to move forward in her life dismissing all the confusion she just had dealing with Samuel Holston. Her mind was now set on Sharan hoping it wasn't too late to make a life with him. He being incarcerated gave her the time to heal and also to comfort a full observation on everything around her. She was now in a phase of her life where she had to be a grown woman now, because she was soon to be thirty in two months. She wasn't going to settle for nothing less, but for Sharan Chambers to be in her life and for her to be in his.

It was going to be a hard road to travel down, but she was willing to take that chance to make the right decisions to succeed in a relationship with Sharan.

CHAPTER FOURTEEN
Keeping It Real

That Monday January 5th Shirley was at work making phone calls trying to gather up Sharan's files from his case. She didn't have any major cases to handle so she was free to do so. After taking care of that business she decided to call her cousin in Dayton Ohio.

She wanted to se if her cousin male friend Doug was still in Ashland Kentucky doing Fed time. She called her job and a woman picked up the phone.

"Hello, Montgomery County Probation Office, may I help you?" The voice was very professional and delicate.

"Hello, may I speak to Bonita Maples please?" Shirley asked the lady.

"Can you hold please so I can transfer the call?" She put Shirley on hold and then someone picked up and it was her cousin. "hello, this is Bonita Maples, how can I help you?" She said.

Shirley hadn't talked to her cousin in awhile. "Girl this is your cousin Shirley." Bonita was talking to a spitting image of her. Bonita was her older cousin, her mother's brother child. "Hey girlfriend, what's up?" Bonita asked her.

"I called to ask you if you were still seeing Doug and was he still in Ashland Kentucky?" Shirley asked her.

"You know he's my Boo girl, but he was transferred to West Virginia about three months ago." Bonita told her.

Shirley didn't want to hear that, because she wanted for her to ride down there with her. "For real girl?" said Shirley.

"Yes and we are getting married when he get out this year in August and the wedding is on my birthday, September the 16th. I'll send you an invitation, but why did you ask me that Shirl?" Bonita asked her.

"Because I have a male friend down there and I thought maybe we could ride down there together," said Shirley which she was now disappointed.

"Oh, I'm sorry lil cuss, but my man is no longer down there. What are you doing tomorrow? I haven't seen you in like forever." Bonita asked her.

"Let me look at my schedule. Umm-tomorrow is Tuesday the 6th, I'm doing nothing," as she was looking over her planner.

"Well I have to come to Cincinnati tomorrow for a meeting in the morning in the Broadway building at 9:00 a.m. and afterwards I thought maybe we could do lunch." Bonita said and it sounded like a date.

"That's fine with me Bonita. Do you have my new office number?" Shirley asked her.

"No give it to me," as Bonita grabbed a pen from her desk.

"It's 513-559-0202." Shirley told her.

"Okay cuss, I'll see you tomorrow, love yah," said Bonita.

"I love you too, bye," said Shirley and they hung up.

Shirley began to piece out how she was going to handle Sharan's appeal. She started to daydream about how she and Sharan's life would be together. She didn't even realize that her love for Sharan was growing wider and fast this soon.

When she snapped out of her daydream she called to check on her friend Renee. She was due in March around Shirley's birthday. Her phone call ended up in an emergency, because Renee went into labor early. She left her office heading to Good Samaritan hospital to meet Rachelle there, Chucky and Renee's mom. Rene was having her baby premature.

She end up having a little girl with a head full of hair. The baby only weighed 5lbs and 8oz. Renee's little girl Shachelle was born January 5th 2002.

…………………………………..

The next morning Bonita called Shirley at around 10:55 in her office. Shirley met her on Fountain Square. They went to the Red Squirrel to eat lunch.

Bonita had on a black and white Apostrophe Hounds tooth blouse, an Apostrophe suit jacket and an all black wool skirt and a pair of leather Apostrophe boots all black with black stockings. She also had a cape coat. Bonita was 5'6", 155lbs solid with a very round shaped bottom. She was very dark skinned complexion like Shirley. Her hair was jet black cut into a style and she had dimples when she smiled.

Shirley had on an Argyle twin set Cardigan and Cami which was tan, black and white. She also had on a black leather skirt with sheer black pantyhose and black pumps.

They sat down at a private booth and ordered their food. You would think they were twin sisters if you didn't know them, because they looked that much alike. They started talking about family and what was going on in the world.

"So Shirley, how is aunt Annie Mae and uncle Melvin doing?" Bonita asked her.

"They are doing fine, I was just down there for Christmas." Shirley told her eating another fork of her food.

"What's up with Trina and Sherrie?" Bonita acquired about her siblings.

"They are fine girl, getting grown and Trina trying to experiment with sex." Shirley said.

"For real? So when are you getting married Shirley? You know you are getting older," said Bonita and Shirley almost choked from drinking her ice tea. She caught her breath and answered her big cousin. "Hopefully before I'm thirty-five and I find Mr. Wrong." Shirley gave a fake laugh and added. "Shit I thought it was going to be this year, I was engaged to this trifling ass Negro I just broke up with." Shirley told her. She paused. "I was going to surprise ya'll, but I found out this Negro had another bitch pregnant and he burnt me Nita. Shit I'm taking antibiotics now," said Shirley.

Bonita touch her hand and said, "Shut yo mouth Shirl, you lying girl."

Shirley batted her eyes and said, "Nita I'm not lying the Negro gave me Chlamydia."

"That's messed up Shirl. So who is this guy you are about to go se in Ashland ?" Bonita asked her. Shirley got quiet and looked down at her plate for only a brief moment and lifted her head with confident and said, "A friend, a really good friend who I've been ignoring for years, but now I think it's time to start paying him lots of attention." She had a million dollar smile gleaming across her face.

"Shit I can't wait until Doug comes home. It seems like all the good men are locked up. It's like they had to venture into hell before reaching paradise." Bonita told her.

"Nita how did you and Doug stay intimate over the years while he was in and out of there?" Shirley asked her, because she loved Doug so much and any other woman would have considered him to be a jail bird.

"Well Doug hooked up conjugal visits for us in Ashland which usually they would only allow married couples, but if his money is right he could make it happen. If you are trying to get your freak on tell him to ask around." Bonita told her.

Shirley just shook her head. "So Nita, what do you think about all the 9-11 stuff going on around us?" Shirley asked her.

Bonita sipped her lemonade and gave a big swallow. She sucked her teeth and replied.

"Shirley this funky ass President of ours is playing a video game with our lives. They let them people into our country and then go over there trying to bully them out their shit thinking they won't retaliate. Our President is a damn fool. We need to impeach his ass before he starts a World War. He keeps playing hide and seek games with Big Ben."

Bonita told her.

"I never thought it would be risky to fly in the U.S. Nita," said Shirley.

"I know, and those sneaky bastards will be back with another attack, I bet you that," said Bonita.

"They are already talking about going over there bombing those terrorist." Shirley paused and said, "So how is Atari doing?"

"She's doing okay. She just moved back to Ohio from Houston after her father died. The baby and her are doing fine though." Bonita told her.

Shirley mouth dropped. "What baby?" She didn't even know that Bonita's daughter had a baby.

"Remember the nigga Snake, Doug's friend that you and Rachelle slept with when ya'll were in High school during the Jazz festival? You know when ya'll were being fast little bitches and he burnt Rachelle." Shirley was shaking her head to tell her yes. "Well when I went over to the Gulf War he was messing around with Atari. He was supposed to have been looking out for her and all along he was fucking my baby." Bonita told her.

"Nita you lying," said Shirley.

"I killed his ass in mama's basement when I busted them fucking and I shot the nigga in his dick. I beat the case though. Then come to find out he got her pregnant," said Bonita.

Shirley couldn't believe her ears. All the time she was running around being Thomas mistress she didn't even know what was going on with her family.

"Damn I didn't know all that," said Shirley.

"I guess you wouldn't, hell you don't come around like you use to, now that you are a big time lawyer." Bonita told.

"It's not even like that Nita," as she cut Shirley off. "Girl its cool, you good with me, it's everybody else in the family who think negative about you, not me." Bonita said. It dawned on her that she did separate herself from her family when she were involved with Thomas over the years. She couldn't dispute her statement realizing she did affect those around her dealing with that married man. They finished their lunch and Shirley walked Bonita to her car which was close by the Red Squirrel. Bonita was driving a 2002 Bravado S.U.V.

"Shirley you call me and let me know how it went in Ashland," said Bonita.

"Okay Bonita, I'll let you know and I'll be seeing you cuss." Shirley hugged her and she got into her S.U.V. and pulled off. Shirley went back to her office.

Shirley started to map out Sharan's case and then relaxed for the remainder of the day. Pamela was on an one week vacation. After work Shirley went to visit Renee and the baby in the hospital. On her way to the hospital she received a private call from Doctor McDonald on her cell phone. Shirley heart started beating fast when she answered her phone and it was the doctor. She told Shirley some promising news that would give her declaration to determine her future. She told Shirley that her HIV test came back negative. Shirley became at ease and was relieved.

Shirley spent a few hours at the hospital with her friend and God child. After leaving the hospital she went to the grocery store out by her house to grab items she needed. Grabbing her grocery's , briefcase and purse she muscled her way to her private mailbox to see if she had any mail.

She found a letter from Sharan along with a few other bills. She smiled, because she knew he had to send the mail over night. She entered her condo throwing the mail on the end table in the living room along with her briefcase and purse on the sofa. She took her grocery's into the kitchen. She came back out to the living room placing her jacket in the closet. She went to her bedroom and stripped out of her clothes. She put on some shorts and a t-shirt. Then she went and put up her few items she purchased at the store and then went to run her some bath water.

She wanted to soak her body in some warm soy milk and fragrance. She grabbed a wine glass and some Moscato she had in the fridge. She lit her candles around the tub, poured her a glass of the wine and then stripped out of her clothes putting her dark melon into the water. After relaxing and soaking in the tub she finally got out and it was around 8:00 that evening. She cleaned the tub out wrapped in a towel. She went and sat on her bed and moisturized her whole body and put on a scarlet spaghetti strap night gown with her grandma slippers. She turned the heat up a notch and went to fix her a microwave Lean Cuisine dinner. After she ate she poured her another glass of the Moscato wine and went into her bedroom with Sharan's letter. It was now 8:45. She sat on her bed with her feet curled under her bottom propped on her pillow. The letter started off explaining the directions and what she could wear to the visit. Then it started to get personal making her

warm on the inside. She started reminiscing about the time she gave him some last year over at Rachelle's house in the guest room and how large he was inside her making her have the ultimate orgasm. She felt butterflies began to form in her stomach. She began to read the next line.

"Shirley you're the harmony to my melody. I like you in more ways than one. How can a man of my stature make you the compass to my heart? I'm patient and know that you're worth preserving. I would like to make you that special woman in my life. You have beauty, class, style and the most beautiful ass I've ever seen. (Smiley Face) I'm on a journey and seeking a mate that's of your stature of being compatible with me. I'm ready to be that parent and share my small fortune with you. My actions will speak louder than my words, all I'm asking is for a chance Shirley. If I could sing I would to you, but I can't so I'm thinking of you and the music we can make together. I know I can love you and I'm shooting for the stars. We shared a touch, a kiss, a night of passion and we experienced tragedy together. I'm ready, Your more than a Jodeci Ballet, and I fiend for your love.
I want to fall in love with you and have a family. Oh on Saturday the 25th is a good day to visit."

Take care of yourself, I love

you.

Always

Sharan
P.S. Write back soon.

Shirley began to form tears in the corner of her eyes. She felt his words and they meant a
lot coming from him, because she knew he was serious and meant every word he wrote down on paper. Shirley managed to write him back that night. She grabbed a pen and her notebook tablet and lay across her bed and began to write him back.

Dear Sharan:
I hope this letter finds you in the best of health physically and mentally. Sharan you are the most incredible man I've ever known. How did you get to be so won-derful? Your words can make any woman blush like a young school girl. I am tru-ly blessed to have you in my life. I hope that these emotions between us last forev-er. After reading your letter for about the fifth time, I just lay in bed and threw the letter over my face and enjoyed the scented cologne you placed on the letter as if it

were you on top of me. Everything you stated in your letter I'm willing to give a try. Well handsome I'm going to end this and get some sleep. By the way I love you too! I know that sound strange coming from me, but I realize that I do have feelings for you. Well take care and I'll see you on the 28th.

She re-read her letter before putting it in an envelope and spraying it with a little of her E. Marinella perfume. She was overwhelmed with the fact that she actually had a change of heart dealing with attractions. Was she beginning to be a woman? Even though she was grown, she wasn't wise enough to realize that attraction doesn't have to do with complexion all the time. Her spirits were lifted and she was ready to gain much interest in Sharan Chambers. She fell asleep that night with a huge smile and a woman who was on a mission.

……………………………………...
...

That Friday Shirley went to work for a half of day. She left work and went shopping out at the Kenwood Mall for a new outfit to go see Sharan. She bought her a pair of tree green corduroy pants, a wool tree green and crème Ralph Lauren sweater and a pair of green suede Eastland loafers for women.

That next two weeks she was going to work getting his case ready to be filed, doing her Pro-Bono work for the firm and be up under Renee and the new baby, as well as Rachelle and her granny. She even went to church two Sundays in a row.

……………………………………...

...Finally the week of the 25th made it and Shirley was excited for her trip to see Sharan. That Thursday she had dropped him a letter off at the Silverton Post Office. She had finished taking all her antibiotic and felt rejuvenated. She had her nails done at a shop inside the Kenwood Mall that Thursday. Friday after work she went and got her hair done by Rachelle. Her friend knew she was going to see Sharan in the morning and agreed to talk to her while she was on the highway. Rachelle and Pedro had just gone to visit him a week ago. That Saturday morning at around 6:00 Shirley's alarm clock went off waking her up from a deep dream that left her sheets and panties wet. She muscled herself to the shower and began to take care of the things she needed to do to get ready for her trip down the highway. After taking a dramatic shower and finishing the job from her dream she put on her under garments which were some sexy French cut panties and a bra to match. She then put on the outfit she bought two weeks ago for this

event. She undid the scarf she had on that kept her hair in place. She put on a little perfume which was Apple
and some lip gloss. She was flawless dressing perfect for the cold weather. She checked her wallet for all her credit cards and AAA card. She took her extra battery for her cell phone off its charger and her phone off the charger. She rechecked her bill fold to see how much cash she had in it. She was set and ready to go. She had gotten an oil change and her tires checked and rotated two days ago. She hit the alarm on her condo to activate the system she hadn't used in months and gently closed the door turning the lock. It was a chill factor outside, and still dark out when she turned the key to open her door of her Lexus. It was 7:30 when she merged on I-275 heading for the I-71 Highway. She saw the sun beginning to rise and shine while driving down the Highway. When she reached the bridge coming out of Cincinnati taking her across into Kentucky she called Rachelle.

"Hello Chelle, get up I'm on the highway." Shirley told her.

"I'm up Shirl, I'm up." Rachelle screamed through the receiver.

"Girl I'm nervous as hell Chelle." Shirley told her.

"Girl it's going to be alright and turn that damn music down." Rachelle told her.

"You know Jay-Z get's my blood to flowing girl. I'll put me on some Avant or R. Kelly in a minute," said Shirley.

They talked for almost an hour and she decided to hang up from Rachelle about a half hour from the facility.

"Alright Chelle, I'm about a half hour away so I'll talk to you later on my way home," said Shirley.

"Bye Shirl and tell Sharan I said hi and we love him." Rachelle said.

"Okay bye Chelle."

They hung up and Shirley cruised on down the road until she arrived at the facility. It was a beige building surrounded by bob wire. She parked in the visitor's parking lot. She got out the car and entered the building and she had to go through metal detectors twice because she had on a wire bra. They searched her thoroughly and then she was able to enter. There were other people in the visiting room when she went in. She took a seat close by a window. They had a courtyard that you could go outside with your visitor and a few trailers on one end of the yard.

Shirley went to the vending machines to get her a beverage and unnoticed Sharan snuck up behind her at the vending machine and grabbed Shirley from behind,

She jumped out of fear. "What the heck." She blurted out.

"Hey baby," as she heard his voice. She turned around to greet him.

"Boy you scared me," as she gave him a kiss. Her actions were out of characters, but she didn't want to waste another moment not being affectionate to him. The kiss was soft and sloppy wet giving him her tongue. Then they walked back to the area she picked out for them to sit.

"Sharan, do you want anything from the machines?" She asked him.

"Not right now, but I do want me some Shirley Thomas." He smiled at her.

"You can have me and some," said Shirley.

"I can?" He looked around confused.

"Yeah goofy! You're everything I ever wanted in man Sharan." Shirley told him.

"I'm glad to know that Shirl."

"Sharan, did you get my letter yet?" She asked her.

"No, when did you mail it?" he asked her.

"About two days ago," said Shirley.

"I'll probably get it today or Monday." He told her still looking at her.

"Well your case is ready to be presented to the Courts of Appeals and I'll do that Monday." She told him.

"Shirl how long does it take for them to hear my case?" He asked her.

"It take up to six months, or a year or even two years for them to make a decision." Her eyes never blinked telling him that.

"That long, I'll probably be home by then," as his expression changed on his face.

"That's why I'm going to file a motion to get you an Appeal Bond. But if not you might be home by the time they rule on your case honey." She told him with concern in her eyes.

"Shirl, stand up and let me look at you again." He told her. She smiled at him with another girlish blush. She stood up and said, "So you like what you see?" She sat back down.

"You know I do," said Sharan with a raspy voice. She thought he was looking quite handsome in his tan outfit that all the inmates had on. His hair was cut in a taper with a small bush where he cut off his braids from the last time that Shirley saw him. His facial hair was nicely groomed. "Shirl, did you send the pictures like I asked you to?" He asked her.

She looked at him and said, "Yes I did, but I wasn't taking any nude pictures boy. I don't know what you and Rachelle was on. I did manage to take some in lingerie for you.

They are enclosed in the mail I just sent you." She told him rolling her eyes and smacking her lips.

"Okay calm down babe," said Sharan.

It was quiet for a brief moment and then Shirley asked him, "Sharan what are those trailers for over there?" She was dying to ask him.

"Oh that's where they let married couples spend the weekend for conjugal visits." He told her.

She already knew from talking to her cousin Bonita.

"For real, my cousin Bonita dude use to be down here. She told me to ask you if they were still hooking it up for non-married couples to get their groove on?"

He looked at Shirley hard and said, "I can make it happen, if that's what you want. I've gotten cool with one of the guards here." he told her.

"So when can we get our groove on? You know I want some of that good dick Sharan." She said with cunning eyes. He was not use to her talking this way towards him. It felt good though and he wasn't going to question it. "It will have to happen sometime in March." He told her.

"Why so late Sharan?" She questioned him.

"It's already booked for February, especially Valentines day weekend, but I'll get us in there you can bet that." He said smiling at her.

"Good I hope it's around my birthday and I can get a big birthday present from you." She smiled at him being seductive and naughty.

Shirley was thinking to herself that it was good, because she would have had her follow up at the clinic and then she could get the okay protected or unprotected sex with him. She had another agenda in mind with him. She was going to try to get pregnant by him. This time she would know for sure who baby it were.

They went out into the courtyard and strolled in the hard brown grass area that was dead from the cold weather. It was like being on a date for Shirley and Sharan. She stayed until 4p.m. that afternoon. When she got back home she called Rachelle and let her know she made it home safe and sound.

For the next several weeks in February Shirley and Sharan talked on the phone and wrote each other letters of love. Somehow on Valentines Day Sharan managed to send Shirley a dozen roses and a huge teddy bear to her office. Shirley knew that he probably had Pedro to do it, but the stuff had a return address in Dayton Ohio.

…………………………..

…

On February 20th Shirley was back at the clinic in Madisonville getting checked out. She had her pelvic exam and Dr. McDonald was telling her the condition of her vagina. She could tell though, because her stuff was back fresh to its normal.

"Ms. Thomas you can start taking your birth control now. The infection is all cleared up," said the doctor.

"Dr. McDonald what about sex and is it safe to have a baby?" Shirley asked her.

"I hope you are going to have protected sex, but you are perfectly fine to conceive a child Ms. Thomas." She told Shirley.

"I just asked and I'll be safe," said Shirley knowing she was lying.

"Okay Ms. Thomas, I'll see you in April around the 20th for another follow up." The doctor told her.

Shirley had her mind made up already. "Okay Dr. McDonald, I'll see you then," said Shirley. She left the clinic and felt like her menstrual cycle was about tot come. She started cramping and it was kind of early for her.

CHAPTER FIFTEEN
Real Talk

The first week of March Shirley was back down in Ashland Kentucky seeing Sharan for her birthday. He had set it up where Shirley could spend the weekend with him in a trailer. She brought groceries and a change of clothes. She was checked out thoroughly by the guards and had to be stripped searched by some female guards. She felt violated when the female guards told her to open up her vagina and cough looking at her with a flash light and then in her anal area. She had an attitude for a moment, but she knew she had to go through with it in order for her to see Sharan in an exclusive manner. Shirley was going to try to get pregnant by Sharan while she was able to have sex with him. Shirley put back on her sexy panties and wireless bra set by Victoria Secret. She carefully watched the female staff stare at her beauty giving them much attitude. Her pubic hair was neat and trimmed, her skin was shining to perfection, looking like silk black velvet.

Then she put back on her white baby Phat doubled breasted power dress that was shortened and accented with gold studs. She placed her jewelry back on and one by one she slipped on her crème eggshell white Stiletto strapless heels.

Shirley gave the female guards the uhn & the awe before leaving out the room they searched her in. She snapped her head back and rolled her eyes walking pass them moving her hips with a thunderous walk.

One of the male guards helped her with her groceries and her duffle bag out to the trailer where Sharan was awaiting her arrival. She had everything she could possibly need to spend the weekend with him.

She entered the trailer and they gazed into each others eyes for a long stare before embracing one another and kissing. She was beginning to perspire just being in his presence. She couldn't believe this was happening. It was her birthday and she was going to get her ice cream and cake all at once. She showered and got comfortable while Sharan was cooking her dinner for her birthday. She was a fan of seafood, so he made her lobster and crab with a special sauce and oriental vegetables. He even baked her a cake. The trailer was equipped with everything.

After dinner they went and got cozy on a small sofa drinking a glass of bubbly. They cuddled and talk listening to Sade. One thing led to another and Shirley found herself underneath Sharan. Before Sharan entered her passage Shirley questioned him about the condom he was about to use.

"Sharan what are you doing with that?" She asked him.

"It's protection, so you won't get pregnant." He told her. She looked away from him. She hadn't taken her birth control since she received her new prescription. He let a lonely tear from the corner of her eye. "Sharan will you give me a baby?" She was still looking away from him. "Shirley I will give you whatever you want." He told her.

Those words brought her eyes back to his. "Well I want to be with child Sharan, make me a baby." Her tears came down her face and he wiped them away, and then eased his tribal piece inside her warm wet passage. "It's going to be alright," as he placed the head inside her. She gasped and let out a tremor. "Umm-umm, oh Sharan, make love to me." She begged him.

He pulled the head out and moved down between her legs. His tongue was insinuating its way into her warm wet pussy and his tongue started tickling all the tender places. When he puckered up, it was a slurp ever so delicately on her pink pearl clitoris, making it feel as if it had tripled in size with his teasing mouth. Shirley screamed in ecstasy, as if all her pent up frustrations went straight to the center of her body setting up powerful series of preliminary tremors. The first spasm started deep within her, even more deeply that his tongue could reach. But they quickly vibrated outward to shake her entire lower body. She gulped and swallowed and twitched and rocked, and it wasn't long before she was out of control. Yes she was cumming furiously down on Sharan's tongue and his mouth. His chin was messy wet with her juices.

"Make love to me baby, take control and make me a baby," she whispered down to him. He looked at her and being submissive to her wishes he knew what he had to do. She wanted it to be a sexual pleasure that neither one of them would forget.

He eased back up on top of her placing the head inside her again. "Fuck me!" She chanted the words over and over again.

Sharan didn't hold back he slid his Stallionesque dick of his into her moist trembling hole and began to move around in it, back and forth, up and down, even in fast spiral corkscrew motions. As big as his tribal piece was, all that energetic stroking made it feel even bigger. Her tight pussy was being stretched to its limit and beyond. She could feel every muscle stretching, every nerve ending lighting up. When he was all the way in-side her, her clit was pressed into his pelvic bone. She was screaming, but she hardly noticed.

"Oh shit Sharan, ooh right there baby, yes-yess-oh-yes, that's it's, make me a baby," as she screamed out in ecstasy the last words.

"Oh Shirley is it good baby?" Sharan was in to it, as he continued to ram Shirley's vagina walls severally. She couldn't even respond, she just tightens her hold on him putting her nails in his back and biting her bottom lip. She grimaced a little from the pain and pleasure. Her body milked him for multiple orgasms, bucking and thrashing underneath him as she greedily hogged his tribal piece for everything it was worth. She didn't know how many orgasms she had, because too many of them were multiples.

"Oh Shirley, I'm about to cum baby," as he began to grunt.

She screamed, "Me too Sharan, oh God I'm cumming, I'm cumming," as her body tighten up and she held him tight. She gripped his butt with her nails.

"Shirley I'm cumming, oh shit I'm cumming," as he chanted it in her ear. She felt him shooting his seed inside her wet passage. "Don't move Sharan, leave it in me." She told him trying to control her breathing. They laid there, as he rested on Shirley's sweaty body.

They had sex over and over all weekend, because Shirley was determine to leave there pregnant. When she left she felt like she had auditioned for an adult movie. Shirley was back down there sleeping with Sharan that following weekend. He had it hooked up for them to do so. They were being intimate up to the time for her next period.

She would notice a change in her body all of a sudden. She was now 30 years old and was celebrating her birthday the whole entire month of March. She would soon find out if she was with child or not.

When her cycle supposed to have come it didn't. Her breast even started to feel differ-ent and her hormones were becoming more intense. She noticed the certain change in her body. She hoped and prayed that she had conceived.

She would soon find out at her next doctor's appointment in April. Instead of April the 20th she was able to reschedule her appointment for the second week in April.

....

On April the 12th Shirley sat patiently in the examining room waiting for the check-up and pregnancy test. She was nervous, because she told Dr. McDonald to check for everything, because her period was late. She was crossing her legs sitting in the gown daydreaming about a family with Sharan.

Shirley was inspired by the new media now, after reading an article on Angela Benton the founder and publisher of Black Web 2.0. Her mind flexed towards success knowing her input and Sharan's entrepreneurship would give them the proper push to be a successful couple having a successful life raising a family. She smiled to herself unnoticed while daydreaming.

She was now hopelessly in love with a man that didn't even desire her taste buds once upon a time. The door to her examining room opened and Dr. McDonald had a huge smile on her face. "Ms. Thomas, you are indeed pregnant. Congratulations! You can get dressed now." The doctor told her.

A tear dropped from Shirley's eye with a sun shine smile. She was happy, as she shouted and chanted to the Lord.

"Yes, thank you Jesus, thank you Lord," as she rocked back and forth waving her fist in the air giving praises to the man up above.

What was suppose to be a check-up turned out to be procreation. She signed up for their pre-natal care at the Madisonville clinic before leaving. She couldn't wait to tell Rachelle and Renee the good news. She called Rachelle at work to let her know she was on her way to the hair salon. Renee was up in Dayton with Chucky showing his parents the baby.

When Shirley arrived at Mother's hair salon she could see it was crowded. Rachelle seen her and waived her over to her booth. Shirley didn't want to tell her the news in front of all these strangers.

"Hey Shirl, what's up girl?" Rachelle asked her stopping with her client for a moment.

"Nothing, I wanted to tell you something." Shirley looked down showing less emotion.

"What is it Shirl?" She asked her.

She really didn't won't to expose her business, but she went on ahead.

"This paper I want for you to look at." Shirley was now looking her in the eyes.

"Well, where is it?" Rachelle was now waiting with her hands on her hips.

Shirley handed her the paper with the facts on it about her being pregnant.

Rachelle looked over it and then paused and regrouped and then she shouted out.

"My girl is pregnant," as she embraced Shirley.

The whole salon froze in still motion to acknowledge Rachelle's out burst.

"Damn Shirl, you and Sharan are good and quick." She smiled at Shirley and she gave a half a smile back. "Chelle I love him, and I don't know how to tell him," said Shirley.

"It would be special if you told him face to face." Rachelle told her.

"I was thinking the same thing Chelle."

"Yeah do that. I'm happy for ya'll. Well next week we need to go get fitted at David and Bridal in Tri-County for our dresses, this is the final fitting," said Rachelle.

"Chelle are the colors still the same?" Shirley asked her.

"Peach and black." Rachelle said and Shirley knew she changed the colors. "Yuk, why did you change the colors?" She looked at her.

"Shirl, it was Pedro's idea not mine." There was a slight pause between them and then Shirley said, "Well I'm trying to get into that Vera Wang dress we looked at in the magazine."

"Girl there you go with that, I got to dress to impress shit," said Rachelle.

"You already know I have to be styling and profiling Chelle."

"Shirl, it's my wedding though." Rachelle batted her eyes.

"I know, but I'm in it." They both laughed.

"Well Saturday we are going out there and Sunday we are having a brief rehearsal. I need for you to help me with the decorations, catering and invitations." Rachelle told her.

"What about Nee?" Shirley asked her.

"She is helping out to since my mom talking about her back is hurting and shit," said Rachelle.

"Okay, well I'm about to go home so I can get some rest and then later call mom and dad to tell them the good news." Shirley said.

"Okay Shirl," Rachelle hugged her friend, "I love you Shirl."

....

Shirley left the salon and went home. She called down to Ashland to make a reservation to see Sharan so she could tell him about their creation and them entering parenthood. After taking care of that business she relaxed and collected her thoughts to try to explain to her mom how she was able to conceive with him and he was incarcerated. She thought long and hard wondering what would her parents think.

She then understood that they did their job by raising her to be a good person. This was her life, her destiny to be who she wanted to be. She took in a deep breath and dialed her parent's number in New Jersey. The phone rang several times before her little sister Trina clicked in.

"Hello the Thomas resident, who dis?"

"Trina let me speak to mom." Shirley spoke into the receiver still of kind of nervous.

"Call back I'm on the phone," said Trina.

"Call back, girl this is long distance you better let me speak to my mama," said Shirley.

"Hold on," as she clicked over to the other line. Trina then clicked back over to Shirley.

"Hello Shirl, hold on, mama telephone, it's Shirley," as she yelled for her mom to pick up the phone. "I got it Trina," said her mom. She was in the kitchen and Trina was in the den.

"Hello." Her mom said to her.

"Mom, how are you doing?" Shirley asked her.

"I'm fine and your granny has been worried about you. You need to go and see her Shirley Ann," said her mom. The phone was quiet for a moment. "Shirley did you hear me?" Her mother asked her with concern.

"Yes ma'am I heard you I will go and see her." Shirley paused and added. "You are going to be a grandmother," as she said in a low tone hoping her mother didn't really hear her, but did.

"I'm going to be a what?" Her mother shouted back through the receiver.

"Grandmother." Shirley said real low again.

Her mother emotions went ballistic. "I knew it, I knew, I've been dreaming about fish lately. At first I thought it was Trina or Sherrie, but it's you. You know Trina is trying to have sex? I found a porno movie in her room. I wonder where she got it from. So who's the daddy? I hope not that married man Thomas or definitely not Samuel?" said her mom.

"It's neither one of theirs mom, it's Sharan's baby," said Shirley.

"Yeah right, I thought he was incarcerated Shirley?" Her mom said.

"He is mom." Shirley confessed to her mom.

"So how did that manage to happen?" She asked Shirley.

"They have conjugal visits where he is incarcerated at and we decided as one to have a family." Shirley told it all.

"Shirley, I don't know about this, even you said he had three years to do, what about out of wedlock? Shirl, you'll be all alone brining this child into the world." her mom told her some true facts.

"Mama, he might be home before our child is born, if his appeal comes through and he get's an appeal bond," said Shirley.

"I'll tell daddy," as Trina cut in on their conversation. She was ease dropping on their phone call.

"Get your nosey ass off the phone Trina, ease dropping on our conversation. Ooh that child is driving me nuts round here. I'll tell your dad and we are here for you child no matter what. I'll pray for yah," said her mom.

Shirley felt relief from her mom's input and the fact she would still be there for her no matter what. She didn't realize that she would probably be all alone when the baby came into the world, being Sharan might still be locked up. Her heart pumped with adrenaline while she was still on the phone with her mom.

"Okay mom, I love you," said Shirley. She was feeling much easier and more confident in the situation she was now in.

"I love you to Pumpkin, you be careful and keep your head up. It's your decision and your life to do what's best for you," said her mom. Shirley insides pled for comfort, but her mind raced with fear. "Bye mom." Her voice cracked in pain.

"Bye Pumpkin and go see your granny."

Shirley sighed and said, "I will."

They hung up and Shirley began to think about what her mother said. Being alone in the delivery room, no Sharan, being alone in Lamaze classes, no Sharan, going through pre-natal by herself and just being a single parent period. It made her think and meditate so she could focus clearly on the bigger picture. Is this what she really wanted? Can she manage until he get's out? The thought was racking her brain until she had a headache. She went to sleep with a migraine and wasn't going to let the fact of him not being there change her mind. She was going through with it knowing eventually he would return.

....

The third week in April Shirley went too see Sharan. When she arrived in the visiting room she saw that Sharan already had a visitor. It was an older woman in her mid-forty's. She was beautiful and a plus size woman. She had a short hair style and was wearing a salmon colored double breasted suit with a black shell and black pumps.

Sharan didn't know she was coming and he didn't see her enter the visiting room. She thought it was another woman he was being involved with and she would confront him right here on the spot. She eased in back of him while he was sitting down facing the lady. The lady spoke to her with a smile. So Shirley waved with a smile of her own to say hello.

Sharan turned around to see who the lady was speaking to. His eyes lit up when he seen that it was Shirley. "Hey Shirl baby," as she stood up to greet her. He gave her a hug and a kiss. They both sat back down with the lady and Shirley was waiting to hear who in the hell she really were, and why was she visiting him anyway. She knew this could've been his mom or sister, because he never spoke of them. So who was she to him, hopefully a relative?

"Shirl, I would like for you to meet my aunt Trisha Proctor, she lives in Dayton. We were just talking about you," said Sharan and his aunt lifted an eyebrow.

Shirley extend her hand. "Hello nice to meet you."

"It's pleasure Shirley, Sharan has told me quite a lot about you." His aunt told her.

Shirley turned to Sharan and said, "I need to talk to you in private."

"Whatever you have to say, its okay to say in front of my aunt." Sharan told her.

She gave him a look of dead seriousness. "Are you sure Sharan?" She asked him.

"Yeah I'm sure, she's like my sister." He told her and she puckered her lips a little and gave a sassy look. "Huhn, read this," as she went in her purse and pulled out the pregnancy paper. He thought it had something to do with case at first. Sharan started to read the paper and passed it to his aunt after he read it.

"Shirl, we did it, I'm going to be a dad. I love you," as he kissed her long and hard. His aunt added, "Congratulations to the both of ya'll. Only if your mom was here to witness her only child have a baby." She put her head down.

"Why can't your mom witness our child Sharan?" Shirley asked him.

"She died when I was around four years old." He had a deep concern look on his face.

"Sharan, I'm sorry, I didn't know baby." Shirley's face was disfigured.

"I know Shirl, it's okay, I'm alright I was going to tell you." He said.

"Excuse me, but how did ya'll manage to make a baby when you've been locked up Sharan?" They both stood up and pointed over to the trailers.

"Oh I see." She smiled at them.

"Yeah aunty where there's a will, there's a way." Sharan was hugging Shirley with one arm.

"I see, Well I'm going to let ya'll be and I'll see you when I get back from Las Vegas."
His aunt told them. Sharan stood up and hugged his aunt and Shirley did the same.

They continued to talk and spent the majority of the day together. Sharan was happy
about the news she brought him. Shirley was still feeling doubtful about bringing their
child into the world by herself.
Out of all the fluff she had previously in her life Shirley was finally looking for some
substance.

……………………………………..

CHAPTER SIXTEEN

Love and Happiness

Rachelle and Pedro had moved the wedding up to May 16th instead of it being in late April. Rachelle's wedding dress would be back in late April early May. Rachelle, Shirley and Renee got the wedding plans in order. Even though everything was back to normal amongst the three Renee still felt guilty for sleeping with Thomas and really didn't know if her daughter was Chucky's or Thomas. Her conscious was killing her. Shirley knew some funny stuff had went on back in late June when she found Thomas watch over at Renee's apartment. They were having rehearsal at Southern Baptist Church on Reading Rd. and Glenwood in Avondale. Shirley had morning sickness and ran to the restroom to vomit.

Renee didn't know didn't know that Shirley was pregnant, because when she tried to tell her she was in Dayton with Chucky's folks. Pedro had Chucky be his best man since Sharan wasn't going to make the wedding.

"Damn Chelle, what's wrong with her?" Renee asked her.

"Probably the baby making her sick, damn I don't know Nee." Rachelle told her and Renee looked at her with the most dysfunctional look known to man or woman.

"Baby? What fucking baby?" Renee's voice was in a high pitch she was mad.

"Oh she didn't tell you, that she was pregnant Nee?" Rachelle asked her. But Rachelle wasn't really paying her any attention, because she was listening to the wedding planner.

"No she didn't tell me shit." Renee was boiling hot. She sat down to wait on Shirley's return from the restroom to confront her. Shirley was sick and wasn't feeling good.

She finally made it back to where everyone was at. Renee didn't waste any time asking her. "Shirl it's like that?" She approached Shirley real aggressive.

"Like what?" She snapped back at Renee. She wasn't trying to hear any nonsense at this moment going through her mood swings.

"Oh you couldn't tell me you were pregnant?" Renee asked her, but it didn't cross Shirley mind, because she thought she did. But Renee's tone set if off and made Shirley catch an attitude.

"Why you didn't bother to tell me that Thomas was over to your apartment and that you probably fucked him?" Shirley was loud and everybody heard her. Rachelle ears were burning from her statement.

It seemed like everyone froze, as the tension was building. Rachelle grabbed the both of them and said, "Pedro, I'll be right back. C'mon Shirley and Renee, we are going outside."

The three women left from inside the church to step outside. When they reached a spot outside Renee and Shirley stood there with their arms crossed with hard stares.

"Now what's the damn problem?" Rachelle asked them acting like the mediator.

Shirley relaxed her arms and said, "Like I was saying she probably fucked Thomas last year. I found his watch in her apartment when we were cleaning up her place after running them dope head bitches out of there," as Shirley was pointing her finger in Renee's direction.

"I probably did or I probably didn't, what do you care ya'll weren't together then nor now," said Renee

"Whether we were together or not." Shirley paused. "You know what, I'm not gone even trip over no man, but I thought our friendship was on another level. I thought honesty and trust kept us together as one, but I see there's a bad apple in the bunch." Shirley eyes never left from Renee's.

"I was going to tell you, I just didn't know how." Renee confessed.

"Yeah right, after you wasn't high on that shit?" Shirley had much of an attitude being sarcastic.

"Shirl stop it." Rachelle cut in. "Na'll Chelle it's cool, I smoked crack, I use to be a dope fiend, is that all you got Shirl? Because I'm waiting to kick your ass." Renee told her, but why did she say that? That sent Shirley to the roof.

"Go ahead and try, you're a bad ass Nee," as Shirley started kicking off her shoes. Rachelle stepped in between them. "Both of ya'll are tripping now, so cut it out. We are like sisters and whatever happened in the past concerning that situation stays in the past, now ya'll make up." She told them.

Both Shirley and Renee stared each other for long moment not giving in.

"Shirl, Nee," as Rachelle looked at them.

Renee put her hands on her hips. "Well Shirl, to confess the truth we had sex, we smoked crack together and he had me turning tricks for crack for us to smoke and that's the honest to God truth," said Renee. You could see a tear form in the corner of her eye.

Shirley was in a mood swing and it didn't matter if she was telling the truth or not, she wasn't on it. She stepped to Renee after looking at her and embraced her. It was like the scene from "Juice" when Q and Bishop got into it and Rahiem made them make up in the living room. Shirley hugged her friend looking up in the sky not believing a word she said. After the drama they managed to have a successful rehearsal. Chucky wasn't aware of what was going with Shirley and Renee, because he was on a private phone call in the men's restroom of the church.

………………………………..

The first week of May Chucky was giving Pedro a bachelor party. Chucky rented the Tandem Hall on Seymour Ave. and Langdon Farm which sat across from the Sunoco gas station and down the street from Roselawn park. Chucky had stripper come down from Dayton to perform. Some of the finest talent in the land known to man was performing.

It was on a Saturday night and he had the hall set up like a night club.

He had an open bar that he furnished for his guest. He bought top shelf liquor and cases of champagne. He bought Bare Foot bubbly and Moet. The same lady that was catering the wedding did the catering for the bachelor party.

It was also his May Bash that he gave every year in Dayton, so he bought it to the Nati and combined it with the bachelor party.

The legendary DJ Ron Hunter was providing the music for this occasion. The crowd was blazing with females and guys. The crowd was thick and the women out numbered the men. They wanted to see the famous strippers too.

Cocaine, Aisha and China Doll were performing.

The first stripper came out on the floor in some red leather high heels boots that came pass her knee. A red army jacket with matching hat. She didn't have on any panties or a bra. She was light skinned complexion with big loop earrings and long blondish hair and green eyes. It was China Doll.

The guys and females were going crazy, whistling and screaming watching her perform. They were making it rain with cash, throwing singles at her feet.

Then another stripper came out looking like Maliah from of those Smooth or King magazines. She had on some Gucci high heel boots, a G-string black thong and a black half cut tank top. She was a butterscotch complexion and very built in the places she needed to be. It was Aisha. She started stripping and dancing playing with China Doll.

They had a few toys with them getting real personal.

Then a mixed female came to the floor wearing a polka-dot blue pair of thongs with no top and a dark blue fur. She had a tattoo of the Walt Disney character who wear wing's and fly around with a wand. Underneath the tattoo it read "**Sexy**". Her hair came down to her back like a brunette. She was stacked in her blue pumps. She had hazel brown eyes and wore a little make-up. She started doing her stuff with the other two women entertaining the crowd. She looked like Vanessa Williams in the face and her name was Cocaine. Some of the women in the crowd were throwing their panties at them.

It was going down in the Tandem Hall. Chucky even had it set up for Pedro to get sexed by Cocaine after they performed. I was a wedding gift from him to enjoy.

Even Boobie, Ren Mack and Sam showed up. Sunny Red, Fleetwood, K.G., Luckie from Millville and Duke Reagan showed up at the May Bash slash bachelor party.

Chucky normally threw this event in Dayton, but now he was down in the Nati. He knew his guys from the Gem City would show up.

Kenny, Don Gotti, Jay-Buxt, D-Boy, Moss Burg, Skane, Bo, Kurupt, S.A., Pearl Handles, Ronnie Roche, Corey and many others. Even a few pro athletes attended the Bash. Aunika, Milan and Deona were off in the crowd . Chucky was drinking straight out the bottle, he had Courvoisier "Exclusif Cognac". He ran into Deona and all he could think about was some of that bomb lip action she was associated.

....

.

ON THE OTHERSIDE OF TOWN in Madisonville Meco was giving Rachelle a Bacheloret party at her house . She had a male stripper by the name of Tubbs from Columbus Ohio doing the party.

They were drinking having a good time getting buck wild. Shirley wasn't feeling good and was off in a corner thinking about Sharan and her unborn child.

Meco, Rachelle, Renee, Anitra, Rachelle's mom and a lot of other hair stylist around the city were taking off their panties for him and acting wild.

Rachelle's mom got her a few feels on the male stripper, touching his tribal piece and chest. She was feeling the ambiance as well as the other females. They were giving him money and one of the females tried to give him a blow job on the spot.

It was a wild night of fun for Rachelle and Meco paid him an extra fee to see him have sex with one of the females in the crowd. He did and she video taped it, because Meco was indeed a natural born freak.

After he finished his show and left the women sat around discussing love, life and loss. It was an emotional time for these women as well as cleansing time.

Being sober for a 7Step program was amongst them and it was like women helping women.

Meco and a few other women stormed havoc when they told the other women and especially Rachelle that their men were probably at that Bachelor's party having sex with strippers they had and everything else. They got all rowed up and took off down to the Tandem Hall tipsy with emotions.

Shirley went home, because she wasn't about to participate in the mess Meco was stirring up. Meco was just upset that Ren Mack got engaged and no longer wanted anything to do with her.

....

BACK AT TANDEM HALL Chucky had let Deona take his temperature by putting his tribal piece in her mouth. Pedro had Cocaine in an isolated room having sex with her and she made him use a condom.

It was like 2a.m. when the hall was slowly losing people making the party almost over when Meco and her ante rouge were pulling up in the parking lot. They stormed in from their vehicles going inside the Hall to see the fella's just sitting around drinking and talking. Chucky's clean up crew was already on the job.

The DJ was collecting his equipment and the caterer was cleaning up, as well as the person he had working the bar which was Fox.

Meco had a look of disgust on her face when she couldn't trash the party and Ren Mack was standing there with his fiancée in his arms. She just walked back out the doors while Rachelle and Renee went to attend to their men and the other women left following Meco.

....

Later on in the middle of May Pedro and Rachelle was in front of the pastor of Southern Baptist church exchanging vows. Rachelle's dad gave her away. He flew in from California. He was now married with a new family and kids. The church was packed to capacity when the pastor spoke clearly to the people who were attending the ceremony. "Rachelle Smith do you take Pedro Willis to be your lawful wedded husband?" She looked at him with a shinny glare in her eyes. "Yes I do." She said.

"Pedro Willis do you take Rachelle Smith to be your lawful wedded wife?" The pastor asked him.

Pedro didn't waste any more time. "I did." His voice carried throughout the church. The pastor looked around and said. "Where are the rings?"

Then Shirley signaled Keith Jr. to approach them with the wedding rings that were on a soft white decorated pillow. "Now place the ring on each other fingers," as they did exactly what the pastor said, "Now I pronounce you husband and wife, you may kiss the bride." Pedro grabbed Rachelle and kissed his new wife, lover, best friend and companion for life. Shirley, Renee and Rachelle's mom were crying for her happiness. Shirley's parent's attended the wedding and her two sister's.

Later on that night at the Hartwell Country Club where they had the reception, Shirley was off in a corner by herself. Rachelle came to comfort her and next to Shirley and rubbed her hand. "What's wrong Shirl?" She asked her.

Shirley had this depressing look on her face. "Nothing Chelle, I'm just thinking how wonderful your life is turning out, hoping mine turn out the same."

"Shirl, it will watch and see girl." Rachelle tried to lift her spirits.

"Well I hope so, because right now I'm lonely and I don't know what to do," said Shirley and she started crying.

"Shirl stop crying, everything will be alright. That baby is going to take you through a whole lot of depressing moods, and your hormones are going to be out of control. It will pass and Sharan will be home." Rachelle told her.

Shirley stopped her flow of tears catching herself. She thought about how Rachelle use to be a brutal bitch when she was pregnant. It made her realize it probably was the baby taking her through these changes all of sudden.

"You would know Chelle, because you were a complete bitch when you were carrying Keith Jr." Shirley smiled a little after Rachelle gave her the middle finger.

"Whatever, c'mon so we can dance and eat, this is my night and I won't my girls to be just as happy as me," said Rachelle and Renee watched from the other side while she was sitting with Chucky. Shirley got up to party with her friend, because it was her friend's night. They had a ball and they took pictures to send Sharan and other relatives who couldn't make the event................

Everything was going swell over June and July. Shirley sister Trina came to spend the summer with her. Shirley's pregnancy started showing, but she stayed down in Ashland

Kentucky visiting Sharan as much as possible.

Trina had experimented with sex while she was visiting Shirley over the summer with a boy who lived down from Shirley.

………………………………...

CHAPTER SEVENTEEN
Tragedy

Shirley's sister Trina had went back home to New Jersey, because school was about to begin for her in the second week of August.

Around the first week of August Shirley received a phone call out the blue when she was over to Rachelle's house hanging out with her and Renee.

They were playing with Renee's daughter Shachelle who was now seven months old. Shirley cell phone was ringing and Thomas home number was on her caller I.D. and she ignored it. Then an unfamiliar number buzzed her cell phone. She looked at it carefully. She wasn't going to answer it, but she did.

"Hello." Shirley answered in a low voice.

"Hello, may I speak with a Shirley Thomas please?" Shirley didn't recognize the voice, but it was a woman's voice, real soft and polite. She thought it was probably a client or someone who already retained her and the woman was contacting her for them.

It was Saturday though why wouldn't they wait until she got in the office Monday morning? Oh well she replied.

'This is her. Mat I ask who this is?" Shirley chose her words carefully.

"I'm Regina, Thomas Patterson wife."

An instant chill went up Shirley's spine. Why was she contacting her, especially now that her and Thomas haven't been seeing each other in over a year?

Shirley stayed with the script, because her guess was as good as anyone else's.

"Regina, Thomas Patterson's wife?" said Shirley and Rachelle and Renee looked up at her. Shirley gave them the big buzz eyes wondering herself. "Okay Regina, how may I help you?" Shirley asked her thinking if this woman was about to question her about messing around with her husband she was going to deny any of it. She had washed her hands of that man and wasn't concern with any of his affairs.

"I found your number in my husband black book, all three contacts, so I tried your office and house and realized that today is Saturday. I'm so sorry I'm a complete wreck right about now," as Regina tried to catch her breath. Shirley picked up on the woman's voice and it sounded like she'd been crying. The woman continued on.

"I was just letting everyone know who were friends with my husband, that he passed away two day's ago." Regina said. Shirley heart dropped and her facial expression let in be known. "Seriously, oh my God," as a single tear dropped from her eye. That really got Rachelle and Renee's attention. They tuned in on Shirley's conversation even more. "What happen to him Regina?" Shirley asked, because she still cared for him a little to have sympathy for him.

"He was found murdered in Walnut Hills in the Setty Kuhn Terrace in his car?" said Regina. Then Shirley thought about the man who was found dead in his car the other day, but they weren't releasing any information on him.

"Do they have any leads or suspects Regina?" She asked her.

"There aren't any leads yet, but his autopsy showed that he was stabbed multiple times and they found crack cocaine in his system." Regina told her.

Shirley realized that Renee wasn't lying about him being over to her apartment smoking crack with her. Shirley knew that Thomas didn't have a drug habit when they were together. "I haven't talked to Thomas or seen him in about a year and some months now Regina," said Shirley feeling more relaxed even though it was bad news.

It wasn't news that involved her of being a home wrecker. Then Regina started venting to Shirley.

"Ever since this woman name Alexis called our home last year talking about Thomas had her pregnant and they were fooling around things went down hill in our marriage," as she started crying again. "I thought it was a joke at first, because Thomas had a vasectomy back in 1998 and there is no way he could get anyone pregnant. But then I caught him red handed with the woman in our home, in our bed. I don't know what the hell had gotten into him," as she had to take a short pause. "I tried to kill them both in our home and to top it off she wasn't even sexy at all for him to be cheating with," as she started crying again in the receiver in Shirley's ear. Shirley thought the same thing, because she saw Alexis the night when she and Rachelle left Skipper's and went to Perkins.

"It's going to be alright Regina," as Shirley was trying to condole her. Regina calmed down and asked Shirley. "Shirley, Thomas had told me so much about you and how you represented their company and are you still seeing Bob who worked with Thomas? I can't reach him and he doesn't work with Proctor & Gamble anymore," said Regina. Thomas and Bob worked together and Shirley had met him once or twice. Thomas had told his wife that her and Bob were messing around eliminating himself from the affair that he was really having with her.

"No Regina, I haven't seen Bob since we broke up like a year ago," said Shirley really meaning since her and Thomas broke up.

"Well I though maybe you could tell him knowing ya'll have history together. The funeral is Thursday the 10th at 9:00a.m. at New Friendship Baptist Church, on Reading Rd. and Whitaker St. in Avondale." Regina told Shirley.

"Well Regina, I'll attend the funeral and I'll try to reach Bob and let him know what happen to Thomas. Thanks for calling and you take care, you have my deepest sympathy," said Shirley.

"Thank you Shirley and any friend of my husband is a friend of mine. Bye Shirley and I'll see you on Thursday," said Regina.

"Bye Regina." Shirley hung up. Rachelle and Renee wanted to know the ins and outs of her phone conversation with Thomas wife. Shirley realized that the baby she conceived last year was Sharan's baby all along, because Thomas couldn't get her pregnant being he had a vasectomy. He was playing her all along knowing she wanted his baby and he couldn't even produce one.

"Well Shirl, what happen?" Rachelle asked her.

"Girl Thomas was the man they found dead in his car stabbed multiple times. His funeral is this Thursday at New Friendship Baptist Church," said Shirley.

She put her head down and Renee wanted to know more, but didn't want to ask her, so she asked her, "What's wrong Shirl, are you okay?"

"Yeah I'm okay, but I just found out that Thomas had a vasectomy back in 1998 and this entire time he couldn't get me pregnant. So when I had the abortion last year that baby was Sharan's. I feel so bad now," as she grabbed her four and half month stomach. Even Renee was relief now knowing for sure that Chucky was the father of her daughter.

"Damn Shirl you were fucking with dope head all this time, like ole girl was on "Waiting To Exhale"." Rachelle started laughing, but her comment wasn't funny to Renee.

"I know ya'll are going to the funeral with me," said Shirley.

"You know we are going you girl." Rachelle told her. "Yeah we are going." Renee added.

She had to go pay her respect to a man that she went all out for once upon a time. They spent the remainder of the day just hanging out until Renee had to leave with Chucky.

…………………………………..

That Thursday morning Rachelle, Renee and Shirley were at New Friendship Baptist Church viewing Thomas body. Shirley had on a solid all black cotton strapless dress and some black leather sandals with the chain Sacoo 1823 by Bolajiz.

Rachelle was dressed in a navy pinstripe, single breasted skirt suit and some navy blue leather wedge sandals by Charles Jordan. Renee had a ruffle cap-sleeve cotton top and a ruffle pull string skirt both pieces was maroon and she had on a pair of embossed leather

black t-strap sandals with the chain detailing by Ellen Tracy.

Shirley never actually seen Thomas wife face to face only from a distance and from pictures.

As the three women were viewing the body Shirley saw his wife sitting in the front row wearing a long halter top cocktail dress of stripes and floral print black and white with a high side split. She had on a pair of leather twist by Mario Valentino, and a black ghost hat. Thomas son and daughter was sitting next to her. His wife was a slender woman with long legs and her complexion was caramel. Shirley stopped to meet her in person. "Excuse me, Regina Patterson," as the lady took a moment to look up at Shirley, Renee and Rachelle. Her eyes were stained red. "I'm Shirley, Shirley Thomas , the lawyer that your husband knew," said Shirley.

The woman's eyes lit up and she stood up and gave Shirley a hug and a smile. She was very tall and was now looking down on Shirley. "Thank you for coming and did you ever find Bob?" She asked Shirley and she replied by shaking her head "no".

"I couldn't get a hold of Bob," she said with a pause. "These are my friends Renee and Rachelle." Thomas wife extended her hand to Renee and Rachelle.

"Well thank you all for coming, the burial is tomorrow at 10:00 in the morning. We are meeting back over here and then going to Spring Grove Cemetery. After that I'm having everyone over to my house in Indian Hills." Regina told them and Shirley knew exactly where she lived in the predominately rich neighborhood out by Kenwood Mall. " I have to work tomorrow, so I won't be able to make it." Shirley said rubbing her belly.

"Okay well maybe you could stop by our house in the near future, here's my address," as

Regina grabbed a pen and paper from her purse to write her info down for Shirley. Rachelle looked at her and smiled, but Shirley didn't see anything funny. " This is my address out in Indian Hills and the house number. I'll be waiting to hear from you Shirley. And by the way, how far along are you?" Regina pointed to her belly.

" I'm five months. I'm due in December. But I'll call you and take care." Shirley was trying to get from in front of this lady, because she was starting to feel a little awkward being she had all that information already. " I will and you do the same Shirley. It was nice to meet you Rachelle and Renee." They nodded to her.

Shirley waved at Thomas kids as they walked back to their seats. His daughter was seventeen and his was fifteen and Regina would be a widow.

She said a prayer for the older man she once had an affair with and his family. She couldn't believe he was lying in a coffin stiff and wasn't moving. She stayed strong and knew then that her life was un bearable and that she had other plans ahead of her.

EIGHTEEN
Back On Track

Shirley was now five months pregnant and had a ton of mood swings. She and Sharan would argue every time she would visit him or on the phone. They were still having conjugal visits , because her hormones were raging and she wanted to have sex every chance she got.

At the end of August Shirley received an invitation in the mail. It was her cousin Bonita wedding invitation. She hadn't talked to her since they met back in January.

Bonita was getting married to Doug Payne an ex-drug dealer out of Dayton Ohio. Shirley was very familiar with her groom, because she had done an appeal for him some years back and he still owed her money for it. The wedding was scheduled to be September 16th at 1:00p.m. Shirley invited Renee and Rachelle to go and Renee was now living in Dayton with Chucky and their daughter.

She told Shirley that she would meet her there on that date. The location was at Maranatha Baptist Church on Wolf Rd. off of Salem out by Shallow Springs. Shirley didn't tell Bonita she was pregnant and Shirley was going to surprise her.

....

Early on the morning of September the 16th Rachelle was blowing her horn for Shirley outside of her condo. She came out in a pink, maroon and scarlet Graffiti maternity dress, with pink leather sandals and a hand bag to match her dress. She was now six months pregnant and looked like she was ready to deliver.

Rachelle was driving her Acura truck and she had on a sheer Olive peasant top, a green sheer patchwork skirt with sequins, gold hoops earrings and a belly chain, some green Armani leather sandals with a green purse.

She had Shirley a small pillow to sit on. Shirley climbed her swollen self into the truck and was out of breath. She cupped her belly and looked at Rachelle and Rachelle laughed at her and pulled off. Rachelle took I-275 W. all the way around to where they could tale I-75 N. going to Dayton passing Hamilton and Middletown. It was 11:30 when they reached the out city limits of Middletown. They decided to eat when they reached Dayton.

It was a beautiful Saturday morning and the weather was rather nice. The temperature was

around 88degress with a slight breeze and less humid. They reached the Montgomery County city limits at 11:55 and Rachelle got off on the 3rd St. exit and went down to the light to turn onto Gettysburg. They went to Hooks restaurant to eat. It was a soul food restaurant that had a variety of items on the menu. Shirley was craving fried bologna and French fries. She wanted to load her fries down with hot sauce and mustard. Shirley was drowning her fries in the mustard and Rachelle was like, "You little pig." "Forget you hussy I like it this way," said Shirley and she kept putting mustard on her fries. Rachelle had just found out two days ago that she and Pedro would be expecting a child. She was now also pregnant, almost a month. Rachelle watched her friend feed her face and then they received directions to Maranatha Baptist Church.

They reached Salem from the directions they took out to Wolf Rd. The church was down the street from a car dealership and an open field. It was packed when they arrived at 1:10 that afternoon. They were playing the Brides anthem when Shirley and Rachelle were taking their seats in the back of the church. Shirley could see the groom who was about to marry her cousin. She saw Bonita's mom and daughter Atari, her sister Annie Fae and her kids as her brides maids and some light complexion woman as her Maid of Honor. She also saw her granny, as well as her mom, dad and two sisters in the crowd. Other relatives were sprinkled amongst the guest.

The groom was brown skinned complexion, around 6'2" in height and about 200lbs. He had on a white and blue tuxedo and blue dress shoes.

"Damn Shirl that Negro look good, he don't look like the same guy we met back in high school. She done hit a lick," said Rachelle as she licked her lips. "He is fine Shirl."

She looked at her friend and said, "He's one of those, I don't want to work kind of guys."

"Oh yeah Shirl!" Rachelle was still eyeing him.

"Something like that, he's an entrepreneur in the illegal business, he has money this long," said Shirley spreading her hands apart showing Rachelle how long his money was.

"So he has dough, it's just dirty money Shirl?" Rachelle asked her.

"Basically." Shirley looked at her.

"Look Shirl, there goes Bonita coming down the aisle, who is that giving her away?" Rachelle asked her. Shirley looked to se it was Bonita's step-dad, because Shirley's mother brother was deceased. "That's her step-dad Chelle. Him and her moms love that Negro she about to say I do to."

They watched the ceremony and after they exchanged vows cameras were flashing like crazy. It was a joyful feeling in the church as the bald headed young Reverend married her cousin who was still carrying her late husband's last name which was Maples.

Shirley was still sitting down when Bonita notice that she was there after they took pictures inside the church. Bonita came to say hello.

"Hey lil cuss, I thought you weren't going to make it. So how did things go with your friend in Ashland?' Bonita asked her.

Shirley stood up and pointed to her belly and smiled at Bonita and said, "I'm due on December the 25th."

Bonita hugged her. "Congratulations Shirl, this is turning out to be the best day of my life after all," said Bonita.

"No congratulations to you. We are going to the reception, Renee is meeting us there So where is it?" Shirley asked her.

"It's out on Denlinger Rd. off of Salem at Burgundy's." Bonita said.

"So where do we go while you and Doug ride around in that Limo doing who knows what?" Shirley asked her and they both laughed at her question.

"Over to mama's I guess like everybody else. She lives on the Coast on Hoover, hold on mama and Doug come over here," as Bonita yelled across the church getting her mom and Doug's attention. They came over to where they were standing.

Bonita's mom was trying to recognize who Bonita was standing with.

"Shirley Ann Thomas, is that you child?" Bonita's asked. She realized is was her and said, "Come here and give your aunty a hug, ooh and you're pregnant too, look at yah all grown up now," as Bonita mom grabbed her and gave Shirley a hug. "You don't come up the highway to see your aunty anymore, just because your uncle is dead don't mean I'm not your aunty anymore." She told Shirley and Shirley looked at her. "I know aunt Bonnie, I've just been busy in the courtroom," said Shirley.

"You ain't been to busy to let some fella knock you up," said Ms. Bonnie.

"You're right aunty, I promise I'll come up more often to visit," said Shirley.

"You better," as she waved her hand at Rachelle and walked to see some other relatives.

"So Shirley we finally meet again." The groom said to her.

"Yeah and where is the rest of my money Negro?" Shirley asked him.

"Two thousand dollars is small change Shirl." He said to her.

"Two thousand isn't small at all and you see I'm carrying for two now." She was pointing to her belly and he smiled at her. "Where's my wedding gift?" He asked her.

"Bonita's is in the truck and I'll buy you one when you pay me the rest of my money Negro," as Shirley had her hand out.

"Enough of that, Doug this is one of Shirley's best friends Rachelle, I don't know if you remember her or not," said Bonita and Rachelle smiled at him and said, "Hi and congratulations Doug." He smiled at her giving her a look of premature thoughts involving lust. "How are you doing Ms. Rachelle? I think I remember you back when you were younger." He told her.

Bonita looked at him and said, "Yeah you remember when Snake took advantage of them when they were teenagers down in Cincinnati that year we ran into each other after the Jazz festival Negro." Bonita told him.

"Yah, yeah, whatever let's get ready to go Nita. It was nice meeting you again and Shirley I'll get you that lil two stacks I owe you. A matter fact I'll have it at the reception for you, if you are going." He walked off. "I hope so Negro." Shirley yelled at him. She gave Bonita a hug and she left with her husband. Shirley and Rachelle started mingling with the rest of the family before following Ms. Bonnie from the church.

They followed her out to the Trotwood Mall where she shopped for about an hour. Then they went to her house which she lived off of Gettysburg on Hoover.

It was around 7:p.m. when they reached Ms. Bonnie house. Damn near all the family was over there from the wedding. They were cooking and playing cards getting ready to attend the reception. Another hour had past by and Rachelle was getting restless and told Shirley to ask her aunt where was a club or bar at around by her house so she could get a drink.

Shirley pulled up on her aunt Bonnie with her stomach sticking out. In her dress.

"Aunt Bonnie, is there a club or bar around here?" Shirley asked her.

She looked at Shirley with a concern look. "For what? You don't need to be drinking child."

"I know aunt Bonnie, my friend just want to go and look around before we got to the reception," said Shirley.

"Well there is a club called the Silver Fox on James H. McGee about four or five streets over," said Aunt Bonnie.

"Which way do we go?" Shirley asked her.

"You go back up Hoover and get back on Gettysburg and then go about a half mile down and you'll run into James H. McGee and the club is on that street." Aunt Bonnie wasn't even looking at Shirley giving her the directions. She was busy seasoning some chicken.

"Okay, me and my friend are going to the Sliver Fox." Shirley said holding her stomach.

"Ya'll be careful and I'm leaving out at around 8:30, because the reception starts at 9, so ya'll be back in a few," said aunt Bonnie.

"Aunt Bonnie we have directions to the reception already and we will meet you out there." Shirley told her.

"Okay child." Aunt Bonnie told her.

....

Meanwhile Bonita and Doug Payne were riding around Dayton parading there new life together. She had been dealing with him off and on for years. Ever since she moved from Louisville Kentucky after almost losing her life to her ex-husband after he punched her in

her stomach while she was seven months pregnant. When she moved to Dayton she was dealing with guys who participated in the street life. She was dealing with a young hustler by the name of Turtle when she caught Doug Payne eye. He plotted on Turtle and killed him off getting Bonita in the process. She never found out that he was behind Turtles death.

....

Shirley and Rachelle it to the Silver Fox successfully. It was a spacious club with a medium size dance floor, booth seating and seating tables. Mirrors were on the walls and strobe lights accommodated the place.

It was a small crowd and a live band setting up. The door man told them it was a cover charge of ten dollars, because Zapp was performing tonight. Shirley explained to him they were from out of town and was just looking around before they went to the wedding reception. Plus the door man was just at Doug and Bonita's wedding ceremony. He knew she wasn't lying and he had seen them earlier at the wedding. He let them in without paying the cover charge. They took a seat at the bar. Rachelle ordered her a

Remy and Coke and Shirley just had a 7-Up. Even though Rachelle just found out she was with child she still took it upon herself to celebrate. Renee had called them and told them she would be out to Burgundy's with Chucky around 10:00. They stayed in the Silver Fox until 9:30 and the band was beginning to play. When Rachelle took her last sip of her drink they departed from the club.

They headed back up James H. McGee to Gettysburg and made a right, and then went to Free Pike where they made a left and then went a quarter a mile up to Denlinger where

they made a right. They were lost, because they found out that Burgundy's was on Free Pike next to an Auto body shop. So they circled back and found it.

Somehow Bonita had given them the wrong directions. It was a gray and burgundy building with a burgundy canopy.

When they entered the club it was jammed pack and the reception was really downstairs.

Rachelle and Shirley went downstairs where the groom and bride were at. Shirley had their gift with her, which was a Vivitar-Vivicam compatible digital camera.

They ran into Renee and Chucky, and they all sat together. Everyone was eating and laughing except Rachelle who managed to get her a nice size cup of gin. Shirley was watching her friend though, as Rachelle was eyeing the best man who was Doug's cousin.

As the night carried on Rachelle was getting loose and she had a chance to get close to the best man. They were on the dance floor and she was all up on him grinding and touching him like she knew him personally.

"I sure would like to see you in a secluded area." Rachelle whispered in his ear.

She was grinding hard on him, she was indeed horny and ready.

"That can be arranged." He told her.

"So how long have you been knowing Doug and Bonita." She asked him.

"Doug is my cousin." He was now gripping her bottom with his hands. She was imagining him getting between her thighs.

"Oh I see, so you're from up this way?" She asked him. "Na'll from the Nati." He answered. She pushed away from him momentarily. "You lying, where from?"

"I'm from all over, but originally from English Woods." he told her.

"So what's your name?" Rachelle was back on him when she asked him.

"My name is Shady Grady." He told her.

"Why they call you that? Because you are to fine to be called anything shady." She said.

"It's a long story, but what's your name and are you from around here?' He asked her.

"My name is Chelle, Rachelle and I'm from the Nati also. I part own Mother's hair salon in Bondhill." She paused and added. "So Shady Grady, do you think you can handle all of this?" as she placed his hands on her ass squeezing her hand over top of his making him feel her soft round bottom. He couldn't believe it, but he didn't back down from her question.

"Hell yeah I can handle all of that and some." he told her.

Shirley saw her friend making her move from a distance and she immediately got up to go and intervene the situation. When she walked up on the two, Shady Grady had both his hands on Rachelle's bottom. Shirley cut in. "Excuse me, I'm sorry about my friend, but she's drunk and mad at her husband, he's around here somewhere and she didn't mean whatever she was telling you. I truly apologize for her gesturers sir."

He pulled away from Rachelle. "Married?" He was in shock.

"Yes she's happily married, with children," as Shirley grabbed her hand to show him her wedding ring. He walked away and so did they. She tried to pull away from Shirley. "Na'll Shirl, I want to fuck him, he's from E.W. down our way." Rachelle said while bending over like she was about to call for Earl.

"Chelle, you are tripping you are a married woman now," said Shirley.

"So, Pedro is probably still sleeping with Shanice," as her words were slurred.

Shirley just looked at her friend with disgust. She sat her down with Renee and Chucky "What are ya'll looking at?' Rachelle asked them.

"Chelle you are tripping," said Renee.

"Na'll that's Shirl acting like a hater and shit." Rachelle said to her.

Shirley went to say her good-byes to her family. Doug gave her the money he owed her. After Shirley talked to those who were important to her she came back to the table.

"Nee we are about to go, she's wasted and now I have to drive us back home. This baby is kicking my butt," said Shirley. Rachelle was lying on her folded arms on the table. She was indeed white boy wasted.

"Okay Shirl. Chucky and I will be here for a little while longer. If you want ya'll can stay over to our place until the morning," said Renee.

"No thanks Nee. I can make it, plus I have something I need to do in the morning and I told Pedro I would have her back early," said Shirley holding her stomach.

"Okay Shirl, give me a hug," as she stood up and hugged Shirley. Rachelle was still sitting there slumped over. Chucky gave Shirley a hug. She went into Rachelle's purse and grabbed her keys to the truck. Chucky helped her get Rachelle to the truck. When Rachelle was secured in the passenger seat she started cursing Shirley out. "Bitch I'm not ready to go, I want to fuck ole boy. You's a hating ass bitch Shirl." Rachelle was drunk. Shirley put the S.U.V. in drive and headed for home ignoring Rachelle until she passed out.

They reached Cincinnati at around 1:30 that morning. Pedro had to come and help Rachelle in the house. Shirley decided to stay over so Pedro wouldn't have to take her home. She had to explain to him why Rachelle was pissy drunk, but left out the other details about her flirting with a total stranger in Dayton Ohio.

Shirley was becoming more aware of her physical change, because her nose was spreading, her feet and fingers were fat and her stomach was out there. She was very mad at Sharan for having her this way, but at the same time she was very happy that her life was now taking its place in the world she was so confused.

CHAPTER NINETEEN
Rude Awakening

Around late October Shirley was at her condo chilling out making room for her baby items and a baby bed Rachelle and Pedro had bought her. She had just finished talking to Rachelle and they were on their way to drop the baby bed off to her.

She was going back and forth slowly moving her well-rounded self across her fluffy carpet. It was a knock at her door that startled her.

Boom! Boom! Boom! Boom!

She knew it wasn't Rachelle and Pedro even though they were like thirty minutes away. She thought maybe it were some kids selling school candy.

She moved to the door. "Who is it?" She was wondering who was on the other side of the door.

"It's me Sam, I need your help."

She was shock, because she hadn't heard from him or seen him since New Year's Eve and New Year's day after finding out he gave her a disease and that he was messing with

Chloe. Her heart dropped. She looked out her peak-hole of the door. He looked a total mess, like he'd been in a brawl. She felt concern not thinking once, if he was on some other dysfunctional behavior. She opened the door. "What happen to you?" She looked at him carefully.

"It was Ox, he put a hit out on me, because I came up short with his money." Sam told her.

"I thought you had your own money Sam. So what are you really mixed up in?" she asked him.

"I was selling a lot of weed for him, I mean a lot." Sam told her.

"So you were mixed up in that bullshit huh?' Shirley was confused, but was wondering why he was really with Ox. Now her wondering was an actuality.

"Kind of," as his eyes traveled down to her stomach.

"So how much do you owe him?" She asked him.

"Like four-hundred thousand." He told her. She couldn't believe it. "Four-hundred thousand," she shouted. "Look Sam I don't need that type of drama out here, I think it might be best for you to leave." She told him.

"Ox doesn't know where you live, plus I just need to lay low for a few days." He said.

Shirley was raced to have a kind heart and even though he did her wrong she still was a good person. "I don't know Sam, that might not be a good idea," said Shirley.

"Please Shirl, I need to regroup and I'll be gone." he begged her.

She thought about it hard and long. She didn't want to be nasty and cold hearted so she gave in. "look Sam you can stay tonight and that's it."

"Thanks Shirl, I owe you one and why didn't you tell me you were pregnant?" She asked him.

"This baby doesn't concern you, that's why I didn't tell you," as she was grabbing her stomach walking back towards her room.

"What, it's not mine?" He asked her5.

"That's right not yours Negro." She said it with a sassy tongue.

"Then who's is it?" Sam asked her and she turned around and looked at him.

"Sam you just need to worry about Sam and what is going on over here." Shirley said.

"You right." he answered.

"You damn right, I'm right. It's old clothes of my ex in the hallway closet I think you can fit. You can take a shower in the big bathroom and not in my room," said Shirley.

"Okay that's cool," as he watched her go into her room. He already knew where the towels were at. Sam went and took a shower and so did Shirley.

When she came out of her bathroom wrapped in a towel Sam was sitting on her bed dressed in some of Thomas old clothes.

"Excuse me Sam, but who told you to come in here?" She asked him.

"I thought maybe you needed help putting on your lotion since you can't quite reach your back." he smiled at her.

"Well you thought wrong. Now please get out." She was now in front of him.

"C'mon Shirl," as he grabbed her arm and threw her onto the bed ripping her towel away. He got on top of her even though her stomach prevented him from straddling her completely. He pinned her arms down by her waist and started kissing her neck.

"Let me go Sam." She said kicking her legs trying to move her neck and face at the same time from him kissing her.

"You are going to give me some of this pregnant pussy." He demanded.

"Let me go Sam, you are hurting me," as she began to let out tears from the corner of her eyes.

"You are about to have some other nigga's baby and you couldn't have mines. Either you're gonna give me some or I'm taking it." He said.

"So you are going to rape me now? Chloe has your baby, that's the decision you made." She said in fear.

"If that's what you call it then yeah, and fuck Chloe and that baby." he said and she could see the devil look in his eyes.

"I don't believe you, you're about to rape me Sam,' as a heap of tears began to flow from her eyes.

Rachelle and Pedro were now knocking at the door and her cell phone was ringing re-peatedly.

Boom! Boom! Boom! Boom!

The knock was clear and loud coming from the front door. Her bedroom door was open and the both of them could hear the knocking.

"Shirley open up, we are here," as Rachelle was calling her name. there were no elec-tronics in the condo and they could hear someone saying something from behind the front door all the way in Shirley's room.

"Shirl, who is that?" Sam asked, as he became a little paranoid.

"It's Rachelle and her husband, they were already on there way before you showed up." She said. That knock at the door made her feel safe.

He knew she was probably telling the truth, because they were still knocking at the door like they knew she was in there. He let her go from his hold and said, "I was just play-ing Shirl."

She knew better from his grip that he was serious. She got up and slipped on a big t-shirt and some sweat pants. She wiped her eyes and put on her slippers. She walked into the living room towards the front door to let Rachelle and Pedro in. Sam was following her.

"You have to go Sam." She said dragging her fat beautiful feet across the carpet and they came out of her slippers because they made her feel uncomfortable.

"Why baby?" He begged.

"I'm not your baby Sam. Leave before I call the police," as she was opening up the door.

Rachelle saw him and was on top of it. "What's going on Shirl, is everything alright?" She asked Shirley looking Sam up and down. Then Pedro slid inside the door mean mugging Sam. "Yeah is everything alright Shirl?" Pedro asked her never taking his eyes off of Sam.

"Yeah, everything is okay. Mr. Sam was just leaving us," said Shirley.

"Damn Shirl is it like that?" Sam facial expression was in fixation.

She looked at him in disgust and said, "Get the fuck out Sam."

He smirked a little and walked passed them and then he gave another grin. Shirley shut the door behind him. Rachelle went and flopped on the couch.

"Shirl, what was that all about?" Rachelle asked her.

"That Negro came over here talking about he's in a little trouble. He was all beat up and bloody, so I told him he could stay the night, and had to leave in the morning. This Negro call himself wanting to take some pussy from me," as she caught her breath. "You can't just help mother-fucka's out now days Chelle."

"Fuck that call the police on that nigga," said Rachelle.

"It's cool, some people are looking for his ass and probably are going to kill him," said Shirley holding her belly.

"I thought that was his Benz out there. It's all wrecked and shot up like its been in a movie doing stunts and shit." Rachelle gave a fake laugh.

"That Negro is caught up in some other shit Chelle." Shirley walked over to her personal chair that it was easy for her sit down and get up out of.

"What you got to drink Shirl?" Rachelle asked her.

"There's some orange juice, cranberry juice and pop in the fridge beside water, shit I don't know, go and see." Shirley told her.

"Damn can I have a glass of orange juice?" Rachelle asked her and Shirley was now sitting down. Rachelle little belly was trying to stick out from her pregnancy.

"You know where it is," said Shirley.

"Bitch you are rude as hell, no hospitality at all," said Rachelle.

"Whatever." Shirley sat there hugging her belly. "Pedro do you want anything to drink?" Shirley asked him.

"I'm cool Shirl. I just want to know where do you want this baby bed?" He asked her.

"Oh, you can put it in my room against the wall." Shirley told him.

"Alright when I go and get this bed, I hope you'll be ready to go Chelle." He told her.

"Pedro you and Keith Jr. are going to make it to that damn fake ass Wrestling bullshit on time," said Rachelle.

"You know we have to go to your moms house to get him and then I have to drop you off at home." He told her looking at her with eyes of impossibility.

"My mother house is on the way fool," said Rachelle.

"Whatever," as Pedro was leaving out the door going to get the baby bed out of the truck.

Rachelle was now in the kitchen getting her a glass of orange juice. She came back into the living room drinking her juice. When she caught her breath she asked Shirley.

"So what's up Shirl?"

"Nothing, just thinking about Sharan, wondering if he's going to marry me, and not because of this baby, but because of me Chelle." Shirley was concern and you could hear it in her voice.

"Shirl that nigga loves you and I know he'll do what's right and his heart has been set on you for awhile now." Rachelle told her friend.

"I hope so Chelle, because right now I'm lonely." Shirley confessed her heart to her.

"You think he's not lonely Shirl?" Rachelle asked her.

"I know Chelle, but I see these new moms out here with the fathers of their child with them and then I look at myself knowing Sharan might not be here for the first two years of our child's life," said Shirley.

"Be strong Shirl, we are here for you." Rachelle told her still drinking her juice. She knew her friend was going through it and it wasn't going to get any easier.

Pedro re-entered the condo with the brand new baby bed .

"Damn ya'll could have opened the door for me." he was out of breath.

"You be fake working out boo, you strong." Rachelle was being funny with her comment.

He took the bed into Shirley's room and placed it against the wall. He came back out and was ready to go. "Chelle are you ready?" He asked her. She looked up at him and rolled her eyes. "Shirl I'll call you later, this nigga is a big ass baby."

"Okay Chelle, I'll be here," said Shirley still holding her stomach, but getting up to hug her friend. She hugged Pedro to.

"C'mon you spoiled brat let's go." Rachelle led the way to the front door. "Bye Shirl," as Pedro left out first. "Bye Pedro."

Rachelle looked at him and then balled her fist up at him, as he walked out the door.

"Bye Shirl, and if that nigga shows back up, call the police," said Rachelle referring to Sam.

"I will and call me later." She watched Rachelle leave down her stairs heading for the parking lot. She closed her door and went back into her bedroom.

She lay across the bed on her side and started to take a nap. She had dosed off for about ten minutes and her house phone rang. The phone rang three times before she picked up.

"Hello." She thought it was Sharan calling.

"Damn Shirl, what were you doing?" It was Rachelle calling her.

"I was taking a power nap."

"Guess what girl, we were driving down I-71 and the police was around ole boy Benz. He was in it and he looked like some one shot him in the head. There were about eight police

cars, Highway patrol and the Ambulance was on the way, you could hear the sirens," said Rachelle.

"Are you serious Chelle?" She asked her.

"Yes I'm serious, he looked fucked up Shirl. Make sure you watch the News later on," said Rachelle.

"I will, but I told you he was mixed up in some other stuff. That's the bad karma he put on himself, oh well," said Shirley.

Shirley didn't have any sympathy for Sam, especially after he tried to rape her. She felt for Chloe being a single parent.

"Well I thought I would call you and let you know. I'll call you later when I get home," said Rachelle.

"Okay." They hung up. Shirley couldn't imagine why Sam was really dealing drugs when his business was the way out. He had a hidden agenda after all that cost him his life.

She peacefully went to sleep not giving it a second thought.

CHAPTER TWENTY
Never Ending Love

That following month in November Shirley received some good news from the Court of Appeals on Sharan behalf. He was scheduled to have a bond hearing the first week of December. Shirley prayed and prayed for this to happen and her prayers were answered. She decided to go tell him in person that second week in November. She was back down in Ashland seeing him. It was a chilly day on this Saturday afternoon in Ashland. They were outside standing under a big tree, Shirley had on maternity blue jeans, hooded Harvard sweat shirt which was maroon and white, and some all white Reebok classics. She had her hair done in spirals, and she had on her Rolex.

Shirley already told him the good news before they walked outside to the court yard. They started talking and the conversation got all emotional.

"Shirley you know I want to marry you, I love you." he told her.

"Do you love me for me, or because I'm carrying your baby?" She asked him.

"Shirley I loved and cared about you before we even thought about this baby." Those words melted her.

"I don't want to be waiting on you and you decide to go elsewhere Sharan."

"Where am I'm going Shirl?" he asked her.

"I know you have other females writing to you and sending you money Sharan, I'm not stupid," as a tear slowly came racing down her cheek.

"So what, you know because I told you. I'm not trying to go anywhere, but home to you." He told her.

"We will see and time will tell," as she wiped her tears away with the heel of her palm.

"What you think I'm lying to you? Are we feeling some sort of insecurity Shirl?" He asked her and her face was still and calm.

"I don't want to lose you Sharan," as more tears started to flow.

"Look Shirl, I want to be with you .You are about to be the mother of my first born child and most likely you'll be my wife, so quit tripping." He told her.

Her tears slowly slacked up hearing him say that she'll probably be his wife.

It caught her attention. "Why did you say probably Sharan?" She asked him.

"Because you have to want to marry me as much as I want to marry you." He told her.

"I do, I'm just scared Sharan, because you might see someone better than me when you come home," she said.

"Shirl, I'm not trying to choose any booty when I come home, but yours. There is no one else who could compare to you Shirl. My concern and focal point will be on you and our child." He told her.

"Can you promise me that Sharan?" She was now sniffling a little.

"I can, but why should I have to swear about my love for you and I know it's true?" He looked at her in the eye"

"I just need that security Sharan, for you to say it." She told him.

"You don't believe me? I can swear now and flip the script later, so what's the difference?" He asked her.

"Just promise me that Sharan, please," as Shirley tears became more intense.

"Stop crying Poohbear," as he called her by her pet name he gave her. "I promise I will never leave you no matter what. Look I talked to my aunt and she's going to go with you to look for a house for us. She has my cars and Pedro has some of my money I had put up." he paused for a second looking at her. "I'm going to call him when you leave to make sure he gives you around eighty thousand and my aunty will fund the rest with money she is holding for me also. The money is for any baby items you need and to size you a ring." he told her.

"Are you serious Sharan?" She asked him.

"Yeah I'm serious. The Feds didn't seize everything, only the little money I had in the bank and twelve thousand I had in a safe at my house." He told her his business.

"I want you to be there when I do that Sharan. Let's wait and see how the bond hearing goes." She said.

"Look I want my child to be in a house when he or she comes into this world and comes home from the hospital." He told her.

"Does your aunt like me? She probably doesn't even like me Sharan." Shirley asked him.

"I told you she's like my sister Shirley Ann Thomas soon to be Chambers." Sharan told her.

"I don't want her to think I'm trying to take your money Sharan." She told him.

"She knows you have a career and your own money Shirley."

"Okay Sharan, but I would rather for Rachelle to go with me to look for a house," said

Shirley.

"She can go, but the reason I was sending my aunt with you was because she's into real-estate." He told her.

"Oh I see, that's fine with me and we can get to know one another." Shirley was feeling kind of at ease.

"That's logic ain't it?" He was looking down on her. "I love you Sharan." She murmured.

He kissed her. "I love you too. Plus I don't want any of your old strange boyfriends showing up at the house," as he smiled at her.

"So Pedro told you about my run in with ole boy?" She asked him.

"No, Rachelle did." He looked at her. She just knew his friend told him.

"Did you get jealous?" She asked him.

"Just as jealous when I told you that other females were writing me." He said.

"Don't get your ass kicked in here Sharan." She batted her eyes at him.

"Yeah, whatever you know the deal. So when are you coming back to see me?" He asked her.

"Hopefully next week and I want some, I've been getting really horny lately. It seem like the closer December get's here the hornier I'm getting." She was snug up on him.

"Okay I guess I'll see you then and hopefully you would have been looking for something nice for that." He was pointing to her finger.

She smiled at him. "What type of neighborhood would you prefer Sharan?"

"Shirl as long as it's a quiet place where we can raise our child, it really doesn't matter." He hugged her as far as her belly would allow him to.

"If you say so." She kissed him long and hard.

Shirley left from down there at her usual time which was 4:00 in the afternoon.

……………………………………..

Sharan waited until 7:00 p.m. that evening to call Pedro. He didn't even bother to call Shirley to see if she had made it home yet like he normally would. He knew she would be over to Rachelle's when he did call like he told her to. He called and Pedro picked up on the third ring.

"Hello," as Pedro picked up. Sharan heard someone in the background crying and screaming. **"No, no I don't believe it, oh God no, please bring her back."** it echoed in Sharan's ear. "Damn Pedro what's wrong with Chelle?" He asked him.

215

Pedro was silent. His voice was shaky as he began to answer Sharan.

"Look Sharan, I don't know how to tell you this, but Shirley is gone man."

"What did you say Pedro?" as his body got numb. "What did you say?' Sharan question him again.

"Shirley is gone Sharan," as he struggled to tell him. "She's dead. She had a fatal accident on I-75 coming from seeing you." Pedro told him.

Sharan shook trying to hold the receiver. "Na'll Pedro you lying right?" He asked hoping he would change his words.

"Sorry Sharan." Pedro said.

"Why man? Why? God give her back to me and take me God," as he screamed through the receiver. He broke down on the spot.

"Sharan, Sharan, Sharan," as Pedro was yelling through the receiver for him.. Pedro could hear him crying in deep pain and sorrow.

"Pedro we were suppose to be getting married and grow old together. I loved her Pedro." Sharan was emotionally unstable. He felt his partners pain.

"I know Sharan, I know. She loved you too." Pedro told him.

The Sharan yelled through the phone again. "Give her back, oh Shirley I need you baby, oh I need you."

Sharan held. the phone not wanting to let go. This was very painful for him and all this time he'd been chasing and wanting her. He put his faith into this one woman and now just like that she was gone.

....
.

Sharan paid for her funeral and the Feds even let him attend the funeral. Weeks later after her funeral he was released on his appeal bond. Four years had passed by and Sharan was out of federal hands completely getting his case over turned.

It was May of 2006 on Mother's Day when he was cruising down Vine St. going to the Spring Grove Cemetery. He stopped in the cemetery to pay respects to his mom as well as Shirley.

Sharan road around to where his mother was buried many years ago and he had a personal tomb stone. He got out of his new E-class 300 Benz he just bought. He was now the manager of the Trap Boys who were doing numbers in the Hip-Hop industry.

He went over to his mother's grave sight first. His mother tomb stone read!

"Clarese Chambers 1944-1982".

Sharan began to talk to his mother that he really didn't get a chance to know.

"Mom I know we didn't get a chance to bond, but I know you are always by my side and I feel your presence all the time. I thank you for being my extra set of foot prints when I was growing up watching over me. I've become a man now and your sister raised me to the best of her ability loving me like her very own. I've made good sense of my life, representing you to the fullest. I love you mama and I will be all I can be." He placed a single flower on her grave and he left her sight getting back in the car. He drove around to Shirley's grave sight which was on the other side of the cemetery. He got out of the car and grabbed two flowers out the back seat before shutting his car door. He sighed into the air. He thought about something that gave him the strength.

"Behold the Lord is doing a new thing. Now that it springs forth, I perceive and know it and give heed to it. He will even make a way for me in the wilderness and rivers of water for me in the desert." (Isaiah 43:18)

When he approached Shirley's tomb stone it read!

"Shirley Ann Thomas 1973-2002"

Sharan then got on his knees and began to speak to her.

"Hey Shirl, what up? I know you are watching down on us and are by our side. I'm doing okay, but I miss you and it's hard not having you around. I'm doing a good job as you can see. I know we will see one another again and I can't wait until that day comes. I will teach the now living self-help, and willingness to succeed in life. I will teach them how to conduct themselves in a fashion that will bring honor and respect to themselves.

How to refrain from committing illegal acts and how to give back to the community. How to give back on a positive note and to build a positive character within themselves. I'm down here doing this for us and ours Shirley and I know you would agree with me one hundred percent." He paused for a moment. "I've created the Shirley Ann Foundation for Dysfunctional Teens and Battered Women." Sharan paused again and then shed a single tear and added. "I have this poem I would like to share with you. It was written by this female name Khalia I.R. Maples, so listen to this," as he cleared his throat.

"It's titled, 'I'm Only Human'." He paused again and then began to read it to her.

"I'm only human, I make mistakes, wrong decisions, but I'm only human. Wrong turns, we all make wrong turns and choices at a point in our lives. But can we

blame them, they're only human. This is not a perfect world even though some people

Wish they were perfect, and that they're oh so perfect. But I'm glad I'm only human. I thought I would share that with you. Anyway we've done the impossible, but we did it. I love you and here is our beautiful daughter that we created out of love. I named her Miracle Shirley Ann Chambers, because she is a miracle to us."

He dropped another tear. "Miracle say hi to your mommy and put the flower right there," as he pointed to the place for their daughter to place the flower.

"Hi mommy, I love you," as she laid the flower on the tomb stone. "Daddy did mommy hear me?" She asked her dad.

"Yes Miracle, mommy heard you and she loves you too." he picked up his daughter in his arms and kissed her and he walked back towards the

car……………………………….....

……………………..……………..

...

This book is dedicated in the memory of Geraldine Pitts my mother and best friend. Love you mom.

To Margret Allen, a paralegal who was loved in the community of Hamilton County. To Keith Caldwell, my childhood friend who got called home after his senior year of High School, you are solely missed.

....

Please look for more books from Imani Books by Douglas L. Maples in the near future. A special note to those who participated in this project. The help and criticism was gladly appreciated. I would like to thank Brooke Scudder, Denise Moore, Tamencia McNair, Billi Jo Louden, Tremayne Griffin and Ms. Brenda Sanders.

About the Author:

Douglas L. Maples has mentored the youth despite his prison terms. He's a motivator and is recognized in the community. He's a graduate of Columbus State Community College and Urbana University.

He enjoys writing Plays and screen plays outside of the many unpublished novels he has written, which includes Bonita, Delight 1&2, Entrance 1,2,&3, Well-Bred and many more. He lives in Cincinnati Ohio, where he's becoming involved in many social and non-profit organizations. He loves to read, watch and play sports and enjoys making his family and friends laugh.

Made in the USA
Las Vegas, NV
21 August 2021

28584272R00122